MW00834301

A Covenant of Spies

A Covenant of Spies

Lies and Consequences Book 4

Daniel Kemp

Published 2019 by Next Chapter
Cover art by http://www.thecovercollection.com/
Back cover texture by David M. Schrader, used under license from Shutterstock.com
Large Print Edition

I would like to dedicate this book to Mr Lee May, without whom I would have finished with writing a long time before this book was published. In the absence of his unflinching support, the world as I know it would not exist.

Other Work By This Author

The Heirs and Descendants Series:

The Desolate Garden

Percy Crow

The Lies and Consequences Series:

What Happened In Vienna, Jack?

Once I Was a Soldier

The Widow's Son

Novellas:

The Story That Had No Beginning

Why? A Complicated Love

Self-Published under the Name of Danny Kemp:

A Shudder from Heaven

Falling Greenhouses and Digestive Biscuits

Teddy and Tilly's Travel Series

Chapter One

August 2007, London, England

"I knew I'd seen him before, but I didn't know where and when until I got back here and ran his name through our computers. Then it all came flooding back. I'm surprised Fraser hadn't known there was a chance I'd come across this chap before, but perhaps his memory is getting as bad as mine."

I was forced to stop speaking by the strange scrutinising stare Hannah gave me, as if it were she and not me asking if I was a fool. "No, Hannah, you're right. If I believed that to be true, then I shouldn't be in the position I am. Fraser Ughert knew exactly what he was doing. The trouble now would be knowing why he wants to play this game?"

* * *

My name is Patrick West. I'm chairman of the United Kingdom's Joint Intelligence Committee, or JIC for short. Everyone with any connection to the security of British interests at home or abroad is answerable to me. Or at least they were, until Fraser Ughert, my predecessor as chairman of JIC—and now in receipt of a gold-lined, index-linked pension that should have paid for something to keep his nose out of the intelligence game—drove down from Chearsley, in Buckinghamshire, and disturbed the peaceful existence I had with Hannah, my wife of three years. I feared that having met with him and his mysterious guest, a Russian named Nikita Sergeyovitch Kudashov at Brook's, my club in St James's Street, London, their names would resonate around those ancient walls for some time to come.

Now I was in the throes of explaining the unexplainable to a woman as perceptive as I and someone more dear to me than anything had ever been. She had converted me from a committed bachelor of almost fifty-five years into a married man and, as such, had accompanied me here to the palatial offices and private rooms in the Foreign and Commonwealth building on my appointment at Christmas time in 2002. Now she was known as not only Mrs West, but as my steward. That was not my choice of description. It was the official civil service name given to the role of the personal assistant to the Chairman of the Joint Intelligence Committee.

As she listened, she poured two large measures of Isle of Jura single malt into the heavy crystal glasses as we sat beside each other facing out onto St James's Park from the sitting room in our apartment, and I began trying to unravel what had occurred, and was likely to. When hearing updates of my work in the comforts of our home, she sat with her shapely legs tucked under herself and one of her slender arms stretched along the back of the sofa. Her hazel-coloured eyes were fixed on me as she swept a strand of long black hair away from her beautiful, shapely face, then laid that face on my shoulder. The time was a little after 1 p.m.

* * *

Not all of what I'd discovered in the time I'd had since the lunch at my club could I disclose to my wife for reasons I will explain as we go through this story of lies and forgotten consequences, but allow me to dissuade you from forming an opinion of me based on that honest disclosure. If you have already done so, then I hope I'm correct in saying you have judged me wrongly. Perhaps you think that withholding information is indicative of having no trust in my wife or not loving her sufficiently. That is not entirely true. However, if you believe me to be sceptical and hesitant in giving my trust, then you are smack on the button as they must say somewhere. I have never trusted a single living soul and as regards the dead, they too are not completely trustworthy.

* * *

"It was 1982 when I first came across him and neither of our names were as they are today. Back then his name was Petr Tomsa, and for the duration of the operation for which I was responsible, Control had named me Frank Douglas. The story he's peddling to Fraser Ughert and me about a NSA surveillance policy code named Data Mining is an extension of their old Echelon programme, managed under what was called the UKUSA Security Agreement, or Five Eyes Pact.

That alliance of intelligence sharing was supposed to be between America, Australia, Canada, New Zealand, and ourselves. I was made aware of the programme in 1973 when I was offered a job in the Secret Intelligence Service by the late and great Sir Dickie Blythe-Smith, who was then the Chairman of the JIC. However, it was not until I replaced him that I became fully aware of some other aspects to the American Echelon programme.

"It was a tiny part of an umbrella initiative code named Frosting, which was established by the NSA as early as 1966 to collect and process data from communications satellites and stations around the world. Frosting had two sub-programs: Transient, for intercepting Soviet satellite transmissions and Echelon, for intercepting Intelsat satellite transmissions. In other words, an early American probe into what can be described as friends' telecommunications between each other's sovereign states. Nosey buggers, the Americans back then, and their impinging on the integrity of friends has yet to change.

"Anyway, that's not the important matter here, Kudashov, aka Petr Tomsa, wants us to extract his granddaughter from the arms of, his words, a powerful Russian politician, in exchange for what he says is her decryption of the modifications the NSA have made to Frosting and the obvious extension of its capabilities. Fraser needs me to sanction the intrusion into Moscow Central's realm of ultimate charge and play his game through. Looked at on the surface, it's a good offer from Kudashov, but I fear there's more to it than the simple exchange it appears to be."

As she shuffled along the sofa, straightening her legs and pointing her feet in stretching movements that captured my attention for a good while, Hannah asked, "Could Fraser's friend, this Kudashov chap, have recognised you from 1982 do you think, Patrick?"

"It was twenty-five years ago and I very much doubt he would recognise me as I saw him from a distance and I can't recall him looking in my direction. We never met face to face. He was mentioned as the expensive 'go-to' man if you were to get stuck in Prague and wanted to get out of Czechoslovakia by the back door. I contemplated using his services when the operation in that country went a bit tricky, but an opportunity arose where there was no need of him. London set me up with a perfectly good route out of the country. Let me expand on that and on my train of thought at the time." I was lying about the escape, which was far from straightforward, but I doubted the lie would be discovered. I had never totally disclosed to Hannah all that brought me to where we were and I thought now would be as good a time as ever.

"My passage to the highest position within the secret world of intelligence has been extraordinarily swift, especially considering how it started from a position far from ideal. At the time of this operation, I was very much the outsider in this intelligence community. I was not fully trusted by my peers, even though what had transpired between the more conventional branch of national security and myself had passed into antiquity some eleven years before. Memories are, of course, a requisite factor in the gathering of, and keeping of secrets; however, I had found a traitor within the Metropolitan Police who was once *on the spy* like me and that makes people like me suspicious, and in some cases, outwardly hostile. My working name for whatever operation to which I was assigned was always altered, but the legend never strayed from my correct age; by then I was thirty-three, and on each trip abroad my passport kept me in the same role, that of a chemical analyst.

"When I was recruited by the then plain Dickie Blythe-Smith, as he was before his knighthood, he said the service wanted me for my degree in chemical analysis; he said that would be of use, but he never said when. Immediately after signing the Official Secrets Act, yet again, I was posted to a company in London where I was employed working on bio-fuels. It was interesting work but sadly not in the same exciting sense as Jack Price and I had got up to in New York prior to my meeting with Dickie in the Traveller's Club, London. Dickie told me I would have to wait for the true excitement; first, I had to do the ground work. I did well in my industry, so much so that within three years I had progressed to working under the head of ICI's research and development team, headed up by a Professor Alan Mitchell. At the beginning, the team I was working with concentrated on specialised polymers and man-made fibres, spin-offs of the oil industry. We focused our analysis into what was out there, concentrating on the bio fuels that could be enabled through chemical engineering, or, to simplify that, changing mineral structures into something more profitable and usable as a propellant. The primary constituents for these experiments were mainly inert substances classed as macro-minerals, as our aim was to engineer those elements into refined fuel sources capable of being installed in places unreachable by conventional power supplies.

"After a few more years, they moved me away from that research and into a high value, rapidly growing market where the products produced had diverse applications in the industrial world. The biggest growth of all was in synthetic organic polymers. With some outside influence, that became my personal speciality and my sole responsibility. This was of course the so-called groundwork that Dickie had mentioned. The intensity of my work kept me fully occupied, leaving little time for contact with any branches of the intelligence services other than a few brief excursions abroad in which I played little part. I was there, I was told, to watch and learn, but it wasn't only watching. I was thrown into a couple of things. All of those precautions, along with the weekend studying and three fake annual holidays I spent at Beaulieu, down in Hampshire, became a huge benefit in the full operation I would undertake in Prague."

Hannah still looked interested, although perhaps that was her congenital kindness or my self-importance misleading me, but either way I soldiered on. There was a part of me that wanted to just get involved with the investigations into this Russian's claims and not share the preliminary disclosures and back story with her, but that wasn't possible because of our closeness at work as well as in private.

"It didn't take much imagination to see that the whole chemical process could lead to the creation of fuel from polymers. All these polymers are manufactured from waste products, which makes the augmentation of this technique imperative for the developing world where there is no oil, or very little. That was what I was endeavouring to achieve: fuel from waste products, or existing bio-diverse products farmed for fuel.

Seaweed would be a perfect example of the sustainable life that is being spoken about today, another would be certain crystals. That's how I got my ticket to be invited to Prague with Professor Mitchell. There is a part of the Czech Republic that is so rich in a particular strain of phosphates and arsenates, that with the price of crude oil climbing all the time, it made commercial sense to mine the crystallised deposits and start the engineering process in what in 1982 was then called Czechoslovakia. Apparently, the location and viability had been common knowledge in the West for some time, all that was lacking from its extraction was the ability to render it profitable. It was to be my role to set it in motion in more ways than one."

Chapter Two

May 1982, Prague

"If every description I read in service files matched the complexity of the ones ascribed to Jana Kava and her brother, Dalek, then I would have had far more free days spent enjoying the pleasures of life than I have been able to. Despite the obvious lack of complications written on the two sheets of paper inside the thin yellowish-brown coloured file, more were hidden from view than I first appreciated."

File coded FlyHi One: First Write 01/05/1981. Updated 01/03/1982.

Starts: Jana Kava, thirty years of age, (DOB 09/08/1951) plain appearance with greying-black hair and hazel eyes. She is old for her age. The subject has high cheekbones, with a sallow complexion to a chubby, heart-shaped face. She has no distinguishing facial features. Comely build, efficient, and reliable in both categories of work.

Her mother was born in Czechoslovakia of German parents and executed 16/07/1963. Tereza (the mother, aged 43) was killed for what was labelled subversive activities almost twelve years after the subject's birth and her father, General Anotoly Vladislav Kava, one-time head of the StB, State Security in Czechoslovakia, disappeared the same day in 1964 as the Russian Premier Nikita Khrushchev visited the site of the updated Warsaw Pact fighter aircraft and trainer, the Aero L-29 Delfín. NATO calls it The Maya. Although retired from the StB, the general was de facto in charge of security at various military sites, including this one. He was also a highly decorated war veteran.

The aircraft is manufactured in a factory on the periphery of the city of Prague, where the retired general also held a post as the Communist Party advisor before his disappearance. That was the ninth of January 1964.

Mysteriously, Khrushchev was not seen in public again in Czechoslovakia until boarding a plane for the flight back to Moscow on the eleventh of January. He was on crutches with his left ankle heavily plastered. According to the official Communist agenda, there were three other appearances scheduled during the week after showing his face at the Aero Vodochody factory. The First Secretary of the Communist Party of the Soviet Union had approximately nine months left in power before being replaced by Leonid Brezhnev as First Secretary and Alexei Kosygin as Premier. All probably just a coincidence, but worth noting.

Personal Life: Jana serves on the central policy committee of the chairman of the Communist Party and at one time the Prime Minister of Czechoslovakia, Jozef Lenárt. She speaks several languages fluently which she possibly practices when in bed with Lenárt. They are discreet in their relationship, but not enough to avoid our notice. He is married and has two children who are both at university in Moscow.

Home bird. She resides in the same house as that of her parents before they died. She is aware of her brother's (Dalek) growing affiliations to the banned anti-Communist movement, Solidarity, started in Poland in 1980. But, and this is vital—neither Jozef Lenárt, nor any other member of the central policy committee know of Dalek's affiliation, or her deception. ... That's how things stand at present. It could be a lever.

Jana Kava is our primary target. However, her brother, Dalek, DOB 19/06/49, is also of interest to us. He holds dual nationality, Russian and Czechoslovakian, and speaks both languages fluently, as well as English and German. His political leanings are the same as his sister's, towards the centre-left; however, according to our placement, he shows significant disillusionment with his Communist Party teachings and we are of the opinion he is now accessible.

File coded FlyHiTwo: First Write 01/05/1981. Updated 01/03/1982.

Starts: Personal Life: Heavily built, but surprisingly deft and agile for his size and slight disability: six foot three inches and sixteen stone, plus a bit. Studied judo, achieving a blue belt before other things took his interest. Black hair, black eyes with a permanent sad expression, which is probably caused by his addiction to alcohol. His face carries no distinguishing marks, is unremarkable and of a dull pale colour. He walks with a limp for no medical reason that we could find, nor do we know of any other cause.

We have no information of his formative years, other than like his sister, he was raised in the family home at number 34 Sámova, Praha 10. It's a beautifully appointed three-storey home on the banks of the River Vitava befitting the offices his father once held. Subject no longer resides at that address. There is no criminal activity recorded against his name. Although he was only fifteen years old when Khrushchev visited, we do know he made quite a noise at the Aero Vodochody factory the next day following his father's, the general's, non-appearance at home. He was called to appear before the local commissar committee of junior party officials to explain his behaviour. He offered no defence and was severely reprimanded, having his junior party membership suspended for three months; however, after an intervention on his behalf by his senior chemical tutor at the Prague pre-University school he attended, that punishment was rescinded and nothing was recorded against his name. We have reason to believe it was Dalek who discovered his father's body. That was on the morning of the twelfth of January, the day after Khrushchev left the country and the committee was convened that evening. The official reason given for the lapse of time between the general's disappearance and discovery, was that he'd died from a heart attack in a part of the complex seldom used by anyone.

Dalek was educated to a higher level than normal. He left the Czechoslovakian university at the age of twenty-one with the equivalent of five first-class honours degrees. One was in chemical analysis. He has occupied the same employment position since leaving the country's education system—Premier Analyst at Bok's Chemicals, Prague. A very prestigious position. He is overall second in charge at the chemical plant and considered to be one of the rising stars in the fledgling Czech scientific industry. We would like that ascendency to be accelerated and we want to know the progression boundaries in the development of your core subject: fuel from waste products.

Sexual orientation: What intelligence we do have on this aspect comes from a source no longer available to us. It suggests both subjects are of a heterosexual persuasion. However, caution must be used with this information as we have no evidence on the ground available to substantiate or repudiate what is in the file.

To Sum Up: We want Jana's signature on our books by close of play. Time is not of essence. Extend your stay at your discretion. What we do want is her alliance detached from her brother. Security is our utmost concern. If, in achieving the compliance of FlyHi One, FlyHi Two signature can also be scribbled in our ledger, then that's an acceptable bonus, but on no account can he be offered the same signing-on fee as his sister. You must make him earn whatever bonus you see fit—within reason. Jana gets premier-class remuneration and five-star handling all the way. One other thing: discretion is of the utmost importance, Douglas. No going off script.

* * *

"That roughly covered the extent of my briefing two days before I departed for Prague, from a Miles Faversham who told me he was the file's compiler and deputy head of the Soviet Satellite desk at Century House. For reasons I'll get to, I couldn't see him on the ground in Prague, so I assumed he'd come by the file information by way of an undisclosed third party. When I left Faversham, my thoughts were centred on the difficulty of the operation. To get one of them to turn against their country was going to be hard enough, but to get two, well, I'll be honest, I doubted I'd be able to do it.

"I hadn't been trained in the persuasive arts. My limited experience at that time was more theoretical than practice. I had no knowledge of operational stuff before I was with Jack Price in New York. That operation was successful as far as Jack was concerned, but it did involve Dickie and Fraser flying out to New York where I'd killed someone and had been previously shot. They got Jack, me and another guy named Job home. Later, after Jack had passed away, I was in on a snatch assignment in Hamburg, which involved the death of an opposing agent in a messy firefight. Then came the other 'look and listen one' in Moscow where I had nothing to do. So I wasn't James Bond by a long way!

"For the job, London gave me a substantial budget to use, but as I say, I wasn't trained to talk people into swapping sides in the Cold War. I wasn't nervous in the sense of not being able to do it, but I was nervous about doing it wrong. I told myself that everyone started somewhere and this was to be my somewhere. Beaulieu was a great institution for teaching trade-craft and being able to look after yourself well enough, so I wasn't frightened by the thought of going, but I can't say I had no reservations.

"The only reason I could think of why they'd picked me for the job was my chemical industrial experience. If Dalek Kava had made such a loud commotion within the higher echelons of the Communist Party when only fifteen, then without question his name was high up on the StB's list and the Russians would have as much interest in him as them. From what I'd read of Czechoslovakia, it wouldn't be a surprise if the StB had Dalek under permanent observation; however, this was my assignment and before I left for Prague I decided to play it as it developed and if need be: ignore Faversham's instructions of getting them both.

"That wasn't my only concern. The briefing I'd been given on the exposé of Jana's affair with a leading politician was too abridged for my liking. For example, why wasn't Jozef Lenárt already 'on our books' and thereby making Jana Kava superfluous to our needs? Also, who was it who found this information and how was it all verified? I asked those question, but got the standard answer to do with pay grades and mine being below what was required. I'm not telling you any of this with the benefit of hindsight, but other things bothered me. Like the fact that Jana, although listed first and made to appear the main target to turn, would in fact be compromised irreparably by her brother's defection. If I turned him then, his sister stood no chance of escaping anyone's radar and would need no inducement to jump ship.

"Dalek held opposing views to his superiors in both the idealistic claims of Sovietism and, as I discovered more as time went on when I was out there, the functionality of Czechoslovakian industrial practices. He was an outspoken individual, owing his freedom more to his father's reputation and his sister's influence than to his own circumspection. On the paper records at the MI6 archives held on five floors of 140 Gower Street, and mysteriously not included in Faversham's briefing notes, Dalek Kava was named as a possible American StB plant. Which could explain why he was still at large. But in other files I looked in, the CIA was said to have no presence in Czechoslovakia. The Director General heading up the seventh floor at Century House Soviet Satellite counter-intelligence would surely not have withheld this information from Faversham's desk, so why would Faversham not show Dalek's status to me? The only answer I came up with was that he and his boss wanted someone flushed out and I would be ham-fisted enough to do it without making it look deliberate. Without asking, I decided to send a gun to the British Embassy in Prague by the diplomatic bag.

"Despite my misgivings with the overall evaluation, I was not going to turn down the opportunity this assignment presented and as you are well aware by now, I've never been shy in putting forward my own spin on things. Especially when it comes to following my heart rather than connecting it to whatever should be inside my brain when it mattered. That particular trait of mine was in some ways my undeniable moral undoing, but also it created a distinct success for the service, or so I thought."

Chapter Three: The Meetings

"My cover for Operation Donor was as a legitimate part of a British delegation attending an international trade fair held in Prague for the month of May in 1982. My branch of science was included alongside a geological surveying exhibition presented by the London Institute of Mining, which in a lot of ways my chemical presentation was linked to. Altogether we were to showcase the scientific excellence Britain was achieving in a variety of ways. One excellence was in the mining of the phosphates and arsenates this country was so rich in. I was to give a speech about our combined efforts and then, at the end of its opening day, I was to be introduced to the Czechoslovakian Minister of Trade.

"Professor Mitchell and I were to be accommodated in the British Embassy and I was assigned to the less classified working laboratories at the Bok's chemical factory as a goodwill gesture. It was an elaborate cover, one I was thoroughly engrossed in. At Bok's, I was to be under the head of research, a man who had studied with Professor Mitchell and knew him well. As per the plan, Mitchell and I arrived the day before the conference and it was at the evening reception held at the Czechoslovakian Ministry of the Interior that I was introduced to Dalek Kava.

"He was an effervescent young man when our conversation turned to the subject matter I was to speak of. My referral to him being young must sound somewhat strange, as we were only a month or two apart in age, but in those far off days I never once considered myself anything but a fully mature man, and those that I came across of similar years were nothing but youngsters with a long way to go in life to catch me up. But with Kava perhaps my estimation was oversimplified as I found his questions refreshingly original and a long way from the insane stupidity of the juveniles I often came across. However, despite his enthusiasm, his overall demeanour was brusque and abrasive.

"The file had him to a tee. I soon discovered his liking for a drink. Those black eyes of his were worrying me as we each enjoyed a beer, and then the customary whisky for me and his favoured choice of vodka. They were so deeply embedded into his smooth forehead, they successfully disguised any emotion I could spot. His facial skin and hands carried no signs of an outdoor life, although there was what appeared to be a sizeable burn above the line of the shirt cuff he had buttoned down on his left arm. I did not ask about that, but I did ask about his limp. He told me it was due to a fall he had when he was twelve years of age. Despite what he'd said, I thought that to be a lie, and sometime after this initial encounter I found out that it wasn't a fall as much a push that had caused it.

"His father, the general, had a violent temper which was exacerbated by his liking for the vodka. Drinking vodka was a family trait, as Jana too enjoyed the stuff, but not in excess like her brother and father before him. The family house had a cellar in which both Dalek and his sister, Jana, were regularly incarcerated when their drunken father was so intoxicated and depressed, that was what he decided. Dalek had, like me, lost three toes on his right foot, except his loss was not caused by a bullet fired in New York. His happened when he was pushed down the stairs to the basement and his foot caught a nail that ripped his toes so badly, three had to be amputated.

"He was a great lover of mottos, was General Kava—introspection being good for the soul was his favourite, and used especially for Jana. She was locked in that cellar more often than her brother, and so Dalek's story continued one night when we were in a sleepy bar in the centre of Prague; she became used to killing rats down there with her bare hands. Jana had lost consciousness one particularly violent night when pushed down the wooden stairs into the cellar by the general and awoke only when a rat was nibbling at one of her fingers. She picked it up and repeatedly smashed it against the concrete floor until her hands were covered in its blood. She then sat motionless and silent, watching as other rats ate its body.

"I shall be completely open with you and admit that it took me a few months to discover why exactly Dalek's comments about the 'West' being decadent and leaderless were so caustic and disapproving, yet carried an air of reverence attached to them. For example, he would quote the record number of unemployed in the UK of that year compared to the full employment of his home country, then go on to deride the jobs his countrymen undertook. He called us murderers when a few days before one of our first scheduled meets, the Czechoslovakian newspaper, *Lidové Noviny*, reported the number of dead aboard the Argentinian cruiser, the *General Belgrano*, which was sunk by a Royal Navy submarine in the Falklands conflict. He then went on to say, rather reluctantly after I pressed the point, that if the Islanders wished to remain British, then the Argentinians had no right to invade.

"In June '82 he was scathing in his attack on the alleged American support for Israel in its invasion of Lebanon that was heavily reported in the press in Prague, but then amusingly added that he hated all Arabs with a vengeance. This professed disapproval of democracy was, I decided, a defence mechanism he'd constructed to deflect his admiration of the 'West' which he could not openly declare, even to his lover, Alexandr Radoslav. The sexual orientation report on Dalek was incorrect. He favoured male company, not female. However, those first few weeks spent in assimilating what I could about him, led to a disclosure that rocked more boats than just mine and also landed me with the prize London said they wanted.

"That outstanding revelation required my immediate contact with Faversham at Century House. According to Dalek, his sister had told him of a Geoffrey Prime, an Englishman, who she said had served in the Royal Airforce Force and worked at the Government Communications Headquarters, GCHQ. She said he spent all that time spying for the Soviet Union. No reference of the highly damaging treason Prime had committed, nor his widespread sexual predatory, paedophilic disorder had been allowed to be published anywhere in the world, but here was a Czechoslovakian telling me about how Prime was to stand trial for treason later this year in November, in London.

"This was the first time he had mentioned his sister, so I played it dumb and told him that I didn't know he had one. He replied she had an important job where she heard things. He went on to tell me she also told him of an experimental site in the Nevada desert where the Americans built and tested specialist spy planes. He was drunk and said he hoped the Russians would bomb it, but thought that wouldn't happen because their bombers would probably not be able to fly that far. It was my estimation that the reason he'd told me these things was to appear more important than he was and, perhaps, get closer sexually.

"I asked how he thought his sister had come by the information about Geoffrey Prime and if he thought the intelligence regarding the site in Nevada had come the same way. He told me this was the first time she had said anything to him more specific about her work or any secrets she had heard. I pressed him on the point of how he was certain she had heard these rumours at work and he just said he was certain. He knew. I then asked him what work she did.

"He was vague, adding nothing more than what I'd read in Faversham's brief assessment and for some unexplainable reason I believed him when he said he had no idea how Jana had come by the knowledge she'd passed on to him. But I wanted him to go further and it was then that he opened up a little bit about what happened to his father following Khrushchev's visit to the aircraft factory where the general was in charge of security. At that stage, all I could get was that the Russian Premier fell from the highest step on an inspection ladder, hitting his arm heavily against a guardrail and breaking his ankle as he lost his footing. His father, General Anotoly Vladislav Kava, was among the party escorting Khrushchev and according to Dalek, shouted all kinds of obscenities at Khrushchev as he lay on the ground, trying to regain his composure before his minders could get to him.

"Apparently, Khrushchev and General Kava had history. Jana and Dalek's father had been in Stalingrad when Khrushchev arrived in August 1942. The battle for that city had already begun and although Khrushchev's role was not major, he and General Kava met several times to discuss strategy and logistics in the company of the city's commander, General Chuikov. The three generals were together a year later in March 1943 when Khrushchev was told of his son, Leonid, a fighter pilot, being shot down and killed in action. Khrushchev, as you would expect, was inconsolable and, in his rage, he ordered the purging of all the senior officers in his son's fighter squadron. Thirty-eight were executed on Khrushchev's orders.

"Early in 1944, as the Russians forced the Germans into a hurried retreat towards Berlin, word reached General Kava that Leonid Khrushchev had not died in combat, but had been liberated from the Nazis who had imprisoned him and where he had collaborated with his fascist captors. Being no friend of Khrushchev, General Kava made sure the news was passed along the correct channels to his friend Stalin, the autocratic ruler of all Russia and of all the Russian military. It is thought that the two friends of many years discussed the penalty to be meted out on Khrushchev's son. Despite pleas from Nikita Sergeyovitch Khrushchev for clemency, Stalin had Leonid shot for treason. General Kava's involvement with that decision was not known to any person other than Joseph Stalin.

"When the Second World War finally ended, Josef Stalin, who held General Kava in the highest regard, posted him to the Soviet political territory of Czechoslovakia to restore the country's military and to take part in overseeing the rebuilding of the country's infrastructure. It was General Kava's reward for his loyalty, but it was there in 1956, three years after Stalin had died, that the faithful general heard Khrushchev denounce his beloved Stalin in a speech he gave when assuming the Presidency of Russia, and the festering hatred grew stronger leading up to the incident that cost General Kava his life.

"The anger the general felt was overtaken by the death of his wife and the care his children needed. Dalek's mother, Tereza, had apparently passed some minor classified information on to the West Germans. Dalek was unresponsive in this matter, as was Jana when I asked her. It seemed as though espionage and subversive politics were never far from this family. It crossed my mind that Jana could be trying to draw me into the open with the information about Prime and the Nevada desert for the StB to pounce and grab me, but that was part of the excitement of being on foreign soil on active service.

"Miles Faversham was as much in the dark about Geoffrey Prime as I was. We, like most in the service, had heard of him, but whatever information there was had soon been stamped upon and the subject banished from the corridors of gossip. The claim regarding spy planes being tested in the Nevada desert stunned Faversham into silence. From the little I knew of him, that was not normal. With due diligence, he passed both items of intelligence sideways until eventually they landed on the Russian desk in the room adjoining his on the seventh floor. Demarcation lines were of paramount importance in the secret intelligence service in those far off days. The custodians of that bejewelled throne asked for Faversham's immediate appearance. When he contacted me the next day, it was all hands to the pumps and a change of course plotted. I was billeted in an old brick-built outbuilding at the British Embassy, but however old it might have looked on the outside, the interior was as modern and secure as anything we had in London, or Berlin. It was on a telephone in the radio room inside that building that Faversham and I communicated.

"My circle of work associates in those days were not influenced by my decisions as they are today, and as much as I tried not to disappoint many of them by suggesting remedies to whatever we were at odds with, I had no idea who or what had persuaded Faversham to come round to my thinking, but I was thankful he had."

"We need to leave Jana where she is at present and we will assess the situation in due time. We do still want her. As for her brother, get as close as you can without spooking him. Inducements to come over are now our second consideration. You must do all you can to discover how this information came into Jana Kava's possession. We want you to encourage more of the same from her. Concentrate on the American Nevada desert end if possible; however, if you unnerve her or her brother, I'll have your head. Is that quite clear, Frank?" That was Faversham's closing statement before replacing the telephone receiver in London.

"Of course, as you know, this was and still is the SIS core dictum—*leave them where they are and play them*—and to be fair to everyone concerned, leaving them where they were was far easier for me than trying to turn them and then get them out of the country. Nevertheless, London still expressed an interest in Jana Kava and to incite anyone against their mother country is never a simple walk-in-the-park exercise. It carried immense risks to those on the ground; i.e. me. But as another of the secret intelligence service sayings goes, everything leads to everything else; I saw it as the most exhilarating and rewarding operation I'd ever been party to. It held huge opportunities for me and as soon it was the settled policy, I set about ensuring its execution; in more ways than one.

"In the commercial world, I was supposed to be in as the British representative on all things to do with energy production and conservation. I was invited a few times to meet with members of the Czechoslovakian government to explain our Foreign Office policy in regard to helping develop non-fossil fuels for the United Kingdom's commitment in preserving the environment. But nobody I spoke with in the Czech government, nor the Russian spokesman, was the slightest bit interested in the natural world. Monetary profit was the only consideration. That also was Dalek's weakness.

"Whenever possible, I championed democracy and all things Western to Dalek's fertile ears and, on the occasions she was there, to Jana as well. I did not need to arraign Communism as Dalek did a fine job of that himself. Despite knowing her brother's hostility, Jana never rebuked him, which I found odd considering her elevated position within the party, as one indiscreet moment from him could ruin her. One warm evening, when I was at Jana's home with Dalek present, enjoying a few drinks, discussing the world's problems and listening to the gentle lapping sounds of the river outside, I was asked a direct question that ended our flirtation with the truth."

"Are you a British spy?" Jana asked aggressively from nowhere.

"Why do you ask?" I replied, but in retrospect maybe a bit too quickly and not assertively enough.

"Because of what you asked my fool of a brother. I think only a spy would want to know where the information I told him came from. In any case, Dalek thinks you are a spy. Don't you, brother dear?"

* * *

"As much as I hate to stop you in mid-stream with this tale, Patrick, you have a 4.30 meeting this afternoon. After that, your presence is expected at the Cabinet Office at 5 p.m. I'm sorry to say the rest of it will have to wait until dinner." The look of affection on Hannah's face when she reminded me of my commitments only served to make me want to share more of my history with her, and starting in the middle as it were, in Prague in '82, was as good a place as anywhere.

Chapter Four: Dead Bodies

My mind was firmly on the streets of Prague as I sat and listened to the regular update on the situation in Afghanistan. NATO was gearing up to take overall control of security in that country, but for the time being, tensions had been steadily rising on the border of Pakistan, with Taliban militants crossing unopposed and raiding Afghan army and police positions, causing considerable casualties. British forces were still stationed in Helmand province in the south of the country, one of Afghanistan's most volatile regions, and the production of opium had reached an all-time high.

At an earlier meeting, I had made a joke about that fact, asking if it had anything to do with our continued presence, but it fell on stony ground and nobody commented or smiled. Those around the table had a spasmodic sense of humour, it seemed, regulated by who cracked the joke. There was no shared humour at this meeting as it was quickly moved along to other subjects.

We had several points of intelligence inside Pakistan, all under one controller who I knew reasonably well, but I had no first-hand knowledge of the MI6 officer overseeing the only source we had inside the Taliban. All other intelligence in Afghanistan came from the Americans via various channels. I gave a short account of the declassified information on what was happening, vis-à-vis intel gathering and distribution, along with a brief summary on the results of two incursions into Taliban positions by special forces operating under the command of the SIS field Controller. The Prime Minister and his press secretary nodded their heads in recognition of my report and the various ministers around the table closed the SIS folders, and the meeting moved on to other matters.

One of the points that was discussed at the Cabinet meeting that day was what to do with the seven Polish soldiers whose artillery battery had mistakenly shelled the village of Nangar Khel in Afghanistan, tragically killing six civilians, including a pregnant woman and a baby. The British Government, along with other NATO countries, were being canvassed for their recommendations as to punishment and although none of it was within my remit, we had intelligence sources within Poland and their thoughts were being asked for. Predominately, our intel came from political sources, but there was a high-ranking military commander being run out of The Box, our name for the Vauxhall Cross home of MI6 headquarters, who was part of an operation on Russian soil I'd met some years ago when he was just a major and I was *on the spy.*

In essence, the collective recommendations from fellow NATO governments was that the seven soldiers should be charged with war crimes and face trial at the UN's Court of Justice in The Hague. As I put forward the approach advocated by our source inside the Polish military, I was painfully conscious of my time in Prague with the Kavas. Major-General Wójcik, my present source in Poland, wanted them to make an atonement in a practical sense, not wasted on some ceremonial display. Poland would supply the monetary resources and building materials for two schools, and his seven troops would assist in building them. If his suggestion was accepted, then perhaps their denouncement would be less allegorical and more beneficial to Afghanistan. All of this debate resonated in a personal sense to me.

I had offered no pageant nor memorial to the person I sacrificed. No stateliness to the bullet that struck the back of his head, taking most of his unlined forehead with it as it exited and lodged in the timber stanchion of the boathouse in which we met. No sound of a gun being fired was heard, nor was a bullet or casing discovered or looked for. Nor was Dalek Kava's disfigured body, which sank swiftly to the bottom of the Vltava River in the early hours of a freezing Saturday morning as I silently lowered it over the side of a small row boat. That was how I dealt with Faversham's order and his Operation Donor. Without following instructions to the letter, I used my initiative and figured that with Dalek's departure, it cleared the way for the conversion of Jana to London's vision of western ideals. But as it transpired, she had visions of her own.

* * *

"Don't patronise me, Jana. I do not deserve that." It was Dalek who reacted first to his sister's accusation of me being a spy.

"Yes, I do think he's a spy, but if anyone can be certain it's you, isn't it? After all, you have your ears glued to Lenárt's phone extensions and your eyes in his memos. You love it, being one step ahead of us less important creatures in the rumour stakes. Can you see it in this Englishman's eyes? Is it in the way he dresses? Perhaps the image of an overcoat collar turned up, standing in a doorway with a burning cigarette between his fingers of one hand as the other rests on the butt of the gun in his inside pocket, hmm?" he croaked at his sister as he stood inches from me his face reddened by drink and flushed by rage.

Jana grabbed hold of my arm, dragging me from Dalek, leaving him alone with his mumbles and complaints of inadequacy and ineptitude of his sister and the Communist regime, to be answered from the vodka bottle he clutched to his chest. What she told me as we walked away arm in arm did not completely come as a surprise.

"He is loud about his weakness and silent about his strength. His work is magnificent, they say. He is irreplaceable or so his boss says. Said as much at all the party committees who sit and want to take his party card away, restricting his ability to work. But he talks and shouts too much and doesn't know when to stop! So far, I've kept him out of trouble and kept myself out of the shit storm that's waiting to sweep him and me away. It's only a matter of time before he's exposed, and then they will come after me.

"Each week, he gets deeper and deeper involved with this Solidarity shit and I can't be sure how long my influence will hold. I've seen some of their union literature at home and when I asked him what it was for, he said he intended distributing it around the city university with his friends as soon as they can all get together. This coming Sunday was mentioned. If that were to happen and he was to be arrested, which the State Security would definitely do, then let alone his job, my job would go as well and we'd both end up a state cell as I doubt he could keep his mouth shut.

"I know exactly how important I could be, Frank. I am in a position of trust within the highest levels of government in this country, but I can also be dangerous. It was I who told my father of Khrushchev's visit. No information like that is broadcast in this country before it needs to be. Yes, his position at the factory was important for security, and he was told of a visit, but he had no knowledge of who was coming. I heard who it was through work. I knew my father hated Khrushchev. He'd told me stories of him often enough. My father was a wicked man, but apparently not as wicked as Khrushchev in his estimation. He knew the risks he faced. He also knew that death was imminent; he'd been diagnosed with lung cancer two weeks before I told him who was the 'important person' we were expecting. Like my father, my brother knows the risks he takes, but that's where the likeness stops. Dalek does not know the consequences. I have no option but to want my brother stopped, Frank. If you want me to spy for you and continue supplying information to London, then I want you to kill my brother."

Yes, that's what she said to me—continue supplying and kill my brother. There was more to come from her.

"I loved him, but how can I now? I have been looking for a way out of the mess he's constructing for us both to drown in, and you're it. I know I'm putting my trust in you to do it, but I have no other choice."

* * *

My attention was back in the room where the upcoming elections in Poland had the attention of the Prime Minister. The corruption that had caused the early calling for a new government must have been foremost in his mind when he announced that the UK would side with her allies in calling for the war crimes of the Polish soldiers to be answered in the Hague, where they were to be denounced in the name of pious correctness.

My thoughts were that if you train a man to kill, don't be surprised when he does, and as men we make mistakes. That's part and parcel of being human. But correctness states that those that are killed, are only those that deserve death as judged by those whose innocence is the greater. I don't suppose the reasons for the Prime Minister's decision was that much different to

Jana's in wanting me to kill her brother. Both were made to conform to an ideological orthodoxy that suited their individual aspirations, but I suffered from no ideology. I just wanted the acclaim of having Jana Kava's political convictions with her hands planted deep in the pockets of the serving Vice-Chairman of the Central Committee of the National Front of the Czechoslovak Socialist Republic, one Jozef Lenárt. A huge feather in my cap if I could pull it off.

* * *

It didn't take long for me to learn just how much Jana was heartless in her approach to everything and everybody in life. She was almost as bad as me. There was a selfish motive behind all she had undertaken since losing her mother, even those basement confinements were for a contrived reason. She would purposely antagonise her father into sending her below the house in order to read the letters he had written when serving in the Soviet army. He had accumulated many about the extrication from Nazi hands of Leonid Khrushchev. Leonid was held by the Nazis at Majdanek concentration camp built amongst the beautiful rolling countryside on the outskirts of the city of Lublin, in Eastern Poland. His father was told of his recapture by the advancing Soviet army and Jana found copies of the pitiful memos sent by Khrushchev Senior to Joseph Stalin, begging for his son's safe repatriation to his father's keeping. She also read a copy of Stalin's refusal, and more importantly, Khrushchev's acceptance of Stalin's order of assassination.

In 1956, General Kava was amongst the select few to hear firsthand the denunciation of Stalin, who to millions of Russians was the divine father of Soviet Russia, and the man Jana's father had faithfully served. The hairs on the back of his neck stood upright in anger as he listened alone on a private radio in the army barracks in Prague. Here was the new Soviet leader telling the Russian people that their war hero had made cataclysmic errors leading to needless deaths and economic waste. According to Nikita Khrushchev, their once worshipped God was satanic. When the full contents of Khrushchev's speech became more widely known, it shook the Soviet Union to the core, but even more so its

Communist satellite allies, notably in central Europe.

General Anotoly Vladislav Kava had stored away a collection of stories in the basement listing riots throughout the USSR when Khrushchev's words were read to special meetings of party members in factories, farms, offices and universities. At such meetings in Georgia, where Stalin was born, members were outraged at the denigration by a Russian of their own national hero. Some people were killed in the ensuing uprisings, and trains arrived in Moscow from Tbilisi with their windows smashed and carriages wrecked. The general unrest in the Warsaw Pact was reaching meltdown in condemnation of new Premier Khrushchev's brand of communism.

In the autumn of 1956, Poland was ready to explode, and in Hungary an anti-Communist revolution overthrew the Stalinist party and government; General Kava pleaded restraint to the Czechoslovakian Communists and, utilising the control he had of the secret police, the StB, managed to deflect the volatile emotions being expressed throughout the country away from revolution, but he did not do that out of respect to the reforming First Secretary of the Communist Party of the Soviet Union. He did it to save a repeat of the deaths of party leaders and political heads that happened in the other countries where bloody revolts had taken place. His opinion had not changed; he hated Khrushchev enough to want him dead.

When Jana heard who was coming to visit the aircraft factory, she started to prepare her father for her benefit with recitals from the 'Secret Speech'. It worked. She told me how the night before Khrushchev's visit, it was her father she suspected to have loosened the handrail on the inspection steps leading to the cockpit of the prototype Aero L-29 Delfín. Khrushchev fell, but only as far as to break his ankle, not his neck. Perhaps the incident might have passed as an accident of unbelievable incompetence had not General Kava voiced his pent-up frustration and disapproval of Khrushchev. He was voracious in his criticism and not selective in the words he used, all of which was probably fuelled by his favourite vodka. Jana had achieved her aim. Next on her self-survival list was Dalek with his loud mouth and his self-condemning choice of associates. She said she had no idea of his StB involvement and I had no desire to tell her. However, I provided her with the means to his removal, plus I held the keys to another kind of future for Jana.

* * *

I thought Miles Faversham was about to choke when I told him I shot and killed Dalek Kava, then weighted down his body and dumped it in the local river. Maybe it was that, or perhaps the fact that I had Jana about to eat out of my hand, but whichever one it was, he was swallowing hard at the end of the telephone connection and gagging on his spittle.

"What was that you just said, Frank?" he enquired hoarsely down the secure line in the basement of the embassy after my coded signal hit the terminal on his desk.

I repeated what I'd told him using a few suggestions as to his hearing requirements then, following an interminably long time, his reply both crushed and infuriated me at the same time.

"You will follow my instructions to the letter on this one, Frank. First we have to get you out safely."

I interrupted, knowing precisely what was to come if my safety was paramount, but Faversham, or more likely the person I could vaguely hear in the background who was directing the conversation, would hear nothing of my claims of proficiency when it came to disposing of dead bodies in rivers.

"We hope you're right, but we're not taking any chances on it floating up and being found. There's a United Nations flight leaving Prague for Hamburg later this evening. The duty officer at your end will see to the ticket and the necessary papers; all you have to do is turn up at the airport and get on the plane. You will be met at the other end and shipped home, literally aboard a freighter leaving early Sunday for Harwich.

"I'll get a communiqué to the ambassador in Prague in an open transmit telling of a sudden death of a close relative of yours in Germany that requires your urgent attention. As it's Saturday today, there's no necessity to advise anyone outside of the Embassy of your departure until

Monday. That delay will also help with Dalek's no show at work. Puts you out of the picture by the time he's missed. Now, as for Jana. This department has all its noses to the grindstone as we speak. We have a local man who we will install as her handler and control. Unusual I grant you, but we feel it's necessary."

"Who's we?" I shouted down the phone line, seething with indignation and anger.

"I'm here on the ground and it's me who cleared her brother out of the bloody way. She's in for a smooth ride as one of ours thanks to me and I know her and, more important than anything, I have her trust. She asked for it and I delivered. There's absolutely no need to change who she answers to and deals with. I have the budget for an extension and I want to work her," I announced, enraged, into the prolonged silence of the phone receiver.

Eventually Faversham replied. "No disrespect, Frank, but you're out of your depth. We have a top-notch guy with an excellent history in this sort of thing on the doorstep ready to step in. We will want you to set her up with him before you leave as the two have never met. Fax me any details of the trade you and she have agreed on so we won't duplicate anything when our man takes over. Ah, just right, I think." He was talking to someone else close by, but out of my earshot when he said that.

"There's a violin concert at the Palac Zofin cultural centre on the Slavic Island this evening starting at 7 p.m. I hope that's nowhere near where you shoved Dalek's body over into the river, Frank. Don't want him floating up during the concert." He laughed.

I didn't, but I pressed and pressed and pressed him about what would happen to Jana, until eventually my threat of not leaving Czechoslovakia worked, albeit not entirely.

"Petr will use her in the same way as you intended, Frank. Perhaps more, but no less, he's skilled in our ways. We have plans for her that I can't discuss. Her brother's disappearance can be accounted for easily enough, so we'll draft the legend and write it off to drink. If, or when, his body emerges and he's still recognisable, Jana can put the gunshot down to someone he annoyed when drunk. A simple solution, all ends tied up!"

None of my concerns were addressed and I didn't buy into what he was waffling on about. Despite knowing I was being given the heave-ho, I wanted to go down fighting.

"So her Control is to be Czechoslovakian?" I asked in a friendly, understanding voice with no mention of Dalek's possible StB connection or the obvious fact that whoever this 'local man Petr' was, could have disposed of Dalek in exactly the same way as I had done. If it was a boxing match, I had Faversham on the ropes, as he betrayed the yearning to gossip that many who can only listen to what filters down from the top of the ladder do if their excitement takes them further than discretion should allow.

"Oh no! Her Control is a blue-blooded Russian. Field name of Petr Tomsa, as I said, but he's top stuff—is our Nikita Sergeyovitch Kudashov. He has ancestral ties to the House of Romanov no less. He was born in the same town, Kalinovka, as Khrushchev was and where the Communist Party insisted that male children took on Nikita as their given name. His patronymic name came from a Sergey Kirillovich, related to a Grand Duke of Russia, but his wife had an even closer link to the Royal Russian family than that. Even so, there you have it. That's the reason his and Khrushchev's names are almost identical. Incidentally, if you can't get on that UN flight for reasons beyond your or our control, he will be the man you must find to get you out of the country. He's accomplished in many areas, Frank."

At the end of that conversation I was left wondering who was on whose side? We had a retired Russian general, one-time mate of Joseph Stalin and murdered because of it, who was once the head of the secret police in Czechoslovakia with his blabbermouth son presumably installed as a StB agent, and whose daughter was only slightly sullied until I killed her brother and set her up as a source of British intelligence. They, the gods of seventh-floor reputation, demanded my prize be handled by a nigh on Russian tsar. Bewildered, I hung up.

* * *

I was in the sunlit, manicured gardens behind the Cabinet Office having a cigarette when Fraser called my mobile phone. He sounded unusually snappy.

“During Operation Donor, did you see Nikita Kudashov, aka Petr Tomsa, before or not until you handed Jana Kava over, Patrick?” he asked as I was wolfing down nicotine and the Prime Minister took an equally important call from his chum, President Bush. Mine and Fraser’s call was not as long as the PM’s. Fraser cut it short after my reply.

* * *

The early Friday afternoon, pre-weekend meeting with the Prime Minister and the Cabinet ended fairly quickly, for which I was pleased, and the stroll through Horse Guards passed in an enjoyable fashion despite my ill feeling about Prague. Faversham’s instructions were perfectly clear; I was to inform Jana of the meeting point and make sure she arrived. My job was then finished.

‘All has been arranged with the duty officer and the ambassador. I want you fully packed, raging to get back home, waiting inside the embassy by the time that concert starts. Okay, Frank?’

Those were the last words I heard from Faversham. When I did eventually arrive home in London, Faversham was no longer at the counter-intelligence desk. Apparently, he'd moved sideways onto the East German desk.

Some three or four years down the road I had some reason to ask for him and I was told he had died from a massive heart attack whilst abroad on company business. It was due to the inherent heart condition he had when joining the service from university. Being grossly overweight had apparently been the cause of a number of minor strokes in the past. From someone I heard that he was first considered for medical discharge when his six-month medical came up, but where he was at the French desk did not carry a HSL, High Stress Level rating. If that was case, I wondered why he was bumped up to the Soviet Satellite desk with the stress that must carry. Everything leads to everything, I reminded myself.

* * *

I had dined and now with dinner ended and alone with Hannah, after the office staff left for the weekend, and the house staff all gone home, my thoughts would still not depart from Prague of some twenty-five years ago. I didn't normally like talking of work after the day had ended, but today was different for several reasons. Hannah noticed my unease and enquired why.

"I don't want to sound unnecessarily worried, Hannah, but things are starting to rattle around inside this brain of mine. Operation Donor won't go away."

"I'm not surprised it won't disappear, Patrick. The part you were telling me before you had to leave sounded exciting but dangerous. Tell me some more."

* * *

Although, at times, I did think of the Kavas after leaving Prague, there were other operations I was involved in to take my mind off them, and then of course, there was Ireland, where I served a great deal of my service time, so they slipped lower in the list of priority as it were. Dalek Kava was not the first I'd killed and he wasn't to be the last. More likely than not, I would never have thought of him and his sister again had not Fraser Ughert introduced this Nikita Sergeyovitch Kudashov to me at lunchtime.

His granddaughter's name of Cilicia Kudashov was too close to the name of our anonymous benefactor we needed to thank for the wedding present of the house in Sussex. At the reception of that wedding, I opened a wrapped box where inside were the keys to the Sussex property and engraved on the lid to the box were the words *From the Home of Cilicia.* Nikita Kudashov had told me at lunch that his surname was an Armenian word meaning home. At our marriage service, I asked Hannah if she thought the gift had anything to do with any relative of hers, from the European dynasty of the House of Hesse, or indeed from her godparents, the Rothschild family? If the gift had come from a member of the Rothschilds, then Fraser and I were aware of a connection going back almost five years to when we were engaged dealing with Iraq and a corrupted CIA file coded Gladio B. Also a Henry Mayler, a member of a mysterious fraternity known as the Rosicrucians, who we suspected of knowing the names of eight families we had strong evidence of, who wanted to influence world affairs to their benefit and theirs alone.

Neither my wife nor I could find the answer to our benefactor's identity when the house was gifted, and nothing had happened since in our marriage in 2002 to alter that fact. Now, with Nikita Kudashov's appearance, I was hoping that might not remain the case, but as my thoughts drifted with the fading sunlit over St James's Park, Hannah brought me back into the world of 2007, reminding me that we were due at a drinks party hosted by the German Ambassador at his country's embassy at ten o'clock that evening. As I was dressing, my private mobile phone rang—it was Fraser Ughert once again. He was as agitated as before.

* * *

"I don't know what happened, Patrick, but you cut me off earlier and I know you're out tonight and time is precious to you, but Molly has put me on a short lead after my visit to St Thomas' Hospital today. They told me, in front of her, to not only take things easy, but give up the pipe and the whisky. Well, I'm not doing that, laddie.

No, not at all, am I doing that. But I have to admit the angina has been playing up recently. I had a bad attack a couple of weeks back. Anyhow, less of the gloom and doom. How did you recognise Kudashov at that park where you sent Jana Kava in? And do you think he recognised you at lunch today?"

The game had started, it seemed.

"London sent a photo of him to the embassy and I was told not to approach, just to point her in the right direction and leave it up to Kudashov to make the introductions. I parked myself up in a position to see them both with a small, retractable, pocket-size telescope I used in those days. It was London who told me of his real name and how he was using the name of Petr Tomsa in Czechoslovakia. Hannah asked me the same question and I gave her the same answer—I doubt he saw me, but I can't be one-hundred percent sure. Now what's all this about your heart? We knew it was no good a while back. Why don't you do what Molly says and put your feet up? You could take up gardening when you can't go fishing. Why associate yourself with someone out of the history books of Century House? Go easy on the pipe and save the whisky for when I'm next there. I promise it won't be long before I'm draining your supplies of the old Jura, my friend."

One question I deliberately never asked and that had never been addressed when Faversham instructed me to point Jana Kava towards Kudashov that Saturday night in May 1982, was how would he recognise her? Nobody told me they knew each other. At the time I remember thinking someone was playing a long game with me, keeping back intelligence that presumably I didn't warrant being told, but as things played out it was pretty obvious there was another agenda in the Prague episode of Operation Donor that neither I nor Miles Faversham knew.

Chapter Five: Victor

The Saturday morning following the reception at the German Embassy, Jimmy, my driver, with Frank, my principal protection officer beside him, drove me to Fraser and Molly Ughert's home in Chearsley, Buckinghamshire, a journey I knew so well. I'd left Hannah in Whitehall and asked her to make a personal call on Michael Simmons at *Group,* where Hannah and I had met. She was my personal assistant when I was the one in charge there and Michael was my station officer. With my elevation he was now the man in charge, the new Director General.

I needed some information that I wanted concealed from both the Director Generals at military intelligence, MI5, and the secret intelligence service at MI6 for a while, and I knew I could trust Michael to deliver on that.

* * *

"Have you considered this request of Kudashov's, and if so, where do you stand on it, Patrick?" Fraser asked as he closed the door to his home, shutting out the hot midday August sun that shone in a heavenly light onto his sprawling estate, some forty miles from London. Our journey had been smooth and uneventful, save for one thing. Michael Simmons' request for a particular paper file from archives had been questioned by Sir John Scarlett, the Director General at MI6, when it had pinged up on his Assistant Director's computer screen. Michael had winged it without mentioning me, but was unable to withdraw it until it had been scrutinised by the head of the Russian counter-intelligence desk, one Sir Brian Macintosh. I was disappointed with that result, but not surprised.

"I'm still working it through, Fraser, and in need of help," I replied to his rugged face, with its blotched drinkers' and smokers' skin and his trademark scruffy appearance.

"Yes, laddie, I thought that would be the case."

"I was under the impression that you were to stop that sanctimonious form of address now that I sit in the chair you once sat in, and I out-rank a retired chairman of JIC. Patrick is fine."

"Oh dear! Bad night was it?" he taunted me, and although it had been a bad night, I would never admit to that being the reason for my tetchy reply. We were at the door to his office, and as he opened it, my nostrils were filled with the tainted smell of violets and rosemary without a whiff of tobacco.

My first question was directed at my own pleasurable pursuits. "If you have given up smoking your pipe, can I still smoke my cigarettes in here, as I don't want to go upsetting Molly in any way?"

"I hope you will smoke them, Patrick. It will cover up the smoke of my pipe and I think I will be in need of more than one refill throughout this discussion."

As soon as we sat, he lit his orangey yellow Meerschaum pipe and I lit one of my cigarettes, but not before pouring two large whiskies from the decanter on the oblong table in front of the unlit fireplace between the two red sofas on which we sat facing each other.

"I was up until four this morning looking as far as I could do in such a short time into this business, and I found a folder inside which were two files, Fraser. One under the name of Nikita Sergeyovitch Kudashov and a separate one marked Petr Tomsa. The Tomsa one dealt exclusively with operations in Czechoslovakia and Poland, but Kudashov's file contained references all over Europe, both west and east. My first reaction was one of curiosity.

"Maybe it was nothing, I told myself, considering Kudashov used another coded operational name I found that he'd been given, that of Ivy; however, I could find no matching case files to that name. There must have been some overlap on an operation similar to the Jana Kava one, where two of his code names cropped up, but no! On the face of it, someone was running one of them, whilst hiding the other. More time is needed for a thorough search I know; nevertheless, I'm far from happy. Until I come up with an end date to the use of the name Tomsa, it could still be going on. That's why I'm here. I came because it's all too close to that Home Of Cilicia with Henry Mayler and that inner Circle of Eight you discovered, who want to rule the world. I thought we'd finished with that as a priority five years ago."

"Have you expressed your concern to Hannah, Patrick?" he asked as the pipe started to emit the soapy smell of tobacco.

"I have mentioned her family name before, but I want to keep her out of it as much as I can and I think not being able to is worrying me the most."

"This is going to be a little indelicate and I'm sorry to say it cannot be avoided. As you know, I've had a considerable amount of time on my hands of late with Molly's insistence on my staying put inside the house. It seems to me I'm only allowed out for doctors and hospital appointments nowadays. No matter, the time has helped me in the investigation I've been conducting into that box you were presented with holding the keys to that place of yours in Sussex. It was something too intriguing to leave alone. A bad passage of history for me, what with Jack Price's illegitimate daughter being killed after she shot one of our targets, that Moshe Gabbai, on Mount Desert Island off the coast of Maine and the estate him being on named The Home Of Cilicia. It's all too coincidental for my liking." His blue cagey eyes narrowed as he ended that last sentence; if he was going to add a reason, he had no time, as at that precise moment the telephone on his desk rang.

Knowing it was Molly's usual method of asking permission to interrupt, I nervously waved at the cloud of smoke above our heads.

"I wouldn't worry, Patrick, she knows I would disobey her with you here."

I wasn't sure how I was supposed to react to his statement. As there was no time to ponder on a response before Molly appeared with a large plate of sandwiches on a trolley with cups and saucers, a teapot, and a hot water kettle under a pretty, embroidered woollen cosy.

"Perhaps tea would be better than the whisky for your heart and liver, but somehow I don't think I'll be persuading you today, Fraser," she said with what I took as a look of admonishment directed at me as she left the room and closed the door silently behind her.

"I think I've upset Molly by coming. You should have given me a clue about that possibility. She's the last person in the world I would want to upset and you know that," I stated indignantly as he topped up my glass.

Fraser and I went back too many years to remember to allow sobriety, or the very few occasions either of us had been drunk, to interfere with the thirty-five guilt-ridden odd years we'd shared. *Everything is inconsequential to a single shared moment in time that has meaning.* We had shared many meaningful moments, some sad, some happy. If it wasn't for the fact that the intelligence service, we had both given our lives to, demanded the capacity of memory most would be unable to imagine, then at least one lie, if not a dozen more, would have led to the friendship's destruction a long, long time before now. Lies were our best friend. They stopped us believing the truth within the lie that everything leads to everything. *In the end, it's the truth that haunts the soul, not lies; they have no meaning, only consequences that in our game, have to be kept secret.*

"She's not upset with you, Patrick, far from it. She was delighted you were coming, only sorry that you wouldn't be staying longer. No, it's with me that her displeasure lies. I do know she's worried about my health, but I can't change the inevitable. I restrict my smoking to one or two pipes a day and a few glasses of whisky. Nothing like the old days."

I interrupted him. "You should stop them both," I declared forcefully.

"And add what, an extra four hours or four days to my life? No, I shall enjoy whatever time I have left doing what I enjoy. Now, less of the morbid stuff and more of the pleasurable. You're right, the files were split, and for one important reason. I believe it was to benefit the Rothschild family. You see how delicate this could be for Hannah if I'm right. We must tread carefully. Let me be perfectly frank here and state that I have no evidence that anyone named Rothschild solicited or stole information from the secret intelligence service of this country. I'm in more or less the exact position of those who investigated Victor Rothschild and his connection to Kim Philby and the rest, before Philby was spirited away to Russia.

"Victor baffled the intelligence services of this country back then and nobody could find anything concrete throughout his life, but it's my firm belief that somehow Jana's father, General Anotoly Vladislav Kava, got his hands on evidence to link Victor Rothschild to the KGB, and he told nobody until his son started to go off line with his support for Solidarity and other liberal pursuits he had, such as his sexuality. It's something I'm working on now this Kudashov has stuck his head above the parapet."

"What makes you think Jana Kava's father, the general and Victor Rothschild are connected?"

"It goes back to my early days in MI5 when the names of the Cambridge lot were on everyone's lips. They were always suspected of having one more in their innermost circle that nobody could get close to. But Dickie Blythe-Smith and I were not like most people. My first meeting with Dickie was like yours—in his club, the Travellers, we became instant friends and that friendship I'm only too pleased to say lasted his lifetime. But I digress, forgive me.

"In those bygone days of the early sixties, Dickie was Deputy Director General of the German desk in MI6. As a favour to a friend, he gave me the name of an attaché at the West German embassy in London who he said had a well-positioned contact in the StB in Czechoslovakia and was willing to trade.

"I'll cut a long, convoluted story short and say that StB contact was General Kava, but nothing came of it. Some years further on, I was invited to listen in on two meetings conducted by Dickie and his duty officer, briefing a man and a woman who I was never introduced to, who were going to Prague to meet with someone and solicit what information they could get on Victor Rothschild. The second of those meetings took place after the general election at the end of June 1970. Dickie called me one night and asked if I wanted to be temporarily attached to the British Embassy in Prague to cover the back door if anything went wrong. Silly question. Of course I did.

"Everything was in place by July that year, then out of the blue Dickie's duty officer calls me up and cancelled the whole op. Nobody ever gave me a reason, but later when Dickie and I worked together on that mission to get you, Job, along with that hare-brained genius Jack Price out of New York—before the FBI got their knickers twisted—he told me he had a call from the then new Prime Minister Edward Heath's office, telling him all funding for any of his overseas operations had been withdrawn until further notice. Dickie was further up the tree by then, but it still came as a shock hearing it directly from Number 10."

He stopped speaking and rose from the sofa, then withdrew a thin buff coloured file from the top drawer of his desk. The probing facial expression at me as he regained his sofa seat needed no verbal explanation. Fraser Ughert had been busy.

"Is that to do with Victor Rothschild?" I asked incredulously.

"Unfortunately, no. It's on Dalek Kava and his sexuality. Thought it might help."

"Yes, I knew Dalek was homosexual. Fraser, and I expect that's a dossier on either Dalek Kava or his lover, Alexandr Radoslav. Or it could be a map of the London Underground, I guess."

"Ha, bloody ha! I expect you know all there is to know about the Northern Underground line. It's on Radoslav, of course. As I understand things from the few files I could read in the time I've had—and remember my access to SIS files is restricted nowadays and has been for some while—you shot and dumped Kava's body in the Vltava River on Saturday the fifteenth, whereas Radoslav was found dead on the following Monday morning, the seventeenth, by the woman who kept house for them both. Now, if you didn't kill him before Dalek or double-back after you did, want to take a stab at who killed him, Patrick?"

"No, I wouldn't. Guessing in this case is far from easy. I'm working on taking a stab at Petr Tomsa and Nikita Sergeyovitch Kudashov, and why the latter was never mentioned in the files, which leaves your question and mine floating in our tobacco smoke."

"Well, that's where I believe the Rothschilds' interest takes over. I met with Kudashov last Tuesday, but more on that later; he says he has no idea London was running two files. How would he, he asked, all smiling and innocent. It's my view that the Russian Satellite desk was manipulated in the Rothschilds' interests by someone as yet unknown. Your question dovetails into all of mine. How about you agreeing to assist Kudashov and work towards what he asked for, his granddaughter's extraction from Russia.

Let's see how many people we can disturb in running that little operation, shall we?"

"You know me, Fraser, I'll be running ops in Hell when I get there. Nevertheless, my weakness for the idea of a daylight raid on the residents of the leafy environs of Guildford will have to be tempered by certainty. I will not sanction anything that endangers anyone in the extraction of this girl in Russia, nor if olden days seventh-floor Guildford reputations are slandered without indisputable evidence. Retirement is one thing. Going looking for trouble without need at your age is another. Let's slow down and have a re-evaluation of what we've got.

"There is one thing that concerns me most at the moment. It is the form of nepotism within the SIS at its Russian counter-intelligence desk. I had someone at Group do some preliminary digging and he found that Francis Henry Grant, the head of that desk in 1982, was stepfather to the present incumbent, Sir Brian Macintosh. Sir Brian's mother Elizabeth lost her first husband indirectly to syphilis. Sir Russell Macintosh was the UK's cultural attaché stationed in Delhi between 1977 and 1979, when he was sent home for medical reasons. It's likely he became infected before the couple moved to India as, when his condition was diagnosed, there was very little the physician could do other than prescribe a massive dose of penicillin. Unbeknown to both the hospital, where he was treated, and the clinician who administered the antibiotic, Sir Russell Macintosh was tragically allergic to penicillin. Elizabeth married Francis Henry Grant in 1981 and Grant accepted Macintosh's child as his own.

"Sir Brian was twenty-four when his mother remarried and never changed his name from Macintosh. Whether he chose to keep his birth father's name to avoid accusations of privilege, or his choice was an honourable decision, is neither here nor there; it should have been examined more closely and critiqued. Is there, I'm asking myself, some link between Sir Brian Macintosh and Kudashov? Or, now as you have introduced the Rothschild name, a connection between them all? Positively intriguing, don't you agree?"

"Even more so, Patrick, as when Kudashov said that he and I had been friends for years, he was lying. The first time I've ever met him was when I told you; Tuesday this week. Lunch at your club was only the second time I've clapped eyes on him!"

"Why didn't you say something?" I asked, beginning to see a joke coming from somewhere.

"Dickie mentioned him a few times and his name crossed my desk, but I didn't want to spoil the fun we can have," he replied, straight-faced.

Chapter Six: Norway

"Kudashov found me," Fraser stated as though I should have already known that to be the truth.

"He says he saw me at your wedding reception at Claridge's and he recognised me from my much younger days in the British legation in Cairo in 1958. He was in Cairo on commercial business, or so he says. He asked the concierge at Claridge's for my address, but came up short on that one. As you know, Marcel is a great friend of Molly and me, and he would never divulge personal information. According to Kudashov, his interest was of no importance then, but four years later his granddaughter, this Cilicia Kudashov, comes to him when he was in his apartment in central Moscow and tells of an American NSA programme that she can decipher. She wants to escape to the West, she says, but can't because there's a brute of a Russian in charge of her department who fancies her, moved her into his luxurious apartment, and wants to shower her in money and furs. Furthermore, Kudashov says she will tell us, if we rescue her, how the Americans have the ability to hack into the mobile phones of international heads of government and most of those involved in NATO. Not really pleasant having one's conversations listened into by anyone, but when done by a so called friend and ally, most disconcerting and downright rude. Makes one wonder if they are on our side at all, but then again I have thought that for years. Mine you, if we found out how to use it—it would pay dividends listening in to a handful of Yanks we have interesting files on.

"Some little time before you were on that operation in Czechoslovakia, I came across an incident with Kudashov's fingerprints on it that flagged up on the counter-intelligence NATO desk I was working at the time. I was in the extreme edge of northern Norway on the border with Finland and Russia. Originally, my role was to work with the Norwegian intelligence service in laying down a 'Stay Behind' line of defensive attributes. It was for the inevitable overrun of Soviet military in that region that could not be stopped, but could be slowed down to enable a counter that might force the Kremlin to reconsider going any further. I was not privy to it all but we were well aware of President Ronald Reagan's belligerence towards Russia and we would not have been at all that surprised had the whole exercise escalated into its worse possible scenario.

"Anyway, back to Kudashov. I was operating along the border with a small group of engineers from 3rd Parachute Regiment and a two-man Gurkha detachment. You would have loved it all, Patrick. War games for the boys. The Norwegians had lit up a recently installed ground-to-air missile battery and radar plotting position. Despite knowing where the damn things were, they had no intel from a ground perspective. It was my job to calculate how easy or difficult it would be to get in and out without being seen and blow the whole place up without leaving any traceable impression. Bear in mind that nobody wanted any stupidity in these things to occur. My written orders were to tread lightly and not to enter Soviet territory. I had no idea how to do my job without entering Soviet territory, so I ignored the written ones that were to save someone's arse and went in.

"I and the Gurkha sergeant got past the wire and inside the base completely undetected. Once settled in there, we went through a couple of routines linked to the remainder of the patrol who were still on Norwegian soil, designed to throw the signature data banks of the radar off-line and bugger up the guidance control on the missile battery. We got out, went back to the NATO command, made my report, then we all went off to the barracks, had a good a drink and knees-up, and forgot about it.

"Two days later, my director at counter-intel was on the phone with a story emanating from a source he wouldn't name who worked inside what then remained of British Leyland. This source claimed that a Labour politician, someone military intelligence were already looking at and code-named COB, gave some photographs to a Communist Party trade union shop steward showing a group of British commandos having breached international law by crossing the Soviet border without a signed invitation. This COB politician chappie told everyone he could that the photograph clearly demonstrated Margaret Thatcher was as much a warmonger as

President Reagan. But he didn't stop there! He stated he had first-hand information that the Red Army had been mobilised and the Eastern Bloc countries were at the highest level of alert they had ever been. War was the next step, he preached, and they listened. His aim, so my director's source claimed, was to cause as much disruption within the Transport and General Workers Union as he could and thereby cripple, or at least disorganise, all movement within this country.

"And this was where Kudashov steps into the game. As my director was telling this story to me and requesting my immediate return to London, it transpired that the Director General at MI6 was briefing the Prime Minister and her Cabinet over exactly the same photographs. Only his information repudiated everything the pictures were meant to represent. The London *Evening Standard* ran the story the government press secretary gave them, with some of the pictures that night, and the national press covered it the following day. I never found out until I was moved up to the seventh floor in 1993 who provided the evidence to prove those photos were false;

afterwards, I was thankful to the man Dickie had mentioned, a certain Nikita Sergeyovitch Kudashov, code-named Ivy, because he not only saved me from a huge rollicking, but saved what could have been an international disaster."

"What evidence did this Ivy have that saved the world from going to war, Fraser? It must have been bloody good."

"The photos that were printed showed soldiers wearing Finish uniforms and nowhere near the border. COB, whoever he was, never had any photos after Kudashov paid him a visit. They were burnt in the incinerator at Century House, Patrick."

"So Kudashov was in London in 1982?"

"Seems as though he was, yes."

"But what do you know of his other code name, this Petr Tomsa, and going back to my question; why did London want the separation? Where is the benefit of having two code names for the same individual whilst overseas and another here on British soil? All I can see is chaos ensuing."

"Precisely, Patrick! Perhaps whoever was behind it wanted chaos. Perhaps whoever designed this chaotic system wants to throw anyone who looks, off the scent. But what's the prize, eh? He, or they, carefully wrote the files so they didn't match. Drafted the operations in such a way they did not overlap. I've read a thesis a long while ago wanting to prove that within chaos there is a degree of order.

"I can't remember if the paper did or did not prove there is, but our job will be to find that order and if what's happened down the years is to the detriment of this country, then we must bring it before the government, no matter who is involved. Let's shelve the mystery into The Home of Cilicia, along with Kudashov's granddaughter for now, and start at the beginning. Tell me about Operation Donor and why you dealt with Dalek Kava the way you did."

And so it was that I repeated the story I had told Hannah the previous day. I expanded on some of it that I had hidden from my wife, telling him of the affair Jana and I found ourselves in, and how her brother disparaged and sneered at her, in bed with the British spy. His insults were becoming more and more personal, and more threatening. He told me how his father the general, when in charge of the StB, had recruited his son into the junior branch of the security service so he could hide his son's indiscretions and disrespect of the Communist Party. He went on to emphatically tell me, in no uncertain words, that Jana was behind their father's death, stoking his resentment when she knew it was Khrushchev who was visiting Prague. He made fun of his sister and threatened to expose her guilt. When I confronted Jana, it was all she could do to refrain from killing her brother herself. That's what led me into killing Dalek. If I hadn't killed him, there's no doubt in my mind he would have put his sister and the operation at risk.

"He was drunk from earlier on that Friday and as the night progressed, so his drunken state worsened, but only into his usual boring anti-Russian rhetoric. There was nothing really unusual in that. But without any warning that I was aware of, he suddenly blurted out some incoherent language, lambasting the Polish government who he said I was helping to keep in power … then he literally threw himself at me.

"Physically he was strong, but he didn't rely on just that. Luckily, I had withdrawn the gun from the armoury in the Embassy the weekend before, as he was particularly abusive on that occasion, but although he quietened down during the week, I'd kept hold of it. Dalek had a handgun, which looked like an old WWII German Luger. He pulled it out from behind, where it must have been tucked in his belt and pointed it at Jana, telling me to back off. I shot him in the head without waiting to see what he was going to do. It was just past midnight and, being the start of the weekend, there was a lot of noise outside when I shot him. Jana and I cleaned the mess, waited until around three a.m. and then I got one of the boats moored about fifty yards from their riverside home. I rowed out to where the River Vltava widens near Wenceslas Square, about half a mile up stream; it was cold and cloudy that early morning and nobody was silly enough to be out to see me. I didn't feel the need to tell Hannah about my intimacy with Jana but, if she guessed, she never said. The other thing I'll say to you about Jana Kava is we must find out if she was in the Czech secret police, the StB. I told my debriefing everything I knew and I never pointed a finger at Jana, but it would be very odd if her father never signed her up."

"Maybe that was the real reason for London's interest, Patrick, but let's put that aside for a while. How far was it from Jana's home to where Dalek and Radoslav lived?" he asked with that avuncular expression I had come to know so well. I could hear the gears in his brain churning over as I savoured his smile with pleasure—*I know where I'm going with this, laddie, and you have no idea do you?* But I did know.

"Do you think it was Jana who killed Dalek's lover and not this Petr Tomsa, Fraser?"

"If that is the case then Petr Tomsa and Jana Kava could be the same person, which would then beggar the question of why send you to Prague in the first place?"

"That question crossed my mind quite a bit. I thought at the time of killing her brother, Jana Kava was already ours and I was sent to clear Dalek out of the way for something else she had to do for London. But if, as you and I suspect, she killed Radoslav, then why use me to kill her brother? If we are to assume Radoslav knew of Dalek's StB connection, which is not beyond the realms of probability, then it follows he would wonder why he hadn't returned home that Saturday morning. We can also confidently assume that Dalek and Radoslav had discussed Jana's relationship with me. But neither Jana nor I knew where their conversation could have gone. The only way Jana could guarantee her future safety once I had killed her brother was to deal with his flatmate in a similar fashion. If I'm right in believing someone in London on the Soviet Satellite desk already owned Jana, then they had no reason to send me out there, but I'm thinking not all on that desk knew about her allegiances."

"That sounded to me that you had that reply loaded and ready to fire."

"Oh, I have more, Fraser. Go one step forward and assume Jana was under suspicion by either the Czech secret police or the KGB; then, whoever was pulling her strings in London, needed her nearest and dearest cleared out of the way before he could be questioned without the blame falling on her. Those running the Soviet Satellite desk start looking for a possible scapegoat if things turn nasty and hey presto, up pops Patrick West as Frank Douglas, already established as a chemical analyst. Send him and see where the ball falls."

"Hmm, interesting! Who set you up in the chemical industry as an analyst?"

"Nobody set me up in it. It's what I studied at Oxford. After women, it was and *is* my premier love."

"How long ago was it you left Oxford and Dickie Blythe-Smith sold you on the intelligence service as your future career move?"

"I left in 1972 and at first went to work with Jack Price in New York, as you know. That was the same year you drove me—from where I was recovering from a busted jawbone and eye socket, as well as the loss of three toes—to the Travellers Club in Pall Mall to meet him."

"I remember that day. You thought you were in for a rollicking, instead of which Dickie offered you a way in to MI6. I'm obviously pleased he did. But back to business. In Faversham's briefing, was there any mention of a date when Dalek Kava began work as a chemical analyst?"

"And there I wonder if we have the answer, Fraser. Kava started work the year before I signed on the dotted line of the Official Secrets Act for the second time, but he wasn't employed at Bok's as an analyst. That information in the briefing file was not entirely accurate. He was, as it said, second in charge of their analysing laboratories, but his expertise lay in what he was: the chemical processing auditor. We shared some common areas, but not as much as the file would have you believe. A small point I know, but if you wanted me as a piece to fit into the jigsaw puzzle, then you'd have to adjust his profile in order to fit me in."

Chapter Seven: Faversham and Prime

Hannah arrived on Sunday morning at Chearsley as Molly was serving her renowned breakfast of poached eggs and bacon fried on her range, with freshly baked bread rolls taken from the oven and still piping hot. My wife was not the only alteration to the environment that witnessed Fraser and me up until the early morning hours in deep discussion and research.

Jimmy and Frank had returned to their homes for a well-earned leave, being replaced by two other principal protection officers who joined the two who had accompanied Hannah on her journey from Whitehall. Molly was beaming a smile of contentment as she dispensed her fare to the hungry mouths, but my mind was centred on a more spartan breakfast scene twenty-five years earlier at Century House in Westminster Bridge Road, a stone's throw from the Houses of Parliament and also our apartment at the Foreign and Commonwealth Office.

* * *

Miles Faversham was a man who appeared comfortable with his size when I met him that day in the middle of April 1982. I estimated him to be nudging twenty stone or more, mid-forties in age, with not a lot other than a huge appetite going for him. The red plastic tray he carried to our table beside a southerly facing window was weighty and full. He scoffed at my meagre choice of tea and cereal before shovelling down what obscenely filled and overhung his plate.

His communications skills were excellent for the typist pool and I mean no disrespect to any of them by saying that, but to me he was too open to be an intelligence Deputy Head of anything, let alone something as sensitive as the Soviet Satellite desk with all the counter-intelligence funnelling through that department. His Director General, or DG, Francis Henry Grant that I mentioned before was, he told me, a very influential man who had promised Faversham preferential consideration the next time a promotion review of the department was held. Faversham impressed on me the importance of full completion with a satisfactory outcome to Operation Donor in order for that offer to materialise. Although I thought him to be totally unsuitable for his position, there was no point, nor any person I could complain to. I was merely a humble yet injurious agent, expected to do what I was told without comment.

Back in 1982, it was not too difficult for an assigned operational officer to gain access to any file held in paper form in the Gower Street archives, but by 2007, when all those records had been converted into digital form, only someone of my present official clearance could access all of them. Hannah had brought the paper file I had previously seen on Miles Faversham with her, as well as a copy of the digital update. Both had every detail about the man who had served within the Secret Service that one would expect.

He had joined in 1963, aged twenty-two, straight from Cambridge University where he had a penchant for languages and the classics. Because of the legendary Cambridge Five, or as the KGB allegedly referred to them, the Magnificent Five, his vetting was meticulously undertaken, with him emerging smelling as sweet as roses. He had been stationed in most parts of Europe, appearing before interview assessment boards each time and further vetted on numerous occasions. As I read on, I found that his achievements were not only restricted to academia. He had a full blue for rowing, being part of the winning boat in the '61 university boat race, so at least at one time in his life he was a fit, athletic man. What, I wondered, had changed to make him the opposite? Additional information included his marital status, married and divorced twice, and his dependants— no children from either marriage.

What *was* a surprise was there were no medical reports or mentions of health checks included in either the old paper file or the computerised one, yet when I asked about his whereabouts, sometime after the adventures of Operation Donor had ended, I was distinctly told by more than one person that he'd suffered a few strokes and was being considered for medical retirement before handling Donor. From the number of people who told me of his strokes, it left little room for not believing it, but then why no corresponding records? As I've previously said he was a big, overweight man when I met him, so his death being caused by his obesity would have come as no surprise but, equally, that obvious debility could have covered something more sinister. I had either been lied to or misled. What else was being covered up?

Inside both case files was the expected service reference to Operation Donor and against the code name for Dalek Kava: FlyHiTwo was the mention of his death—eliminated by an external asset. Asset, not officer, that distinction deflected his murder away from me. It went on to say that his body was successfully disposed of. Against Jana Kava's code FlyHiOne, was a one word explanation: present. There was a peculiarity to that declaration in the digital file that fitted into today's framework—an StB investigation into Dalek's disappearance and the murder of Alexandr Radoslav. The disappearance of Dalek Kava did not appear to have been extensively investigated, but that was not the case with his lover. Jana Kava was interviewed following the discovery of Radoslav's body. Her alibi was the thing that connected the 1982 operation to the reason we were sitting in Fraser's office discussing our next step over the extraction of Cilicia Kudashov.

The last time Jana saw Radoslav, as recorded by the investigating Captain Milan Tříska of the Státní Bezpečnost police at 19.35 Tuesday the 18th of May, was on Sunday two days previously, just before she left her home for the hospital to be beside Karina Kudashov, wife of Ludvík, who gave birth to Cilicia seven minutes before noon on Monday the seventeenth. In her recorded evidence she stated she had seen her brother with Radoslav leave 34 Sámova, Praha 10, together around 11 a.m. Sunday, saying they were going Radoslav's apartment. They both were in good humour and although they had obviously been drinking, both were upright. She and Karina were old friends and she'd promised to be with her throughout her labour. The Captain praised her for her openness and complimented her on the friendship she had with Karina Kudashov—they were a wonderful family, he said.

Her evidence stated that she stayed with the Kudashov family for what remained of that day and for the night. She left for work on Tuesday from their home. She had no idea where Dalek was, but offered the informed opinion that he might be in a ditch, drunk! As far as Radoslav's murder was concerned she had no idea whatsoever who might have killed him, but when Captain Tříska put the proposition to her that perhaps Dalek had killed Radoslav and then committed suicide somewhere yet to be found, she reluctantly agreed that could have happened. *'Unfortunately my dear brother was never a stable man when on a drinking spree, which was every weekend and most weekdays.'*

The police report that I read established three things of importance: one, Cilicia existed; two, the Kudashovs were known to the StB and to Jana, and; three, Jana Kava was not requested to return for further enquiries. The question over who was using who and for what purpose was even higher on my list of considerations.

* * *

With the benefit of hindsight it's now clear to me that Faversham was most certainly being used, and his death conveniently erased him from any enquiry. When we met, he struck me as man without a purpose, stuck in a job that demanded usefulness and integrity. There was no passion in his crow-black bulging eyes with heavy, hooded eyelids that were unresponsive as he read from the file. There was no emotion to his softly spoken voice on delivering his briefing. The only time I can recall him showing any sign of not being a disillusioned robot was when I asked what he did before having one of the main chairs at the Soviet Satellite desk.

He was positively loquacious about how it was he who informed the German authorities of a Red Army Faction proposed rocket-propelled grenade attack against the US Army's West German Commander, a Frederick J. Kroesen. He gave me chapter and verse on how the information on Brigitte Mohnhaupt and Christian Klar, the two suspected attackers, had arrived on his French desk and the name of the French agent who had penetrated the German terrorist organisation. It did cross my mind about how secure a link he would be to have at the London end of Operation Donor.

When I contacted Faversham from Prague and explained Jana's revelations about Geoffrey Prime and the American spy plane facility in

Nevada, the mental picture I had of him as my Control gave me no confidence as I listened to his advice, having told him I'd shot one of the targets he wanted me to turn. I wanted to conduct the exchange by the pre-coded fax machine, but was told to use the scrambled phone line instead. I couldn't hear another person on the telephone line, but that does not mean there was none.

* * *

After surviving the circuitous route and passage aboard the freighter to arrive in London from Prague, one of the first things I did was to try to find how Geoffrey Prime had been caught and what he'd done. What he'd done was the easier of those two aims of mine. He had learned to speak Russian at a language school in order to be posted to RAF Gatow in Berlin, Germany, where most of the radio traffic came from Russian-speaking East Germans. Once he was established at Gatow, Prime worked exclusively as a radio operator, monitoring Russian voice transmissions from the other side of the wall and passing the ones he selected on to GCHQ. On his return to Great Britain, he was transferred to a division of Government Communications based at St. Dunstan's Hill in the City of London. It was here he started to photograph highly sensitive government transcripts and pass them on to his Soviet handlers in exchange for money.

He had tried, unsuccessfully, to convince the KGB officers he met that he wanted to spy for Russia for ideological reasons, but they never trusted him, insisting they paid for what he gave after they analysed it. That distrust the KGB had of Geoffrey Prime never wavered, but that never stopped Prime. When he was posted on to GCHQ, Cheltenham, he continued to pass on information for money to his handlers.

The damage done by Prime when at Cheltenham was considerable. I discovered from another file Hannah had copied that he was vetted and acquired American security clearance, after which he was appointed to work inside a highly classified part known as J Division, an American specialist telecommunication department. This clearance enabled him to interpret collected unencrypted telemetry from Soviet missile launch sites gathered from US satellites, as well as intercepted radio communications from VHF and

UHF wavebands and microwave telephone communications forwarded on from RAF Menwith Hill, in Yorkshire, part of the United States Air Force Intelligence Surveillance and Reconnaissance agency where their Frosting and Echelon programme originated from. He had every means of communication we and the Americans used to transmit and receive at his and his Russian friends' disposal to do with as they pleased.

One of the systems Geoffrey Prime used to decipher UK/USA intelligence signal traffic led to his most damaging disclosure to the Soviet Union. It was the revelation of a programme designed to track the secret radio transmissions of Soviet submarines. He used a computing machine that Alan Turing, whilst at Bletchley Park, had developed to break the 'Enigma Code' during WWII. Ironic when you think that the English-born Alan Turing's work helped Great Britain to victory against fascism and the English born Geoffrey Prime's abuse of that work could have helped Communism defeat the freedom Turing worked for if war had broken out between NATO and the Soviet Bloc. Prime was a pernicious and careful spy, beginning his trade with the Soviet Union in 1968 while in West Berlin with the RAF and finally ending his alliance in 1981 when he was paid the sum of £4,000 for that tracking system.

The 'how' he was caught was the odd thing in what was such a devious and complex scheme he had devised for the espionage side to his life. For example, he was not caught at any meetings he had in Berlin, or Vienna, or Dublin where he met with his Soviet handlers. Nor was he caught using empty Coca-Cola tins to pass microfilm at dead-letter drop-off points. It's arguable that, without a psychological disorder being his Achilles heel, his downfall would never have happened. He was allowed to indulge in both his treasonable pursuits and what was diagnosed as a psychological disorder, by the inefficient safeguards to the safety and welfare of the public that were in place during this time. In fact, it could be said—nobody cared.

Prime had a paedophilic interest in young girls. In 1982, the police had an anonymous phone call, giving his car registration in response to an appeal for witnesses to an assault on a young girl whilst alone in her home in Hereford.

He was interviewed at a police station, but released. In the official reports on the affair, it's said that Prime later confessed his predilection to his wife, who then reported his disclosure to the authorities.

When police searched the house, they found incriminating evidence of his spying activities beside a card index of some 2,300 girls he targeted by using the telephone to find his victims. Although sentenced to 38 years in prison, he was strangely released after serving only half of those years. By 2007, he had been released from prison for six years and I figured the best way to discover the circumstances about his capture was to ask him. But I had another prey on my mind to start with.

* * *

It was Hannah who broke into my thoughts before I had spoken of them.

"There are a few things we need to do before we blindly rush and ask this Geoffrey Prime questions we have not as yet identified."

Fraser lit his first pipe and joined the discussion with some sage advice.

"True, yes, I'm not sure Prime would have the answers, but it's a good enough place to start. Jana Kava giving you information of Geoffrey Prime's future appearance at the Old Bailey is not exactly top-floor confidential stuff is it? It's more like a … *see what I have* kind of thing. No!" Abruptly he stopped speaking and stared at the blank sheet of paper in the notebook on his red leather-bound blotter. "I reckon some-one gave her that snippet of information about Prime, knowing full well the extent of the dam-age Prime had done at GCHQ. Someone's play-ing a game trying to make us believe that's the only intelligence they had. Whoever gave her that information knew more than just a future court hearing."

I interrupted him. "That was my guess when I was in Prague and Dalek told me what Jana told him. Initially, I thought he'd got it wrong and Jana had told him more, but he said no and I believed him, as he then opened up about the US Nevada site. There was lots of detailed infor-mation in what he said his sister had told him. To start with, he had the technical names of two US spy planes tested out of there. He knew the radio frequencies and methods of transportation used to ferry the framework of the planes to the place, as well as other stuff attributable to the site management.

"I asked him what the two of them were doing at the time Jana had told him, and if there was a particular reason why she told him. By that stage he wasn't very comprehensible as he'd been drinking for most of the day, but despite that, he was certain she told him of Prime's court appearance a few days after I had met them both. That would have been around the second week after I arrived. She never instructed him to tell me either or both of those things. In his words—he just felt like it. The two stories were of course important in different ways and I can't tell you why I thought it, but I believed the Nevada test-site information came from a separate source than that about Geoffrey Prime. It's just a hunch, as the Americans might say. Anyhow, I passed on some very explicit details to Faversham about the Nevada desert site that will not be in the file we have. It will be in a higher classified one than this."

I picked up the two-inch-thick red paper folder I'd been referring to and nonchalantly tossed it away on to the sofa behind me. "So far I'm sticking with my theory that Faversham was a front for someone able to work the seventh floor and the whole episode of the apprehension of Geoffrey Prime was done simply to cover up someone nobody discovered at GCHQ because nobody looked further than Prime. He was charged, and the door was slammed shut on their disgrace. I'm leaving Prime for now, and not only because of the taste his name leaves in my mouth. I'll start with Nikita Kudashov and see where that goes, Fraser."

"Yes, you could be right about nobody looking further past Prime. There was a lecture given to the East German security service, Stasi, by Kim Philby the year before Prime was eventually caught. In it Philby attributed the failure of the British Secret Service to unmask him as due in a great part to the British class system—it was inconceivable to them that one born into the ruling class of the British Empire could be a traitor. That despairing judgement could equally apply to Prime. The early eighties were strange times,

Patrick, ones best forgotten but learned from. But I do know someone who dug deeper than just accepting Prime," he replied with his craggy face turned towards the window.

Chapter Eight: Monday's Ethnic DNA

I arranged to meet Kudashov at the place he was staying. It was what we called The Russian House—number 17 Craven Hill Gardens, Bayswater, Paddington. Russian instead of Russia, because most of those who stayed there for any length of time were from a past age rather than being relevant to the present or the future. Whether or not that summary applied to Kudashov, I was about to find out.

Number 17 was in the second of two well cared for gardened rectangles of Victorian-built properties in a tall long terrace of five-storey buildings, which mainly served as private apartments, hotels, consulates and the comfortable London retreat for wealthy Russians seeking an audience with HM Government. No one tried to conceal the place, why would we? It was convenient for us to see who we had staying and was of interest to those inside the Russian Embassy a short walk away. As of yet Kudashov had attracted no interest from the Russians. Our ministerial car was parked in the nearest spot to number 17 and Hannah strolled the short distance to the front entrance to the building with Frank at her side. I could have sent anyone with her as I had no worries about her safety, but I thought Frank would reassure Hannah and if she needed it, boost her confidence.

I had learned over our time together that although she had never been instructed in the arts of interrogation, her quiet reassuring voice lured the unsuspecting into revealing more than I, along with most other interrogators I knew, would extract without the use of force. With Kudashov we needed soft hands, and who better to approach a member of the Romanov family than one with the same kind of prestigious ancestral ties as his? In Hannah's case, her lineage was to the ancient European House of Hesse, connected by marriage to the Rothschild family. My thoughts were that our wedding gift of the house and grounds near Hassocks, in Sussex, must have come from one of Hannah's Rothschild relatives purely because of the cost, over three million pounds' worth of luxury. Hannah

Sofia Rachel Landgft, to give my wife her full name, was, I thought, my ideal weapon to open up Kudashov's particular box of surprises.

* * *

I had the pleasure of attending a meeting once in the Russian House when Fraser Ughert was a mere section head at Group and I was, for want of a better word, his heavy. In those far off days nobody had invented the phrase principal protection officer. The world was less complicated back then. My principal, Fraser, was there, so he told me, to meet a retired Russian translator who had worked at the Polish Embassy here in London. That was the extent of my knowledge, but he might just as well been there to see the Russian President and hand over the Crown Jewels for all I knew.

What I do know is that it was a hugely impressive place. High vaulted ceilings displayed magnificent paintings of mystical dragons that appeared to be two feet above your head and about to grab you in their open mouths. Marble floors and painted marble pillars. Three life-size sculptures of Lenin, Pushkin and Rimsky-

Korsakov were there separating the formal lobby from the carpeted, elegantly appointed reception area. I knew as little about Russian furniture as I do now; however, to my unaccustomed eye the highly ornate tables, chairs, and side cabinets looked distinctly of an Eastern design and the ebony coloured desk at the far wall was, I was told, when I asked the brute of man who followed me everywhere, Empress Alexandra's desk from the Romanov's Winter Palace. I did not stay long that day as Fraser's translator was not there.

On the return journey to the building that then housed Group, hidden within the Ministry of Agriculture and Fisheries in Whitehall, we were informed that a person of his description, but not of the same name, had boarded a flight for Ottawa, Canada. A little later on that far flung day, whilst sharing with Fraser a brand of whisky the name of which I've long forgotten, I learned that the man Fraser had an interest in had managed to leave a tape-recording of all that was required to 'burn' a Polish official at their embassy in London.

On arrival in Canada, the translator was immediately driven to the British High Commission where he made a written statement confirming the name of the politician who was selling Polish secrets to the French in return for a considerable amount of money traceable to an account in Geneva. I can't say who was pleased and who was not in that exchange. All I can report is that the chorus of congratulations heard from Fraser Ughert's offices travelled substantially further than the Bear and Staff public house, Craven Hill Gardens, where the two of us were enjoying any echoes two full glasses of whisky might make as the contents were greedily consumed. All I was able to do this time was pick out Hannah and Kudashov's conversation from the echoes in the marbled reception on the tape-recorder she carried and we were listening to.

* * *

"I shall come straight to the point of my visit, Mr Kudashov. I'm here to find a sustainable and adequate reason for this country to become involved in the extraction of the person whom you say is your granddaughter, one Cilicia Kudashov, daughter of your son Ludvík, and his wife Karina Kudashov, from Moscow, or any other part of Russia. We believe there has to be something other than this Data Mining, which although it's intriguing, is a process we are aware of. But our door is far from closed to you. We are in the market for other wares you may have to offer as you have certainly piqued our interest. Please, trade away."

She had not disappointed me. The recorded conversation was a long, drawn out affair of almost an hour or so where neither of the participants felt able to finish the negotiations in one sitting. It was when I was beginning to tire of references to Kudashov's ancient relatives and long lines of historic confrontations between various titled European families with nothing being added to Cilicia's relevance to us, other than her communications skills, that Hannah altered track and asked what I had requested.

"When you met my husband last Friday you were with a friend whom you claimed to have known for a considerable time, when in fact you had met for the first time the previous Tuesday. A rather unusual mistake to make, Mr Kudashov.

It is also recorded that you may have seen my husband in the past, in another country, but you made no reference to that sighting. Is there a reason for these omissions?"

He went into his shell for a while, denying that he had ever seen me before, until Hannah asked again, this time dangling more than a carrot. "My husband would very much like to meet with you and discuss both the past and the future, but I have nothing from our discussion to offer as an incentive for him to alter his busy schedule. Your granddaughter has an obvious appeal to us, but as I already said, we do know of the NSA programme and we are aware of their capabilities. I need something of a higher value to serve to capture his interest."

"Would the body of Dalek Kava be of interest to you both, or your husband as your husband, or your husband as the chairman of your joint intelligence committee? Which person named Frank Douglas would fear the discovery the most, do you think, Mrs West?"

* * *

Hannah arranged the meeting to take place in my club at lunchtime the following day. She accompanied me and I was reintroduced to Nikita Sergeyovitch Kudashov. I sat with my back to the sun as if I was a gunslinger about to draw on a card cheat.

"Frank Douglas in Prague and Patrick West when home." His eyes were squinting into the sunlight, but the hawkish brown colour was still distinguishable amongst the lines of age that crisscrossed his mottled face.

"It's a question I've always wanted to ask a spy, and that's do you ever get confused by all the changes of names you must go through, Mr West?"

To assimilate information about the character of a person you're sitting opposite to from just the face and eyes was a custom I was familiar with, and so I tried it with Kudashov. His eyes registered excitement as well as disappointment, which was clear when I replied to his question with one of my own. On first appraisal I thought both sentiments to be genuine. In regards to his face, there was little movement to reflect his emotions. The lines around his mouth showed more frowns than smiles and so it was at the table we shared. His offer was certainly tempting. Any intelligence on rivals or friends and enemies is never to be sneered at, but be that as it may, the offer of a benevolent hand should always be tempered with circumspection. If there was nothing else discernible from his facial appearance, there was experience etched deeply into every line of his skin.

"But surely you would know the answer to that, Mr Tomsa. Were you not also Petr Tomsa in Czechoslovakia, as well as being Ivy in other theatres of global influence?"

"My code name was, as you know, Ivy, but I'm guessing you spent your time in many aliases. As far as the name Petr Tomsa goes, then I know nothing of the person. If your intelligence has me posing with that alias, then someone has screwed up in a big way. Either it is intentional misinformation or you have a really crap filing department within the SIS."

The summer sun faded behind a dark dense cloud threatening to add more showers, and I instantly felt the irony of trying to discover secrets about another country and in another time, whilst there was something hidden away as a secret in my own. Most things in the intelligence game are based on assumptions and theories; once one of those theories is proven correct, a piece on the chessboard can move, but the art is knowing which chess piece to move and where to move it. I was spared making that decision for the time being, despite the fact that Petr Tomsa had only a Czech and Polish file, yet the man sitting in front of me was who Miles Faversham had detailed as Jana Kava's Prague Control. It did nothing for my appetite. Who was Petr Tomsa if not Kudashov?

"It would seem I have been allocated a second token of information to barter with, Mr West, or are you simply speculating on the name, Tomsa? Perhaps now would an appropriate time to be less formal in our discussions, Patrick. Please, call me Nikita. It's what my friends call me."

"I will, and now we've got that out of the way, can we discuss the real reason for your visit to this country?"

"There is an old saying in Russia: even a good horse can stumble. You will find this Tomsa without too much trouble, I'm sure. Probably a silly administrative error made in a filing department, not important. However, you will never find what I have to offer without my help, Patrick. Let me be honest here. I am not a scientist, and I cannot give you the scientific breakdown of the list of sequenced eukaryotic genomes and ethnic DNA that has been assembled and experimented with in the laboratory that I have knowledge of. But what I can tell you is from the solid information I have been given, the work on these chemicals in that place will become more lethal to human life than any nuclear threat has ever been. I was disgusted by what I discovered and I'm determined to make it known, but despite my abhorrence I cannot allow my name to be disclosed whilst I have family that are beyond my protection."

"By that you mean Cilicia, or is there someone else as well as her?" It was Hannah who asked the family related question.

"I refer to Cilicia, yes. I lost my son and his wife some years ago when the aircraft he was flying crashed near the Russian border with Finland. My wife died some considerable time before that sad happening. My dear granddaughter is all I have left in the world. She is precious to me. I will not leave her in the position she is."

"Following on from what you've just said, can we assume this laboratory is in Russia?" she asked.

He did not answer the question. "I have a good, well-practised memory, but it's not as it once was. I forget things now that I would not have done when I was a field agent. Here." He reached inside the breast pocket of his suit jacket and removed a torn, perforated sheet of note paper on which were four outwardly innocent words: Diatom, Apicomplexan, Microsporidium, and Leishmania Major.

I knew the last one to be a parasitic protozoan, a microscopic, one-celled organism that can rapidly multiply in humans and can be the linchpin to many devastating diseases. "What do these organisms have to do with ethnic DNA you mentioned, Nikita? I noticed you stressed the word ethnic when you were speaking."

"Ah, there you have the reason for my disgust and one of the reasons why I'm here. I did consider going to the Americans with what information I've found, but I'm scared they might use it themselves. It really is as dangerous as I've indicated and I will not put my trust in them. The British had a sense of loyalty and honour at one time. I'm hoping that it is still alive here anchored in you, sir."

I went to speak but he would have none of it, waving my attempt away. He continued speaking after our plates were cleared and the club sommelier poured the remnants of our wine into our glasses. "I understand the work in the laboratory that I know of is towards targeting particular population groups with a ricin base virus engineered as a eugenic weapon, which is possible to immunise against. So the country that unleashes it can vaccinate their own military beforehand. In theory, if this weapon is fully developed, it can determine who is killed and who is left alive without damage to the infrastructure. Now, can you see what a time bomb I have to offer for my granddaughter and me to live in peace and quiet together?"

"I can, yes. Do you know how long it will be before this scientific project becomes a viable weapon?" I asked, swallowing hard on what he'd said.

"I was in the hands of a reliable source when I was informed of this. She told me it could take anywhere between five and ten years, maybe more, maybe less. The science of discovery relies on skill as well as luck and we all three know how luck can alter our lives in the click of our fingers. All I know for sure is that it's underway and prospering. In my expert's opinion it should be stopped before it has a chance to snowball." His expression had a grave countenance whilst he detailed the threat we faced, but then had a laughing smile to it when he finished.

"You must excuse my ineptitude with your language, but I think I've heard that word, snowball, used in such a way here in England."

I ignored what needed no response other than praise for what he already knew was anything but inept.

"Has this anything to do with what your granddaughter has to offer us with the Data Mining, or is this purely an addition to what you say she has to offer?" Hannah asked.

"Yes, of course, it's in addition. Yes, it is, Mrs West. The two are separate. I'm just the go-between. I know very little of the specialised work Cilicia does and even less of the experiments into the eugenics. But I want Cilicia out at any cost and I can provide something extra to galvanise your interest."

"Go ahead, Nikita, we're all ears," I agreed nonchalantly.

"My source from the laboratory told me that the Kurdish population was to be the first target for this eugenic cleansing agenda, and the chosen area for its inaugural testing was the south-east of Turkey."

"I know very little of Turkey and even less of the Kurdish population in the region. However, would I be correct in assuming that the laboratory producing all that's needed for this genocidal attack is sited inside Turkey, or at least close to the Turkish border? Give us some clues, please," I implored him.

He didn't fall for it. "Of course you know nothing of Turkey and its Kurdish population, Patrick. And it naturally follows that your lack of regional knowledge would extend to not knowing anything of the south-eastern area of Turkey being the capital of the once Armenian Empire and known as The Great House of Cilicia. I'm sure you've never come across that before." A mischievous grin covered his face, narrowing the shape of his eyes and adding extra lines to his forehead. Another area where he was not inept, and that was in playing me. He hadn't finished.

"Nor of course would you know of an Armenian German by the name of Henry Mayler, Patrick. Or, come to that, anything about his connection to the Rosicrucian Fraternity. I should have known that you are purely the symbolic head of the best secret service in the world and somewhere you have hidden the real chairman of the joint intelligence committee." The smile had left his face, but the mischievousness still remained in his voice, taunting me over his lack of response to my plea for more clues.

I left his denouncement unanswered, hiding my astonishment at his comprehension of an operation that had consumed my and Fraser's energy and deliberations for a considerable time by signalling for my club account to sign, then asking a question myself that was away from the subject he had brokered. He had shocked me with the disclosure of Henry Mayler's name, and the region of Turkey he had mentioned had been discussed exhaustively five or so years ago with an Assyrian billionaire and Samuel Rothschild, a relative of Hannah's. Kudashov had covered enough today without the need for opening up another subject on the periphery to the eugenic programme underway and the Data Mining of the NSA. Mayler could wait his turn.

"My wife tells me you were implying that I might have had something to do with a body that was found in Prague. Dalek Kava was the name you mentioned and I'm at a loss to know why you would associate a dead body with me?"

His derisive laughter reminded me of Fraser's characteristic laugh when in possession of knowledge of which he knew I had a little, but he more, and aware of how he'd loved to educate me further. Kudashov's supercilious manner was more practised than Fraser's, as his grin lasted far longer than my friend's.

"I was the head of the Municipal Police in Prague for a good while, Patrick. I still have many friends there. It sounds to me that your intelligence system is in need of an urgent overhaul if you haven't got that on file. In that capacity I had very few dealings with the StB, but when I did, I think I was useful to this country of yours. Yes, an unrecognisable corpse was found earlier this month by a dredger working the River Vltava, as it does every August without exception. When I was told of the body, I remembered how Jana Kava had been questioned over her brother's disappearance and suddenly it all fell into place."

It was my turn to laugh, which I did with great gusto, causing some club members' heads to turn in our direction.

"Wow, now who's speculating? That's one huge accusing step into the unknown. To start with, how can you know it's Dalek's body?"

"That was quite simple. I contacted my friend from the science laboratory, Patrick; she ran the DNA and found him."

"And what do you know of Jana Kava?" Hannah wanted an answer.

"Very little now, Mrs West. I lost touch with her when London moved her to Poland. I think it was before the riots in that country, maybe July or early August '82, but it could have been late June. It's a long time ago, but when she was relocated, I'm sure I was still with the police in Prague. But wasn't it very close to when you hurriedly left Czechoslovakia? I would have thought you'd know more of Jana Kava's service life than me, Patrick, including her movements."

This time it was a quizzical look he used to express volumes of his apprehension in my intelligence department's knowledge which, fortunately, my answer appeared to put an end to as our conversation drifted on to Cilicia's position in Moscow Centre and the high ranking official she was involved with, and his expected reaction to her departure.

"He will probably order the launch of several intercontinental missiles, but luckily for us he does not have the launch codes, Patrick."

* * *

Hannah met Michael Simmons at Group's headquarters in Lavington Street, at the Borough in South London later that Tuesday afternoon and started to download all they could access on Jana Kava, Ivy, and Petr Tomsa. In order to get the information to me without anyone at Vauxhall being aware of it, they sent it in encrypted form via Sir Philip Noble, whom I had appointed to the job at the Auxiliary Intelligence Service in Greenwich when the previous DG moved on.

Sir Philip was an old friend from my Oxford days. He sent the files to a grumpy acquaintance named Adam, the senior administrator for all that originated through, or was sent to, Group. If anyone could hide encrypted computer information, then he could. It was not that I distrusted anyone in the wider Intelligence Service, there was no reason for that. I simply wanted to keep it to a small body of people for now and in that way keep things quiet in case it all went wrong.

Adam was the man who knew everything about everyone. He was the one who hid everything from those who didn't need to know what he knew, and said nothing to those in the know or out of the know. He was the one-man distribution hub when I was at Group. He was true to form when I contacted him with an outline of my scheme of events.

"Why the effing 'ell is the head of everything that's holy channelling ancient files addressed to himself through someone as lowly as me? I can understand you wanting my great lord at the gold-plated, top-notch, effing money-swallowing Greenwich facility to endorse what you're up to, but not using dear Adam to hide the bloody info. Why don't you just lock up everyone there is until you find who's guilty of stealing the toilet rolls from the F&C bathroom and then send them on the next clipper to Australia?" He stopped a moment for breath before slightly changing his tone. "Can I have peek inside one or two of these folders before I hide traces of them for you? Just for old time sake, eh, Ezra old chap?"

My biblical name of Ezra was from my street days when I was attached to Group. Five years had passed since those days, but no matter how many years were to float away on The Thames, I would always be *on-the-spy Ezra* to grumpy Adam. When I said no to his request, I was entertained to an abusive selection of words that reflected his abhorrence of rejection that, if recorded in script, would scorch the paper they were written on. Adam was a good sort. The trouble was, he knew it.

Chapter Nine: Peaceful Countryside

Fraser was sitting at his desk, staring at the computer screen in front of him when I arrived mid-morning on Wednesday, having left Whitehall in Hannah's more than capable hands. I wasn't expecting any communication from Sir John Scarlett at the Box, Vauxhall Cross, but if we had inadvertently ruffled his feathers, then I knew I could depend on Hannah having the perfect riposte for any questions he might have. As I closed Fraser's stout office door and was on my way to gather up the whisky decanter and a glass before sitting in one of the comfortable sofas and pouring myself a very large glass of agreeable Scotch, he turned to face me and loudly proclaimed, "Nothing!"

"Yes, nothing," I grumbled in reply. "We have legends galore on Ivy as Ivy or as Kudashov, but not a grain on Tomsa other than the name printed at the top of two blank reports. Why would that be? There is no name on the report of

Jana Kava going missing on the first of September '82 in Gdańsk, Poland. Again, no name of who reported her as never showing up for a debrief after the riots. That intel must have originated from her last handler, but whoever that was, it wasn't Kudashov or Tomsa. I don't like the way it's stacking up, Fraser," I declared as he lifted his own glass of whisky in a sign of greeting.

"At least we can have a stab at where Kudashov's science lab assistant might have got Dalek Kava's DNA now. And Kudashov doesn't know she's dead? Come on!" he exclaimed. "Are you of the same opinion as I am—this mysterious laboratory is somehow connected to this missing information in these case files?"

"For the moment, yes I am. Which means we have a lot of digging to do and we have another conspiracy on our hands. All we can do is hope this one does not go higher than the old seventh floor," I solemnly replied with a deep sense of foreboding.

"I'm seventy-seven now, Patrick, against your—what is it, fifty-eight? Of those seventy-seven years, at least fifty were spent in various capacities inside our external intelligence service. I worked for departments that had sub-departments, sections, regional desks and outside branches. I served on the nineteenth floor for two years at Century House. I even attended meetings on the top floor when old Dickie Blyth-Smith was the Director General. Anyway, apart from all that historical trip of mine, there are several classified divisions of staffing that can only be opened with your signature, along with that of the Director General of MI6 and that of the serving Prime Minister. We have to open this inquiry up to Sir John Scarlett. If for no other reason than my theory about Jana Kava and Petr Tomsa being the same person is gaining ground every time I think of it. We also need to find out who was the duty officer on the Russian Satellite desk when Miles Faversham told you of Petr Tomsa. Human error cannot be ruled out of course, but until we have some names then we're stuck."

"Not completely! We have Kudashov knowing that Jana Kava was posted to Poland."

"Yes, we have that and we can gain some traction there, but we need the name of who posted her and who was her Control officer in Poland. Also, we need to know if Kudashov really did stay on in charge of the local police in Prague when she left."

* * *

The Prime Minister was in Washington, DC, where he was spending more and more of his time of late. The lack of evidence of WMD in Iraq, or anywhere near that country, beyond the weapons of annihilation that Fraser and I had discovered, had led to a great deal of speculation into his suitability to continue as the Head of Government in the national press, as well as questions on the subject inside both Houses of Parliament. The atmosphere between the security services and the PM's office was not good. Some heads of departments had been coerced to agree with government spin-doctors that WMD had existed, but were destroyed before the war began; others knew the truth.

My name and position in the SIS was not known outside of Whitehall, nor was there any knowledge of those weapons Fraser and I had unearthed known beyond specific government posts, and I was under a strict code of conduct never to react to newspaper reports, as were the Director Generals of MI5, MI6 and GCHQ, who were similarly restricted in comment. However, the PM, and those close to him, resented his intelligence community and did all they could to belittle them in damning innuendos leaked to the press. I was particularly disliked within the plethora of government spokespersons, but the feeling was mutual with me being a lot less diplomatic than them.

The anthrax-loaded artillery shells Fraser and I had discovered in the Straits of Tiran and the phosphorous shells and artillery pieces overlooking a garrison of American troops in Afghanistan, were hardly the Weapons of Mass Destruction that the United States and our government alleged Saddam Hussain was targeting the West with, but attempts were being made in Whitehall to allow that information to be leaked to the press. I was not the only one to believe the WMD did not exist and this was merely an effort to cover some people's backs. I had the power to impede the disclosure by redacting all the files that covered that exercise of discovery. That I did, but not without consequences.

* * *

Between the intelligence communities of the United States and ourselves, the endeavours of the eight would-be world-controlling families in what Fraser had named as the Circle of Eight, to influence and then control world opinion at the start of the Iraq War, had been squashed and obliterated. Henry Mayler, the man behind the threat those weapons had represented, was no longer alive to endanger the world. Despite this, the administrations of this country and the US had no other choice than to continue down the hole they had dug, searching for a negative and shouting down those who said WMD never existed. The weapons that were in the redacted file could have given some validity to the government's claims, but not after I got to them. Even so, we could do nothing to impede the invasion and occupation of Iraq that went ahead as detailed inside the corrupted CIA Gladio B file Fraser Ughert had found. However, it was there that the plans of this Circle of Eight families had been stopped, or at least for now they had.

* * *

Fraser was right, I could no longer exclude Sir John Scarlett from our investigations, if only to get hold of the information on the staffing at Century House in 1982 we needed. At the same time, I did have concerns about the length of time it would take to get the PM's signature. That fear did not materialise. I had reason to marvel at the speed my request was sanctioned by the Prime Minister's office as the evidence I'd given in camera to the Hutton Inquiry in August 2003, concerning the sudden death of Dr David Kelly, a world respected authority on biological warfare employed by the British Ministry of Defence, I was reliably told had not 'pleased' the government, and I was further informed that my name was no longer included on any 'cocktail party list'. I didn't cry when I was told that news.

Within the circles I moved in, it was decided before the inquiry sat that Dr Kelly's death was to be registered as a suicide and, then after, I had given my sworn affidavit it was decided that evidence related to the death, including the post-mortem report and photographs of the body, should remain classified for seventy years. When this was announced to the press, it caused widespread conjecture that the government was concealing evidence of some kind. They had a right to question the government on that decision. I was called before a Civil Service inquiry and asked to elaborate on what I had told the Hutton committee in confidence. As it was held in private, I refused. I believed that no one at Number 10 forgave me for my part in the Hutton Inquiry, but as governments along with Prime Ministers come and go on a fairly regular basis, but Director Generals of the intelligence gathering service and, especially the incumbent chairman of the joint intelligence committee are immune to such whims, I wasn't bothered in the slightest.

What I did find difficult to live with was the name of Miles Faversham's boss at the Russian Satellite desk he manned after reading those staffing files: Lieutenant Colonel Jacob Ward. I looked him up. Ward was an American CIA operative. Nowhere on his partially hidden service record was there mention of him in charge of a department inside MI6. This was going to be a hell of a deep mystery to unravel.

* * *

"I have Hannah working with the Foreign Office trying to discover whatever there is on American personnel seconded to military defence intelligence in 1982 and then being handed a seat at a desk in Century House. I'm also wondering if this Jacob Ward brought his own American staff. Were we running alive with CIA agents? I would have imagined he'd need some familiar faces around but, if we had been smart, we would have slipped someone a bit sharp in there. Did you have any unusual dealings with the Ministry of Defence in or around the date I was in Prague, Fraser?" I thought it to be an innocent enough question; however, it turned out to be anything but.

"Not in May 1982, no, but I was thinking about your time on the Czechoslovakian operation a moment ago. Further into the summer that year I was the liaison officer between Group and the Ministry Of Defence. At the time there was huge unrest and uncertainty in Poland and many of the surrounding Warsaw Pact countries. It all came about after the founding of the Solidarity Trade Union in the Lenin Shipyard in Gdańsk, two years previously under the leadership of Lech Wałęsa. For a couple of years, the Soviets instructed the Polish government to watch and see what might happen without forcibly closing the trade union down. They gathered names and did what they do best, threaten to kill, then sat back and waited for it to wither and die. Except this time was different; it grew in size both inside Poland and beyond.

"The time it all started to boil over coincided more or less with you being in Prague. The Polish government had tried to abolish the movement and calm things down by installing martial law at the end if the previous year, but that hadn't worked. When the trade union proposed to hold massive demonstrations, the Russians ordered their Polish subordinates to mobilise the army and dispatch tanks to quell any riots.

"President Reagan was supporting the breakaway unionists with rhetoric and bags of money. He had the CIA deeply involved in Poland, on the ground and through diplomatic channels. They were stringing at least one senior officer of the Polish General Military staff that we knew of, and it was the CIA who influenced the decision of the ruling government to declare martial law. In Washington that was seen as a better alternative than the Poles inviting the Soviet Union to send troops to intervene. I believe you were in Poland by the time all this was starting to hot up, Patrick?"

"Yes, I was there when it all kicked off very badly in Warsaw. My orders to travel out there came in late July and I can tell you the exact date as well; it was the 29th. I know the date as it was my birthday. I'd only been home a few weeks before I got the recall signal. I was thirty-three that year and living every moment as if it was my last. And to be truthful," I was smiling as I recalled the moment, "the following day might well have been my last had not those travel papers arrived at my apartment by courier. I was in bed with a married woman, but not just any married woman. Her husband was a very close friend of Charlie Richardson, the South London equivalent of the Krays. But his wife was worth the risk.

"If I remember correctly, the main demonstrations took place on the last day of August 1982, by which time I was well settled into the legend London had given me—working for what was then Beechams Pharmaceutics Company extolling their products to the Polish chemical industry and government departments. The brief I was given was to get some microfilm on a new encrypted radio coding the Polish military were using out of the country. I met with my mark as news broke of a student being shot not far away from where we were. It already seemed as though all the security service, the Esbecja, were concentrated on demonstrations, but when the news of the shooting broke, order was thrown out the window. The Esbecja cracked down everywhere they discovered more than two people together. It didn't take much for them to start piling into people, swinging their batons at anything that moved. In Warsaw the tension had been building for days, with propaganda broadcasts both for and against Solidarity supporters. The threats the Polish government were making sounded real to me. Some of that disruption went a long way in helping me. I made the meeting point without fuss and the exchange went sweet as a nut. I left the country on the Monday when the disturbances in the capital had quietened down, but the nervousness was still tangible enough."

"Were you made aware of what it was London gave you to give away for the exchange of this microfilm?"

"A big paper envelope stuffed with dollars, Fraser. I saw it counted, sealed, and sent via the diplomatic bag. When I picked it up at the embassy, it was counted again and I signed for ten thousand dollars."

"Hmm, would you say the meet and exchange went easier than you anticipated?"

"I hadn't anticipated any trouble. What are you getting at?" I asked and immediately read his mind. "Are you thinking the demonstrations were arranged as a diversion so I got the code to that radio traffic without a hitch, because if you are, that's going way beyond anything I've known. Do you know something you're holding back on me?"

"I'm not, no, but less than six months after your microfilm encryption exchange, there was a NATO exercise where I know from first-hand knowledge that the so-called undecipherable new coded data the Soviets were employing was being broken all along their radio frequencies as they were being used. GCHQ were running numerous forages into their transmissions and relay stations, but holding back from sending them off stream and thereby warning them. The NSA were linked in via Menwith Hill and, as far as I was aware, it was the first time the Echelon part of their Frosting programme was in use via facilities based in the United Kingdom. It was being aimed at every Soviet satellite and then turning the Russian signals into unencrypted scripts that we then read at leisure.

"Nobody confided in me as to how that was done and where all the information had come from, but I do know we had broken into the Frosting programme sometime in the seventies and although those new Soviet codes were only exclusive to us for the opening few hours of the exercise, we did not share what our chaps decoded at Menwith Hill with anyone. Those signals went straight to the top floor and the Prime Minister. We were watching the Soviet armed forces answering their telecommunications and switching on lines of radio communications and radar beacons through every stage of their alert status. All the systems they had in use were ours to manipulate, had we wanted to. The screens I was privy to showed so many new green and red lights, it looked like some psychedelic lighting to a nightclub. To limit the access to that level of intelligence to just ourselves for no matter how long came from way up high, Patrick. I would say the Poles had trialled that new coding in Warsaw before the Soviets adopted it throughout their military.

"As I said, we had it on our own to play with for a few hours, but eventually all of it had to be shared. Part of my responsibilities at Group was to report activities to the NATO staff at Strategic Studies within the Ministry of Defence. I was the link man and the one at the other end was an American—said he was a naval commander, name of Forman, Commander David Forman. He never said, but he probably arrived with the Air Force lieutenant colonel you mentioned. Thinking back to that time, there was one thing about Poland that was exclusively American. That was their overhead satellite pictures. Under a treaty obligation, they were supposed to share all photographic intelligence with our Ministry of Defence Intelligence Fusion Centre, but nobody could be certain how much they really passed our way."

* * *

My mind was working in double quick time over what Fraser had said and what was missing to complete the picture he had painted. To obtain a new Soviet Union radio signal coding was a coup of gigantic proportions, the like of which was rare in the extreme, so could it be within the bounds of possibility to assume the climax to the student and trade unionist demonstrations was organised to coincide with my operation into Warsaw? Could the death of a student nearby be so arranged as to cover the exchange of money for secrets that could damage the Eastern Bloc for years that followed? If the answer was yes to either of those propositions, then why entrust a mission of such importance to a relatively inexperienced officer such as me? Someone either had huge faith or was hoping I might balls it up.

Chapter Ten: The Lodge

Hannah's car pulled up outside the gated entrance to The Lodge, the name of our mysterious wedding present just outside Hassocks in West Sussex, at precisely 11.03 Thursday morning. We were due to entertain Hannah's only brother, his wife and two children for the weekend, with my two favourite sports of shooting and riding included on the agenda. She varied her routine as much as she was able, making it not every weekend that we stayed in the house, nor were our plans written on any schedule that could be seen by anyone. It was always a spontaneous arrangement whenever the pieces of our two lives fell into the right place.

Although forewarned of her arrival some ten minutes prior, and in receipt of the registration of her ministerial car, as her driver turned into the lane leading to the property, one of the two armed guards stationed in the gatehouse exited and positioned himself where the car would stop before admittance to the property was possible.

At the same time as he left the gatehouse, nearby cameras were concentrated on the entrance and the alert status was moved up to its highest position. As per the rehearsed routine, after the occupants of the vehicle produced their security passes and satisfied the waiting guard's inspection, he radioed for the high ornamental gates to be electronically opened. Inside the motionless, highly polished, black sun-reflecting car Hannah sat alone in the rear, with her principal protection officer in the front. The day was sublime, and according to the meteorology office the weather was set fine to continue for the coming week.

* * *

The main part of the red-brick house was built in 1763, as attested to on the keystone in the arched portico above the four wide-bricked steps leading up to the black gloss-painted front door. The first registered owner of the property was a Lord Richard Montfort who was, according to the records, an aide to King George III. As much as Hannah had searched the archives for that name, it was impossible for her to find how

Montfort aided the King, or come to that, any Richard Montfort who fitted into the timescale, leaving it all as an ongoing investigation into who he was and what exactly he did. In addition to that intriguing missing part to her research, all subsequent records had been mysteriously destroyed until the 3rd September 1989, when on the death of its last owner the property was transferred to—the state.

Luckily I'm not a superstitious man like Fraser, but had I been, then I might have found it very worrying that the last registered owner of The Lodge, before the state took possession, had the same surname as the person who had purchased a London residence for Henry Mayler's grandfather and his family in the 1950s. One of Fraser's other superstitions that again I did not share was with numbers. And here we had a conundrum. The London home of the Maylers was also transferred to the state when Henry, the last of his family, died and the date of that transfer was similar to the transfer date of The Lodge—divisible by a number important not only to Fraser, but to the Rosicrucians as well, the number three.

* * *

There had been two extensions added to the main building since its inception, both of which were solidly built and in keeping with the original Georgian architecture. Even so, despite those extensions, the house itself was not huge, nor was it small. There were four bedrooms, four bathrooms, a more than adequate kitchen, a large dining room and an intimate sitting room along with an office. All those rooms, on the ground floor, had open fires in inglenook fireplaces. Before we began our 'occupancy', all the draughty sash windows were replaced by security triple-glazed projectile resistant ones, white-framed, conforming with a stretched Listed Building requirement that took the status of my job into account. The place provided not only somewhere secure to unwind, but comfort and in the most part, provided work did not interrupt us, tranquillity and enjoyment.

The original tall, thick, matching red brick wall surrounding the property was completely intact, as were the old stables. One of the stable blocks housed part of the screening points for the outside surveillance cameras and another a twenty-four-hour manned communications station. All the equipment in the modernised 'stables' was replicated inside the basement of the main house. The centralised basement area was connected by tunnels to all the other outbuildings, nine in total. Of those nine, five were self-contained cottages converted to house three Ministry of Defence security guards in each. This effectively meant that eight guards were patrolling the periphery of the house at all time. One of the remaining buildings continued to be used as stables for the two mares Hannah and I would ride when time and conditions allowed. Another of the remaining buildings was the garage. It too was connected by an underground passage to the main house. There was one other complex of rooms leading from a separately accessed tunnel. Those rooms were to be used for a specific purpose, hopefully never in Hannah's and my time. They were designed to sustain life in the event of a nuclear war.

Beyond all these myriad of buildings there were eleven acres of green open grounds on which a neighbour grazed his sheep and when we could, Hannah and I rode and shot at clays for enjoyment. The neighbour in question was a Special Branch officer whose daughter undertook the livery of our two horses. There were additional mounted cameras that overlooked each and every one of those meadows as security had been placed on the top of the list when the house was gifted to us.

* * *

The coincidence of Oswald Raynor being the man suspected of firing the fatal bullet into the head of Grigori Rasputin, the Russian mystic and court advisor to the last Tsar of Russia, being the same as the last owner of The Lodge was not lost on me, nor was this cursed number three that played such a huge role in the Masonic and Rosicrucian life of Mayler and the Circle of Eight. But whatever was behind the words, The Home Of Cilicia, was not going to be discovered by running away from any serendipitous connections. We had enjoyed our three years of tenure, taking delightful long weekend breaks in the Sussex countryside, and it wasn't written on any agenda of ours to change that enjoyment.

* * *

In the back of the car Hannah had the files on Lieutenant Colonel Jacob Ward and Commander David Foreman along with the ones that Michael Simmons at Group had unearthed on three other Americans that, although not working on Operation Donor from any seventh-floor desk, were included in the signal traffic from the CIA outstation that was permanently manned near Admiralty Arch at the opposite end of Whitehall to the apartments Hannah and I had. There was something else she had brought with her: the address where Geoffrey Prime was living. Unfortunately, however, none of what she had on the seat beside her was she able to give to me in person.

The bullet that killed her went through the rear side window into her temple and exited through the other side of the car, embedding itself in the trunk of a sycamore tree thirty yards from the where the guard had stood. He was now kneeling on the tarmac road facing the direction of the kill shot. He never had a target.

* * *

To be intimate in a long-term relationship with any woman was always going to be a step too far in my line of work. It was never a rule of course not to get as deeply involved as I had, but it was a fact that if you did, you then had a weakness that could be exploited. I was never one to obey rules or take notice of facts thrown at me derived from someone else's 'life mistakes' because it was expected. No, that was not me. But the moment I heard of Hannah's murder, I wish I had taken notice of a puerile silly fact because that's how I felt—defenceless to the charge of being exploited by my own ego in ignoring my responsibly to those around me.

Chapter Eleven: Death Played a Card

Even though I had never received any formal education in the art of either telling lies or adopting different individualities, I had, through the persistent rehearsal of both, acquired a master's degree in fabricating the truth and adopting expedient identities. Most of my artistry I'd found to be natural and pure in the way that nothing was ever forced or appeared to be faked. That attribute had been the pivot around which my career had blossomed, but there was, and is, no point in attempting to mislead oneself and in this narrative there is no point in me lying to you. I will be open and honest and say that my first thought, when told of Hannah's death, was for myself. I would be on my own again. Which was something I had usually relished. It was, until our marriage, the way I liked my life to be. In fact, being on my own was my absolute preference to being in any sort of closed-off relationship, but somewhere along the road of an ageing self-discovery, my predisposition was totally transfigured overnight, waking the next morning to find a yellow-coloured ring uncomfortably around a finger on my left hand and my life devoted to a single person.

Yes, I was sad that Hannah's life had ended at such a young age, and sad for the members of a family that she knew, and for those who knew her, but my life was not ended and if it had been love that placed that ring around my finger, then love should have nailed it there. We are all alone at one time or other in our lives and as much as I told myself that's what I wanted, I needed all my ability to lie to believe it. Normally, over time, a lie becomes cemented to the memory. It becomes your truth, your way of life. I did not have time to falsely justify a lie. Whether it was false or not, there was a truth I had to live and live it I would applying all the experience that had been thrown at me.

Death had taken yet another fine, beautiful woman who had shared part of my life and left a bloodied stain on it to blend with each of the others and choke me. I knew love, and I knew the taste it left when drowned by blood. What

I didn't know was how to turn my back on it. When death finally remembers my name and calls for my life, I would like it said that my blood flowed through the lives of others in a positive way. I did not enter the life of another person to suffocate whatever was inside of them.

* * *

After the manner of a life-shattering telephone call screaming death down the invisible line at me came the prosaic reporting of other procedural requirements from the scene of a crime relating to a member of the intelligence kinship: there was no sign of Hannah's killer. No abandoned rifle or spent cartridge case. No picturesque, unusually broken twigs lying where the killer had made an entrance to the woods, or even an escape. No signed confession pinned to a tree. No, none of that because according to the expert assessment, this was a professional kill by someone who knew more than just Hannah's habits; they also knew the exact specification of the glass of Hannah's car.

All ministerial vehicles, along with those of top civil servants when going about official business, were fitted with laminated glass, which could either absorb a bullet, or if it was fired at from an angle, deflect the bullet. However, Hannah's car reflected her position on the civil-service ladder, having cheaper, thinner laminated glass than mine and the likewise privileged others. In some sort of defence, I could claim that my knowledge of that subject was woefully short, but it shouldn't have been, should it?

The shot that killed her had been fired at the required, exact right-angle, shattering the glass of her window. The Home Office senior pathology team attended the scene as soon as possible and despite every method they applied, the calculating and measuring of the passage of the embedded sycamore bullet was at best difficult, and at worse impossible, owing to the degrees of deflection my wife's skull would have caused to the bullet's flight. This matter-of-fact information made the position of the assassin harder to trace because of the thickness of her skull.

Perhaps it was the length of time since anyone close to me had died that stirred a sense of outrage on receipt of the news delivered in such a tactless manner. Or maybe it was because Hannah's murder was the only one where I was not present or attended the scene immediately after the murder without the necessity of a vocally expressed report. But on replacing the telephone, I felt the chill of the realisation of death of someone so close come over me as I sat on Fraser's comfortable office sofa, whisky glass in one hand and a burning cigarette in the other, watching Molly furtively glancing at Fraser with a look of crestfallen acceptance on both their dispirited faces.

The solemnity of the moment we shared was shattered by yet another phone call. The Chief Constable of Sussex Police, who was the officer in charge, blamed the adjacent woodland to the north of the property, left untouched by the security assessment officer, who had to gauge risk against this rural protected area of beauty, for providing cover for the assassin. Notwithstanding the obstacle this presented to his men, one of them he proudly proclaimed, had found a sealed envelope address to me pinned to a tree from where the sniper had rested the rifle that fired the .308 soft-point round that had shattered my wife's beautiful head and killed her instantly.

Inside the envelope was a sheet of scrap paper on which these few words were typed: *If life is the greatest gift of all then death is its most grateful recipient. Only when life is ended can we escape from the ramifications of death, Mr West. It's now your turn to suffer.*

* * *

I excused myself from the Ughert's company and went to the bathroom, where I shed a hundred tears of remorse. But again, if I'm to tell the truth and not a self-effacing fabrication of it, I'm not completely sure they were all for Hannah. It's more than likely, most of those tears were for myself, because it was I who killed her by falling in love.

* * *

Jimmy, my driver, was a dependable, level-headed type of man with the sort of stalwart personality that made him ideal for being a principal protection officer and driver, but the look of bemusement on his face when I declined his offer to drive me to The Lodge from Fraser's turned that perception on its head. He resembled a little boy who had lost his toy. Frank, his fellow protection officer and all-round man of steel, although seemingly equally puzzled, was not as reticent. He decided to ask with a sombre but melodic ring to his question, 'Would you not think it best to visit the scene, guv, before returning to London?'

I prided myself on being a polite man under most circumstances and unquestionably when only civility was called for. Understanding of one's fellows' needs and wants, aspirations and limitations, coupled with their ability to manage the pressures of the outside lives in which they lived, was of equal significance to my dignity and self-esteem, particularly since becoming the shortened version of 'governor' to those I was on the most familiar footing with. *Courtesy Before All Other* was one of the many epigraphs engraved in stone or wood I'd seen during my educational years and it could and should have been my maxim, my family insignia, but because of various episodes of life, some to do with me and some not, that honourable dictum did not adorn a crest of the West family. Nevertheless, I had curbed most of the intransigence and some of the irascibility that had attached itself to me because of past indiscretions on my part. Unfortunately, the day of my wife's murder was not a day where convention played any part.

I will not bore you with the flow of expletives that left my mouth, nor the extent of the fury I dispensed on both my loyal, most trusted aides. I will merely leave it to say that when my senses returned to where they should have been, I felt cold and shivery through the disgust of myself and nothing but admiration for the two whom my anger had unjustly targeted. It took me some time to calm down, during which I waved Fraser away from joining my solitary company, walking alone with nowhere to go and a head full of nothing but sorrow. As I've intimated, the problem was I couldn't work out who the sorrow was for, and before I could move on, I really had to.

* * *

For the first few miles of our silent journey returning to London, I toyed with the idea of ringing Sir John Scarlett from the car phone, acting as though I was calm as a mill pond in arranging to discuss the 'staffing files' he'd got his hands on but, try as I might, I wasn't in a good enough place mentally to carry the pretence off; that was until the unexpected happened and he called me. I quickly pulled myself together before taking his call.

After the predicable commiserations and his laboured utterances of comfort, I broached the subject of the current investigations into the ancient Operation Donor together with Kudashov, his offer, and his granddaughter Cilicia. Had it been possible to hear the beat of his heart, then I'm positive it would have been beating fast enough to pass for a plausible percussion display a concert drummer would have been proud of. Had I told him everything about our Russian friend, then I might have had to face the charge of manslaughter.

* * *

He and I had a strained working alliance. In all reasonableness, I could not have expected anything other. His service record put him ahead of me by most criteria applicable in promotional matters and judged accordingly, but I had leaped over him into the only remaining position above, and I felt he had not settled well with that hierarchy formation.

When I was first appointed, he was supportive in a reassuring manner, somewhat avuncular and encouraging as a relative might be from the touchline in a game of schoolboy rugby, but I never thought I had his full backing. My impression was that he was hoping I would fail and, as a result, he would be asked to take my place. After all, it was he who had the in-house, managerial experience. I came from the street and could only offer an operational perspective, thorough though it was. There was of course another rival for the Joint Intelligence chair and that came from the Director General at internal military security, the MI5 chief, Sir Elliot Zerby.

From him I felt less antipathy. Indeed, I thought there was a resigned liking. However, over the four years that have passed since then, I feel that Zerby was simply happy where he was when I ascended to Fraser Ughert's throne, Sir Elliot's thirst for power being quenched. Both Scarlett and Zerby were a lot closer to retirement age than I and, whereas my age difference to Fraser's made him the closest thing I'd had to a father, the differences in years between me and the two heads of the departments below my own made me very much their younger sibling. In reality, it had not taken me long to establish myself in the chair of JIC, but that was not achieved through any sense of subjugation. I confirmed my position by, I hope, the harmony of a shared purpose. However, being the type I was, I always kept an eye on my back.

* * *

I arrived at the Foreign and Commonwealth building apartment, adjacent to my offices, as soon as the weight of traffic and propriety had allowed me to leave Fraser and Molly. Although there were many international agendas on my mind, they had become mere distractions when it came to finding Hannah's killer. Taken literally, the words written on the white woven writing paper inside the murderer's envelope referred to the assassinations Fraser and I had ordered in the hunt for the elusive Circle of Eight and towards the subsequent discovery of the lethal weapons trained on unsuspecting victims.

It matters not if it was collective decision of all Eight of those despots to murder my wife or just one of them who had ordered Hannah's death as an act of reprisal, I held them all responsible. Hannah's relatives, the Rothschilds, were I believed part of that Circle, although up until now I did not think their involvement held the same threat of some others. I had met with Samuel Rothschild when the weapons Henry Mayler had assembled were made known to the American Chief of Defence Staff and the syndicate Mayler worked with was dismantled. Samuel Rothschild was a reassuring connection to reality. I held no suspicions of his involvement in this heinous crime. Given all that, it was still my intention to put an end to the mystery surrounding our wedding gift of The Lodge. As I had abandoned all thoughts of her assassination being connected to the Rothschild family, I hadn't abandon those thoughts towards the Rosicrucian fraternity. I could not. But sometimes that which is the most obscure is the obvious, and the opposite of that is also true.

* * *

Hannah's collection of departmental files, some with spots soaked in blood that no amount of wiping could completely erase, were on my desk when I arrived in my office after first composing myself for an hour or so in the memory-laden apartment. As I open the first mustard coloured folder, a pencilled note of Hannah's dropped to the floor. It was impossible to stop my eyes following her distinctive writing and as it settled beside my foot. I started to cry.

Chapter Twelve: Thursday Evening

I had managed to shuffle the staff between the Greenwich Auxiliary Intelligence Service, the AIS, and at Group, thereby allowing for the temporary promotion of Michael Simmons to fill Hannah's position here at Joint Intelligence. He wasted no time in arriving and, within minutes of him stepping inside the offices, I'd set him to work looking into Nikita Sergeyovitch Kudashov's data files, trying to find if there was any traceable rationality for his antagonism towards American intelligence and his preference to us. I also needed knowledge on where his British cover of 'Ivy' had taken him, especially when it came to his travels in Russian territory. Sir John Scarlett was due at my office in two hours. I needed a wise, all-knowing ear in the Foreign Office before I met him and I knew just the man.

"Yes, Patrick, I can fill in some of the spaces without you spending hours researching the period. 1982 was a very volatile year. It can be summarised by a few words; unemployment was rocketing at home. Margaret Thatcher was stamping her authority by sinking the Argentine battleship in the Falklands War. The left-wing, murdering terrorist group, The Red Brigade, was sending shivers down every civilised person's back, and Ronald Reagan was pushing the boundaries before starting World War Three. As if all of that was not enough to worry about, Israel invaded Lebanon without letting us know."

He was being sarcastic about the last thing, but for a while his phlegmatic diplomat's face had me fooled. As he carried on, he smiled; however, I wasn't sure if the smile was because of my stunned expression or simply because he felt he was back in the time when he held positions of great responsibility.

"I was a private secretary at Number 10 in those days. There weren't many days that were uneventful. Yes, now, your question. The invasion of Poland, that wasn't an invasion. It was an invasion in the sense that Russia sent military advisors and some chaps in dirty overcoats who looked dark and threatening, but the Poles used their own security and military forces to quell the riots. At one point, dear old Uncle Ronnie had thoughts of stepping it up a few gears, but thankfully his foreign advisors got a word in his ear and he dashed off to his country retreat to speak to the Israelis. We in the UK calmed everything down as much as we could.

"I wasn't part of the innermost sanctum, but despite not knowing all that was going on, I can tell you this much. We had permanently open lines from the Cabinet to the War Office and NATO along with a private link to wherever President Reagan went. As you know, in the United Kingdom we don't use the DEFCON, the defence readiness condition that's used in America; we use a more straightforward threat status, even so our threat status was severe and the US was at DEFCON one, their highest ever. War would not have been a complete shock." A grim expression filled his face. It didn't last too long.

"There was one comical occurrence just after *HMS Conquer* sank that Argentinian battleship that I recall. At a press conference, a reporter from the Guardian asked if the UK had her whole nuclear fleet of submarines at sea. 'We wouldn't have a fleet of anything if the socialist party your rag supports was in power, would we,' the parliamentary press secretary retorted, to which most in the room laughed.

"Of course we did have the whole fleet at sea, but not because of the Falklands skirmish. It was because of Reagan and his military exercises. They were extensive and very frightening. I'm sorry about your wife, by the way. It must have been a terrible shock. I hope you're able to keep busy. That's the only way known to man to overcome the loss of a loved one. I have the documents you requested here, Patrick. I would have thought this to be somewhat strange reading material for you at this tragic time."

I left my old Foreign Office acquaintance and met with Scarlett, armed with a little more knowledge than I had previously.

* * *

Sir John Scarlett had lost his wife to pancreatic cancer quite a few years before my marriage to Hannah, but neither he nor I had ever mentioned his past, nor shared any time away from our intelligence service responsibilities. It was a known fact he was a gregarious type, loved company, and since recovering from the loss of his wife, socialising with pretty young female companions. The latest to grace his arm was a very lovely brunette named Julia. Each had been vetted in much the same way as Michael Simmons had on his promotion to become my steward. Although our investigative procedure in the examination of those about to be privy to secrets of national importance was extensive and thorough, I for one was never completely satisfied and, as a consequence, treated everyone with suspicion.

In Scarlett's case there had been rumours about his loyalty, as there had been about mine. Doubts had arisen about me because of the meteoric rise I'd taken through the ranks. Scarlett's were on account of his dalliance with a variety of beautiful women. We had both been the subjects of exhausting inquiries and exonerated from any suspicion; however, my overall concern lay with the integrity of the committee, who judged the investigations and who wrote their clearance. Despite my misgivings, I wasn't looking to start a fight with any of them; for now at least.

* * *

Sir John had immaculate dress sense, which was accentuated by his tanned complexion come by, I was told, the amount of time he spent on his yacht in the Solent. Ever since I was conscious of sailing yachts, the wind in their sails and the noise of rushing water as the bow beats through the waves, I'd wanted one of my own. Maybe one day, I mused as I both admired his sense of style and loathed his acquiescence to the social divide.

For our business discussion, he wore a blue and grey striped linen suit, blue shirt with his Eton school tie. He even wore the college striped socks paired with his highly glossed, polished dark brown brogues. He was a prominent man who carried his prominence with distinction. He would, I suspect, be the first to admit that his years in service to the Crown had benefitted him well, as his chubbiness attested to. His liking of fine claret was a thing around which legends had been built. Fortunately, my apartment housekeepers were well versed in providing liquid comforts to the grandees of the various Civil Service departments entertained in my fine bedecked rooms.

After filling two glasses from a forty-three-year-old Château Margaux, that if told of the price I would probably die, we settled down to our discussion, facing each other from opposite sofas. The vision of Hannah always choosing to sit where he now sat was imprinted on my mind and would not budge. I felt compelled to explain. His reaction was one of complete surprise. There was a genuine sympathetic tone to what I had expected to be insincere platitudes and, to his suggestion of a simple switch of seats, I gratefully accepted and then felt miserly of my assessment of him. But business is business on the road to everything, so it was not long before we were recalling operations where our paths had crossed in one way or another, with me citing the St Petersburg operation we both were involved in when a Hungarian air force major wanted a way out of the Warsaw Pact military. I had held his hand on another freighter into the same port of Hamburg, and then it was the plain John Scarlett in those days who we'd met at the dockside and took over. We drank a toast to that success and a couple more toasts for operations we had collaborated on. The more memories we shared the closer I felt, but still that feeling of a distanced distrust remained.

* * *

The handwritten note of Hannah's that had caused me such distress was her explanation of how little of the Operation Donor was collated in draft. She went on to suggest that one reason could be answered by her reference to Scarlett being designated as the senior duty officer assigned to the Soviet Satellite desk in 1982, the same desk as Miles Faversham, but one step below him. However, that decrease in serving rank meant that overall Scarlett had more of a workload than Faversham.

* * *

The Americans were signed in as honorary Defence Intelligence staff, which made it simple to explain away to any unauthorised inquisitive looks. At the bottom of the note she had meticulously written, she'd scribbled—'Needs Scarlett's clarification.' It did indeed!

"Yes, that was my role for your Operation Donor, Patrick. But of course you were under a different name then, weren't you: Frank Douglas, wasn't it?"

"I was, yes. Let me compliment you on a marvellous memory. What I want to know, John, is why were the Americans allowed to take an interest in me and a Polish girl with possible StB connections?"

"It wasn't a memory from twenty-five years past. I read up on the operation last night. It's a good job you gave me that chance, otherwise I would have looked a complete idiot round about now, which wouldn't do at all."

His obvious enjoyment of the wine was shown by his replacing the small amount he'd tasted before he opened a red leather-bound well-used notebook with a stub of a pencil in a matching elastic holder at its side. He thumbed through some crossed-out pages until he arrived at the unfinished page that was in current use. He glanced at that opened page as he continued.

"According to what I read there was a US naval commander, David Forman, overshadowing Miles Faversham, who liaised with Fraser Ughert at Group, who in turn was the operation link to the Ministry of Defence. But both Forman and Faversham were under an American Air Force flyer by the name of Jacob Ward. I have him down as a lieutenant colonel, but I'm sure your investigations uncovered his CIA credentials."

"CIA hierarchy carrying British passes stamped Defence Intelligence staff, yes I saw that. Almost fainted when I did, but I survived. I also saw mention of the Joint Air Reconnaissance Intelligence Centre." I had read the brief report that Hannah and Michael's research on the Centre had uncovered, along with the background on the next point I put to him.

"There was a round-the-houses account of how some photographic imaging from Poland found its way to the Imagery Control Commission at an RAF post in Germany. Other than the length of the report, which as I said was very longwinded, there was nothing unusual, except where those images began their journey. From Ministry of Defence Intelligence, not as would be the normal procedure from the duty officer Soviet Satellite. But I'm ahead of myself somewhat. Correct me as I'm going along on this, John." We locked eyes at that stage, but his attention returned to his wine as I continued.

"Whilst I was in Czechoslovakia on the first phase of Operation Donor, during the month of May 1982, I was strictly British interest, nobody else looking in and making suggestions. Then, when I was sent to Poland in late July, the CIA were invited to run along with us? Have I got that right?"

A strained expression accompanied his reply. "I'm not too clear whether they were invited but, as far as my knowledge goes, they certainly were not in operational control. I was second on that with Faversham out on point.

"Okay, John, I'll come back to that if needed. But for now can you explain why the same operational name was kept when it took place in two separate countries with a gap in time in between both operations?"

"Sorry, can't answer that as I've no idea. I must admit it seems strange looking back on it, but a lot of stuff seemed strange to me around that time."

"An interesting answer." I hadn't expected so much candour from him. "Was there anything in particular that stood out as strange?"

"Some of the Falklands stuff coming out of that CIA station that's still here near Admiralty Arch was in dangerous conflict with some of the Argentinian stuff. Some of it was going out from that base to a unit the Americans had hurriedly assembled in Bogotá, Columbia, easily read by the Argentinians because it went out in decrypted Spanish script, laying false information that was very easily cheeked. The PM loved it of course, but we hadn't asked for anything on that score and when it came to repaying that credit note, I can remember the cost and thinking she had caved in too readily. But that's not what I'm here to divulge, is it, Patrick?"

"I haven't asked you here to divulge anything sensitive to those unfortunate times, John. I simply want any clarification you can throw on what seems to be a curious decision in coding two operations by not only the same name, but by sending the same officer into the two separate countries involved. Looking back on it, a little dangerous and certainly unorthodox, I would have thought. Are you aware of any particular reason for sending me in on both operations?"

The same screwed-up expression proceeded this reply. "Not that I know of, but your question shows either a lack of confidence in yourself or excessive confidence in thinking you were important enough to be set up. That's if you're going down the road of some sort of in-house organised conspiracy to drop you in it."

"You're full of surprises, John. I hadn't thought of it that way. A conspiracy you say? Well, perhaps I was the carrot and Faversham had the stick, eh?"

I took time out to refill my own glass. I offered to fill his half-empty glass, but his hand covering the top and slight shake of the head signalled his refusal. Maybe it wasn't as good as my palate suggested. "I was thinking it was just a fuck up at the satellite desk," I declared, on setting the bottle back on its silver coaster. "Any ideas why the CIA had a chair on Operation Donor or was that an example of lack of confidence the top floor had on the satellite desk?"

"I can't answer all of those questions, as I was the humble desk duty officer who was told what to do. If those photographs you referred to, did or did not emanate from my position with or without my signature on them, then that's what happened, but I'm buggered if I can remember that far back. I read nothing of that in the Donor file I found. What does it say in the logbook descriptive account listing the imaging?"

"Not much, John! Apparently, there was an over-fly of Gdańsk by an NSA satellite and the pictures magically found their way to one of our Joint Air Reconnaissance platforms in Germany, as well as presumably to the NSA, HQ at Fort Meade. What little wording there was suggested that someone at your desk had messed up."

He fidgeted on the sofa, uncrossing then crossing his legs, and straightening the creases in his trousers. He flicked some cotton from his jacket sleeve, then with a distinctly annoyed expression, continued. "As I said, it was a long time ago for my memory cells I'm afraid, but in those days as duty officer I was not involved with the drafting of policy. As you must know, I would have been told very little of the mechanics of the operation. Before the CIA were included, I remember being one of a number of intelligence staff briefed on the top floor by the retiring chairman of the Joint Intelligence Committee, Dickie Blythe-Smith, that an operation was underway in Prague with one of our officers on the ground, so the whole of that area was out of bounds to everyone else. The coded message that was to go out to all stations home and abroad was—the outside playground is busy. Seek permission before using equipment. In those days, that was our standard stay-out-of-the-way message. But neither Dickie nor our own Director General in the Soviet satellite office said a word about what kind of operation was going on, and nobody gave away any details to me.

"A month or so later when the Warsaw part of the operation kicked in, Blythe-Smith had gone, or so we were told, and our DG was promoted to chair of the Joint Intelligence Committee in replacement. On the satellite desk we had a temporary Director General, a man named Hugo Glenister. That move of Glenister's shocked me as well as most in the Soviet Union department. He had the dubious honour to be the ex-Director of the Middle East desk. A bottomless pit of secret intelligence service dreams.

"Shortly after he took over, Glenister paid my office a visit, must have been sometime in early August as I would have been in Falmouth for the last two weeks of August for the sailing regatta. I had a small boat in those days and raced her whenever I could. Sorry, I wandered off subject." The wine was back in favour as now he felt confident in filling his glass and topping mine up.

"When I was thumbing through the file notes last night, I did look for a date, but couldn't find it. Anyway, that's when he told me of the Ministry of Defence interest and we had CIA at operational status in the building that, in his words, were assisting. As you would expect, no specific operation aspects were discussed or mentioned. He told me that I was keeping the duty officer role, but Faversham had been removed. Didn't say why and I never asked." He leant back and enjoyed his taste of the wine with a cheerful countenance.

"I'm afraid the only one who could tell you the unabridged story of Operation Donor is Dickie Blythe-Smith, as I'm positive Hugo Glenister was only following a dictated script. But wasn't dear old Dickie the man who recruited you from

Jack Price's Royalty mob way back when?" He knew that was the case, as did most people in the SIS.

"He was, yes," I replied, as a previous chapter of my life with a woman I loved dying in the car seat beside me passed across my memory, to vanish into the tobacco smoke above my head.

"But of course Dickie's dead," he added. "So I guess your questions will end there, unless of course Fraser Ughert has any additional input."

"Did you and Fraser work together on the first part of the operation, John? The bit in Prague?"

"No, I don't recall working with Ughert on that. We worked together on several ops, but I'm not sure that was one. I would have to look that up, Patrick."

"No matter. We can return to that later if need be. But you were the duty officer on both parts of Donor. That was right?"

"It is to some degree. I came in on the Prague end when you had to be extracted. Faversham was a bit out of his depth as I recall. Before that happened, then no would be the answer. I was on the main Russian desk, working a different operation than the one that was happening at the satellite desk. In essence, I was duty officer to both desks, as the whole of the seventh floor was short-staffed for some time, but your Donor operation was not under my direct control. I was told early on that Faversham had it all in hand, needed no support."

"You were told that at the beginning, were you?"

"I was, yes, and your follow-up will be—who told me Faversham needed no assistance? That came from my Director General; Francis Henry Grant."

"Okay, thank you for that. I will follow that up. Faversham was still acting as my Control and handler when you took over?"

"Yes, he was. And he was sliding down into the shite. It was he I gave the instructions to of how to set your asset and the stringer up, and then how to get you out."

"Was it at that point you became aware of Nikita Sergeyovitch Kudashov, aka Petr Tomsa, or did you have knowledge of him before the handover?"

He took a deep breath at this point, turned in his seat and with glass in hand, looked far into the distance, towards Buckingham Palace beyond the trees of St James's Park. "I'm having to think hard here, Patrick, but it was at that point, yes. I had not heard of Kudashov before the handover and I have never heard of Petr Tomsa. Since taking over the Director Generalship of the SIS, Kudashov's name has crossed my desk a few times. Back then, however, Faversham came to me and explained your situation. He said Francis Grant had given him Kudashov's name as the local asset the department would be using in the event our officer needed out in a hurry. He was, he was told, in charge of the civil police in Prague. No better man, I thought.

"Anyway, I instructed Faversham to contact Kudashov using the in place protocol and set the wheels in motion. He went through the normal channels and away you came. If I remember rightly, Kudashov assisted in arranging the travel papers for your Czechoslovakian asset to enter Poland. Searching my old memory banks once again, my department has authorised two operations involving Kudashov. The ones I'm thinking of were both on Russian soil. I can copy over the details of his connection to the SIS when I'm back at my desk."

"That would be good, thanks. I'm still a little confused with some points though. Miles Faversham for example. Why was a man who was so manifestly ill prepared put in charge of my safety? It was always going to be a difficult job, that could and did turn into something far more dangerous."

"Not my place to call it on that one. Top floor chose the players. I was, as I said, told what to do and in any case, I came in at the end of that phase of Donor."

"Okay, let's skip to phase two, the Warsaw exchange. Dickie Blythe-Smith had gone, so had Faversham. You said you thought Hugo Glenister was reading from a prewritten script. By that, I took it you meant all of the Warsaw part was planned before he took over. Is that right?"

"I would say it was, yes. No disrespect to Hugo, who I didn't know that well but, in my estimation, he was the type who reacted to situations rather than drive them forward. A steady hand on a plan. Not the spontaneous type you want in charge when the plan goes wrong, which we both know is how it happens most of the time." He was positively oozing friendship at this stage as the expensive vino was disappearing at a respectable rate of knots.

"Who would you say was in charge when the Warsaw part opened up? Was it the retired Dickie Blythe-Smith or the American and his staff, do you think?"

"Hmm, odd sort of question for you to ask, Patrick. It was Dickie Blythe-Smith's operation and Blythe-Smith's plan. In retirement and to the grave I would have thought. That was the man he was. He wouldn't have let it slip from his grasp just to go fishing every day. He was possibly coerced into accepting the Americans on board for some political reasons, but most certainly they were not in Century House as controllers."

"Are you sure, John? It's just that those NSA satellite pictures somehow ended up with us at the signals intelligence unit at RAF Gatow in West Berlin. I can't see how that could happen. Did Dickie plan that as a going away surprise do you think, or was human error playing a part?"

"Are you trying to trip me up here, West?" I suppose I should have been aware that accusation might have happened, but at that point I wasn't.

An aggressive scowl forced his upper lip to curl inwards and his jaw to clench. He pointed the index finger of his left hand me at me and the gold wedding band he still wore caught the sunshine pouring in through the unshaded windows. "I thought I had come here to broaden your perspective on a twenty-five-year-old operation when you were being run from London in two satellite states of the Soviet Union, part of my field of influence and professional interest. I'm not sure I want to be interrogated on some supposition you hold regarding the CIA interference being," he paused, thinking of what words to use, "duplicitous and with me mixed up in it." Without finishing what little there was of his fine wine, he hurriedly rose from the sofa, making his way towards the door.

"It will be a shame if you leave, John, as I'm not implying anything along those lines. I know who Lieutenant Colonel Jacob Ward and Commander David Forman really were and I know why

Jana Kava told her brother of the Nevada site. What I'm hoping is that you know more than I do about why they threw us Geoffrey Prime's name?"

Despite regaining his attention he did not retrace his steps. He jerkily turned around to face me and stood wide-legged with his arms crossed, staring down at me. "That would depend on how much you know, West. I'm not a lover of fishing. I leave that for others. As far as I know, I serve the Crown as you do. If you have doubts on my loyalty, speak your mind, don't play games with me."

"I'm not accusing you, nor hinting at disloyalty, John, but I am certainly saying you know more than you're willing to divulge. How about we trade? Jacob Ward was a Deputy Staff Director of a special unit code named Winding Clock. David Forman had a navy rank but was Deputy Director of Internal Affairs at the CIA when he came over here. Quite a twosome to wind up some students into demonstrating in the cause of democracy, don't you think?"

"How did you find all that out?"

The look of bemusement on Scarlett's face carried no deceit in his question. He did not know. Nor did he know the other piece of the jigsaw that Hannah had found. His aggression had now given way to inquisitiveness, he returned to the sofa opposite me, and I refilled his glass with what little was left in the claret bottle. From a box on my desk, I took two cigars and after using my lighter, I passed it to Scarlett. When he was happy his cigar was alight, I continued my narrative.

"From what I was told when I was in Prague, I formed the opinion that the Americans had a leak at their testing site in the Nevada desert and they also had someone planted in GCHQ. I believe it was the CIA who gave Jana Kava the vague information about Prime having a forthcoming trial date. Guesswork about the trial, but no matter. When I passed that information on to Faversham's desk, it led someone here to believe Kava knew more than she did. They waited to see who reacted when it hit London, and how and to whom that leak was passed on. Again I'm guessing I know, but Prime's exposure came about through the NSA's Frosting Echelon programme and it was a payment they made for outing the mole they had in their Nevada site. Do you think I'm on the right track and, if so, do you recall if they caught whoever it was leaking from their test site, John?"

"Yes, you are close to the right track and yes, they did catch their leak. Or so the information that filtered down to my position indicated. But of course nobody confided in me directly. I was not of any significant importance in 1982, but you still haven't told me how you got all this."

He was fidgeting again, somewhat uncomfortably with his glass when he asked. I left the second bottle of Margaux unopened, deciding it was too good to share and I'd uncork it when Hannah was home. Then the realisation of her murder hit me harder than the blow that broke my jaw and dislocated my eye socket delivered by a knuckleduster in New York at the same time as I was shot in the foot. My mind held a picture of her head covered in blood as I reluctantly opened the second bottle and forced all my memories to wait as I pulled the cork.

"When my wife was alive she and Michael Simmons looked into the first part of Operation

Donor and came up with some very intriguing intelligence directly influencing the second part. Are we getting close to that trade I mentioned, John?"

After swirling the wine around his glass, then savouring the bouquet, he emitted a long-suffering sigh, and the sands parted in the Nevada desert as the first sample passed his lips. "The CIA's leak was a woman," he announced after exhaling from his cigar. "She'd been under surveillance for some time before they got here, but they had nothing solid on her and were beginning to doubt their internal intelligence. I was informed this was to be their last crack at her. The CIA attachments to the post over here were regularly changed, so she wasn't spooked when she was transferred from Langley. They asked to use our asset and I was told Dickie signed it off. I imagine he traded it for what they had on Prime. If you were to ask for my opinion on how part two of Donor played out, then I would have to say that Dickie was running it, even though he was away from the building. I guess you can understand how that can happen with you and Fraser Ughert being so close. Have you finally been able to get him out from underneath you? I guess it must have been awkward."

He stopped speaking, scrutinising me with the kind of pitiful gaze one might use for a hospital patient with a broken leg, and for an equal length of time I wondered who that pity might be for. "If you're as wise as you seem, Patrick, you will keep your friendship with Ughert even tighter if he has indeed accepted his retirement. You will be in need of a friend in the dark days that follow the loss of a loved one. I had my boat and the sea for company when my wife passed away. It took me about six months, I think, to realise I needed more than just that. I needed the distraction that came with a beautiful young woman in my bed. You may be different and can cope with your loss with more conformity than I could. Personally, I don't give a damn about what people think of me. I can enjoy life with a clear conscience. I loved my wife when she was with me and she loved me. I love her now in death. She was not the type of woman who would want me to grieve for what life I have left. I did not know your wife well, West, but if she was similar in her views to my departed wife, then do not grieve for long. Life is too short to be washed away in tears."

I took his compassionate and sorrowful words on face value; indeed, they carried a great deal of sense. Despite feeling a degree of empathy towards Scarlett, I didn't fully trust him when he entered my office and nothing had happened to change my view. I did not address his remarks about death. I left them where they were, a private matter between the two of us.

When he carried on with our discussion, he seemed in a dispassionate mood. "When your signals from Prague reached the satellite desk, they were automatically decoded and shown live on the CIA staff's screen in the office they occupied. She was one of them in there and it did the job. She couldn't understand how a Czechoslovakian that we were working had intel on the site in Nevada because she hadn't shared it with the Czechs. She got too worried for her own good. That night she was followed when leaving Century House and her tail found her using a call box in Lambeth North underground station. She wasn't there to make a phone call. Her Russian handler had followed the group of

CIA agents she was in to London and the two of them had arranged to use the phone box as a drop-off if the occasion arose. It was Forman who picked her up with a coded message inside a telephone directory. The implication that was passed down to me was that they turned her, but once again I wasn't in the direct loop on that. I can add one pointer though. Internal Security barred the Americans from placing the tube station on watch. MI5 had it on a warrant as under surveillance. I know for a fact they had quite a result following on from the CIA's success in finding their traitor." He hadn't finished and nor was the wine.

"In all probability, by now you have discovered the family ties between Sir Brian Macintosh and the Director of the Soviet Satellite Department in '82, and again yes, I was on good terms with Macintosh's stepfather, Francis Henry Grant. We did discuss you and what you'd achieved out in Warsaw before he was lifted upstairs. I didn't know then, but I do know now the full story of Jana Kava and her brother. His final outcome in Czechoslovakia was also discussed, but that discussion took place on the top floor. It was my first and only visit up there when Grant took over. Your action in Czechoslovakia was commendable, Patrick, but in Poland you excelled yourself. No operation could better that … incidentally, in case you never knew. Hugo Glenister's temporary posting lasted for eleven years, by which time we'd all moved to Vauxhall."

"Were you included in the selection of the personnel for Operation Donor in any way, John?"

"No, and those insecurities are on show once again, Patrick. Having now genned up a bit on it all, it was Dickie who signed you up for it, if that's what you're asking. He sent it downstairs, listing his needs of a professional and you, he wrote, were the best. In the margins he added the postscript of—best since Jack Price. He also posted Glenister to replace Grant. Musical chairs for the VIP big players."

"That was kind of him. I'm flattered. Useful to know, but I want to discuss the Geoffrey Prime message and how might the Americans have known of him, John? Is there still something that you're not telling me?"

He emptied what was left of the wine carefully into our glasses before he exposed a little more of himself. “If I was a betting man, which I’m not, I’d bet my life savings on you knowing nothing about Prime. Can you remember the precise words Dalek Kava said about the man, Patrick? No, well I do because I read it this morning in the case file. He told you Prime was to stand trial in November. There was no date set for a trial and, as of May that year, it was undecided exactly what to do with Prime. Jana had told her brother what her Control had told her. But what was her Control telling us? Dickie set a ball rolling in 1982, but I’ve no idea in which direction it went, or if it stopped. When Prime’s name was mentioned, Dickie initiated a covert inquiry into a number of names Prime had listed as possible future blackmail targets who were still working at GCHQ. That list led to five employees being demoted and losing their security clearances. I’m now wondering if one was missed or deliberately left in situ.

“I was Director General on my floor when the GCHQ thing went live. Dickie had retired and telephoned to arrange a meet in a café near Holborn Station. All bloody Beaulieu tradecraft, smoke and mirrors, and what have you. We met and he instructed me to write up a report as none of those five names, or anyone else in GCHQ, were under pressure from the Soviets. However, from the conversation we had, I think there was another file which he wrote himself and placed under a hundred-year seal. He would often write files himself when he was in one of his famous uncommunicative moods.

"Obviously, I was never shown that file and I still haven't seen it, but in it I believe is the name of another spy of perhaps even greater importance than Geoffrey Prime, and who had a much wider access within GCHQ's remit. This of course may be one of those serendipitous moments that happen in life, but the Director General of GCHQ disappeared whilst holidaying alone in the Pearl Bay region of the Everglades in Florida, round about the same time. The signals of his overdue return home flashed red on everyone's console. A day or so later, there were signals bouncing around saying he could have been murdered and his body washed away from something called a *stilt house*, where he was staying in Florida. The things are called 'Chickee' huts apparently. Very eloquent name.

I can't wait to go," sarcastically he added. "You can watch the alligators swimming past underneath whilst sinking a pink gin as the sun goes down. I can't imagine anywhere worse, but luckily there's no accounting for taste, is there? Whatever happened, I think it was late February 1983 when he disappeared."

"If it was more recent, we would have to investigate, but I think we have more pressing concerns, John. One would be the name of Jana Kava's Control in Poland. Did Dickie let anything slip on that at all?"

"Dickie never let anything slip, unless he wanted to mislead someone. I don't believe he would divulge a thing he never wanted to, even if he was burnt at the stake. In those bygone days, when the scribble pads next to the telephones had 'Top Secret' embossed in them, there was only one person Dickie Blyth-Smith trusted and I think you know who that is, Patrick."

Chapter after Twelve: Salmon Fishing In Norway

"Nobody from GCHQ was swallowed by an alligator in Florida that I know of, Patrick. There was none cleverer than Dickie Blyth-Smith in the misinformation game. You're right. There was a Russian mole with access to sensitive sections in GCHQ who was further up the food chain than Prime, but it wasn't the Director General, Bernard Nicholls, who was as loyal as they came. Let me tell you a story involving the greatest man I ever came across in this business of ours."

Fraser was in his element of storytelling of past victories of his greatest friend and long-term incumbent of the chair of the Joint Intelligence Committee being made a peerage on his retirement. According to Fraser, Dickie Blythe-Smith was to the intelligence service what Robinson Crusoe was to shipwrecks: inseparable.

"During his first term in office, President Reagan authorised the US navy and air force to lay underwater tracking beacons stretching from Greenland to Norway in order to detect Soviet submarines leaving the major northern Russian ports. It worked, but not for long. The Russian navy plotted them on their maps and then whenever they needed inaudible passage from ports such as Murmansk, decommissioned the beacons by sending a constant sonic microwave signal that, put quite simply, knocked them out. The Director General at GCHQ, this Bernard Nicholls, the same one who Dickie subsequently told everyone had been turned into alligator belts, bags, and boots, came up with a better idea—a line of three signal delineated beacons from the north of Norway across the Barents Sea to the island of Svalbard and onto the northernmost inhabited place in the world at Alert, in Nunavut, Canada. The important difference between this and the submerged beacons was his idea was above ground and, apart from three signal masts that could pose as anything from a clothes pole to a television receiver, there was nothing tangible to interfere with. However, there was one weakness; if one transmitter was tampered with, the other two could not hold the system in place.

"Don't ask me the intricate parts to how it functioned because I haven't got a clue, Patrick. But work it did. Dickie and Bernard aired the idea with the Defence Intelligence Service who weighed it up and, when satisfied, presented it to the Foreign and Commonwealth Office as their own idea. The Foreign Minister summoned his head of the Joint Intelligence Committee, Dickie Blyth-Smith, and he said he'd sound out likely partners.

"That one weakness to the system was ironed out when events turned everything better over a quiet drink and dinner at Dickie's London club. Bernard Nicholls declared a passion for a hobby Dickie indulged in: salmon fishing. It just so happens that in the River Alta, in Norway, one finds some of the best salmon fishing in the world and if Bernard Nicholls were ever to move to the stunning-all-year-round landscape, with the magnificent skiing in winter, and he got bored with that river, then there was plenty more all around, along with the sea. As the wine flowed and the conversation was only interspersed with the scented inhalations from cigars, Dickie put a proposition to his guest—become one of the most important men in the Cold War.

"The Norwegians, although allies of ours, have to consider their near neighbours the Russians. The two countries have always had a hostile relationship, with the Soviets regularly flexing their muscles along the one-hundred-mile border, and as I've already described to you, we're not averse to the occasional trespass onto their territory. Dickie and I travelled together to Oslo and met with heads of the Norwegian intelligence and heads of their defence staff. Everyone jumped at this new proposal of Bernard Nicholls with one proviso: the number of people who knew of it was to be kept to the absolute minimum. As I've said, there needed to be three transmissible points with all three being erected in places of negligible habitation, thereby minimising local interest, but the call for clothes poles being erected in areas where hardly anyone lives could cause some concern elsewhere. Permission for the first two, Alta and Barentsburg, were no problem being Norwegian territory. Alert in Canada would not, according to Dickie, present any difficulty, but to keep secret the purpose of all three, might.

"This project was far too sensitive for politicians to be mentored into its serviceability; that precept applied to Americans or Canadians, as well as ours. Dickie saw a possible opening into the new Strategic Defence Initiative Organisation that was being mooted in American circles. Bernard Nicholls could, he told Dickie, use their proposed space programme capabilities to safeguard what he had invented. The initial concept he'd had, this Delineated Signal Intelligence Gathering or DISIG, to use its acronym, required a feet-on-the ground base to analyse the data produced from the signal encrypted delineation, but if satellites could be utilised, then the analysis could be done in a detached location anywhere in the world. All that was needed was a building on top of which could be placed something that could easily pass as a simple television receiver. Hey presto, no one's cage rattled and a network capable of imagery detection way ahead of the game went on stream."

Fraser was positively drooling with pride as he resumed after a satisfying taste of his whisky and pipe. "Again, I found myself as Dickie's chosen travelling companion, only this time our destination was that part of America we are all familiar with: the revered George Bush Centre for Intelligence in Langley, Northern Virginia."

He gave me one of those condescending 'have you been there' looks—the ones where his bushy eyebrows almost touched his greying hairline and his hazel eyes took on the size and stare that could make a stranger believe him to be mad.

I shook my head to answer the unspoken question and he ploughed on. "Of course there was nowhere near Langley that could shine a torch to the powerfully majestic beauty of Norway; however, we could not find the powerhouse we needed in mountain-lined fjords. We hoped we could find it in the CIA funding. We were showered with grand hospitality and congenial acquiescence for all the proposals hallowed Dickie put forward. They loved it so much they paid for its installation in a purpose home for Bernard.

"The widower Bernard Nicholls had overall control from a nondescript timber-framed house built on the outskirts of the small town of Alta.

There were no wires leading to or from his house, or aerials of weird construction mounted on it or nearby. Nor was there any discernible difference to the small television reception boosting satellite dish on the roof of his house to his few neighbours' houses. He told his friendly Norwegian neighbours, whose language he spoke enough to be understood, that he was a retired travelling salesman from Scotland who loved the outdoor life Alta offered him, with the salmon fishing and skiing being his two favourite pastimes. Everything fitted and worked perfectly.

"It was during the NATO exercise of '83 that Dickie's little baby paid off big-time. The Soviets knew nothing of Bernard Nicholls and his undulation detection proficiency. Thinking the seabed beacons were easily decommissioned, twelve nuclear submarines in two staggered groups of six, sailed through the Barents Sea, heading east towards America and the same number sailed south towards the UK and French ports. As soon as Bernard's detection project noted all the submarines, a rebounding signal was transmitted via satellite to NATO Command Headquarters in Brussels. Immediately, two UK Nimrod aircrafts and three USA P-3 Orions, all of which were in the air, were notified from a special incident room inside the American Pentagon. All five altered course, set to intercept. As the Soviet subs passed from Russian waters into international ones, each aircraft dropped predetermined patterns of sonar buoys around their individual targeted submarines or, in one case, a congested pack of three. As soon as the buoys hit the water and 'pinged' the targets, the captains of each boat opened radio contact, broadcasting on acknowledged Soviet distress wavebands contacting the Northern Naval Base Headquarters at Severomorsk on the coast of the Barents Sea, north of Murmansk. Without ceremony, each boat was immediately ordered to return to Russian waters.

"Bernard's design worked on the same principle as the beacons laid by President Reagan. They both picked up the noise that submarines made as they stealthily moved into the open sea and towards their target. Having no visible 'beacon' it was indestructible and impossible to disable, even if Bernard Nicholls' home had been discovered. Where he lived was merely a place he could view his invention in action by a series of blue dots that would appear on his adapted television screen whenever he was alerted by a prearranged code from the Pentagon sent over the telephone line.

"However, the Soviets attempted to quieten their submarine acoustic emissions based on knowledge an American navel warrant officer, by the name of John Anthony Walker, gave to the Russians for what he called ideological reasons. It took a fair amount of time for the Soviet navy to implement all of the intelligence Walker gave away, but eventually the noise was significantly reduced. Because Walker was persuaded to tell his interrogators the full extent of what he betrayed to his Russian masters, Bernard Nicholls' procedural structure was capable of absorbing the necessary changes to its propulsion recognition, and it's still in operation as we speak. Today, we are now able to detect each and every Soviet submarine's incursion from Russian waters through an improved twenty-mile response area from a dedicated satellite that supplements his Delineated Signal Intelligence Gathering. I've no idea how long we will be one step ahead, but

I do know that without the foresight of men like Dickie Blythe-Smith and Bernard Nicholls, the Soviet Union would still be hammering at our front door."

Fraser had travelled down to London that Thursday night to stay and keep my mind working. Really it was his lame excuse to smoke his pipe and drink more than he should. When I suggested that as the motive, he replied, "Nonsense! I'm coming to keep that mind of yours moving along in the right direction." But nothing about direction was included in the first words he said when I opened the apartment door to him.

"Look here, Patrick, nobody will blame you in the slightest if you ease back on all that's on your desk. Delegate those that are important and put the others on hold. Move Kudashov to one side and let the police do their job in Sussex, old son. Take some time to grieve, but not tonight. After I've gone try not to be on your own too much."

Sagacious advice perhaps but, in general terms, I was not a very sociable person, which Fraser was aware of, leaving me confused as to what to do with his advice. Work and Hannah were the cornerstones of my life. Alone. Perhaps that was where I was meant to be. Without my wife, only work remained to sustain me.

I was delighted to see Fraser and revelled in his story telling, but his fixation on the Rothschild family entered our conversation too soon for my liking. The name reminded me of Hannah and I did not want to think of her or who might have killed her. It wasn't a case of refusal to accept her death, or ignoring facts. Call it what you like, but I just did not want to think about not being with her. What I wanted to do was to confirm my suspicions over who handled Jana Kava when she was in Poland before I was needlessly sent out there. It could only be one person—Kudashov—and if my suspicion was right, then Jana Kava was indeed Petr Tomsa as Fraser first suggested, but where was the point to that? It was as I was opening yet another bottle of my favourite tipple, a forty-year-old Jura single malt from the generous stock someone in the civil service had signed off on, that Michael Simmons entered.

* * *

He carried good and bad news. Francis Henry Grant, the Director General of MI6 at the time of Operation Donor, had died shortly after his promotion to the chair at the JIC. There was nothing suspicious, Michael added, as though that was about to be a question from either me or Fraser. When neither of us asked, he added in a conspiratorial voice, "There was no autopsy report in the file. The cause of death was recorded as heart failure due to atrial fibrillation. According to the death certificate, he could have had an irregular heartbeat for some time and not have attributed the symptoms to anything serious."

I had asked Michael to conduct his inquiries away from any intelligence department's cybernetic signals and communications. Keeping it as secret as we could. It worked. At last, he had good news to impart.

Hugo Glenister was alive! Something as simple as a search through the Ministry of Defence superannuation payment accounts revealed the whereabouts of his bank, along with his home address in Farnham, Surrey, ten or so miles from Jack Price's nemeses of Guildford, where according to the cynical old Jack P, *all the wankers in the service lived.* With Dickie Blyth-Smith cold in the ground, along with John Scarlett's ex-Director General, Hugo was all I had left. I hoped that at the age of seventy-eight he remained in as good health as Fraser, who was one year his junior.

Chapter Fourteen: Hugo's Conservatory

The waking hours of morning brought no respite from pity. Shared coffee, shared conversation. Shared schedules, shared objectives—shared love, all sharing was missing. Tears were uppermost on my schedule that Friday and I vowed not to shed any. That vow lasted until I was in the bathroom amongst Hannah's toiletries and the scent of her. I'm sure this will sound harsh, but as I saw those things, I had no choice. I phoned housekeeping and asked for all of her clothes and accessories to be boxed and moved to The Lodge, which was still condoned off with teams from forensics crawling all over and around the place.

Friday was to be the first day of my being a widower. Fraser Ughert and I had stayed awake until past one in the morning, going over and over and over again what we knew and what we didn't. However, not even we could delay the inescapable movement of time. I had politely refused to bury my head away from the real world and leave others to do what I should contribute to. Every government minister or head of the various departments I had regular dealings with, shared the same thoughts as Fraser when they were in contact with my office—take time out. I thanked them, saying I would consider it. The Prime Minister had called during Thursday evening, offering for the second time his condolences with the advice I was bored with hearing. The Cabinet Secretary was tactful and gracious in his offer of sympathy; however, being a matter-of-fact civil servant, he was the only person who never advised me to take time away from my post.

* * *

The one thing that stood out more than anything else in Fraser and my exploration of the facts was there were more of what we *didn't* know than what we did. If only the great Dickie Blythe-Smith had left a time capsule somewhere obvious for me to find, or Jack Price was still alive with his intuitive sense of the iniquitous, or my old soldier friend Job, from Group.

Job's answer to a problem was far more direct than the others I've quoted. He would have smashed a few heads together to sort the wheat from the chaff. Even though that approach was not alien to me, in this past time-encased dilemma I had no heads to smash.

I have never offered excuses for rage that was warranted. But when Fraser left for the separate apartment next door to my own that Thursday night, leaving me in the one Hannah and I had shared for such a short period of time, the rage I vented at the unchangeable fact death delivers, meant nothing in palpable terms to anyone but me. Despite that being true, I could feel my own physical presence in my rage melting as my voice calmed before I finally fell asleep with the battle of loneliness being conducted inside my head with the many anguished voices that permanently lived there.

* * *

Fraser arrived for breakfast as I was on the balcony with my umpteenth cigarette. The fact that I was smoking more than normal annoyed the part of me that would say I'm strong and dependent on nobody, yet that belief was drifting on the smoky breeze as I exhaled, watching it go. Through the open doors I heard him shout that Michael Simmons had been in touch, saying there was no news from the Sussex Constabulary, but Hugo Glenister was pleasantly surprised we were coming all the way to Farnham see him and looking forward to our visit with great interest.

* * *

"I retired when I was sixty-five, young man. I was offered a very enticing retirement package and I had no reason, nor ambition to stay on. The top-table position, the one you hold now, young man, was offered to me the year before I left in early '94. That was to be our final year at Century House. To be brutally honest, the job would have been too much for me. I loved every second I had in the SIS, but I was never happy in charge of any desk in European foreign intelligence. I'd done just over eleven years in the temporary posting to the Soviet floor and, quite frankly, I wanted the end to come. The Middle

East was bad enough, but running everything as chair at Joint Intelligence then, thank you, but no thank you. I heard that you'd stayed past retirement, Ughert. Good for you, it's obviously suited as you're looking in very good health."

There must be something in fine malt whisky that kept these two septuagenarians in such fine mental condition, I thought as I watched Hugo pour generously large measures of his favourite tipple, a fine aged Macallan, into three glasses, placing the bottle next to an ice bucket in the middle of a circular marble table surrounded by four soft-cane chairs in his conservatory. The windows looked out onto an immaculately presented cottage garden with roses, climbing plants, and summer flowers naturally interwoven. The colours were strengthened by the penetrating sun, particularly around the ornamental pond and fountain, the splashing of which could be heard through the open door.

"I remember that overseas excursion your PA mentioned on the phone last night very well, West, but I only came into Operation Donor when it was halftime. Apparently, it opened in Prague and was being carried over into Warsaw as an add-on. If I recall correctly, it kept the same coded name even though there was a month or so in between. I'm afraid if you're going to ask me why that was, I have no answer for you as I couldn't understand the reasoning for it either. Your operational name was Frank Douglas and you want to know about your handler, hmm ..." he paused, but not for long. "He had the same name as a town in Kent. Hang on, let me think. Faversham, yes, that was his name."

His wide angular face with the greying eyes of age shone almost as brightly as the sun as the laughing smile erupted on finding the name in his memory banks. "I believe he died not long after I replaced his DG on the seventh floor. Shame when the young die. Big fellow, as I remember, very obese. Stuck in a chair for too long, no doubt. Not the size of chap you forget that easily."

Nor was Hugo. An extremely tall man—I'm not short by any means—but he towered over me at six foot seven at least. I couldn't imagine it was just the garden that kept him as physically fit as he looked, but whatever it was, it was working for him.

"I was told the field officer was back in the UK when Faversham was stood down and I took overall command of the desk. Part of my instructions from the top floor were to keep John Scarlett on as duty officer as he had first-hand knowledge of the show. I believe he has a knighthood now. He was a little slow for my liking, but obviously his methods suited someone. Anyhow, I was told that all things to do with the officers' home welfare arising from loose ends in Prague, Scarlett was to deal with it. Something to do with a shooting that wasn't scheduled. The Czechoslovakian operation sounded as though it went a bit sour to me."

"Why did you say it went sour, Hugo? Did you hear details of something going wrong in Prague?"

"Not specifically wrong in that respect, no. More than anything, it was the atmosphere on that floor that bothered me. It would not have been unusual to find some resentment with the department head coming from outside as it were, but it wasn't just that. There was no banter on the floor. No smutty gossip, not that I'm into that sort of thing, but you know what I mean.

So and so was seen with so and so, and so and so is knocking off someone's wife who's having an affair with so and so. That sort of office chatter. Nothing like that on the Soviet satellite desk. There was nothing I could put my finger on. I got the impression that Scarlett was looking over his shoulder all the time, frightened to piss the Yanks off. As DG, I kept out of it and let Scarlett have the lead. Originally, when I was posted there, I was informed I was to be a short-term solution, but I must have done something right, as I stayed for quite some time, as I said."

"A notable achievement, Hugo, considering your stated dislike of power chairs. Was it Dickie Blythe-Smith who persuaded you to take up the posting, and was it he who filled you in on the Prague end of things, or did the two you meet as the show was running?"

"We never met at all, young man, and I was always sorry for that. You see, I knew Blythe-Smith by name only. Not only was his reputation first class with dazzling honours, but it was he that everyone was measured by, in lots of ways. That was another thing that surprised me. Somehow or other, here we were with the Yanks sitting in on one of our operations and the top floor being aware. When I was on the Middle East desk, we had officers on the ground that were engaged in live, highly sensitive operations, and my staff and I kept it all to ourselves. At no time was I made aware that we shared information whilst the op was running with partners if it wasn't overlapping. That was the conclusion I came to; Operation Donor was impinging on an American action that was going on.

"I'm sorry to say that the Americans being there didn't fit well with me or any in my department. Maybe that's why the floor seemed stifled. I would have loved an audience on the top floor with Blythe-Smith to sort it out, but he had vanished into retirement." With deliberation I nodded my head, adding as I did, "Yes, I see, Hugo. I can totally understand your dissatisfaction with the situation. I'm sure Fraser and I would have felt the same."

I turned to Fraser and he had that all-knowing look of his plastered across his enigmatic face. It was my show, he'd said in the car as we pulled up. '*I'll play the serious role of Rodin's Thinker, while you play the court jester to Henry II, Roland*

The Farter. Look him up afterwards.' I hadn't a clue who Roland was, but I understood what Fraser meant.

"I'm not trying to put words into your mouth, Hugo. I just want to recap and make sure we all know where we are. You thought the Americans were in overall control of Operation Donor in Poland when you switched over from the Middle East desk to Soviet Satellite? Would you say that was the impression you had?"

Glenister's sizeable presence made the conservatory, at the rear of his charming detached home in the picturesque countryside of Surrey, seem a lot smaller than it really was. Despite that feeling of economy of space, his contribution to my knowledge was far greater than I could possibly have hoped for.

"It was more than a feeling, Patrick. It was a fact and, as I've said, I was not comfortable with it, but I stuck it out. The actual briefing I had came from the departing DG, Francis Henry Grant. I can't forget that name. In my youth, I spent a year at university in Ontario in Canada, and whilst there, I had a bit of fun serving in what was called the Fort Henry Guard. It was an entertainment for tourists, nothing more. Lots of drum noise and marching stuff. Yes, sorry, back to the debrief. Grant told me the Yanks were totally in command. However, the rationale in the file was ambiguous over that decision. Nonetheless, the CIA was on our territory and Grant spelled out the sequence of command in no uncertain way—them first, me second, then Scarlett. Despite them being first in the chain of command, my only instructions would come straight from Grant. No direct orders would come from the Americans. As you can understand—odd."

"A strange set-up indeed, Hugo."

We stopped speaking for a moment as we both gazed out onto the noisy fountain, neither of us troubled by the noise, simply fascinated by it. Fraser followed our stare, rising from where he sat and making his way towards the pond.

"Are there fish in the pond?" he asked as he was walking down a short flight of steps into the garden.

"As long as the herons haven't stolen any."

I returned the conversation to Operation Donor. "I'm sorry to load you with Russian names, Hugo, but I have no choice. Did you come across the name Nikita Sergeyovitch Kudashov at all? I have the names written down on some notes, if my Russian pronunciation is too rustic for you."

He waved away my suggestion to withdraw some papers from the document folder that rested against the side of my chair. "Not necessary, your Russian sounds fine to me, Patrick. Yes, I know that name. He was the Czech agents' handler before I arrived. Again, this is only from a briefing, remember, and it was twenty-five years ago. I saw nothing written down. I understood he had the Prague end for us."

I tried to hide my look of utter bewilderment the best I could. Maybe he had it mixed up, I told myself, ignoring the fact that up until that moment he had confirmed everything we knew, so why should he now be mistaken? Before I realised what I'd done, the file with Hannah's written notes of names was on the table beside his half-empty glass. Obviously, somehow I had put it there and opened it, but I had no answer to when or how. My hands were working independently to my brain. Without asking, I filled his glass and mine, adding what remained of the ice to mine. I sat waiting for a response with my glass nestled in my hand, but not daring to move, as no matter how melodramatic this might sound, I sensed a hand on my shoulder. I turned my head slightly, away from the pond, and there stood Hannah, as clear as day.

At that moment, Glenister spoke. "Yes, that's the same name and the one above it—that one," he pointed at the name of General Anotoly Vladislav Kava. "I was told he was the agent's dead father."

I blinked and Hannah had gone.

"In respect of the handler, Hugo, are you sure it was agent that was mentioned, not our asset or operative? This Kudashov fellow was our agent's handler. Was that correct?" Fraser was standing in the doorframe facing inwards and I looked at him as I asked. His look of concentration reflected what was racing through my mind and making my fingers twitch in excitement.

"I'm positive, gentlemen. I did know the difference in those days. I had enough agents to deal with in Palestine, Lebanon and the rest of Middle East. Yes, agent it was. He or she was one of ours."

"I bet you did have agents and officers in the field from your Middle East days, and I bet those names were just as complicated as Russian names, if not more so." I smiled and hoped I had reassured him and settled my nerves. "I have another name, but this time it's Czechoslovakian and my Czech is useless nowadays." I took hold of Hannah's notes and my inside froze as I pointed. Those nerves were far from settled. "Did you ever hear that name mentioned, Hugo?"

"I never heard it spoken, Patrick, but I saw it written down on a classified memo on Lieutenant Colonel Ward's desk."

When I was *on the spy,* and things became tense or exhilarating, my breathing and heart rate slowed to tortoise-like speeds. I was told that was an advantage, but I didn't know if the slowness of them now would be an advantage. "Do you recall seeing anything else written on that memo, Hugo?"

He stared out of the window towards the fountain and cascading sunlit water, but his focus was inside an office twenty-five years ago, not his own, and in a building he couldn't wait to leave.

The silent Fraser, who had retaken his seat to my right, had told me he'd met Glenister a few times on service business, forming the opinion he was a diligent, measured man in the dealings the two had had. I was hoping Fraser's estimation was correct and Hugo's dedication to details was still available to me. As I was thinking my question had defeated his memory, he slowly turned his head towards me motioning it up and down ever so slightly, raising my hopes.

"Do you know what, I do know more. In situations like this, I try to visualise the scene where I was. Put myself back in time and into the space I occupied. Very rarely does it not work for me and thankfully this is not one of those times. Neither the lieutenant colonel nor the naval commander were in their office so I had ample time to look, and look I did, Patrick. I was a nosy bugger back in those days." His infectious smile seized hold of both Fraser and me, easing the tension we shared. "It said—no show Petr Tomsa at Battery. Strike zone empty. I was a bit of a sports fanatic all through my life and I believe they are baseball terms."

The smile had disappeared from Hugo Glenister's face, replaced by a strong impassive bearing, one I imagined he carried throughout his service years. My breathing was at its slowest. "This is going to be a difficult one to answer, Hugo, but I'm going to ask it anyway." My smile was not as genuine as his had been, but he returned it just the same. "Have you any idea of the date of that memo?"

"More than an idea. I know *exactly*, young man. It was the first of September 1982. That was the same day the Israelis entered Southern Lebanon and pushed the Palestine Liberation Organisation out of the country. My old desk had alerted me of the situation out of courtesy, and although they had up-to-the-minute reports, I thought the Americans might be able pull strings and find more information for me. It was the reason for me going to their office. An ex-wife of mine was an American-Jew and she was serving as a field intelligence officer in the Israeli military when the Israelis invaded. That was perhaps the main reason I'd been given the Middle East desk."

Chapter Fifteen: Fall-Out

After leaving Hugo's genial hospitality, I spent the remainder of Friday with Fraser and Molly at their home in Buckinghamshire, supposedly in research, absorbed by the information on a computer screen, but in truth I was wasting away the hours before an inevitable return to solitude in a once happy environment. As much as I loved Fraser, I found his predilection for any involvement of the Rothschilds with the Cambridge spy ring of the sixties debilitating and hard to bear. Although I held his logic in the highest regard, I could not see the sense in going back so many years in order to harden up 'proof' that had been constantly denied.

During the preceding early morning hours that we and a bottle of Jura had spent together, I toyed with the idea of flying off somewhere to wipe away my memory of Hannah. How far would I need to fly to completely erase my past? Not only the one I'd shared with Hannah, but the history I had with the other voices that hid in my mind until they hammered at my conscience? But the impossible was beyond what I could achieve as I did not possess that amount of detachment or insensitivity. Or did I? As the night closed in and the dark descended on the Whitehall apartment, I realised I could not be that person. I was cruel to her memory in removing her possessions to Sussex. The wiser thing to do would have been to keep them, as they would have been comforting and not crushed me with sentiment.

Having arrived at the conclusion that I needed a new approach to the situation I was in, I carried it further and decided there was no amount of whisky that could drown either the tangible or the intangible memories that remained. I resolved to turn my back on that remedy. What I did try was to return some of the unanswered calls from her family. Her brother was the first name on the lengthy typed list left on the blotter of my desk and he was still awake.

* * *

To begin with, he expressed his sorrow for Hannah's departure, but it wasn't long before a degree of spite found its way into his empathy. *Why did she marry a man who would expose her to so much danger* was only one of the accusations he found to aim at me. I finished our exchange after another insinuation as to her welfare, which I found one too many from an uninformed source, even allowing for his grief, which by then I found insincere. *The newspapers said her car was fitted with inferior glass compared to the top civil servants who need protection. Couldn't a man in your position ensure my sister's life was adequately secured from an assassin looking for revenge for something you had done? It was you who murdered her and I hope you can live with that guilt.*

There were several ways I could have reacted to that remark. One would be to forget it and move on, leaving just another disgruntled encounter behind me lying in the passage in life. Or, I could have noted it mentally and tried to reconcile family differences that occur in the heat of moments of despair, when outrage might subside when rationality returns to fill a void. Another way, and perhaps this was the best way I could have dealt with it, was to send a car to take her brother somewhere quiet and find out how he came to think that revenge could be a motive.

Until I'd met Hannah I'd had nobody in my life to worry about. Nobody to care for or to care for me. I had never experienced the fear of not being able to reconnect with a person I'd left at home, because there was no one to go home to—until, that is, I said those two small words of *I do* in a church, facing the woman I was smitten by. Now my best friend, my lover and wife had gone and I was left with more anger than any brother could imagine in their wildest nightmares. It was not my responsibility to open his eyes to the brutality of life and to the savages that I had lived with and walked amongst. Yes, Hannah died because of an action I had sanctioned, but Hannah knew the life she had chosen and she also knew I wasn't about to leave it.

I shredded the note of names my secretary had left, not returning the calls from Hannah's sister, her aunt and the three Rothschild godparents who had either contacted the Home Office to find a phone number or had my private mobile as a contact. If I wanted to be with Hannah, then it was to Sussex and The Lodge I should go.

* * *

Ever since Thursday's horrendous incident, the risk factor I presented had notched up a degree or two on whatever it was that Special Branch used to measure how my safety was represented to them. In response, I was assigned two extra cars, four police motorcyclists, and five extra protection officers to look after me. By the time I had reached a decision to travel to Sussex, both Jimmy and Frank had been stood down for the weekend, which disappointed me greatly as they knew my temperament and how best to deal with me.

I needed friends but had none other than Fraser. There were of course colleagues in the same job as Fraser and me, but I didn't count on them as I did on him. It was a conscious choice I'd made not to make friends with any person from the day my last friend, Job, passed on. I felt close to him and to Jack Price, who died before Job. Both those deaths had an effect on me that neither the death of my father nor my mother ever had. I never needed to ask the service psychologist, who anyone involved in a shooting incident had to see, why it was that killing someone had no effect on me, but the loss of a friend did. The death of a close friend hurts, that's why. Having no friends saves on the Kleenex.

I believe to know oneself is the most difficult aspect of life. One can learn most things from others and, if one is clever, one can learn how and where to discover that which cannot be taught. A single person can create unique works of art of many descriptions, but if the individual elements are combined it may tempt the critical part of the person to alter over time. The trick is to know what made up the original, and to be able to do that one must be absolutely certain of the instinctive characteristics. I had known every tiny detail that constituted my complexity, until the slight alteration I mentioned chipped away at it each time I had thought I was in love. On more than one occasion, the object of my affections had died in similar ways to Hannah.

The beautiful Kerry, whom I'd found in Ireland, had trespassed into my heart before being taken from me in excruciating pain, inflicted in the name of freedom by people Hannah's brother had no knowledge of how vile humanity could be, as he hurled insults in the wrong direction. Fianna, another from that beautiful enigma of an island called Ireland. Sitting beside me with her head blown off, slowly sliding down the front car seat towards me as Job dragged me from the car. I was lucky that love only touched me three times. The other voices came from loves of a different sense. Desire, yes, intimacy, yes, fondness, yes, but devotion and adoration, then no. But honesty could not always satisfy a protesting voice.

Friends are a nuisance. They are a weakness in my trade and love is a traitorous emotion that I should have fought harder to resist. I had heard love described by many people caught up in many differing circumstances.

Once, on an assignment into Southern Ireland, the officer I was assisting wanted to tell me his life story the night before we went 'live' on an execution of an IRA brigade commander. He and his wife had a newborn baby, three weeks old and, to make matters worse, he was given the chance to sit this operation out because of that. But he was good at his job and he thought it his duty to say yes, sir, please, bring it on, sir.

The hit was easy, they said. Every Wednesday morning, the brigade commander went to the first Mass at his local Catholic church. That's where it was to happen. On the dot of 6:15 our man's car pulls to a halt outside the church. His minder and driver have a quick look around and then he steps out of the car and onto the pavement. We had done everything by the plan, by the book; nevertheless, someone had blown us.

My fellow officer, the father of the three-week-old son, crossed the road from behind the van I'd parked thirty yards north of the kill zone. I was to cross from the front. My door was open and my gun was in my right hand as my colleague raised his gun to fire. Without warning, three men appeared from inside the church. I got one in the chest as they, and the two with our target, fired. I saw my colleague hit several times before the gunfire was concentrated at me. I got away two more shots, hitting the target on his shoulder and his driver in the head. Those still standing retreated to the church doorway. I reloaded and kept laying down a covering fire as I dragged my man into the van from the passenger side, ducking under the wide incoming fire, and drove away from the scene unscathed. He was dead when I got to safety.

That experience taught me the lesson that I never forgot; the one where being in love was for others, not me. He had shown himself too quickly at the scene. Had he waited a split second longer, when I was fully out in a position to fire a kill shot at our target, then I believe we both could have escaped, but I think he had his mind on things other than the plan. The grief that man's wife must have suffered when she was told of her husband's death must have been the same as I now felt but, strangely enough, whatever sympathy I might have had for her then now vanished, as though it was never there. The choice of abandoning commitment had a lonely consequence that now drove away any equanimity I could find for myself. There was no help to expect from Hannah's Landgft family, but there might be clues to who presented the keys of The Home of Cilicia in her private possessions that were now at The Lodge. I decided to look and disregard sentiment.

The first possession I looked for was her computer, which she was constantly using in her research into the ownership of the house. I found the file and opened it … opening yet another surprise.

* * *

Oswald Raynor, the last owner of The Lodge, had not died intestate with the property being dealt with as bona vacantia. Raynor had gifted the property directly to the Prince of Wales. That came as a shock. I imagined there would be very few on the Prince of Wales' staff who were empowered with the authority to transfer property from his estate. At some time, I must find whoever had signed the transfer papers.

I looked again at those numbers of 3/9/1989, remembering the date of 'Petr Tomsa's' nonappearance at the baseball Battery or Non-Strike terminology points: 1/9/1982 both divisible by the Freemasonry number three, and was surprised at how I'd missed the dovetailing of the Tomsa date into the conspiracy. As I stared more intently at Hannah's findings, I wondered if Fraser had missed that as well. There were too many numbers that had connections to Mayler's branch of Freemasonry to be just a coincidence, but how could it not be so?

I started to recall my adventure with Jack Price and his continued reference to The Firm, the name he used for the Royal Family, and how tightly meshed and secretive they were, but he had penetrated that secrecy, turning what was a weakness into a strength that I managed to make use of at my meeting in the Travellers Club with Dickie Blythe-Smith.

My first meeting with Dickie was in a hotel room in New York, with Jack, Job, and Fraser all rushing to collect luggage to make the flight from America back to London. He was inquiring after my welfare, worried that my busted cheekbone and broken eye socket, along with the missing toes, would curtail my ability to fly. Jack Price passed me two syringes filled with morphine, his last two. Neither Dickie nor Fraser were aware of Jack's incurable illness. When he told them of his impending death, Dickie Blythe-Smith made a comment to me that I failed to see the point of then, but now I do—*know everything then nothing comes as a surprise.* However, that had a sting to it that Dickie hadn't seen coming; the secret I kept in my back pocket that only Jack Price and I knew of.

* * *

I was jolted back to reality by Fraser's phone call. He wanted to know how I was doing. "I'm doing just fine," I said as the extent of our shared incomprehension of the surprises kept hitting me, making me want to scream. The recurring number three had been a surprise. Nikita Sergeyovitch Kudashov's knowledge of Henry Mayler had been another surprise. Hannah's death had been the biggest surprise of them all.

"I'm doing just fine," I repeated the reply as Hannah's brother's accusations were overcome by my flippancy. I had used her for my own convenience, that of shutting myself away in the arms of love until an all-knowing Russian arrived in London with tales of Cilicia, and perhaps an assassin following his every footstep. My muddled memory of repeats, clues, and unanswered questions was in danger of being drowned by partially controlled tears.

* * *

Those confused thoughts had been with me when I arrived at The Lodge. Approximately thirty minutes later another car arrived and a hooded passenger, wearing handcuffs, was escorted into the nearest outbuilding to the main house, down several flights of winding stairs, then along a brightly lit corridor and finally into a room where the hood and handcuffs were removed. The first person he saw was me.

His dark brown eyes blinked rapidly and, when fully adjusted to the light in the room, he scanned his modest surroundings of what the inventory of the house stated was the Safe Room, a misnomer as there was more than one room, as the doors that led off attested to. There was sufficient space to comfortably accommodate up to eight people and sufficient provisions to sustain them for two years. It was the 'fall-out' facility, excavated in the grounds of the estate to withstand a nuclear attack on London and the South East. Although, as I say, the furnishings were functional rather than sumptuous, they were perfectly suitable for the purpose.

My visitor was not to be subjected to any physical attack, but he seemed to suspect as much as he repeatedly claimed to have a delicate heart condition that could lead to his premature death if abused.

"Your file says nothing of a heart complaint. Something new, is it?"

I asked as I occupied one of the soft upholstered chairs opposite Nikita Sergeyovitch Kudashov, and together we began trying to unravel a twenty-five-year-old mystery.

"My humble apologies, Mr West. That was my cowardly defence mechanism kicking in when put in the back of the car and hooded. I am not a man equipped for torturous pain, but I don't think you're that kind of man. A strange way to do it, but you have presented me with a chance to extend my condolences for the tragic loss of your wife. However, I doubt you have brought me here to listen to my compassion in your time of loss. But perhaps you've brought here because you believe I killed her?"

"I have no reason to believe that at the moment, but who knows how my mind might work as we conduct our discussion. Let us start with a lie and see where we go. Why did you lie when you said you didn't know who Petr Tomsa was, Nikita?"

"It was important that you found it out for yourself. If I had told you who Petr was when you first asked, then I believe you would have closed your mind to everything else. Now, hopefully, you can begin afresh with a clean mind."

"And would you have a preferred point where you would like to start with it all, or maybe you would like to start with what you're not telling me? Because I think there's a helluva lot you're not saying."

Chapter Sixteen: Microfilm

"I was London's operative way before anything started involving you and the Kavas. It was I who was the author of both the reports that appeared in the classified files you read on Jana Kava and her brother Dalek for the operation London coded as Operation Donor. Although this operation commenced in May 1982, its real beginning can be traced back to 1944 and to a small town in Scotland, where a British army colonel named Maurice Buckmaster trained a Czechoslovakian woman, who was to become Jana and Dalek's mother.

"It was from that Special Operations Executive camp that she said her goodbyes to Buckmaster and, under the name of Tereza Místek, took to the skies to be parachuted into Nazi-occupied Czechoslovakia. Tereza was twenty-four years old when she arrived in Prague in her SOE role as a courier between the Czech and Slovak resistance and their soon-to-be liberators, the 9th Soviet Army Group, commanded by General Anotoly Vladislav Kava, who was to become her liaison officer. It gets interesting, doesn't it, Patrick?

"Tereza's cover from the Scottish school was excellent and it did not take her long to exceed all Buckmaster's expectations, as he originally marked her as Not Ready, before being persuaded to the contrary by Vera Atkins, his counterpart in charge of the female section. They were all part of Winston Churchill's 'Secret Army' ready to *set Europe ablaze* as he told his Minister for War. I shall not bore you with any details of the exploits she endured during the final months of WWII, but it led to Tereza marrying General Kava a year after the war ended. Not even he knew that she was London's long-term plant inside what was to become the Czechoslovakian corner of the Soviet Bloc. She wasn't executed for distributing subversive material as I wrote it up in the Kava's file. She was executed for telling the truth.

"One night during one of her husband's increasingly violent alcoholic periods of abuse, she went searching for a way of striking back at her husband. She hadn't the strength to fight him off, nor gun or knife to finish a once love-filled marriage now turned into a bitter violent one, where she and the two children suffered at his hands as his depression-induced attacks got worse and worse.

"In a loud, rasping voice she told him of her spying activities in his domain of Czechoslovakia and how those activities of hers had helped to fight against the Communist dominance of Europe. Yes, she cried out, I told London everything thing, no matter what.

"There was nothing more damaging or hurtful she could have thrown at him. His blows of temper that hit her were less painful now she knew how much she had repaid his brutality. It was his turn to be hurt, but that pain turned to retribution. He gagged and tied her hands, pinned the Solidarity leaflets he'd found all over her clothing, then marched her to his army barracks and there, after forcing her to kneel on the parade ground, shot her in the back of her head. All that is true, Patrick West, because he would not have killed his wife for having leaflets. Who would do that? But he would kill her and gag her if she had confessed to having been a spy.

"I saw her shot, and the abhorrence I felt towards Stalin and the system he believed in was reinforced a thousand times. I was disgusted by how mankind could act in defence of a murderer and tyrant. It was I who loosened the bolts of the inspection ladder where Khrushchev slipped and then voraciously abused Kava for his incompetence, so much so that it almost came to blows before two of Khrushchev's bodyguards dragged the general away and shot him. He deserved that and more for what he done to Tereza, a kind woman who I never heard speak ill of anyone. I didn't watch Kava die that day in the factory, but there was no need to follow the First Secretary's hoods to know what was about to happen. Hearing the argument was enough for me. But had I needed proof, it lay on the mortuary slab an hour after his body was found, where I was summoned to appear in order to increase my police education."

Kudashov was genuinely sad as he leant forward with elbows on his knees and head in his hands. At this point of time, coffee and sandwiches were brought in and placed on the dining table pushed against one of the wallpapered walls. As the tray-bearing officer left the room, Kudashov rose and examined the small array of books on display on the shelves along the adjoining wall. He poured himself a mug of coffee and returned to his seat.

"It's possible for me to tell you stories of Tereza Místek as Tereza Kava that would take hours of your time to hear a fraction of her accomplishments during and after WWII, but that's not the period of European history that interests you in this matter regarding my granddaughter, Mr West, is it? Incidentally, is it permissible for me to be informal in the way I address you? Or should I forget Tuesday's meeting now I'm your prisoner?"

"Prisoner? No, you're my guest, Nikita. Forget Tuesday, no, not at all," I replied. "We need to broaden our outlook, that's all. Be as informal as you like and please do carry on, but before we go deeper into this, tell me how Jana Kava came to be known at the Soviet Satellite desk by two code names? The one on the file you claim to be all your work—FlyHi One, and Petr Tomsa, the name London gave me as your coded name?"

"Puzzle, isn't it? But London also gave you my name as Nikita Sergeyovitch Kudashov, did they not?"

"They did, yes."

"Then, do you think you had a dummy working that desk, Patrick, or did he tell you something you shouldn't have known? Was your handler that clever, do you think? If he was not that clever, was there someone else who was?"

I was imagining Fraser sitting where Kudashov sat, as it seemed to be the same sanctimonious smile on his face when he asked that all-important question. Yet another I had no answer to. An expression conveying knowledge beyond my limitations was a trademark of Fraser Ughert's that he often used, but if the boot were on the other foot and I knew more than he, his defence was to deflect the question by either asking one of his own or simply ignoring it. I chose the second option, adding a bottle of whisky and two glasses alongside the food, and offering cigarettes as I advised him to continue in unveiling the intrigue that lay ahead.

* * *

Although Kudashov condensed the parts of the story that had no direct impact on the present day; it still took hours to tell and even more for me to fully comprehend its importance. He started it somewhere in the middle with Jana Kava, who had been a member of the StB as I'd suspected. The association proved to be a strength to her in respect of credibility for her intelligence gatherings, but it also led to a meeting that was not planned. It was during a drop-off intended for Kudashov that she met her nemesis, an American. Officially, the CIA was never in Czechoslovakia, but there was an American embassy with diplomatic staff and an ambassador who had an eye for the women and the scent of promotion. Kudashov told me the ambassador's name, but it's not his name that was important. What was important is what he did. I shall call him Jack.

Jack emerged from a meeting with the mayor of Prague and for a reason known only to himself, wanted a smoke. It was a beautiful spring day, so he shunned the comforts of the embassy car, preferring to stretch his legs. He started his stroll around a pretty city park towards one of the wooden seats in the arched alcoves that lined some of the walls. He hadn't planned to sit there, just walk past, but no matter, that's where history was changed.

Ambassador Jack saw Jana Kava rise from one of the benches, leaving an open packet of cigarettes with only a few of the contents gone. He did what every gentleman would do. He picked them up and called to her. At the precise moment he waved that packet in the air, something fell from it and unfortunately for Jana, Jack recognised what it was. From that moment on, the intelligence Jana gathered from her position serving Jozef Lenárt and his fellow members of the Communist elite was shared with Jack and his CIA buddies in America, as well as with her London contacts.

For almost a year, everything was going as well as it could until London heard from Kudashov, telling them of Jana's brother's consorting with representatives from the Solidarity movement and generally making a dangerous nuisance of himself. They wanted to know how Kudashov had permitted such a valuable agent as Jana Kava to be compromised. They asked him to deal with Dalek himself.

He made as many valid excuses as he could, but London insisted that it was his problem and his to deal with. Eventually, left with no other choice than to agree and risk everything he had worked for, Kudashov told London the truth about the American involvement and how that would make it impossible for him to take care of Dalek.

* * *

"I'm sorry for the interruption, Nikita, but once the CIA had their hooks into Jana did they not trawl around and find you in their nets?"

"No! I was not known to the Americans at that stage and I held out from telling London about Jana being compromised for as long as I could. I could not be completely sure though that the Americans would not tell the Soviet Satellite desk in London. The CIA only heard of me because I couldn't kill Dalek Kava. I told London the full story of Jana's American connection when I told them I couldn't. That's when they told me they were sending you."

"Who are 'they' in that context?"

"The Director General, Francis Grant. I had word passed to me from the British embassy by way of my usual contact. I saw you when you were at the trade conference and once when you were with Dalek in a bar. You two were about to leave when I arrived. The next time I saw you, you were watching Jana and me together at the Palace Zofin on a Saturday night, but I haven't got the date of that meeting handy, Patrick."

"Was it Grant who gave Jana Kava the additional code name of Petr Tomsa?"

"No, not London that time. That name was given her by the CIA. Your next question would be when was that, I presume?"

I nodded my head in acceptance of his presumption.

"This I do know as it was on the day my granddaughter was born. My granddaughter was healthy, as was my daughter-in-law, so I was superfluous in my son's house and in everyone's way. I left and was on my way home when I was approached in the street. There were two men, neither of whom did I recognise, nor could I now. The shorter of the two said they knew I was London's man and they told me they had Jana on their books. It was then I heard the name Petr Tomsa. They told me to tell London that name so the wires didn't cross."

If I tried to hide the fact that I was confused, it didn't work. "Yes, I'm at a loss to know how they knew about me as well as you," he stated, but I wasn't convinced.

"Why did they ask you to tell London the code name and not notify London through accepted passages, I wonder?" Although my question was spoken aloud, I didn't really expect an answer, however Kudashov provided one.

"They never said, Patrick."

I left all the additional questions I had hanging in the cigarette smoke and whisky fumes, allowing Kudashov to continue with his account of what occurred. As he did, more things became clearer. According to him, it didn't take much time for London to discover it was a CIA agent who had introduced Dalek to Solidarity.

Although the Americans were thin on the ground behind Soviet lines of influence in the eighties, their level of incompetence was astounding. Nobody had bothered to find out all there was to know about Dalek, and they had no idea of the damage his affiliations to that banned movement could cause to Jana's safety. There was absolutely no mileage in Dalek holding a Solidarity member's card. It was fraught with danger. However, with them now included, it was unrealistic for London to handle her alone; hence, the US Air Force lieutenant colonel sitting at the Soviet Satellite desk in Century House. It was American government policy not to get their hands in the grime in Czechoslovakia or anywhere else in Warsaw Pact countries, that's the reason I was sent to Prague with a concealed agenda to the mission.

Not only was I not told the true reason for being sent, I was given an inept handler on point whilst I was there. Having avidly listened to what Kudashov had to say, I could understand why it was played the way it turned out. My problem with all of it was—why was it necessary to make my instructions so complicated? Why not just send me to kill Dalek Kava?

I never made Kudashov aware of the full extent of deceit that was the foundation of my briefing before I left for Prague. To be honest, I wasn't sure if I had seen through the slyness of it all, or been informed of the real objective behind sending me, I would have refused and not taken the operation. Equally, I'm not sure I would have acted any differently once I was in Prague. I achieved what was required by a twisting route compared with sending an assassin, it's true, but that was not where Operation Donor ended, nor was it Miles Faversham's end. His end, I suspected, came later from an induced heart attack.

Hugo Glenister had stood Faversham down, but kept John Scarlett in position. Kudashov knew them all, so I asked him why was that? Receiving no answer, I repeated what Scarlett had said about how he believed Glenister was working from a prewritten script, and would he like to add any comment? Again, nothing was added to the subject. Despite there being a gap to Kudashov's all-round knowledge, there were other matters he had opinions and answers on; particularly the role of the American CIA in it all.

Poland, with the fuse starting to burn under the Communist government by the Solidarity movement, was President Reagan's target from the offset when Jana Kava was recruited.

It was to become a portion of the icing on top of the CIA's cake. They already had a voice inside GCHQ ,whose back could be covered by exposing Geoffrey Prime, and they had a Soviet spy inside their agency. They could and did use the situation in Prague to find the spy they had in their organisation, digging a deeper hole for the one they were using against us in GCHQ to hide themselves in. Prime's exposure was a cheap price to pay.

The US handler in Prague instructed Jana Kava first to go to Warsaw and then on to Gdańsk and do as much as she could to incite the students to demonstrate in support of Solidarity. Their reasons for that were not sensible and, at their worse, downright idiotic. According to Kudashov, they gave Jana precise instructions where to be in Gdańsk on the first of September '82, making it easy, so he alleged, to murder her and cover their tracks.

"In my mind, I'm sure the CIA marked you down as the possible fall guy when they became aware of you. No one can be one hundred percent sure how it was to play, but my money is on London insisting it was you who made the pick-up of the radio coding at the main train station in Warsaw. In that way, whoever was in overall control in London, pulled you away from the murderous American hands."

* * *

I had nobody to ask if Nikita Sergeyovitch Kudashov's theory was correct, but I did know that at the time of the operation I was naive enough to think that only the London desk could know of Warszawa Centralna being the location of the signal coding exchange. At least the answer to why Kudashov had come to me for help in his granddaughter's escape and not the American CIA was getting clearer, but how did he have that information, even allowing for the twenty-five years that had passed? For the next citation of events, I wanted to tackle his suspicion of a secret sect within the Rosicrucian fraternity and a dislike of the number three. But before we got to that point, there were other topics on his mind.

"I would imagine that I'm being kept somewhere below your property in Sussex, The Lodge. A gift from The Home of Cilicia. Do you think that was just an intriguing random choice of words engraved on the box, Patrick?"

I didn't ask how he knew, but Dickie's words of *know everything then nothing comes as a surprise* were tailor-made for Kudashov.

"If I were to tell you where you are, it would make the use of the hood somewhat silly and make me appear a bit of a fool. Yes, the naming of the gift is intriguing, particularly with your surname deriving from the Armenian word for 'home' and your granddaughter's name of Cilicia. Was it your gift to Hannah and me, Nikita?"

"If only I had that quantity of money, plus that amount of leverage on the Prince of Wales."

Had I have been sitting on the edge of my chair, I think that last piece of knowledge might have tipped me out. Could my flippant thought of Dickie's phrase being tailor-made for Kudashov be right? He had more to offer.

"But perhaps leverage is the wrong word. Please don't offend me and look as though I wouldn't know about the Prince of Wales. I know much more than you might believe."

Yes, I thought, *you do. Everything does lead to everything if you know what everything is to start off with.* As I was thinking about that, his smile creased his eye-line, forehead and seemingly every muscle in his face. He continued speaking before the smile totally disappeared. "Maybe it was the Prince himself who gifted it, Patrick? Have you considered that? Did not the Windsors change their name from the German Saxe-Coburg and Gotha, when WWI broke out? Have you thought of a family connection along those lines? Perhaps those of the House of Hesse and the Saxe-Coburgs are related by marriage?"

I had discussed the possibility with Hannah one night not long after our wedding. As I remembered that discussion, I thought of her and I felt cold as I did. I changed the subject from me to him. "You may have a point, but my initial thoughts were on your relationship to him through the Russian tsars. Are you a close friend of the Prince of Wales through your Russian ancestry, Nikita?"

He sniggered derisively at my question, declining to answer before his rhetoric carried on. "The United States Army Group Europe had its HQ in and around Frankfurt in the region of Hesse in Germany until I think it was 2002, but well before that year came and went, the CIA had established an outpost, close by in Mannheim. Ostensibly, they were there to protect American interests in Germany and her immediate neighbours. The contingent of agents was small for such a huge and complex mission: twelve pairs of boots on the ground and four pairs of dainty shoes. Their mission was accomplished by the cooperation of the National Security Agency and the forty-four operatives they had working their Frosting project from above an innocent garage, where the gainfully employed mechanics below had no idea what was happening above their heads. Some other people never knew either. Only one of America's allies in NATO had a clue what they doing above the garage and that was the West Germans. Not even Britain's GCHQ was allowed to know everything the NSA were up to. But Patrick, the Americans would not have exposed Geoffrey Prime had they not needed to.

"My granddaughter has a comprehensive list of their present targets, along with every code they used since 1982. Every message they sent and every name and organisation on their list of people of interest. She has copied the complete works they have. In a safe deposit box in the vaults of a place called The Metropolitan Security, in Cheval Place, Knightsbridge, there are two folders of decrypted NSA signal-branded messages to CIA outstations in various parts of Africa and the Far East. Take them and see what your own analysts think of them. If you still want to talk, I will understand how valuable you rate her. As I told you, she has the profile data needed to decrypt their latest information sweep, this Data Mining. I have given you the facts about the eugenic programme and I am willing to trade more on that, but I must press you for a decision about Cilicia, Patrick. She is my main concern."

It was a sincere appeal he made and one I took seriously; however, he knew as well as I that these things didn't happen in the time that had just passed. Cheval Place needed a visit.

"I am in consultation with a colleague about your granddaughter and a feasibility report based on Moscow for the extraction has been compiled. We have worked it up on the assumption that Cilicia is not allowed to travel away from Moscow or anywhere on her own. At first sight, the prospect for success does not look favourable. The advice I'm getting is that central Moscow should be avoided if at all possible. But we're still working with it. What is not feasible for one man can become feasible for another. I can assure you, Nikita, when all the issues in the programme are smoothed away, I'll come back with a proposal, but we are not at that point yet. One outstanding question that requires your deliberation is the answer to who donated The Lodge. I think you know more about the wedding gift of that house in Sussex than you're telling me."

The pensive expression he wore gave me cause for hope about the answer I searched for, except that wasn't the reason for his silent thoughts. They dwelt on a previous chapter of life that took another hour to be aired and examined before weariness overtook me and my eyes began to close on his narrative. We parted company a few hours before dawn, he to sleep in one of the 'Fall-Out' bedrooms and I to retire to a single bed in a room on the first floor of the house as far away as possible from the master bedroom Hannah and I had shared. Her haunting cries knew no boundaries such as walls and doors; nonetheless, not even they could not keep me from the sleep I desired but dreaded.

Chapter Seventeen

Gdańsk

Late on Saturday morning I had two telephone calls, one immediately after the other. The first was the more straightforward. It came from the relatively new department at the AIS, Greenwich. The encoded signals contained in the two folders Kudashov had told me of in a safe-deposit box at Cheval Place in Knightsbridge, had been rapidly decoded by their state-of-the-art analytical computers and proven to be every bit as accurate as his granddaughter's decryption. The spatial diagnostic telecommunication readers were the finest anywhere to be found in the western world. Although the intelligence in the signals themselves did not add up to much value for the time we were now in, they would have had a bearing on many matters in the years they applied to. We now had thorough confirmation of Kudashov's assertion about his granddaughter's capability.

The second call confirmed Kudashov's account of Tereza Místek's training and affiliation to the SOE. This part of our investigation was collaborated by the keeper of the Czechoslovakian Special Operations Executive's records at a place named Morar, a small village on the west coast of Scotland. The custodian of what was left of the history of the organisation was a Scottish lady whose grandfather taught the skills needed with radio equipment, along with how to code and decipher messages to the agents that were parachuted behind enemy lines. It was with a very proud voice she told me over the phone line some of the history of her grandfather's association, including his role in the training of those who assassinated Reinhard Heydrich, one of the main architects of the Holocaust in Prague.

Unfortunately, she informed me, most of the files of SOE exploits were destroyed in a fire in 1946 at the place they were kept in Baker Street, London. The remainder were 'weeded through' before either being shredded and burnt, or tucked away out of sight under a one-hundred-year ban on publication. When we finished speaking, I was totally satisfied with Kudashov's explanation. I sent word to the protection team to make him as comfortable as possible, with exercise being restricted to the Fall-Out areas only. I told them to laugh at his jokes and tune in to the Russian news channels if he wanted that, but for now I had no need of his company and, in some ways, his presence reminded me of Hannah.

A good part of the day was spent on the telephone chatting to the heads of government departments, as well as acquaintances in the UK military, along with the Director of the CIA in London who, using the word loosely, was a friend. I spoke to the Special Branch Commander who was now in charge of the search for my wife's killer. They had no suspects, but they did have one slight lead; a grey van was seen parked on the outer edge of the woods on three occasions prior to the Thursday Hannah was shot. It was parked there the day of her murder.

A lady who exercised her dog regularly had given the police the first two letters of its registration number. It wasn't much, but at least it was something. I had news of more substance from the Civil Aviation Authorities who returned my call around lunchtime. After contacting their counterparts in Norway, they were able to confirm the wreckage of a Cessna 172 found near a place called Grense Jakobselv, close to the border between Norway and Russia, in January 1997. The flight plan listed two passengers, surname of Kudashov, and a destination of Kramvik north across the Barents Sea. No survivors were found, but there was something else discovered that was of immense interest that I had to put to Kudashov at our next meeting.

* * *

The government's secret chemical research facility at Porton Down, Wiltshire, confirmed my fears that the chemicals Kudashov alleged to be in use in laboratory trials were capable of causing severe damage to the human DNA of the host, if subjected to the end product. They could give no formula of effectiveness, nor rate of growth of the parasite, but in simple terms, one was a parasitic cell that would create an infection. One of the chemicals would increase the rapid growth of the infection, causing devastation to the human genome in its wake, and the third, the unicellular

Diatoms which, on the surface at least, appeared the most innocuous of them all, would be the element that would hold the manufactured chemical together for the alteration of the DNA to successfully occur. Frightening, as the only possible purpose for the completed synthesis was confirmed by NICE: to be used for the breeding of a human race an elusive few desired.

Sir John Scarlett returned my call, providing more information, this time on Kudashov's movements made on our behalf since any reference was made to the code name of Ivy. I ran a comparison check between the dates he'd provided and the sites of 'known to be' active biological weapon laboratories that were listed on the file I was given on Thursday evening, originating from the Foreign and Commonwealth Office. There were two matches. The off-putting thing was they both were in Poland. As the CIA had a partial hand in the running of Jana Kava in Poland whilst I was there, I wondered if they knew of more sites than the FO had listed and Kudashov had strayed across their path as well. In order to clear that detail away, there was someone to meet that I would rather stay away from, but couldn't. I found the resolve to call and arrange to meet with him: Spencer Morrell, the Director of the CIA in London.

He had met Hannah several times and had attended our wedding. My messages on the Whitehall screens, and on my mobile phone, were full of ones from him of condolences and concern. After the customary exchanges, we agreed to meet that evening for dinner at Scott's in Mayfair, London.

* * *

I had first run into Spencer at the scene of an attempted assassination of the Israeli ambassador outside the Dorchester Hotel in June 1982. I had been home from Prague a few days before being assigned to the team who arrested the perpetrators. We met again five days later, when President Reagan visited our shores, and I was on his protection detail. There was a twenty-year gap before our paths crossed again when in 2002. I was in a pub in Derry in Ireland, and a nail bomb decimated the collective clientele. Morrell was on his way there to liaise with me and another

Brit *on the green*, as a tour of Ireland, with any connection to the IRA, was called.

The date of June 1982 was smiling at me as it slowly travelled around my mind. I was home from what I believed was a successfully completed overseas mission with a page-long index of phone numbers of attractive women to further my education with, and no time for Jana Kava and her dead brother to get in the way. As so often in recollections of pleasant times, something comes along to disturb it. I remembered a conversation Spencer and I had whilst engaged in the craft of babysitting at the Houses of Parliament. He with a President and me an Iron Lady to look after. Morrell alleged that MI6 knew of the conspiracy to kill the Israeli ambassador months before it happened but, he said, they were stood down from intervening by the British government. He went on to allege the government wanted to assist Israel in the dispute with the PLO.

The attempt on the ambassador's life was used by Israel as justification for the 1982 invasion of Lebanon and the beginning of the war. Morrell had inside information that the Iraqi Intelligence

Service was behind the assassination attempt and they too wanted the PLO out of Lebanon. But for them it was for political ends in neighbouring Syria. This gave rise to an interesting question—was Miles Faversham shunted from his Middle East desk in May '82 because of Her Majesty's Government's knowledge, and if so, was that the reason for him to die?

* * *

We had got past the tragedy of Hannah's death and were into the main course from Scott's menu by the time I raised that twenty-five-year old allegation of his. If I were to be asked why I didn't believe his face of astonishment, then an answer would fail me. But some things in life, and particularly the business I'm in, are beyond explanation. By the time we reached the dessert course, the murky darkness was clearing slightly.

"There was a hell of a stink over here in the press about it, Patrick. I'm surprised you can't remember. It was started by some questions put to Prime Minister Thatcher by some lord of somewhere I've forgotten the name of. It was notable because he was in the House of Lords when he asked it and beyond your archaic laws of slander. He had Palestinian connections and wanted to draw Thatcher out about what he alleged was a cover-up. Of course, nothing happened. After a day of headlines in the national press, all was forgotten and swept away."

Morrell was coming up for air every now again, leaving the sweet smell of his treacle pudding and custard to waft across the table and fill me with envy as I cast my eyes at the bleak coffee I'd chosen with Hannah's words of warning ringing in my ears: *just by thinking about sweet puddings is enough to put weight on, Patrick. Stop being wicked and stop thinking of them.* I told myself at least I had a brandy on which to sulk. He did not stay submerged in the custard for long.

"June that year was dominated by the Falklands War and all the comings and goings of diplomats to see your PM. Reagan sent down instructions for us to help out where he could, but he was pulling back on full Presidential support, worried about drawing the Soviets in. Chile was also on your side, which helped you a lot as the Argentinians kept some of their elitist mountain army divisions back on the border, worried

Chile might take advantage of the situation and invade. But you had no British Commonwealth down there and most, if not all, South American countries were lining up against you. A couple of them even offered to send paratroopers when things looked dodgy for the Argentinians. It was a tough time for us in the CIA keeping a lid on things."

His sarcasm released an unrestrained and hearty laugh that for reasons best left unsaid, always reminded me of the Soviet-made heavy machine pistols the IRA got from Libya. We confiscated a few and used them ourselves. My stomach was churning over by the time he stopped laughing, and it wasn't due to the food.

"Did you ever run across a Russian name of Kudashov, Nikita Sergeyovitch Kudashov, Spencer?"

"It's good that your Russian is better than average. For a minute there, I thought you meant that little bald-headed guy who used to slam his fist down and shout a lot about Cuba, name of Khrushchev. I know he was nasty. How about the one you're talking about; is he a nasty Ivan as well?"

"Did you get a chance to look up the name I gave you, that one I thought was a US agent in Poland and Czechoslovakia?"

"Yeah, the Petr Tomsa one. I did look. That was an interesting one. A little beyond what I'm supposed to do, but hey, that's what friends are for, right? We had him, but not for long. Apparently, we poached him from your lot when you weren't looking. Lasted from sometime in May '82 until around September that year. No printed signatures on his sign-up papers and no existing retirement package. Came and went like a winged Pegasus disappearing into the night sky."

I was into my second brandy as Spencer began his first. Time to savour revelations of how Jana Kava (as Petr Tomsa) functioned within the CIA, and to see if the brandy would make Kudashov's name be inadvertently mentioned.

* * *

Spencer Morrell had an annoying characteristic. He had an irregular need to clear the back of his throat, which not only broke up his sentences, making the conversation difficult to follow, but often caused alarm to those unaccustomed to his *ahem*, which was proclaimed loud and distractingly. Notwithstanding that impediment, some very interesting new information was revealed that evening as a result of my wallet being emptied on glasses of expensive booze. One tale he told was of what must have been Jana's last report as a CIA agent on the 31st August 1982, the same date I was in Warsaw. He said it had the highest classification, with the name of a Polish colonel redacted, but not the name of Petr Tomsa as the field operative. It did not take long to find out why that was.

Jana was in Warsaw on British business. She was there to meet a Polish army colonel attached to the Soviet 8th Army Group. The colonel had met Jana twice before, but each time she had been with her brother. On those occasions, Dalek had passionately spoken of the Solidarity movement, attempting to persuade the colonel to incite unrest within his army contingent that would coincide with the planned uprising. London's interest was centred on when the colonel was officer commanding the forward communications headquarters position overseeing one of the biggest military exercises the Soviets had ever organised. It was staged in and around Gdańsk.

One objective was to show the West how strong and flexible the Red Army was, but another reason for choosing Gdańsk was to show, beyond doubt, what sort of strength the dissent students in the Solidarity movement would face if they tried to overthrow the Polish government. It hadn't worked. The protests went ahead and much blood was spilt. Whether or not the colonel's sympathy lay with the anti-Communist Solidarity students and supporters before the riots or after was never said, but there was no military uprising. None of that information was included in the CIA report. I had it in a corresponding file attributed to agent Ivy, London's code name for Kudashov.

The following was essentially the same in both reports, the one I had on file from Ivy and Spencer Morrell's spoken account. At first, the colonel asked Petr Tomsa the whereabouts of Dalek Kava. He was told he was hiding in the university, having escaped the security services when they forcibly broke up the demonstrations. He was further told Kava couldn't come out of hiding, but any message he wanted to send to him would be passed on. He blushed and looked embarrassed by Petr's oblivious recognition of emotional feelings towards Tomsa's brother, but he successfully reassured him that all was well. This was where the reports differed.

In Spencer Morrell's account, Petr Tomsa told his CIA contact that the colonel wanted to defect to America. He needed instructions on how to combat the security ring the Polish security services had established around the US Embassy in order to stop the students approaching. He said he had most secret information and wanted to come over straight away, but only if Dalek Kava would come with him.

In the MI6 file I'd drawn from the archives, there was a different story about the information this colonel had. In this report it said the colonel gave Jana the English code name of an American who was a highly placed operative working inside GCHQ in Cheltenham, on America's behalf. That's where my information came to an end.

There was nothing recorded that Spencer could read of what transpired at that meeting. He had no idea that the colonel had given

Jana the coded name of an American spy inside one of this country's most secretive establishments. Nor was he aware of what I strongly believed—another part of the CIA being responsible for the murder of Jana Kava. The secret Soviet radio signal coding I sent to London on that same day had not been released to any other agency by the time Jana was killed, and at that stage I couldn't work out why she had been murdered, but murdered she was; I was sure of it.

Kudashov said he sent the signal of Jana's meeting to the Soviet Satellite desk on the 31st of August, which meant that both Glenister and Scarlett would know the coding used to conceal the name as soon as my signal was decoded, but there was no record of Jana's Warsaw signal being received at that desk on the date in question. In fact, according to every logbook I could find, there was no Warsaw signal sent to London Control other than mine. Were three people lying or had Dickie Blythe-Smith still got his hands in the pot, even after leaving Joint Intelligence? Were Kudashov and Dickie Blythe-Smith playing games?

I needed to discover why was the Imagery Control Commission in Germany sent pictures from an over-fly of Poland by a NSA satellite, and why did they find their way to one of our Joint Air Reconnaissance platforms? Rattling bones were gaining prominence inside my head. In Sir John Scarlett's words, Dickie Blythe-Smith was running the Warsaw operation whilst in retirement, and Scarlett thought he had set a ball rolling that was yet to stop. Why, Dickie, *why*?

* * *

I convinced myself I had found the ball Dickie had started to roll and I was at the beginning of the hunt for its end. Maybe my persistence had prised open only a smidgeon on the books of untold secrets involving this country and our ally, the United States, but it was enough to whet my appetite for more thought-unlocking brandy in the long lounge of Hannah's and my Sussex home, where some of our shared memories floated in my cigar smoke.

* * *

I was in the gym around six a.m. and then had breakfast with Kudashov that Sunday morning at about eight, but before either of us could enjoy what was offered, I had to listen to his complaints. They ranged from being held a prisoner against his will to not having a drinking companion for the plentiful supply of vodka in the cupboards, and he would prefer it to be his long-time partner who would be concerned for his welfare. I settled that by informing him that we had told her he was away until at least Tuesday, helping the newly arrived Russian trade under-secretary to acclimatise himself to London's hidden treasures.

According to the background I'd read, he had been active as a field agent for almost forty-five of his seventy-odd years of age. He had never been apprehended in any country he had operated in, which were exclusively Warsaw Pact countries and Russia itself. Dangerous places for even the best professional. My own record of fieldwork was nothing in comparison to his, and my experience as an interrogator was minimal. Could that be the reason why he chose me to come to and present his story? I tried to put those self-doubts behind me, taking this as an ideal opportunity to find out if my hidden theories were right.

"Tell me some more about Cilicia. Was she staying with you when her parents died and was it you and your wife who raised her after that plane crash of theirs?"

"Yes, she was and yes, we did, Patrick. They were on a fishing holiday in northern Norway. It was something they did every year since Ludvík had got his wings four years beforehand. He loved flying and they both shared a love of Arctic fishing."

"Did he get that love of both things from you or your wife?"

"Not from either of us, no. Karina's father was the keen fisherman as I remember, but sadly after the accident we drifted apart. I hope that doesn't happen with you and Hannah's relatives, Patrick."

I didn't want to speak of Hannah to him or anyone. "How long did Cilicia have with you both before your wife passed away?"

"My granddaughter was twenty-one when my Anna died. It was true she had another year to do at university, but she was already working in the counter-intelligence surveillance section of the Federal Security Service at Moscow Centre. Her whole education was aimed at that position and the technical qualifications she would need. In Russian universities, such courses are much sought after," he proclaimed with obvious pride.

"I imagine they are, Nikita. I find it strange that you've never mentioned your wife before. How long were you married?"

The conversation drifted along cozily, with him sharing some fond memories of their wedding and honeymoon in the Sudetes mountain range, near Germany. Memories of other holidays were like photographs spread before me, along with general recollections of happy times; each one was like a dagger stabbing at my heart.

"Anna was my connection to the Russian Romanov family, you know. It was she who was the daughter of a legitimate cousin of the last Tsar. I can't be sure of course, but I think it was because of the tsarist connection that I was never suspected of being a spy. They probably thought I wouldn't have the balls as you would say in England."

I was pouring more coffee as I asked how his wife died.

"She committed suicide when I wasn't at home with her." He fell silent and motionless.

I shared the grief that death brings. Perhaps it was speed of his reply, or the tone in his voice, but there was something wrong in that confession.

"I'm so sorry. I should have read all the records, but what with everything that's happened of late—well, time has not been that kind to me. Did that happen in—what I've read—sounds like a very prestigious apartment you have in the centre of Moscow, or where you lived in Prague? Oh no, of course, you moved from Prague in the same year as Jana Kava went missing in Poland, did you not?"

In Kudashov's red file, the one that should have every detail of an agent's history, his wife Anna died in the apartment he and she shared in Moscow some twenty-one years after he had left his role as police commissar in Prague. However, as I've said, I didn't believe her death was recorded correctly, but I didn't know why. We locked eyes, with him trying to discover exactly what I knew without answering my question and me trying to dig away at the covering that hid the real Kudashov. It was I who spoke next.

"Our Civil Aviation Authority turned up a really strange twist of fate when they contacted their Norwegian counterparts to verify your son's air accident in 1997."

He did not avert his attention from what remained on his breakfast plate.

"There was another accident involving a modern version of the aircraft your son was flying. It happened on the Sunday of last week, two days before you reached out to Fraser Ughert. The pilot was killed, as was his only passenger, a woman in her fifties by the name of Claudette Avogova. Perhaps you could shine a light on that name for me, Nikita." I stood and looked down at him before continuing. "But no, I don't need your help just yet. Claudette Avogova died in 2001 whilst in Sierra Leone. The Norwegian police traced the body to a classified CIA file, which we managed to access. Normally I wouldn't get involved in a case like this as it's way beyond my realms of interest, but there's something else in that incident that the Norwegians reported."

Although anyone would show some form of interest to this story of intrigue, Kudashov showed no sign of any. His eyes were empty of remorse and the detached expression he wore on his angular, ashen coloured face did not alter in the slightest until I introduced the Norwegian report.

"As I said, something else is strange other than the similarity of the make of aircraft involved in this latest incident. The woman carrying Claudette Avogova's passport boarded her private flight at a place very near to where your son and his wife's aircraft crashed ten years previously. It's so deserted in that region that they took the precaution of recording where they were heading each day with the Norwegian Arctic Rescue coordinated from Narvik. We were able to take a look at the copy of the log your son and wife registered with the Norwegians whilst on their fishing holiday.

"I had my people take a close look at one place in particular … named Nikel, a few kilometres over the border from Norway into Russia. The place where Avogova's aircraft took off from. It's aptly named as they found references to the nickel mining that went on there for hundreds of years. They had Russians, Finns, and Germans all fighting over who had sovereignty of those valuable mines. Even us Brits were there at one stage digging out the nickel, but nothing on why Avogova and your family would want to go anywhere near there. It seems a very popular place, does the Arctic Circle. Any ideas you'd like to share with me as to why that might be, Nikita?"

Apparently, he had none. But he did have demands. "When you do eventually devise a plan to get my granddaughter safely away from Moscow, I must be told of it at least twenty-four hours beforehand. If that does not happen, then a piece on the chessboard will not move in time and, in consequence, it will jeopardise the whole game, Mr West."

* * *

As I left him, and walked the fluorescent-lit corridor to the staircase to the house, it was apparent that no matter what I used as a distraction, all I could see was Hannah's smiling sculptured face that fateful Thursday morning as she left the Whitehall apartment on her way to the offices and then onto our home here in Sussex. Her elegantly tall, curvy body, her long black hair with her porcelain white skin was kissed by the sun as we had breakfasted together before a call from the Cabinet Secretary delayed my departure. I had mouthed a silent *no*, in reply to her scribbled note of: *Do you need me to stay*?

On her notepad I wrote back: *I'm holding for the PM. He needs updating on Iran. With luck I'll be at The Lodge for dinner.* I signed that off by drawing a heart on a separate sheet of notepaper. She marked that page with five crosses, as kisses.

As she walked away I stood watching her, first to our office and then through the outer doors to her car that waited in the courtyard below. We had planned to return to Whitehall late on Monday, ready for work on the Tuesday. Nothing was on my desk to prevent that break, nor was there anything on the intelligence radar to unduly worry over. Very seldom had we travelled to The Lodge in the same car, but how I wished we had, then either I would still have her beside me, or it would have been me killed if we'd used her car. Both options were better than the apparitions that now devoured me.

Chapter Eighteen: The Levant

Frank and Jimmy were back on duty by that Sunday afternoon and it was with them that I travelled to Fraser Ughert, first depositing Kudashov at the deportation centre in Croydon on the way from The Lodge, on the grounds that his detention was conductive for the public good, and he needed to be kept in a secure confinement, pending expatriation.

At Chearsley, Fraser's Circle of Eight was up for discussion with a previously investigated American and Russian pinned firmly to our agenda. They had both first crossed our path five years earlier when the three of us, Hannah, Fraser, and I, successfully managed to stop the aspirations detailed inside the top-secret, corrupted CIA file—Gladio B.

We were fortunate in preventing the vast majority of the short-term aims of Gladio B, and in the process we believed we had deterred one particular man who would have been crucial to the long-term aims as set out in that file. That man was Tucker Stoneman, a Rosicrucian, with access to the Panamanian bank accounts holding a sizeable part of the trillions of dollars Donald Rumsfeld had identified as missing from the US defence budget. Rumsfeld, a former American Secretary of Defence, went on to allege that the biggest threat to world peace was his own country's military and intelligence bureaucracy. His speech was made the day before the Twin Towers attack and, as a consequence, passed without much notice. Although Tucker was, at the time of our first investigation, the Democrat Party's presidential candidate, he was not in this inner circle of Fraser's, but he had connections in very high places that could well be part of the Eight families, who were behind the objectives of the corrupted file.

When Kudashov spoke of the eugenic manufacturing laboratory he had either knowingly, or unwittingly, connected the Gladio B file to the here and now, as one section proposed that those deemed to be *undesirable,* in the Elysium that was to be created, were to be sent to parts of eastern Turkey, northern Iraq, western Iran, and eastern Syria along with Pakistan, India and

Southeast Asia, all of which were destined to become a cesspit for the human beings not required by those Eight families of world builders.

I have never been a great believer in providence. However, Kudashov's appearance in London telling about a granddaughter named Cilicia and the subsequent murder of my wife was anything but a coincidence. With hindsight, I should have realised Kudashov's appearance could have been the catalyst to something else, but hindsight is a friend who's never available when he's needed. I was taught that maxim of *everything leads to everything* until I could recite it letter by letter in double quick time, but where was its corporeal worth? If the truism in that statement was correct, then could her murderer be closer than I thought?

Hannah had no enemies, whereas I had many. Luckily most of mine were not capable of a murder of this precision, which not only needed the keen eye of a sniper, but also required money and logistics, which were only available to a very few I'd run across and were still alive. Five years ago, I had authorised the murder of two associates of the inner circle of families suspected of having objectives amounting to such desolation, suffering and injustice on this world, it could never be imagined in any dystopian nightmare.

The first man who was eliminated was an Israeli businessman, a justifiable kill, whilst holidaying on an island off the coast of Maine, North America, and the other was a man in a Paris hotel room, the main coordinator of fundraising for the Palestine Liberation Organisation. Although they came from opposite ends of the political spectrum, they shared a love of the wealth that money could buy and the destiny it could ultimately control. One of the people that was used on that operation had died near the scene of the Israeli shooting, her dead body being disposed of in the water close to Mount Desert Island, as the surviving perpetrator made his escape.

A British submarine had recovered her remains, but we could not be certain nobody had identified her before that could be done. The Israeli was staying at an estate named The House of Cilicia. The closeness of the wording on the gift box and that estate had not escaped me at the time of our wedding, but the name of Cilicia had occurred so many times during the investigation the three of us had undertaken, I lost no sleep over it. Now, however, his killing took on a completely new significance.

The MI6 officer who murdered the PLO fundraiser in Paris and went on to partner our commissioned killer at Mount Desert Island was, in due course, engaged in a game of exchange with Mossad, the Israeli Secret Service. Politics being what they are, an ever-changing scene of self-interest, the assassination in Paris was done in exchange for a favour that suited our Foreign Office in the affairs of state; however, that was where the leak of our sponsored assassination must have been. I needed to speak to Christopher Irons, our man *on the spy* with our Mossad friends.

It had taken from late Thursday evening until the very early hours of Sunday morning to catch up with Irons, who was on a covert mission in Iran. Yes, he confirmed that he had told his Iranian contact, who had then told Mossad of the Paris success and, yes, he knew a man who might have sold that information on. That man was beyond Christopher Irons' immediate reach.

Despite that inconvenience, he knew of someone who could influence the situation.

By the time I arrived at Fraser's home, I had most of the information I needed. Christopher assured me that the man who sold the information of my involvement in both killings to Hannah's assassin did not have his name. All he had was a description dating back to the year 2000 when the two had met during the War in Eritrea. The man we were after had killed the commander of one of the main Ethiopian Army groups along with his deputy. Mossad had sanctioned and paid for that operation and that's how Christopher's agent, who was connected to Mossad, and the killer came to meet.

For all this man's assassinations, including Hannah's, he only conducted business by fax. Christopher had the fax number address, an empty launderette in Bagdad where the words—Defenders of the Levant—were painted in red on the wall facing the door. The launderette's address was worthless without extensive enquires being made and I was uncertain as to how long it would be before this killer would strike again. I instructed Michael Simmons to set up a task force to include Interpol and the Iraqi police, and search for answers. In the meantime, Fraser christened Hannah's murderer, Solidus.

He told me he had taken it from the name of the first chairman of the KGB—General Ivan Aleksandrovich Solidus. I waited for an explanation but, as with most of Fraser's discoveries, it came at a price. I watched as his normally studious facial expression gradually changed to the one bearing his distinctive trademark—*I know more than you and I'm keeping you in the dark until I decide to include you.* He took an inordinate time before he did include me in his secret. However, there were other facts he was willing to share whilst he kept me waiting.

* * *

"I have found out who Claudette Avogova was, Patrick, and I think I know why Kudashov came to us." I was interested in his first discovery, but not his second, as I doubted he had grasped the full intricacy of that word—*why*—when applied to Kudashov and, if he had, then I already knew the complications behind that decision.

Although already knowing Fraser's opening remarks about Avogova, I did not interrupt. What he then went on to tell me was of immense importance.

"Claudette Avogova was Italian by birth, but British by marriage. She was a bacteriologist who worked at Porton Down research laboratories and who died in 2001 in Sierra Leone. She volunteered to join part of a scientific team put together by the United Nations to work on finding a cure for a virus that escaped from some chemical vials stolen from a ship that had docked at Freetown, Sierra Leone. The stolen vials, twelve in all, were in transit to the Brazilian archipelago of Saint Peter and Saint Paul for destruction, from Murmansk in northern Russia. The woman who died in the aircraft crash was in the same profession as Avogova, but her name was Paulette Simona.

"If you remember back to that tale I told you of me and a Gurkha sergeant skipping over the border in Russia ... well, from that operation I made friends with a Norwegian counter-intelligence officer who helped me out on this one. Did you know the Norwegians have the fifth largest intelligence service in the world? You wouldn't think of that unless you took into account the closeness to Russia and the fickleness of their neighbours, Sweden and Finland. Anyhow, I doubt you need a geography lesson to go with the whisky. I asked the chap I know and he tracked this Simona woman down through fingerprint data to a CIA register of the Directorate of Science and Technology, where she's recorded as an inspector. Smart work on his behalf, eh? That leaves us with the question of why would anyone want to pose as Claudette Avogova?"

* * *

I gave Fraser each one of the recordings of my conversations with Kudashov from his arrival at The Lodge until I took him to Croydon. We were still recording in the car on the way there, and Michael was at Group downloading information of use from more agencies than our own. Following a few formalities at the South London detention centre, I had Kudashov taken in an unmarked private ambulance to a part of the Beaulieu House estate, on the edge of the New Forest in Hampshire, where he could be kept safe away from prying eyes and assassins' loaded rifles. I had no idea how much danger Kudashov was in until most of the story had unfurled. Although completion was still a considerable distance away, at least it felt as though this rolling ball of Dickie Blythe-Smith's was closer. Kudashov was right in assuming that I would never have believed him until certain things had been established as true. I would have considered a lot of it as a fairy tale.

Given that I had no way of knowing Kudashov's life was in need of protection when he arrived in this country, the same rationale did not apply to the Ugherts. Fraser needed no warning. His home was already as secure as it realistically could be, but I'd taken the extra precaution of saddling Molly with eight static guards. Her kitchen skills would delight them all as well as, hopefully, driving away Fraser's protests of being self-sufficient with security.

* * *

I had a communication in answer to one of mine from the Ministry of Defence, intelligence section. In the listings of service personnel they supplied me there was one stand-out name that I could hardly miss—Jacqueline Price, head of C-section photographic analysis, Germany, in 1982. Jacqueline instead of Jack, with Price as her surname! How close was that? I knew the two were not related, but where else would Dickie hide a secret than some place we both knew? The trouble there was how did he know I would still be in the SIS business? At the back of my mind something, or someone, said: it wouldn't matter if you were not. How on earth would I interpret that? I read on without addressing those issues.

Jacqueline retired full-time from the Civil Service roughly two years ago, remaining on their register as part of the Board of Commissioners of what was called Sentinel Development Policy, whatever that was. She lived near Windsor, Berkshire. Could it be luck that Dickie found a Jacqueline for Jack, leaving the clue staring at me from the personnel page? Or, had there not been a Price in the Ministry of Defence, would Dickie have continued to look to find an alternative?

* * *

Fraser wearily removed his thick black-rimmed glasses and wiped his eyes with a scrupulously folded and ironed chequered handkerchief. It was approaching six o'clock in the afternoon and I too was suffering from fatigue. Ordinarily, I would have left Chearsley and asked to be driven back to Whitehall, which was considerably nearer than The Lodge, but these were not ordinary days. With Jacqueline Price of Sentinel Development living in Windsor, which was not that far out of our way to Sussex, I suggested to Jimmy we go there. Frank remarked how exhausted I looked when I gave Jimmy the address, but I shrugged his observation off, saying I would grab a nap in the car.

I watched as our journey was lodged with Special Branch and the vehicles that now travelled constantly as my escorts, took up their position front and rear of my car. The blue flashing lights of the motorcycle outriders were switched on and away we went to Berkshire, or so I thought as I lay out on the rear seat and closed my eyes. It was Frank who disturbed my thought-filled solitude with an urgent message from Sir Elliot Zerby at Thames House, the MI5 headquarters.

There was, he said, a credible terrorist alert for Victoria railway station. The threat originated from an organisation calling themselves the Defenders of the Levant.

Chapter Nineteen: Gunfire

Destination Windsor was scrubbed, as indeed was Sussex. It was to Whitehall that the convoy returned. I quickly changed and freshened up, then used the underground tunnel from the Foreign Office building and emerged in the offices of the private secretary to the Prime Minister. After an intolerably long time spent briefing the PM from the information that Zerby had given me, I escaped back to the apartment in the FO building. I consulted with both Zerby and Simmons over the security arrangements at the site of the threat: Victoria railway station, along with arrangements made at all ports of entry and departure in mainland Britain.

Special Branch, along with every department of interior security, was being stretched once again by a succession of penny-pinching governments who sought popularity rather than security as their number one priority in order to continue in the 'power' it wantonly craved. Having agreed on the measures taken to face this latest terrorist threat, I gave in to the utter weariness I felt, but as tired as I was, I could not bring myself to sleep in our bed. It was to the second apartment I went, hoping to find what rest I could.

I was awakened by the ringing of my private mobile telephone. I glanced at the small square, digital clock; it was 08.03. I'd slept solidly for nine and bit hours, but still felt shattered. It was Michael Simmons on the other end of the phone. He had confirmation of a Polish Army colonel of the same name as the colonel Jana Kava had met, being arrested by Russian KGB officials on September 3rd 1982, whilst in barracks in Kaliningrad.

Kudashov had told me of this during our conversation; however, he had added that the colonel never reached the KGB interrogation station on the perimeter of the base. He had, according to Kudashov, bitten on the potassium cyanide L-Pill he had hidden in his mouth. I had searched all that was recorded of his and Jana Kava's meetings and there was no record of us supplying him with a death pill. If we hadn't supplied him with the lethal tablet, then the Americans must have, making the Polish colonel a CIA operative all along the way, but did we know that?

I thanked Michael and returned to our once shared main apartment, marvelling at its tidiness. I showered in the now minimalistic bathroom, minus all Hannah's toiletries, and was sitting at my desk by nine-thirty that Monday morning. As I sat there, reading my computer screen, the realisation of being on my own and lonely whilst so much surrounded me, was a consciousness I had not anticipated. It's not always the big occasions one shares with another person that the unconscious mind clings to until the space it occupied is empty. Often, it's the little things one shares that stay the longest time in one's conscious state, hammering in one's skull to be remembered. The first thing Hannah would do at the start of a working day, when we were at our separate desks divided by an unmovable wall, was to send a heart in a message along with an X as a kiss. It was through a combination of repetition and love that I looked at my computer, waiting for them both, knowing that neither would come.

* * *

Variously coloured signals from Thames House filled part of my main computer screen, awaiting my attention but, despite the importance they represented, it was another message on another screen that captured my attention. It was an eyes-only scrambled message for me from the personal secretary to the relatively new Prime Minister. There was to be a special security conference called for late September, where I would be required to give an overall view of the intelligence reports emanating from Iran in respect to the United Kingdom's support to any firm US proposals for an invasion mounted from neighbouring Iraq. I wondered if this had anything to do with the update in my briefing of the situation I'd provided him.

* * *

The thought that Hannah's assassination was a mistake and the assassin intended to kill me had been considered by Special Branch, and in their opinion rejected, however it did leave me feeling that I should want to be dead in her place. But I didn't. I was alive and I was happy to be so. Being alive was not my fault. Or was it? If I'd dreamt at all since Hannah's death, the dreams were harmless and forgotten as soon as I woke. Nevertheless, my guilty apprehension was not completely obliterated by smothering myself in work. With a terrorist threat that linked the assassination of my wife to the writing inside the Bagdad launderette, I convinced myself that I needed to do more.

* * *

The signals from Thames House all referred to the problematic situation at Victoria Station and now, more than ever, the thought of why the assassin had not tried to kill again was pounding at my brain. Perhaps this was his way of pulling me into the open? Victoria Station remained closed and taped off to the public whilst the bomb disposal teams went about their painstaking and dangerous job looking for evidence of the bomb the message to *The Sun* newspaper from the previously unheard of Defenders of the Levant stated was concealed there.

I wanted to see if I could be of use in drawing him out into the open. I called Sir Elliot Zerby and told him of my idea. He wasn't in favour, but after some haranguing, he agreed to speak to the Metropolitan Police Commissioner who could move some police marksmen from the rear to the front of the station. He would also authorise additional bums to the seats of the surveillance monitors. I called Frank, expecting to hear his displeasure with my plan but I heard the opposite. He was up for it. *Oh yes, guv, Jimmy and I will fancy that!*

* * *

I wanted my arrival to be as conspicuous as possible. A cavalcade of five was arranged, blue light flashing, sirens blasting vehicles, with armed police outriders escorting me on the short drive from the Foreign and Commonwealth building, making as much noise as possible. When we arrived, our escorts peeled away as only our vehicle was waved onto the station forecourt. With screeching brakes and an expertly executed handbrake turn, Jimmy parked our vehicle slap-bang in the middle, allowing me to get out on the side overlooked by the adjacent and cleared London Transport buildings, with Frank alighting on the station forecourt side. The plan was to draw a sniper's bullet, but not for one to hit me. Although I was wearing a vest and protective helmet, the calibre of bullet used to kill Hannah would penetrate anything we had available.

There were seven police marksmen plus Frank scanning the overlooking buildings for movement, along with several others on static positions around the station. The whole area was swamped by cameras. As I neared the end of our car, I caught sight of a uniformed police officer walking towards me from the shadows of the overhanging station façade into the sunlight. He walked into a line screened from my direct view by Frank and an armed police marksmen. Instinctively, I knew something was wrong. In reality, everything was happening at a walking pace, but reaction time was flying past as it had happened the last time I was in a kill-zone. Despite my history, no longer could I be included on any list as proficient. Where before, in my active service life there was never a doubt, now the doubts were drowning me. I tried to shield my eyes from the sun, but they were watering at the intensity of it. My legs started to feel as though they were made of jelly as I tried to move towards what I knew to be the oncoming assassin, keeping the car between him and me.

In a steady, unhurried pace he broke cover from behind Frank, starting to raise his machine pistol as he did. From somewhere a deeply installed inherent sense compelled me to shout: *Down*! *Gun*!

Years of pain-filled training, supervised by seemingly spite-ridden physical training officers, saved my life. I drew my own weapon, then threw myself to the tarmac forecourt. I heard the closeness of zip-zip-zip as the first three rounds of volley fire he got away passing close to where I lay behind the rear wing of the car. The dislodged stones lashed at the underside of the petrol tank. I had no target as I couldn't see anything, but I heard the deafening sound of a pistol fired tight to my left ear, then I felt a great weight on top, propelling me further to the ground.

* * *

I was shot in the left leg, inches above my ankle, and luckily the bullet passed straight through the flesh without hitting bone, leaving just a hole of a wound that needed little treatment at St Thomas' Hospital other than some stitches, painkillers and antibiotics. The only one else who had been hit by gunshot fire was the murder-intent gunman, whom Jimmy had killed with a single shot to the head. It was that shot that had deafened me just as he had fallen on top to act as a shield against any more gunfire.

The gunman's name was not Solidus, it was Aybak Khoury. He was born in a small Israeli town named Shalom, near the border with Lebanon, in September 1978. There was a record of him being detained by the invading American military near Kabul, Afghanistan, in 2001, but nothing of him being involved in anything of a similar nature anywhere. Mossad had him on file under what they called a 'yellow' flag, which I was told amounted to no more than being a person of interest. Special Branch was aiding Scotland Yard in tracing how he came by the uniform and security passes found on his body. I was told the serial numbers on the gun had been removed, but there were car keys and a hotel pass in a pocket of his. Photographs were being shared with other agencies, along with Interpol, and the usual graphics were underway. There was no 'hard evidence' linking him to my wife's assassination; however, his affiliation to the Defenders of the Levant was, although technically circumstantial, deemed sufficient to wind down the investigation.

* * *

I was pleasantly surprised by the first call of congratulations I received while I was still at the scene. It was from the Prime Minister. I was being treated in one of the ambulances that were there on standby when he called. Although my ears were still blocked and I couldn't understand all of what he said, I'm sure I sensed an unusual amount of relief in his tone of voice as he praised my initiative and what he called my bravery. He briefly mentioned the Middle East in its widest terms, but nothing about the forthcoming party conference or its agenda.

Sir Elliot Zerby was the next to call. After I refused his invitation for lunch at Shepherd's, a popular restaurant nearby, he offered the dining rooms at Thames House for an informal meal, as he put it. I refused that offer too. Had the Queen rang, which was not likely, I would have turned her down as well. My three missing toes to my right foot were now joined by a hole in my left leg, which did not make me the most cordial person to be found in Victoria Station that day.

I'm embarrassed to admit only mawkish thoughts were filling my mind as I watched Jimmy from the back of the ambulance as a pretty young paramedic was applying a pressure bandage to the wound in my leg. He was with Frank, making written statements in the Incident Command Centre beside the station where inside the bomb disposal team had located and defused a Semtex bomb of significant size. Despite it being someone close to me who had saved my life, I didn't know what to say and how to thank him. Furthermore, he was the last person I wanted to see. My animosity was childish I knew, but I didn't want to speak to him.

The paramedic nurse was speaking to me, but I could not properly hear what she was saying through the blockage in my ears, which kept coming and going. She smiled and pulled the rear doors closed, shouting *good to go*, to the driver then the siren wailed and we were off. I was fully conscious with the morphine taking away what pain there was, but be that as it may, the movement of the ambulance seemed to be pushing death to a pinnacle beyond my reach.

I was heavy-hearted and miserable, beyond any commiseration I might hear. The orderliness that had constituted my life since marriage was destroyed last Thursday, leaving only the state of death to hold me together: Hannah's death and now Aybak Khoury's. Looking back on the events of that morning, I realise my resentment towards Jimmy was because I was so close to the person who had murdered my wife without it being me who took his life away. I was too slow. But it was my heart that was the grateful recipient of Khoury's death.

The rest of the day flashed by as if it was a mere second of normal time. Constant phone calls were either made or answered with Fraser being the main caller, patiently holding while other calls were taken, then discarded. My honest answers to his questions of how I felt was that I didn't know. Responsibility was something never far away from me since leaving university and losing both parents, but the responsibility for losing Hannah was a heavy load to carry without being able to adequately express the utter confusion going on inside my mind. With the death of the assassin achieved, perhaps now I could find a way forward into solitude. Early that afternoon my hearing had fully returned to normal and I finally made it into the main apartment without the constant feeling of guilt. After I made my inner peace with Hannah, it was to Fraser I turned to chase down the closure of what surrounded Kudashov.

* * *

General Ivan Aleksandrovich Solidus, from whom Fraser had taken his soubriquet for the killer, and Jana Kava's father were, according to my confidant, great friends and colleagues during Stalin's reign of power in the Soviet Union. Unfortunately for Solidus, he lost his position after the Cuban Missile Crisis. Fearing for his life during another of Khrushchev's temperamental purges, Solidus allegedly buried some compromising documents that conclusively named Victor Rothschild as an agent of the KGB. Future blackmail was his reason, in case he needed Rothschild's financial help in escaping from Russia and setting up somewhere warm and inviting. However, Solidus figured there could be a far greater advantageous use if ever he needed to embarrass Khrushchev.

It was Fraser's contention that in early 1961, General Ivan Aleksandrovich Solidus told Khrushchev that his KGB had incontrovertible information directly from Rothschild that the American government intended to station a squadron of Pershing nuclear-tipped, medium-range ballistic missiles at İzmir in Turkey. Just a little over two-thousand kilometres from Moscow, roughly half the distance Cuba is from Washington DC.

Khrushchev did not believe the new president of America, John F. Kennedy, would position nuclear weapons in Turkey and thereby threaten not only Warsaw Pact countries, but Russia too. He was wrong and the opportunity to bargain away the threat passed when the missiles were installed at the Turkish military base. Cuba, Ivan

Aleksandrovich Solidus, told Khrushchev, was a lost cause before the ships carrying the Soviet nuclear missiles left harbour. *'Comrade First Secretary, the Americans have their weapons pointed at us already. They can fire at any moment if they are pushed too far. We, on the other hand, must sail across the Atlantic, unload and position our missiles. It is a bluff we cannot win. Their weapons could annihilate all the silo stations throughout the Soviet Bloc.'*

Fraser was using facts to substantiate his argument about Cuba and Turkey, but using guesswork when it came to the conversation Khrushchev had with his head of the KGB. None of his hypothesis was unreasonable, provided his General Solidus had the information Fraser claimed he had from Rothschild. His assumptions did not stop there. He quoted dates and venues where General Ivan Aleksandrovich Solidus and General Kava had been together during and after World War II. I replied that it was not unusual for generals to meet. He had me beat on that.

Fraser tied that knot of the alleged friendship with an intercepted message dated the 29th

March 1963. It was a happy birthday wish sent by General Solidus, who was commanding an Army group in the Ukraine, to General Kava who was in Czechoslovakia. It was signed: *From your dearest friend.* Perhaps an innocent address, but in the spying game it's the minutest of gestures that count. Fraser surmised what Solidus would tell his 'dearest friend' about his survival ticket. Depending on where the conversation took place, Solidus could even have shared the unabridged version of how the Americans were allowed to station their Pershings while First Secretary Khrushchev's reactions were inferior to those of the American President.

I had heard and read chronicles of Dickie Blythe-Smith's prowess in the game played by spies. Once I was the beneficiary of his organisational skills, but if half of what Fraser and Kudashov wanted me to believe was true, then this matter involving the Kavas was one of the biggest sagas of smoking mirrors ever played by anyone anywhere. The trouble was I couldn't work out why Dickie wanted to play it.

* * *

A message pinged red on my computer at 3.10 in the morning, waking me instantly. A red ping sounds similar to a fire alarm signal, which during the day is more bearable than the same alarm sounding in the quietest hours of the morning. It was from Special Branch headquarters, containing an itemised list of all that was found in the hotel room the dead terrorist had rented near Victoria Station. There was no evidence of the assassination of Hannah in the room. No residue of a firearm being discharged on any clothing other than what he wore at the Station, and the gun he carried in the attack on me was not the weapon he used to assassinate Hannah. That gun was not found. Special Branch listed the property discovered in the van his keys fitted. It was a grey van, matching the description of that seen near The Lodge, and two letters of its registration matched the same two the police had already.

Chapter Twenty: The Game

Whoever thought that nothing ever happened on a Monday had never earned a wage working in the intelligence industry. My 'bravery' of the morning had lost its noteworthiness by the afternoon. The telephone conversation I was having with Fraser was cut short by my senior secretary's unannounced entrance to my office.

"I'm sorry to interrupt, sir, but the PM needs you now. He was most insistent and sounded distinctly angry. He said to tell you to come immediately."

Haste was not a motion I applied to any given task or pleasure I indulged in; in fact, on more than one occasion life had shown how foolhardy haste could be. There are plenty of jokes, alongside moral stories on the subject of how being slow and careful is far better than being fast and reckless. I will add one story to those detailing the actions of a person we have already met in this tale of mine: Spencer—ahem—Morrell.

It happened in Londonderry, in Northern Ireland, known to the security branches as simply Derry. I had been Officer Commanding in Ireland for a few months, going about the business of tracking terrorists without too much interference. I was to introduce Spencer to my lead ground officer responsible for watching three separate cells of Provisional IRA. The CIA were instructed to exchange information concerning the people of America who bankrolled the violence and death the IRA inflicted on the legal and moral inhabitants of Northern Ireland and to the government in Westminster. But the CIA were also on the ground in the Emerald Isle to put names to the faces of the terrorists in case, one day, they sailed across the Atlantic.

Spencer was the personification of the easygoing. On the day of the meet, he had strolled to the Erin Arms, the place we were due to get together, taking twenty minutes longer than if he had taken one of his station cars. The bomb that killed five and maimed the same number spared me, but not completely; it took away a kidney. By luck, it spared my leading ground officer. Had Spencer arrived five minutes earlier and used the door from the tarmac road instead of the rear door from the alleyway where he'd walked, then he would have caught the full blast of the nail bomb.

It was with my normal steady speed that I journeyed along the interconnecting tunnel that many of my predecessors, along with Foreign Office Ministers and others, had travelled. With each echoing step that sounded heavy on the bricked passageway, I imagined Fraser's eyes staring at his ceiling while listening to the tapes I'd had couriered to him of my conversation with Kudashov.

* * *

"Our family name is not Kudashov at all. It is Mecklenburg from the German aristocratic line of heraldry. My family abandoned Russia in 1905 following the Bloody Sunday massacre of that year. Although my memory of my grandfather is shrouded by time, I remember my mother telling me that he was a wise man with great vision. He told everyone that Russia would never be the same again after that sad event and we should go. Of course he was right and by the time his prophecy had come true, the Mecklenburgs were scattered to the four corners of the world.

"I was told that the reason why we settled in Czechoslovakia was that we had influential relatives in Prague. Our relatives had retained the Mecklenburg name and were, so I was enlightened, the virtual masters of that country, along with the country of Austria. Notwithstanding that fact, Grandfather judged it best to keep our name, but distance ourselves from them. I was never told why and still don't know the answer to that riddle.

"Over the years that followed, money bought us the positions my elders required. I was born the day before Germany invaded what was still then the unified Czechoslovakia. The most inopportune time for so many, but for us it was different. It was not so much our heraldic line that made a difference, although that did not interfere, but it was our wealth and the influence it buys that kept us from the inequities of what occurred for the next six years. My eldest brother, Philip, had gone to England before hostilities broke out and it was he who sent word to me, during the height of the Cold War, to spy for your country. We were nothing if not pragmatists, and it wasn't hard to see that as Nazism had failed, so too would Communism," he smiled, and I bought it.

"No, I joke, Mr West. We were Royalists at heart and besides, Philip went to England in 1937 to marry a cousin of your Prince Albert. We Mecklenburgs swayed with the times and adjusted to them. Hence the change of name from Mecklenburg to Kudashov conveniently done before the Red Army took over the whole of the Czechoslovakian countryside."

* * *

"In the beginning I performed small duties for MI6, using the tradecraft I was taught by a man who called himself Rose. I must admit I found that name somewhat effeminate, which was not helped when he said that my code name was to be Ivy. You must understand I was young and impressionable when that all happened. I was making an uninformed judgement because I wanted a really red-blooded name and an equally manly named handler, not Ivy and Rose! No matter, it worked well enough.

“The game began in earnest in early 1981. Rose—I hate that name—left instructions for me to become friendlier with the family of the one-time head of the country’s *Státní bezpečnost*, the StB for short: one General Anotoly Vladislav Kava. I had made his acquaintance much earlier than this. The first time I met him was when I was twenty-four and in the middle ranks of the civil police. I was ordered to escort him while he marched his wife to the army barracks, where he shot her. It was either that evening or the next day I accompanied my father and mother to the Kavas’ home to offer our condolences to Jana and her brother who, of course, were merely children at that time. I lost touch with the family after the general was himself murdered at the aircraft factory.

“However, by the time London instructed me to intensify the slight acquaintanceship I had with his family, I was in charge of the civil police force in Prague. Everything went up a notch or two when I started dealing directly with London Control, who urgently wanted Jana Kava, and they wanted me to convert her in any way I saw fit. The best way into her was through her brother. I told her I would incriminate him by planting Solidarity movement propaganda leaflets and have him arrested, then handed over to his late father's StB. The StB were renowned for their long memory, and following the incident with Khrushchev at the Aero Vodochody factory, the Kava name was no longer highly respected in the State Security. The fact that I knew him to be homosexual would not have helped his cause once in the StB's hands.

"I told Jana what she already knew; as a consequence, her position would become untenable. I was successful in the conversion, but I only saw her as of low-grade value. After all wasn't Russian intelligence the big game? But it wasn't as clear cut as that. From that moment on, things changed considerably for me. London stepped up the pressure. I cannot give you proof, but I sensed a change in emphasis on what London wanted. This would be sometime around late spring, early summer of 1982. London changed from attention on local topics, such as general conversation she'd overheard at party headquarters, or better still at the StB offices on Wenceslas Square. All of a sudden, they wanted to know if her father had known and corresponded with a KGB general named Ivan Aleksandrovich Solidus.

"I had no idea why Control asked that question until Jana told me of a letter addressed to her dead father with a Soviet army hammer and sickle seal on it, with the KGB badge. She'd opened it. It was from that General Solidus and she still had it. Dalek was still sharing the family home with her then, so she waited for him to leave and met me near our usual spot beside the river. Inside the letter, General Solidus told of a place near his Moscow apartment where he had buried some information about Khrushchev. London's ears picked up! *Go on they said, find us more.* So I did. In another part of the letter it said that if ever the documents were discovered, then Russia would become the laughingstock of the world because of what happened when Khrushchev was in charge.

"The following week, I was told that you would be part of the trade delegation that was coming to town. London said to stay clear of you. Leave you to deal and don't interfere. You know the rest, apart from one immensely important detail known only to three people: my Control, myself and now you, Mr West. As I made contact with Jana Kava after you and she parted company in Prague rather hurriedly on a Saturday night, I was told to move to Moscow and by whatever means available find the information that General Solidus had buried. I did. And I think that's one of the reasons why my life and my granddaughter's life are in danger. There is another reason that I think it's more pressing."

* * *

As my stroll came to an end and the elevator rose to the PM's personal secretary's office, I imagined Fraser Ughert salivating by now as the deviousness of Victor Rothschild was uncovered and one more piece of his jigsaw fell nicely into place for his memoirs. I was thinking of the place on the tapes Fraser must be listening to of my conversation with Kudashov as I waited for the elevator to my audience with the PM.

* * *

"I think you were suspicious about my wife's death when we spoke of it and if I'm right I know why. In the MI6 file you have on Ivy, the death is recorded to have happened in Prague, but that's not the case. She died by her own hand in our apartment overlooking Polosk Park in the centre of Moscow soon after we moved there in October 1982. My wife's passing was written up the way it was to save me from whoever it was in the CIA who killed young Jana Kava in Gdańsk. London were covering my back by throwing misinformation at the CIA computers. That's the more dangerous pressing reason I mentioned. I think the CIA have caught up with me.

"Anna's heart was broken when she saw what Lenin and his Bolsheviks, then Stalin and the war had done to Moscow. In 1985, things started to ease up in Russia because of Gorbachev's glasnost and his opening up of East-West dialogue. I was one of the lucky ones and allowed a travel pass out of Russia. When I was in Czechoslovakia, things were different. But to get a pass out of Russia, well, I was lucky. It seemed as though the decadent aristocrats of yesteryear were back in fashion. I followed London's orders by hiding the Solidus papers on me, travelling to Switzerland where, after some very elaborate precautions I met a man named Macintosh, but his name was not that and neither of us needed a mackintosh that gloriously sunny day overlooking Lake Geneva."

I asked Kudashov for a description of Mr Macintosh and it quickly became obvious who he was. Mr Macintosh was Miles Faversham and the place abroad where he met his death was Switzerland. I could think of only one person who could pull the necessary strings to get Faversham to Switzerland and leave no trace in a file or document within the secret intelligence service and that was Dickie Blythe-Smith. What I couldn't work out was, why send an overweight desk man?

Just as I trying to fathom out why my control officer for the first part of Operation Donor was possibly murdered, the elevator had risen and as its doors opened there sat the PM's secretary ostentatiously checking his watch.

Chapter Twenty-One: Codes

The Prime Minister's questioning alternated between why had I not briefed him on the special forces incursions across the Iraqi border into Iran, to could we find some connection between Aybak Khoury and his Defenders of the Levant with the Iranian National Guard, whom the American President Bush wanted to declare as terrorists before he found a real reason to invade their country?

"He's gaining more and more support for an invasion of Iran, and I'm hoping we can use the Victoria Station bomb incident in some way to help him. Israel is on side and if there is to be an international alliance again, I want the UK leading from the front. There's more business to come our way if we are among the first in the country, West."

The PM wanted me to contact the Egyptian lawyer who was director general of the International Atomic Energy Agency and persuade him to speak in favour of an American-led intervention in Iran when the IAEA met the following week. I suggested it would carry more weight if it came from the Minister for Foreign Affairs and, when he prevaricated, I flatly refused to do it. The disagreement became heated and where once I might have gone too far, I was held back by thoughts of Hannah's anger at my indiscretion when I returned to the apartment. But she wasn't there, was she? Nevertheless, my resolve to remain judicious persevered and I left his office saying that I would see what I could do in respect of the IAEA.

There are many entrances and exits from Number 10 which are shielded from intrusive eyes and I was met at one by the returning team pairing of Jimmy and Frank. We swapped updates of the morning along with verification of health issues, and I thanked Jimmy for the deafness I temporarily suffered from. Less sarcastically, I thanked him for his awareness and accuracy. As we made our way on the journey to Windsor, and the awaiting Mrs Jacqueline Price, I was saved from further elaborating on the simple 'thanks for what you did, Jimmy' by my phone bursting into life. I was anticipating Fraser, but I was wrong, it was Michael Simmons.

"I'm pleased I found you, sir, and obvious congratulations about this morning. I hope the leg's okay. Listen."

Nine times out of ten he started a conversation in such a way: *listen*. It was infuriating and for the umpteenth time I reminded myself to say something to him. My nerves were grated.

"I know this is old hat, sir, but I think I've turned up something from a search I conducted using the AIS monitors at Greenwich and the advanced geospatial intelligence they offer. It threw up something that could be of interest connected to the 1982 Israeli insurgence into Lebanon. Someone gave us a heads-up four months before that war commenced. The information I uncovered included specific details of ensuing PLO movements. One route of withdrawal was a supposedly protected route to a Syrian village called Harfa.

"Sixty-three escaping PLO members were met at that village and completely wiped out. With obvious reasoning, the Israelis were blamed for the massacre. Not only did that blame come from the higher echelons of the PLO, along with the Syrians who threatened reprisals, but from the American government. But it was not the Israelis who ambushed the PLO. Signals I've downloaded conclusively show it had been a prearranged operation between Syrian special forces and a department in the American National Security Agency.

"We have decrypted the NSA signal sent to Damascus from Royal Air Force Menwith Hill, sir. It has been encrypted into the databanks at AIS Greenwich, marking all the CIA pings they used in those days as verification. We also have the original coded script that Menwith Hill relayed back to the American army intelligence and security command at INSCOM headquarters, Fort Belvoir, Virginia. Signal analysis of Echelon, and can I add—with Frosting on top, sir." Michael had a sense of humour it seemed. "I've copied the case files and consigned them for your eyes, Mr West. I'm at Group at the moment. Do you need me at Whitehall, sir?"

As I told him that I didn't need him at present but might do later, we were joined by what the PM's secretary had told me were to remain as my permanent police outriders and escorting vehicles. Their presence made me feel important, but it also intensified the feeling of loneliness.

* * *

The door to number 74 Rydal Drive, Windsor, was opened by a woman I knew to be sixty-seven years of age, but whatever it was she dieted on made her look at least ten years younger. Her long blonde hair sparkled as the afternoon sun struck her, lighting up her face and briefly showing the brilliance of her blue eyes before she shielded them from the glare. As she did, I briefly wondered if it was the air quality away from London that made a difference to her and Glenister's appearance.

"This will give the neighbours something to natter about," she declared as those blue eyes scrutinised the convoy of vehicles blocking the road with the motorcycle escorts at each end with flashing blue lights and an armed police officer at her gate. "Please, come through. I've prepared a tray of cakes and biscuits. Would you both like tea or coffee to go with them?" she enquired politely.

I asked for the coffee, excusing Frank from either, saying he was here just to look around, citing that morning's terrorist incident as a reason. Whilst he busied himself with security matters, I thanked her profusely for allowing the visit and followed her into the kitchen. I mentioned I'd seen her work record and noted how accomplished she had been in applying her talents in the various photography intelligence fusion centres, as well as Military Intelligence Section 4 during the years that were of interest to me.

As Frank poked his head through a doorway, announcing the place to be 'all clear, boss. Mr Price is in the greenhouse,' I had a distorted picture of Jack Price at eighty years of age tending tomatoes, and then I thought of how many times Fraser had shouted down the phone connection on the journey here. "I told you Victor was clearly in on it from the start," and I wondered how I had connected those two images.

Jacqueline was placing the teapot on a tray as I was visualising Fraser jumping up and down in front of his computer screen, punching the air as if he'd won a boxing match. Molly was probably there, or on her way, to quieten him. Maybe she checked his blood pressure or administered any of the tablets he had to take daily, anything to avoid exacerbating his heart problems. When he finished congratulating himself on his wisdom over Victor Rothschild, he was most probably rattling off the questions I should put to Jacqueline Price about the 1982 signal, and in his voice I could hear the excitement of predicted pleasure in Jacqueline's twenty-five-year-old memory.

"Of course she'll remember it, Patrick. It wouldn't be every day of the week a section head of photographic analysis in Germany gets a coded signal with the Century House SIS logo somewhere on it, asking her to keep her mouth shut about a secret. Of course she'll remember. Hugo Glenister just remembered a name, so why won't she remember a signal? How could she forget that?"

I had not shared Fraser's confidence when we left Hugo Glenister's conservatory, but as I followed Mrs Price into a large sitting room, my confidence was growing.

"Will your husband be joining us?" I asked.

"No, I told him this was old ministry business and to clear off." Her smile was not only genuine, but had been in use many times, judging by the way the creases were etched around her eyes and mouth. "He would probably be in his greenhouses all day if I let him." The smile remained and, if anything, it became more intense and sincere. "He spends a lot of time in there now. It's the tomatoes you see. Tomato rot is around at this time of year. It's been very hot in there. Whereas I have my project that's tied to the Ministry, his hobby is gardening. We've been married too many years to get in each other's way. I can introduce you if you want?"

"Perhaps later, if there's time." I wanted her to take the lead as I didn't want my visit to appear as if it was an inquisition. I took my coffee and a digestive biscuit, then sat back in the soft armchair opposite hers.

"Now, Mr West, what exactly can I do for you? Your secretary was rather secretive about it, but I can understand why that was. By the way, I saw the BBC News coverage of the Victoria Station incident. Am I right in assuming the man you came with was there, as someone looking distinctly like him was?" she stated emphatically.

"He was, yes. A very upsetting time for all those involved, I'm sure." My presence at Victoria was censored from any news broadcast both at home and abroad.

The coffee was good. Made from the same filter thing we had in the F&C apartment. Where did the 'we' come from? There was no 'we' any longer. As long as my thoughts were kept in my head, I was okay. I ignored those notional questions and concentrated on why I was there. Jacqueline Price understood the reason for confidentiality; could that be because she remembered the signal?

"But sorry, I'm taking up too much of your time. It's the signal you're after of course."

Bloody hell, Fraser was right; she does remember. Can I jump up and down in delight, or does the death of one's wife preclude all celebrations?

"You're after the bounced signal that was addressed to me, section head in Photographic Analysis, but wasn't meant for me. It came with instructions in plain English to hold on to it without showing it to anyone. There were two aerial photographs that, again, I was told to keep until a later date. All of that stuff was typed, but there was a handwritten note as well."

Could one faint if one was sitting down? I held my coffee cup tighter in case that happened to me. "Do you remember what that written note said, Mrs Price?" I adopted an ostrich's approach by averting my eyes from her, hoping she would not recognise the nervousness I felt.

"I still have it all, you know. I wasn't going to chuck any of that away. I used to muse over what sort of spying caper I was caught up in. I don't suppose you can tell me, can you, sir?" I felt her eyes on me and I returned her stare with an answer to her plea.

"It was important back in 1982, the Cold War days and all that, but now it could be an embarrassment to a Russian official at the United Nations. With all that's happening in the Middle East, we cannot rock any diplomatic boats in the peace process that we and Russia might propose."

"I completely understand, Mr West. Peace is a quality we all strive to achieve for more reasons than one. Would you like another coffee while I fetch it from upstairs? It won't take me long, but I thought it safer to wait until your arrival before I got it ready. No good having it lying around then finding pressure of work causing your departure to be cancelled."

Having praised her for the quality of the first cup of coffee, my refusal of another seemed impolite and I'm sure Hannah would have disapproved, but I managed to take the edge off any discourtesy I'd caused by commending her carefulness. "You are very wise, Jacqueline. Who knows what might have occurred."

My patience was at breaking point, plus the hole in my leg was throbbing like mad, which was my fault as I'd forgotten to change the morphine patch an hour ago. Thankfully, she wasn't too long.

The message showed both the coded version and, after being transliterated into plain script, it read: *Keep until the West arrives.*

"Obviously at the time I received it, I had no idea what that meant nor, of course, the other message. But as soon as the official from the Home Office confirmed it was your secretary who called me, I knew you must be the one this is intended for. I put it all together in this envelope for safekeeping. I hope you don't mind me checking up on you?"

I think I murmured—not at all on taking her trophy into my possession. She looked tremendously solemn on the exchange, leaving me to marvel at how unflustered we both were as I removed the contents from the cherished envelope and spread them onto the dining room table. The handwritten message read: No One Is More Important Than Each—NOMITE. I almost fainted.

The photographs showed images of Jana Kava. The first was a continuous reel showing Jana walking into an open, abandoned building site, kneeling on the ground, where indicated by the man at her back holding a gun, and then the same gun being pointed and placed at the back of her head and fired. The second photo was a single frame showing her body spread-eagled in a pool of blood. In that second photograph, the face of her killer was clearly visible.

"A terrible thing for you to see, Mrs Price. I apologise on behalf on my department."

"There's absolutely no need to apologise, Mr West. When I was in the photographic section I'm very much afraid to say I saw far worse images than these. I hope you're able to save the situation with this," she stated as I lamely stared at the photographed face of another cold-blooded killer.

* * *

This time I was sure I saw Fraser hop in delight as he opened his door to me some forty minutes or so after leaving Windsor. I hope it never ceases to amaze me how much time a police escort can save on a car journey. I was pondering on that fact, also wondering how fast the police motorcyclist could get the photographs from Windsor to Image Recognition and how long it would take to find a name to match the face of Jana's killer, when all of a sudden there he was in all his smiling scruffiness, shuffling from foot to foot.

Despite my amazement over the speed of police escorted travel, I had no doubt Fraser's smile would have lasted for the time it might have taken me to walk the thirty odd miles. His *I told you so, didn't I* was the first utterance I warded away before Molly appeared with a tray full of plastic glasses and jugs of fresh lemonade for the outriders and protection officers. Molly was the type of person for whom onerous was not a word she would recognise. Everything she did was done freely, joyously, and with a selfless heart. Hannah was the same, and I was only just winning in pushing her memory to the back of my mind. I realise that will sound harsh; nevertheless, that's what I needed to do.

* * *

I can't recall whether I lit my cigarette first or it was his lighting of a hidden pipe; no matter, it was he who toasted me with the Jura for the capture of Hannah's killer and the tracking down of Jacqueline Price. Perhaps the ball was slowing as the path forward was becoming clearer. Fraser and I set about seeing how far forward we could see.

* * *

"I got my signal containing the new Soviet Union radio coding off from the British Embassy to the seventh floor on the afternoon of the thirty-first of August. The same day Jana Kava hands Kudashov an encrypted message from her Polish colonel, naming the American in GCHQ.

Although that message was in the new coding, it never hit any screen. I can't think of a reason for that other than Dickie wanting to keep that name to himself and Kudashov somehow sending it without passing through counter-intelligence.

"These photos of Jana Kava meeting her end are dated the following day. The only reason for ending her life must be because she knew something she wasn't supposed to and must have something to do with the Polish colonel. But is that why Dickie sent the photos to Jacqueline Price at the Imagery Control Commission in Germany? I know these are big assumptions, but let's go with it for a while. Dickie takes over the running of Kudashov when something or someone spooks him regarding your man Rothschild. Word comes back that there's a letter in Jana Kava's possession and London instructs Kudashov to get it by any means. How am I going so far, Fraser?"

"Aye, I'm following you, Patrick. Carry on," he replied studiously.

“Right. Let’s get going then. Michael has been doing some digging into the past from old Hardballs’ legacy, the AIS installation at Greenwich.”

“Heard anything of the bastard, have you, Patrick?” I anticipated his interruption as Geoffrey Harwood, alias Hardballs, was one of Fraser’s pet hates.

“No, I’ve not heard a thing. I expect he’s in some South American jungle, setting up communication stations for the natives. Can I carry on, or are you going to butt in wherever you please?”

“How’s the leg? Need more whisky, do you, to take your mind off it?” he asked.

I was thankful for it being warm when I was shot and it not being in the damp of winter when the rheumatism in my right foot and right leg was at its worst of being debilitating and painful. If I’d had that to endure, as well as the wound in my other leg, then I could guarantee my irritability would have been bordering on the obscene. I poured a large glass of pain-removing Jura and moved the speculation along.

“Michael Simmons found an internal GCHQ intelligence report dated June 1979, alleging some pirating of hypersensitive analysis of Iranian intel transmissions received at a UK listening outpost at RAF Cyprus. An investigation was undertaken straight away, but wasn't ended in my opinion until Dickie told Sir John Scarlett to write it up as a Nil-Find and Dickie closed the real case file with a hundred-year seal. Most of that is factual, so here comes my hypothesis.

"The Americans get edgy when the investigation starts to really get going at Cheltenham, so they come to an arrangement: 'We'll give you a name,' they say, 'if you help us find a rat at home leaking secrets about a spy-plane factory in the Nevada desert.' We might have known of that desert facility already but, if not, we would have known eventually, so it's no great loss to the Americans them telling us, but they stand to gain an awful lot on the GCHQ front if we stop looking once they have given us Geoffrey Prime. They made a mistake though. Dickie didn't stop looking. He stopped when he found the real mole.

"This is where my train of thought is coming up against a wall and I need your help, Fraser. I can't place the Victor Rothschild of the sixties in the Geoffrey Prime timeframe of the GCHQ of the eighties. Nor can I find a reason for needing confirmation of Rothschild's involvement with the Cambridge Five. I think you have the answer to that one and there's maybe more you need to reveal now."

Chapter Twenty-Two: Revelations

Fraser had the room, and the room consisted of only me. I certainly was not sorry I was alone as his stories were always told in such a way that other considerations were forgotten or pushed aside for a different time. In my case, that applied to Hannah and my leg. As it was obvious Fraser and I were going to drift past midnight in our examination of facts and theories, I stood down Frank, Jimmy and the rest of my escorting cavalcade, accepting Molly Ughert's offer of a bed for yet another night in peaceful Buckinghamshire.

When Dickie Blythe-Smith sat in my chair of the Joint Intelligence Committee, Fraser Ughert was Director General of Group. They were the greatest of friends and trusted each other and nobody else. Victor Rothschild's friendship with Kim Philby, one of the Cambridge Five, was a similar kind of relationship, but built on reliance not respect.

On 12 December 1957, Aileen Philby, Kim Philby's wife, was discovered dead in the bedroom of her house in Crowborough, Sussex. Her friends believed she had killed herself with drink and pills. However, the head of MI5 believed she had been murdered by her husband, or a friend, because she knew too much. Kim Philby had no money of his own to speak of, but somehow he found enough to set up home in a village outside of Beirut, then took an apartment in the Lebanese capital before travelling extensively throughout the Middle East, always in a rich degree of comfort.

By January 1963 it became clear that Philby's spying activities for the Russians had been discovered and he had no choice but to leave his new wife and Beirut. Using what was suspected to be a combination of Soviet influence and Rothschild money, Philby was allowed by MI6 to escape through Syria, then overland to Armenia, and then to Russia. The security service did not want an embarrassing public trial and it was decided that it was not the time to look too far into the class-ridden secret intelligence service.

However, two men did look: Fraser Ughert and Dickie Blythe-Smith. Both were in different departments of internal security. That was where the fascination with Victor Rothschild began for them. For Fraser, it led to a disciplinary hearing that set his career back a few years, allowing Dickie to race ahead in the promotion stakes. Perhaps it was Dickie being older that made him the diplomat to Fraser's youthful 'bull in the china shop' syndrome, but neither strategy unearthed any concrete evidence to confirm the pair's worst fears, that Moscow had a prodigy planted inside British intelligence, but the pair smelled something odd and refused to let it lie. If, they argued, they could prove Victor Rothschild was the sixth member of the Cambridge spy-ring, they could confirm that the thirty-year-old American university graduate who started work in the same J30 section of J Division 'Special Sigint' at GCHQ four years before Prime was posted there, was the real McCoy, planted by Moscow with help from Rothschild's recommendation. Dickie could then confirm the name when he received the coded signal I sent from Warsaw on the thirty-first of August. The question left from that argument was: what was hidden in the NOMITE signal that then went to Jacqueline Price?

* * *

"I can understand what you were trying to do about Moscow's intervention inside GCHQ, Fraser, but why didn't Dickie tell you the name of whoever it was in there, and why enmesh it such a convoluted way as this? It's making me ask if the mole inside GCHQ was American or Russian? No One Is More Important Than Each, or NOMITE, was Jack Price's name for the group he enrolled me in before we went on the operation in New York. That ended up with you and Dickie coming out to America. It's also where my fictitious sister Fianna died. Now there is only you and me alive who know what the abbreviation stands for," Fraser interrupted me.

"I had never heard of it until you just mentioned it, Patrick." We were walking in the fresh evening air of summer, but it wasn't helping to clear away the mist in my mind.

"Okay, so that leaves only me knowing it. So why on earth send something to someone who he had no idea would still be around to find it?" I was talking for the sake of it, throwing words at a puzzle, hoping some might stick to a place on the board. Fraser wanted to play the same game.

"My first thought is that does not sound like Dickie at all. There wasn't much spontaneity about him. He was a meticulous man, where it was details that held the importance for him. Mind you, I know he admired Jack Price. Mentioned his name to me many times in a reverent kind of way. Used some of Jack's operations as examples when giving lectures at Beaulieu House. There were two things he prized in service officers and both he said you had in abundance: composure and the ability to react to the situation. That's why he bumped you up into the full blown intelligence service. You've come a long way, Patrick, with a few bumps along your road, I'll grant you. You will get over Hannah, you know." It looked as though he was about to let sentimentality in the door.

I slammed it shut. "How did you like the tapes, Fraser?" I asked needlessly, but it did take his mind back to where I wanted it.

"Loved them. I could picture it all unfolding as I listened, especially the rift between Khrushchev and the staunch Stalinists. At the time, that rift almost led to another Russian revolution. I didn't know the full history of the Kudashovs, but they were certainly a resourceful lot to survive both Communism and Fascism. One can only imagine how much hatred General Kava had stored away to scream and shout at Khrushchev as he did. He must have known it was the end for him. Brave man to do that." By the reflective expression he wore, it was clear we were edging back towards sorrow.

"Shall we make our way back, Fraser? I could do with a livener."

"So I could I, dear boy. By the way, were there any more tapes of your conversation with Kudashov, as he had me drooling over the prospect of him making the connection between Rothschild and GCHQ?"

"There's one, yes, but he doesn't mention Rothschild. He does, however, shine some more light on why he came to us and it involves the death of Paulette Simona, aka Claudette Avogova in the aircraft crash on the Sunday before he met you. I'm sorry for not telling you sooner, but what with everything else that's been happening I'm getting dizzy with it all. The tapes where Kudashov tells me the final parts of his story I've had to lock in the vaults at the Foreign Office, for reasons that will emerge as we go on.

"Having listened to him, I'm in agreement about his life being in danger; hence, the trickery in first taking him openly to the deportation centre at Croydon and then sending him to Beaulieu in the back of the coroner's van. He's safe in the New Forest for now at least, but I believe he's in more danger than he realises. And what's more, if my worse misgivings are true, then so is his granddaughter. But I wish I knew it all.

"On the day the final bricks of the Berlin Wall were carted away, Kudashov was in the Federal Intelligence Service offices in Cologne, Germany. He was there on our business unconnected with the demolition. As you have been aware for some years he was our eyes and ears on the German and American relationship to certain countries in the Middle East. In short, during the Cold War, Kudashov was our insider in the West German Federal Intelligence Service. I've read the case file of how it was he who supplied the information about the assassination attempt on the Israeli ambassador in London in June '82."

"Yes, Patrick. A devious man is this Kudashov, and a very clever one as well. A political decision was taken after I presented the information and it went before the Cabinet. I can only remember Dickie mentioning Kudashov the once though. It was in connection with an operation he was running in Odessa, independent of those at the Russian desk. Never told me what it was of course, and I never knew why he told me the name of Kudashov, or Odessa. When I was chair of JIC, I saw Kudashov's name a few times forwarded on from the secret intelligence service, but he was not involved in anything major like this."

* * *

I loved Fraser Ughert like I would a father, and to me I guess he had become that figure in my life. I knew his moods and I knew how good he had been as chairman of joint intelligence. His was a huge role I had to fill. From the day I accepted the position I had sought Fraser's advice whenever I thought he would add something I could have missed. We had reached his office by the time we resumed our conversation. I started where reminisces had taken over.

"Because the final parts of the Berlin Wall were still being demolished, the West German intelligence service had their attention elsewhere and Kudashov says he got a glimpse at a reel of microwave radio signals emanating from a NSA relay point in Mannheim. He photocopied one. But his luck didn't stop there. The NSA signal operative had left the coding running on the screen for all to see. He added that to his miniature Minox camera. When his granddaughter was safely ensconced in Moscow Centre, he gave her what he photographed that day. He doesn't know the technical terminology for what she did with those encrypted codes, but in them she identified signals linking the laboratory at Nikel in Russia to a part of the American CIA and our friend, the Russian oligarch Bohdan Dimitriyevich Valescov, from poor old Henry Mayler's Rosicrucian order.

"Kudashov has heard of Valecov and heard of his fortune and the ways he protects it. You see, Kudashov is of the same persuasion as you, my friend. He believes Valecov is one of that eight number of immensely wealthy families who wish to further their worldwide hold on the rest of us.

"I haven't got it all from Kudashov about what he knows of Nikel, but he admits that his initial designs for the information he was compiling were selfish. He became interested in the area when his son and his daughter-in-law's plane mysteriously crashed near there. He believed then, and still does, that Ludvík and his wife Karina had nothing to do with the laboratory. He also believes that they may have seen something on their fishing holiday that meant their plane had to be brought down. In the crash report he saw, it noted that a fuel line had a clean cut to it. This, he suspects, is a clear sign of sabotage.

"He met Claudette Avogova at a party that I haven't yet had a chance to look into. That's one of the points I need to discuss in the future. As we know, the real Claudette went missing in 2001 and so Kudashov not only worked with her, but also with this Paulette Simona. I want that to come from Kudashov slowly. There is one thing he has said about Paulette Simona that's interesting. Her identity had been changed by the CIA, but she never attended any face-to-face briefing, nor knew her handler by sight.

"She was presented with an inch-thick dossier, told to read and digest it by her flight time, which was the following day. She rightly assumed a cover name would be needed because of the sensitivity of the work, and it was a formality in the way it was handled, but luckily for us she was wrong. We have a friend who has a friend in the CIA's Directorate of Science and Technology who's looking into it as we speak."

"Do we know how her plane was brought down, Patrick?"

"The Norwegian civil air authorities examined the wreckage and wrote it down to engine failure, but I've requested they hold on to what they have until an air investigation team from Farnborough arrive. The earliest time that can happen is Friday. I wouldn't be surprised to learn it was shot down. It might be difficult to discover as it sustained heavy damage when it crashed."

"No, nor would I be surprised," he mumbled as his pipe smoke swirled around his head. "Did Spencer Morrell say that the CIA had a look at the name Jana Kava was given in Warsaw and passed on to Kudashov?"

"He says no. Says that any Jana, as Petr Tomsa, file he has, was heavily redacted from our end. He's playing the knowledge they had of Kudashov close to his chest. Can't say I blame him either. Least said, soonest mended kind of thing."

"Okay, yes, I can get that too. So how many people saw the coded name that Kudashov got from Jana Kava and sent to the Soviet Satellite desk, Patrick?"

"Only two, Fraser. Kudashov and the only one who could decode it—Dickie!

Chapter Twenty-Three: A Cup of Tea

"If you're sure the only time Dickie mentioned Kudashov's name to you was in conjunction with an operation he was running on his own in Odessa, Fraser, then whatever code was being used then is how he had the name of the insider at GCHQ sent directly to him from Warsaw. That way, it would have avoided touching Sir John Scarlett's desk or any on the seventh floor. He and Kudashov had a previous special code for the Russian op and worked it up again. You said yourself that Dickie never did things, or said things, without having a reason. He was laying the ground for something he might, or might never, have to use by telling you of Odessa."

My conjecture was met by a hard, dubious look on Fraser's face that remained when Molly opened the office door and sent him to bed. I begged permission to use his computer, adding I would curl up in an armchair when tiredness overtook me. He scowled his agreement, adding as Molly defiantly stood in the doorway, hands on hips, "If you find any dirt on the Macintosh name used in Switzerland be sure to keep it for me to look at." I had forgotten about him!

* * *

Although it was late, I sent a message off to Michael Simmons to look into all he could find on Sir Russell Macintosh of the Diplomatic Corps and send his results directly to Fraser Ughert. I very much doubted Dickie had instructed Miles Faversham to use the name without there being a hidden agenda, so I hoped whatever Michael could find would give Fraser some useful reading. As for me, I went to find this friend of a friend I said we had inside the CIA's Directorate of Science and Technology; it was to be a tough task as I hadn't anyone on the inside, but I did have Spencer Morrell. It was a little after half one in the morning when I sent a message off to him hoping, but not expecting, a reply later that day. One came back on the screen from his terminal straight away.

'Sunday last, we were put on the highest internal alert status because of a possible missile strike over Norwegian airspace. It was a civil aircraft that was brought down, flying out of Nikel, Russia. The flight plan registered Torp Sandefjord in southern Norway as the destination. There was one passenger on board, an employee from the CIA's Science and Technology. We're looking into her record of assignments. Is it you that's asking or your Government, Patrick?' he asked and I typed *me*, then pressed the send button.

My mobile phone rang; it was Spencer.

"On the surface this looks big, but I'm caught in the crossfire here and nobody is telling me much. My office got lumbered into handling the inquiry as we're the heaviest staffed in Europe after Berlin, who can't deal as they're working on something else. It sounds as if you're more up to speed on this one than me and have probably worked out it wasn't a Brit named Claudette Avogova on that flight.

"We contacted the Norwegians and then ran all they gave us through everything we've got and came up with nothing other than a confirmation on the passenger's name—Paulette Simona. To make matters worse, we have the passport holder Claudette Avogova registered with the Directorate of Science and Technology, as well as Simona. The records show she is the Technical Analyst Manager at the Directorate's regional office in Oslo, Norway. I've heard of the Science and Technology department, but I'd never had dealings with them.

"On paper they are pretty innocuous. From what I can understand, they deal in making signal traffic easier to send and receive, and they deal with any technology issues our agents encounter. I'm still getting info on her role in Oslo, Norway. The higher-ups at Langley are a bit touchy about filling in the details for me on this one. I guess you've heard about the flight departure point, this place spelled Nikel in Russia. I would be mighty glad if you could send any intel you have on it to me, Patrick, as we don't seem to have shit here. There have been overflights of the place since the name pinged up in Langley and I've seen the analyst's reports—nothing. There's been some large construction near a lake that's not in keeping with the surroundings and what appears to be another nearby site that's recently broke ground, but apart from that there's not much else there other than a few homes, an airstrip, road in, the same road out, and a small harbour."

I asked him why he thought it was a missile that brought down the flight and he confirmed the notification I had seen from RAF Menwith Hill of the traced trajectory of a surface to air missile they had intercepted from a previously undesignated source outside of Luostari, not far from Nikel. As the aircraft was registered to a Russian oil magnate named Bohdan Dimitriyevich Valescov, there was no complaint made to the Russian ambassador in Washington DC, as the CIA would never admit to one of their officers working anywhere on Russian territory. From the remaining conversation, I couldn't be sure if Spencer was telling the truth as he knew it, or was aware of the significance of Nikel, but for the time being I had no choice but to accept what he said as he said it.

* * *

There was a message remaining from Monday, sent from Sir John Scarlett's office that I had not seen. It was headed: The PLO.

Aybak Khoury's family had, so Scarlett's report alleged, been expelled from Israel during the 1982 war with the Lebanese and the PLO in particular. His mother and father had not survived that upheaval, dying on the route they and many others were forced to take to Amman in Jordan. Aybak was four years old when that happened and nursed by his sister until she too died, by which time Aybak was old enough to look after himself on the streets of Jordon.

His sister's life was taken by the remote control she used to detonate the bomb she wore outside the American compound in Amman. By the time Aybak was seventeen, he had been in Israeli custody on seven occasions, but never held for a crime. Scarlett had run down six assassinations where Aybak was and could have been directly responsible. He was, so the report went on to emphatically demonstrate, a hired killer only a few could afford. MI6, working alongside other worldwide agencies, was looking at possible principals. It was the principal behind Dickie Blythe-Smith's message of NOMITE to Jacqueline Price that was on my mind as I curled up on the sofa-cum-daybed in Fraser's office and fell asleep without once thinking of Hannah.

* * *

I awoke that Tuesday morning with a head full of ideas; the trouble was Fraser had his own all to do with Sir Russell Macintosh, and he didn't want to hear mine. Frank and Jimmy were back at work, starting off the day eating Molly out of house and home, with her contented smile as they did.

"Would you like everything for breakfast, Patrick?" she asked with a wholesomeness about her the world needed to adopt, or at least the two newscasters on the television playing in the kitchen who loved to make all their morning viewers miserable. After consuming so little food the previous days, but drinking so much whisky, I gratefully accepted the offer, sitting back and listening in to the sporting news Frank was extolling.

Fraser made a hurried appearance, hoping it was not he who had awakened me; nevertheless, he added he was pleased his office was cleared of vagrants. At first I simply smiled at his attempted humour, but something triggered my eyes and nostrils into gear, and at once I knew to what he referred—me! I needed a shower, a shave, and more than likely the third 'S' that army drill sergeants are keen on mentioning so indecorously on parade grounds throughout the world. Having heard no complaints from any other person, I concluded that his lack of office ventilation had exacerbated the problem. I should have thought of this last night before staying too long as I had a long day in front of me, and the last thing I wanted to do was waste time.

* * *

I travelled from Clearsey to Whitehall straight after breakfast but, despite my swiftness, it wasn't until almost eleven o'clock that I could journey on to Beaulieu to see Kudashov and perhaps put some things to rest. There was some news about his granddaughter that I could relay to him and, if I was careful, I could omit telling the parts that he would not like to hear.

It was a glorious day as we set off with a now perfunctory escort of armed motorcycle police and ever-present SO9 Special Branch vehicles to accompany us.

A hot sun beaming down from a cloudless sky greeted me as I stepped from the car, walking the short distance to where Kudashov waited in the gardens, full of summer colour. The first thing he asked was how the plans to extract Cilicia were going. I'd had the best two officers Sir John Scarlett had at foreign intelligence, both well known to me, in Moscow for the past seventy-two hours. The first officer was the man who killed the PLO treasurer in Paris and then assisted in the kill in Maine, America, a few days later. The other man was who I was talking to in the Derry pub when the nail bomb exploded. He was also included in the last operation Fraser and I ran against political corruption. Liam Catlin, of Derry fame, was who I first spoke of in relation to any forthcoming operation in Moscow.

Liam, with three lamp-burners from Group, was watching the movements of Cilicia Kudashov, twenty-four hours of the day. One of Group's lamp-burners had an additional local contact, an entire family he had run for years who interchanged with our personnel on a normal irregular tag routine. The party had an operational van, plus two other vehicles at their disposal. Lines of communication from the van to Liam's fixed location were sealed and secured. The other officer on the ground worked alone. Christopher Irons had earned his reputation for excellence the hard way.

In terms of age, both Catlin and Irons were getting on a bit—the wrong side of forty—but for any assessment of skill, tenacity and effectiveness, then both were in their prime. Irons had always been a loner. He'd been of service in most countries throughout Europe and the Americas, but predominantly his expertise was of use in the old, and now the new, Russia. He had many disguises, ranging from a travelling musician to a poet in the more liberal Soviet community. For this operation, he masqueraded as a municipal housing inspector, carrying all the correct paperwork to fit his vocation with telephone numbers that went straight to the console installed in our observation van. Playing this role, he paid a visit to the prestigious block of apartments in the Kitay-Gorod area overlooking the Zaryadye Park where Cilicia Kudashov lived. He had 'accidentally' bumped into her the day before my visit to Beaulieu.

Nikita Kudashov and his granddaughter had formulated a means to communicate when he had left Moscow for London. A secret word the two had dreamt up was to be said by a third party by way of introduction and as Cilicia's proof of identity. Christopher Irons knew the word—*articulate*—and made contact.

All this information delighted Kudashov so much so that when I hedged my bets over when Cilicia would be invited to leave her position in Russia, he wasn't as disconcerted as before. I managed to move the conversation on before his calm mood altered. We went over the exchange in Warsaw once again as we strolled through the magnificent rose garden in this private part of Beaulieu, away from public gaze.

"Tell me more about Odessa, Nikita. Did you and Dickie devise a code for that mission that was subsequently used for the signal traffic from Warsaw?"

"Numbers from letters, Patrick. Simple and easily remembered. We'd used it before a couple of times. One thing you must understand before we go any further and that's Dickie and I go back a long way, you know. He was twelve years older than me and a lot wiser when we first met, but I was a quick learner and he was a good teacher. Our first meeting was at a police conference in East Berlin of all places. I had graduated straight from the academy to the investigative side of the civil police, working my way up under the influence my family had that I've told you of. The reason I was instructed to travel to Berlin was 'to further my police education alongside my security counterparts,' which meant, buy their patronage for a future date that might become useful. You know what I mean.

"Dickie Blythe-Smith said it was my brother Philip who first made the English security services aware of me and apparently they marked me down as a possible candidate for long-term activities. He was so laid back. Said he'd come into East Berlin to meet, have a chat and a cup of tea. I can never forget that. Such a civilised man in a far from civilised world. He sold me on all the right things and hey presto there I was, an international spy! You say *on the spy*, don't you? I must be truly honest and say that I've enjoyed every heart-thumping, dangerous moment. But having led you on since our first meeting, I can understand how you might distrust that statement and me in general. Let's start at the beginning of your friend and mine's relationship and, just perhaps, I can reveal something about Dickie neither you nor Fraser Ughert ever knew."

Chapter Twenty-Four: Granitnyy

"Odessa was a big gain for us, Patrick, one of the best, but Granitnyy was the breakthrough moment for me. As I progressed through the Czechoslovakian civil police, so my contacts in the StB grew larger and, more importantly, I got close to military intelligence here in London. Dickie was my Control and apart from my brother, whom I never heard from, the only one I knew in England. Our exchange of intelligence was difficult but not impossible. I had police business beyond the Czech border, in Poland, East Germany and, on very special occasions, in Austria.

"There were three murders committed in Prague in 1976 and one of the suspects escaped across the border with Austria, which meant I went to Vienna to liaise with the police there, who had a similar situation only in reverse. It all became quite convenient. That's where Dickie and I set up the sting in Odessa. The Czechs and the Russians rotated officers above a certain rank in all branches of the military, security services and police. By 1975, I was on that rota, so was a KGB officer stationed in Odessa, but in May that year he was working within the StB in Prague. During the normal course of events we met several times and by the time he returned to Odessa in the Ukraine we had developed quite a friendship. The following year, I was posted to his home town and this KGB officer invited me to his celebrations of being promoted to lieutenant colonel. I went, but I didn't stay long. It was held in a male-only brothel. I made my excuses and left, unseen by the lieutenant colonel.

"But I didn't go far. I climbed the drainpipe to a second-floor window where he was with someone I didn't know, but they seemed to be getting on well, if you catch my meaning. I photographed them together. Before I returned to Prague, I left a copy of one of the photographs for him to find. When I was back at my post he called me and, almost in tears, he pleaded not to show them to anyone or he would be shot.

"Dickie said he made hay with the first batch of documents I left in dead-drops in Vienna for him to find. It took me the best part of a year to find out what the silly English expression of made hay, meant.

"There was no ceremony of course, but I was signed on full-time in the SIS after that major coup. When Dickie was promoted in the SIS, he continued as my Control and handler while our little sting bore fruit. But I lost touch with the KGB lieutenant colonel sometime around '79. I made tentative inquiries and found out he'd died. Although Dickie continued for a couple more of years as Control, eventually my handlers changed within the set up and I only met with Dickie once more, and that was in Vienna after he sent a man named Macintosh to Switzerland for the papers General Solidus hid."

I asked him why he had played so many games with the different emphasis he implied London took when Jana mentioned the letter, and how that conversation was designed to lead me to believe his Control had changed. He made an interesting reply and one that should have filled me with self-belief and confidence, but it didn't and I had no idea why.

"I wanted to see if you were as good as Dickie said you would become if you did survive. And not only have you survived, you've excelled yourself. You know, Patrick, Dickie had your back through every step of Operation Donor."

He stopped speaking to look me up and down from head to toe and then in reverse order, as if there might be a sign of resilience or longevity hanging somewhere loose from my clothing to prove Dickie right. When he was satisfied I was a mere plain human, he continued. "I wasn't anywhere near London when the Soviet Satellite desk became aware of the American interest in Jana Kava, but I have some knowledge of how they work, and Dickie knew precisely how they would react if their agent got blown and you were left standing under the searchlights. At best, you'd plead for mercy from the KGB and at worse, well, you don't need me to explain what would have happened.

"I would bet everything I owned on it being Dickie who insisted you made the pick-up at Warsaw central railway station, unbeknown to the CIA. That way, he pulled you away from what they were up to in killing Jana in Gdańsk.

If you had stayed in the open in Warsaw, I'd bet everything on them throwing you into the place where she was shot.

"What's more, Patrick, Dickie knew you would take care of Dalek Kava. I know that because we discussed it when he told me he had selected you for the operation and told me to draft those files. That was done in London in 1981. By then, I had one of highest clearances possible to have in Czechoslovakia and I posted myself to the Czech Embassy as head of security for a month. I ran internal checks and simulated counter-intelligence exercises to keep them busy, and I think they were all pleased when I slipped away to put Donor together.

"There was one thing, of course, he could never know about you and that's if you would stay the distance and piece together what this is all about. Well, he was right in one respect. You've come this far, Patrick. I wonder if that brain of yours will go that bit further."

We were sitting on a wooden bench beside a fast running stream full of different breeds of ducks, as well as swans and their cygnets. A cooling breeze was blowing that ruffled the long grass and reeds at the water's edge. Nothing, it seemed, could trouble Kudashov's philosophical frame of mind.

"Do you know who was the plant inside GCHQ, Nikita? Was it obvious by the coding of the signal that was passed to Jana, or did you have to wait until Cilicia could decode it?"

He laughed heartedly, throwing his head back as he did so. Some ducks were not so amused, flying off to the opposite bank. "No, Patrick, but I did hope Cilicia could have deciphered it. You must remember that Sir Richard Blythe-Smith did not receive that knighthood of his for being a fool. Yes, no need to look so surprised. Of course I knew of it. By the time Cilicia had the coded signal I'd lost all my interest in it. But there must be something you know more about that signal, otherwise the mystery ends here. Dickie had faith in you. He showed that when he was alive, and I bet he showed that before he died. Somewhere in this mystery there is a message only you would know, Patrick. Find it and work out what it means."

He was right, but I kept the Jacqueline Price message to myself and altered course with the rest of the conversation. I went back to my line of questioning about Nikel. Whatever it was that caused the sabotage of his son's plane, I knew Kudashov would have gone looking.

"The plane was examined and that cut fuel pipe was found, leading the crash examiner to conclude that's what brought about the sudden loss of altitude seen on the radar, and then the crash. If that was true, someone had a big reason to want to do it, but I was not going that far north and freezing my nuts off on guesswork alone. The police said they had no jurisdiction in Russian territory where the fuel line may have been cut, so it was left.

"Then something happened three years after the disaster that changed things. In late November 2000, I was invited to watch the rocket carrying the first crew to man the Space Station as it flew above a small village called Granitnyy, north of Murmansk, in what I was told was the clearest and cleanest air on the planet. It was spectacular with the Aurora Borealis over my left shoulder and the dramatic rocket's propulsion trail through a billion stars straight in front. Beautiful! I was among a hundred or so guests of a Russian we have mentioned before—Bohdan Dimitriyevich Valescov. I mingled, I opened my eyes and ears, and I found a man who was injudicious with his conversation when a glass was in his hand. It was he who told me the name on the laboratory at Nikel. It's one that may touch a nerve: Zaragoza, Patrick. If I'm correct, that's where the founding lodge of the Rosicrucian order can be found."

Some people have an annoying habit of displaying their grasp of a situation of which they think you have only partial knowledge, with a facial expression that resembles a gorilla about to pass wind. Kudashov's face reminded me of a picture I'd seen in a magazine purporting to represent such an event.

"Yes, I do know of Zaragoza, Nikita, but I'm wondering why you do and how you do?"

"Let's just say I know and leave it there for the moment, Patrick. I will explain later if you require me to." He still had the haughty look and his arrogance had not subsided.

"Okay, I'll go along with that. Did you meet Claudette Avogova at this party in Granitnyy?

"Yes, I did. A really lovely lady sadly blessed with a huge heart and it was that sensitivity that took her to volunteer to go to Sierra Leone. No one could allow her to leave and connect what was happening with the Ebola virus in Sierra Leone to what she'd seen in the operation at Zaragoza. What would happen if she reported all of that to her colleagues in the World Health Authority at the United Nations, or to those she could be in contact with at her old post in Porton Down? And that's why she never showed at Torp Sandefjord airport after February 2001. Instead, Paulette Simona arrived with Claudette's paperwork. Someone inside the CIA saved the legend of Claudette to avoid anyone getting suspicious."

He took one of the cigarettes I offered, and as I was about to light one for myself, he took hold of my arm to pause briefly in the peaceful stroll we were undertaking.

"I started to worry when Claudette told me she was part of that UN team, but there was nothing I could say that would change her mind. She was set on going and that was it. Our conversations about what happened inside the Zaragoza lab were never conducted in a clandestine manner; it was simply a woman telling a man about the fears she had in her work, mainly about the development of certain strains of biochemicals that evolve best in the environment created by the inert gases inside disused nickel mines. There were two underground shafts below the Zaragoza buildings where those experiments went on. In the main building where she worked, the work was concentrated on antidotes, vaccines and antibiotics. They were her priorities."

We continued our walk in the sun.

"One day in December 2000, she told me she thought that a new strain of a deadly virus called Filoviridae was being created inside one of those shafts. She'd overheard two microscopists speaking of a single-stranded negative-sense ribonucleic acid based virus. Apparently, that strain needed World Health Organisation permission to be developed, but by the sound of these two, none had been sought. Her alarm bells were ringing louder when she heard of the Ebola outbreak in Central Africa.

"When it became clear that vials containing the virus had been stolen from a shipment originating from Murmansk, she knew Zaragoza was to blame, but she was the type of person who blamed herself for not warning anyone. She was naive in thinking she could escape from those who arranged the theft from the ship in Freetown and then distributed the twelve vials. There was no escape. I became aware of her death sometime that year and a part of me wanted revenge for such a pure-hearted individual as Claudette. I think you can empathise with my feelings, Patrick."

I could, but I didn't say as much.

"From then on Torp Sandefjord became my second home. To go to Nikel was out of the question. As I've said, I had some idea who was running the show and therefore had no desire to be seen by anyone there, so for months I just watched the arrivals at Torp Sandefjord from the Zaragoza lab. There was one regular traveller. I had the flight details checked and the passenger was listed as Claudette Avogova. I approached her and told the imposter that I knew she wasn't who her passport said she was and threatened to tell the Norwegian authorities she was a Russian spy. I told her that in all probability they would take her somewhere isolated and very cold to shoot her, but not to shoot her dead. In the stomach, I said, then leave you in agony to bleed to death.

"It didn't take any more threats of mine for her to come round to my way of thinking and we picked up where Claudette had finished. Paulette became my high priestess with the eugenic engineering and wrote it all down for me. As I said, she never knew for sure who gave her the identity, but she did know who signed her transfer papers to the regional office in Oslo. Her name came from a CIA sub-divisional office in the Transportation Department in Virginia. I haven't got any reach inside America, Patrick, but if you and Fraser Ughert want that name, then that's where you need to look."

We were at the rear entrance to the main SIS building of the Beaulieu House Estate and I for one had a thirst. I suggested we took our work inside, but Kudashov wanted extra time to tempt me with one more thing, away from anyone else.

"It's not that I distrust anyone in particular, nor would I like to malign the staff here that look after me, but sometimes one must think of one's own self-interest above all else. Cilicia is my main concern and the one I'm most worried about. It's been a week since I reached out to Fraser Ughert and although I do appreciate how complex and difficult it's going to be to get her out of Moscow, I would have hoped that we'd be further down the road to her freedom by now. There is more I have to offer that would satisfy your own national interest and Fraser's cliquish interests, but that's not available until Cilicia is here and settled. I may also be able to shed light on the conundrum about that wedding gift of a box of keys."

I made him a promise to do all that I could with his granddaughter and the eugenics programme. I could do no more.

Chapter Twenty-Five: Mayor Swan

In 1969, the American President Richard Nixon banned the use of biological weapons, but that declaration only applied to stockpiles of such weapons on American soil. Of the more commonly known, such as weaponised Saxitoxin, Ricin, T-2 Toxin, along with a variety of virus infections, including six species of the Ebola viruses, huge amounts were not only stored by ruthless individuals, but manufactured by them as well. The nickel mineshafts at the Zaragoza Laboratory site were an ideal place for their storage and, as it turned out, they were also an ideal place for their destruction, but before I could have them obliterated, I needed proof of what Kudashov told me was true.

Cilicia Kudashov along with the acronym of NOMITE were both important issues to be resolved, but neither was as important as the destruction beneath the frozen waste at Nikel. I judged it to be prudent to organise the raid at the same time as arranging for a sample of the laboratory's work to be independently analysed. I had Christopher Irons in Moscow, who was more than capable of planting an explosive device inside a tunnel or the main laboratory or both, come to that, but I couldn't order him to do that. To sanction an attack on Russian property on Russian soil was tantamount to issuing a declaration of war and something any UK Prime Minister would never do however, it was something Fraser and I would do if it was proven to be necessary to save human life.

* * *

Fraser had read all Michael's findings on Sir Russell Macintosh, along with his son Sir Brian, and had come up with a surprising synopsis.

"I believe Dickie used the Macintosh name for Kudashov's Switzerland meeting because he wanted someone to look into Sir Russell Macintosh's diplomatic career, Patrick. I've found another anomaly. In 1977, Sir Russell met with the same newspaper reporter several times following Indira Gandhi's defeat in the general elections of that year; nothing unusual in that I guess, until you discover who that reporter was and what he subsequently became. The man's name was Vyacheslav Trubnikov. He was the Russian representative in India of *Pravda*, the official Communist newspaper.

"On the 25th July 2004, Vladimir Putin sent him back to India, only this time he was to be no journalist. He was appointed to the post of the Russian Ambassador to India. But let's go back to 1977, when Trubnikov was working for the First Chief Directorate of the KGB. I can't find any file we have about him, other than an updated one that states he was in the same department as Vladimir Vladimirovich Putin. To get more information seems to be beyond my retirement status, but I'm hoping you can get what's there for me, Patrick.

"I can't remember exactly what was said, but Dickie did mention Macintosh's name. Said something about there being an odour about the man's name. Most people knew he had contracted VD, so I assumed that was what Dickie was talking about, but now I'm not so sure. I have an inkling it was in some way to do with Francis Henry Grant, but I need your help. As we've said in the past, there was nothing Dickie did or said without having a reason."

I couldn't argue with Fraser on that point, so after outlining the semblance of the plan I had, I loaded Michael Simmons with the task of finding all he could on this Trubnikov. Whilst Fraser ruminated on my idea to blow up the Zaragoza laboratory, I took the first of two calls that evening from Christopher Irons. He'd spoken to someone who knew something of the laboratories at Nikel. This person, who Irons said he would trust with his own life, knew the site to have too much sophisticated security for a one-man demolition operation. Irons wanted a specialist team assembled and assigned to the job. Despite the risk, Irons wanted to do a solo run at the laboratories from the Russian side to get that sample I needed before any operation took place.

His second call came an hour or so later. It was to confirm reservations he had made for me and a serving British army officer for dinner later that night. It was with someone he said I knew and he could thoroughly recommend.

* * *

"I've had a cursory look at the satellite picture, Mr West, and I don't see any reason in the slightest why this operation would not be successful. Do you know how many people will be on the surface at the target?"

I replied that I had no idea.

"Then I take it you have no intel on security in place at the tunnel end of the target area either, sir?"

I shook my head in denial of knowledge, adding that I might have a better idea in the near future.

"I see. However that plays, do you accept there will be an issue with casualties?" His eyes carried a hard, emotionless stare that was anything but questioning to that emotive inquiry.

I added a simple, "Yes. That's acceptable," knowing my reply carried enormous human consequence.

"And what sort of window do I have to organise this operation, sir?"

"There is a proviso. A sample of what's in those labs should be in the UK by Sunday latest, possibly late Saturday. Authenticity of the sample will take less than hour. There is no doubt in my mind of the lethal consequence if what's manufactured there is allowed to progress. However, we do need proof of its capabilities. Allowing for that formality, I want everything in place within the next forty-eight hours and the expedition to go live this coming Sunday, major." I did indeed know Major Swan and knew him to be a highly reliable professional soldier.

* * *

That was all to come. For now I was with Kudashov at Beaulieu, with more to hear of his sad story.

"When Paulette told me the full extent of the demonic master plan behind the work that went on at the Zaragoza lab, I asked her why the laboratory technicians continued operating the eugenic breeding programme devised by Bohdan Dimitriyevich Valescov and his cohorts. I don't think I can ever forget her words, Patrick ..."

'I heard so many reasons. Money was the most popular mentioned. For some though, it was a moral duty to control breeding in order to increase those with desirable characteristics. The reason I found the most depressing were from those that

fully embraced the science, saying how we needed to kill off a few billion people that in their opinion were useless. Obviously, the few billion that needed to be removed did not include themselves. The whole programme was accepted as though it was just another day at the office.'

* * *

Liam Catlin had a new office in Moscow, only his was in the back of a nondescript van. He and his men, with the local family's help, had drawn a map of the Kitay-Gorod area with special regard to the exits from the apartment block leading into the Zaryadye Park and, from it, past the pedestrianised areas, onto routes where an 'abducted' Cilicia could be picked up without attracting too much notice. For five consecutive nights Liam had run a simulated exercise of extraction from Cilicia's accommodation. The favoured route was to use Star Square, then away from the city using Ulitsa Varvarka and the train to Vnukovo International airport. There was one safe house to fall back on if things went wrong, the home of the family helping them.

Christopher Irons made the introductions between Cilicia and Liam, and the three of them established the trade rules of the operation.

The family that Liam had working with him walked the route with Cilicia, interchanging every now and again so as not make anything look suspicious. With imperceptible nods of the head or small hand gestures, the 'lamp-burners' were pointed out to the 'escapee' and the final agreement on the operation was fixed. Christopher reported that Cilicia was a calm woman not likely to be fazed by the simulated act of abduction. All was arranged for the Monday following the operation at the mine. We changed from the initial plan of Sunday as there would have too many people off work strolling through the park. Monday was judged to be overall the quietest. I never told Kudashov when either operation would be live.

Before either of those events took centre stage, Michael Simmons had the Vyacheslav Trubnikov case file—it was still open, under Sir John's signature. Before speaking to him, I read through it. Fraser had been right in his assumption about Dickie Blythe-Smith wanting Trubnikov's name out in the open. But it wasn't for any straightforward reason that Fraser could imagine. As far as Sir John Scarlett was concerned, I wanted all he had on Trubnikov and I wasn't very patient in asking for it.

* * *

Hannah was fading from my mind, but had not yet joined hands with the other sad loves that had passed into the crevice marked 'confusion' floating around my head before settling in a corner and knocking loudly to be let out. Although our apartment did not pose a risk to my sanity any longer, it still threatened me with memories that appeared more in the dark than in the light of day. I had sat with the Jura and glass, reading Trubnikov's file for more than five hours, fighting against turning off the lights and retiring to bed. I wanted to think of her, but not as I thought of myself—as her killer. In my mind's eye, it was my face lying against the stock of the gun and my finger on the trigger as it fired. I'd watched her head disintegrate as the soft-point bullet hit it, slamming it against the opposite window to rebound and settle somewhere on the seat. It was a vision that was in my eyes whenever I closed them. It never went away.

* * *

There was a distinct irritation to Sir John Scarlett's voice when I called at six-thirty that morning. After calling me a few names, he told me how Vyacheslav Trubnikov had been a long-term target of the Russian desk, but his posting to India could not have come at a more fortuitous time for them, along with various other government ministries. Commercial trade with the once dominion of Great Britain had dwindled in a fast decline and the Foreign Office had given him the task of acquiring whatever inside knowledge they could obtain as to the cause. Vyacheslav Trubnikov could be a valuable commodity to have in finding ways to corrupt purchasing officials. Scarlett had been given a special fund to achieve success. Russia had become one of India's main trading partners, more for imports of goods than exports and it would be beneficial, he told me, to have the Russian ambassador on board to swing things more in our direction. I was aware of substantial government funding for that kind of dealing, but I didn't think I would be any good at bribery for trade favours. I wished him luck with all that.

As I was replacing the telephone receiver and considering my inadequacies in politics, I wondered if Sir John's department would use the same trade-craft for the betraying of commercial secrets as they would in the incitement of betraying a country. I concluded I was stupid to think there would be any other way. Equally stupid was the deduction that Dickie Blythe-Smith could have any notion that Vyacheslav Trubnikov would become pivotal in a trade war between Russia and us in 2007, with India as the prize. But where was the reason for the disclosure of Trubnikov? There was nothing in what I'd read of him, nor what Scarlett had told me, to shine light on why a man working in the First Chief Directorate of the KGB was so important in 1982 that hiding his name beyond the SIS was Dickie's first thought.

Chapter Twenty-Six: NOMITE

Later on Wednesday morning, I decided that with the promise of extraditing Kudashov's granddaughter from Russia shortly to be fulfilled, and plans for the destruction of Zaragoza in Major Swan's capable hands, I would spend my time trying to find the reason for Dickie's use of the message—No One Is More Important Than Each—the pseudonym used by Jack Price that was so mysteriously sent to Jacqueline Price. Trubnikov would have to wait his turn.

I first met Jack at a property he owned in Soho, in the heart of London, and it was shortly after our meeting that he introduced the acronym of NOMITE to me. Fraser said he had never heard it before. There was a faint possibility Jack might have mentioned the word or phrase to those he knew in Soho but, by now I reasoned, the ones I remembered would all be dead. I knew for a fact that on his death the apartment in Soho was sold and the revenue was divided equally between three friends of his who worked in that area.

At the time of gifting his flat, it was thoroughly searched by all four of us looking for clues as to his wife and children's addresses in Canada, but nothing other than a few questionable bottles of supermarket whisky was found.

His wife had left him, as had his two children and, for reasons I'd never got my head around, he had taken a liking to me, so much so that the house he had in Woolwich in southeast London was bequeathed to yours truly with instructions to sell it and put most of the money in the bank, for as he profoundly explained: *No one gives you an umbrella on a rainy day, son. You keep the money that's left to buy yourself loads of umbrellas. Then when it's raining, go stick one up a Guildford's arse.*

He used the name of the Surrey town of Guildford in a derogatory manner when referring to the top brass of the secret intelligence service. They all seemed to be living in and around Guildford when he was part of the same intelligence service.

A portion of the sale proceeds, a sum of five thousand pounds, he left to the church where he was to be buried and to pay for his funeral costs and the two plots he acquired for himself and Job, his indispensable right-hand man, whom I've said I had the pleasure of knowing. Before I sold the terraced house in Woolwich I painstakingly went through everywhere, looking for further clues to his life than the few he'd given me or I had discovered as we'd gone along trying to unravel a mystery that started in Vienna, Austria, in 1945, one in which my own father had a role.

Jack Price was a complex man in his professional service life, but the reverse was true for what private life he allowed himself to have. He had nothing of interest in my search in his belongings in either of his homes. But there was his notorious triangular-framed chair he'd moved to the more countrified air of southeast of London rather than leave it in the 'nightish' realms of Soho. I kept it for a few years, but that too had eventually gone to a curiosity shop, which was fitting, owing to my curiosity when I first saw it.

Jack died in 1973 and to my knowledge from that year onwards the word NOMITE had never been aired, but Dickie had remembered it, even though it was probably only once mentioned in his company. He was there watching over my shoulder when I signed all the official documents required of me by the secret intelligence service, but how on earth could he know that I would still be in the service twenty-five years on from when he sent the photographs and the critical message to Jaqueline Price? The answer to that was that he could not know. So why put in so much effort?

I was writing notes of papers putting places together where Dickie, Jack and I might have been at the same time, or if visited separately having a common denominator. One leapt from the small pile. Dickie had been one of the few who, like me, had attended Jack Price's funeral and interment held at St Michael's Anglican Church, East Wickham, not very far from Woolwich. We had light-heartedly discussed Jack's arrangements when lunching at the Travellers and I sarcastically suggested he took the title of Lord Woolwich when his inevitable investiture would be due. There was no doubt in my mind Dickie would have remembered the church all right. He remembered everything, did that sly old fox. That's where he sent the message about the hidden traitor in GCHQ. It had to be!

* * *

It was well past lunch when I could finally prise myself away from the responsibilities of chairman of the JIC and set off for the church. Frank and Jimmy went looking for the churchwarden as I visited Jack and Job's graves. For some silly sentimental reason I had brought two bunches of flowers, knowing full well that there were no vases to put them in. Having no other choice I laid them on the ground, wrappers and all.

"I say! Would you mind awfully taking the flowers out of the paper and the plastic, and putting all the rubbish in the green wheelie bin over there against the wall, please? Leaving it where you have means the paper and plastic will get blown everywhere if it's windy and up here, and on this hill we do catch the wind a lot."

He was a tall thin man, with a deep commanding voice, wearing a black cassock down beyond his knees with the sleeves rolled to the elbow with a loose clerical collar. His head was shaded from the hot sun by a white Panama hat. He had been behind a huge oak tree in the corner of the small cemetery and seen me before I had a chance to see him. His reproach made me feel uneasy as he walked towards me carrying a small bin stuffed with waste paper.

"I'm sorry if I sounded a little brusque just then, but paper in general is the bane of my life. If it's not inside the church being delivered by the postman, it's outside. Confetti is lovely, of course, but when it gets everywhere it becomes an intolerable pest. Whatever you do, don't start me on plastic! If only it wasn't used, then it would not be left lying around."

The lenses in his black-rimmed glasses were thick and concave, making his grey eyes seem larger than in truth they were, but nothing could disguise his young age. Even though it felt disrespectful, I asked —"How old are you, vicar?" removing the flowers from the wrapping as I did.

"I'm twenty-nine. And now you're looking somewhat perplexed and disappointed. Here, let me take the flowers and spread them out for you. That way I can make sure what's in your other hand gets disposed of properly. No disrespect intended in that remark. Which grave are they for?" he asked, his manner now subdued.

"They are for the two of these. I had the privilege of knowing both men." Waving my arms, I indicated the two headstones in front of where we stood. "I owe you an apology," I added, "but I was hoping the vicar here was older than you. You're right, yes, I was disappointed. Sorry I was so obvious, but I always assumed vicars to be old. Anyway, my wife, Mrs West, died last week and I was hoping you might have a plot where she can be buried. She would be close to both my friends and I'm sure she would have welcomed that."

"I'm sorry for your loss, Mr West, but as for a burial, then I'm pretty positive the church cemetery is full, but the right people to speak to are at the council offices who deal with those matters. I can give you their telephone number if you wish. I will have it somewhere in the vestry." His eyes begged for company and I was not about to disappoint him.

We were walking towards the main church building when he turned to face me. "Sorry, but your name is West, is that right?"

"It is, yes. Why, does it ring a bell?"

"It does somewhat, Mr West. I took over the parish last year from a minister who had devoted thirty-eight years to serving the name of God and the parishioners of East Wickham and beyond. A very honourable and humble man was Reverend Martin Jenkins." He crossed himself, then looked at me. "Martin left an envelope addressed to a Patrick West. Could that be you?"

I told him it was, showing him my Home Office pass with my name and photograph on it.

"In that case you must be here for the envelope he left in my charge. It was open, so I looked inside. It had a sort of Christian message if I remember rightly. No one is more important than each. I'm pretty positive that was it. Probably meaning: there's nobody more important than the person beside you. Is that about it, do you think, Mr West?"

"It's not far removed from that, vicar, yes."

We passed Frank as we entered the church and he asked, "Is everything alright, sir?"

I said it was, which stimulated the vicar to ask if I was a man of importance.

"We are all important in our own way, are we not?" I answered.

"Indeed we are, but I can't think of too many people who would have a message sent to him via our sacred church dated twenty-five years ago. At least, that is the date on the envelope. Was it a Christian message or could it have referred to some sort of Marxist theory?"

"I not aware it had either connection. It was designed for a small group of people who shared the same purpose."

"Well, we're here now, Mr West, and at a guess, I don't think you will want the council's phone number for your wife's laying to rest."

We had arrived in the vestry.

"I think it's the letter you're after and nothing else. Not my concern of course, it's just that I think I'm in the middle of some sort of espionage hurly-burly and it's caught my imagination."

I smiled and tried to look uninterested in his supposition, but that charade was ruined when he handed me the opened envelope with Jack's motto typed on one sheet of paper inside above one solitary name.

"Who sends a note with an anagram and a name written on it that's picked up twenty-five later other than a spy?" he asked, tilting his head to one side with a smug grin on his face.

By now I'd had enough of his arrogance. "If I were a spy, vicar, then I would hardly admit it, would I? If true, that could amount to treason, as would you divulging anything that's happened here today. I advise you to forget about the envelope and its contents. That advice is not only applicable to legal obligations you are bound by, it is also for your own safety. This subterfuge was to hide a particular secret that needs to stay hidden. You will receive notification of those restrictions from the Home Office as soon as I leave. Please, do follow the advice. You really do not want to be on the wrong end of the Official Secrets Act, I can assure you of that."

* * *

I looked at that meaningless four-letter name a thousand times on the drive from the peace and restfulness I'd found on a beautiful hot sunny day in the shade of a church on the outskirts of London, wondering what surprises were waiting to be discovered. In the meantime, I phoned ahead and ordered all we could find on GCHQ during the seventies when Geoffrey Prime was in

J section through until 1982, when Dickie's message was mailed to the Reverend Martin Jenkins.

Chapter Twenty-Seven: Vyacheslav Trubnikov

It was one week to the day of Hannah's death and the funeral arrangements were finalised. She was to be buried in the Hesse family mausoleum at their stately home in Brockenhurst, in the New Forest, Hampshire. Hannah's older brother and Samuel Rothschild, one of her godparents, had organised all the necessary arrangements. I wanted the operation at Zaragoza and Cilicia Kudashov's staged abduction over and dealt with before my mind could manage to say goodbye to my dead wife.

I instructed the pathologist not to release her body until the Tuesday following on from, hopefully, the successful outcome of both those operations.

I had not contacted Hannah's brother, who lived at the Manor, since his rude denunciation of me. I rectified that on Thursday afternoon after spending part of the morning in consultation with Sir John Scarlett at his ultra-modern offices at The Box, Vauxhall. Her brother's complaints had, for the time being at least, diminished, leaving his demeanour far more conciliatory than a week ago on the evening of his sister's murder when we last spoke. He accepted the necessity for the length of time before her entombment, adding his praise for the swift operation in identifying and disposing of her killer. He seemed to know that I was present at Victoria Station when that occurred. I neither cared, nor knew, if he was guessing or had been told. But by the time we finished speaking, I was satisfied that any disagreement between us had been settled and Hannah's funeral would pass without any unnecessary animosity.

I found Sir John in one of his flag-flying patriotic moods, celebrating an anniversary of an unsuccessful attack on the SIS headquarters building by the IRA. It wasn't the anniversary of the attack as such he was celebrating, but the apprehension of the three men who carried it out. He was smiling as he recalled their capture, but his smile faded when I repeated the reason for my visit.

"I've looked into this Vyacheslav Trubnikov and it seems that your department missed a trick in 1979, John. How well did you get on with Sir Brian Macintosh's stepfather, who was head of this department at that time?"

"Francis Henry Grant? Yes, I told you that I remember him. He was a standoffish sort of chap. He came up through Eton and Oxford and was a bit harsh on those having anything less of an education. He and I got on well enough and if I recall correctly, he was great friends with Fraser Ughert. Probably Ughert would give a clearer picture than I, but are you suggesting incompetence on his part or something worse?"

I didn't answer, but went a different route. "Reading between the lines of a communiqué from the Indian Embassy in Delhi, dated January 1979, addressed personally to Francis Henry Grant and automatically copied at the Foreign and Commonwealth Office, it would seem that Russell Macintosh was aware of the relationship that was building between his wife, Elizabeth, and Francis Grant. Mrs Macintosh was often in London, staying at the family home in Chester Square, where Grant was, as noted in

Trubnikov's file, seen on numerous occasions. Unfortunately for your ex-head of station, living opposite the Macintosh's London home was the Member of Parliament for Kidderminster, a friend of the Home Secretary and one of the men who had appointed Grant to his intelligence position. Maybe Elizabeth Macintosh mentioned it to her lover and he was of the opinion that the upper class don't tell tales on each other, or maybe she never knew who her neighbours were, but I doubt that very much. Which leaves only my first conclusion: Grant could not have cared less, relying on the upper class not telling tales on their upper class fellows.

"If the Director General of Soviet counter-intelligence was not clever enough to realise he was cheating with the wife of a chap who had neighbours overlooking her front door who knew the Home Secretary—a man her husband had gone to school with, and being the same person who had appointed him—then that would be why your department missed the trick with Trubnikov. Because Macintosh was in love with the Russian journalist, and his love was used by the First Chief Directorate of the KGB in

Moscow Central ... possibly by no other than Vladimir Vladimirovich Putin.

"The proof of Grant's incompetence is right there in the files, John, except they are not listed under Eton College or Oxford University, or past unethical behaviour of heads of station. They are in letters sent from two disgusted members of Sir Russell Macintosh's staff at the Indian Embassy in Delhi addressed to the Foreign Office and forwarded on to MI6. You told me you've been wanting Trubnikov for years, well your department had him, but never looked past the colour of the school tie.

"Take a look at the Indian sub-file at the Foreign Office of the February of that year. It's not digital, John, it's typed and a little long-winded. I believe Dickie Blythe-Smith knew of Trubnikov and what was happening with our cultural attaché, and used methods outside of house to deal with it. I'd love your thoughts on the matter when you have time.

"Right, let's move on and discuss this Iranian thing that the PM wants done with the International Atomic Energy Agency. Have we anyone close to the Director General of the IAEA through diplomatic links or someone we could use in his role as a lawyer? I need to have something on the table by Monday next week at the latest as I'll be seeing him at Hannah's funeral the following day. Of course, that's if I can avoid seeing him beforehand. Thank you, incidentally, for accepting the invitation on behalf of the SIS. Is it Julia you're fetching with you?"

"It is, yes, and I don't wish to appear insensitive, but we won't be staying after the church service, Patrick. The weather is forecast to remain as is, with the addition of a stiff breeze for the whole of next week. My yacht is moored very close at Bucklers Hard on the Beaulieu River. I thought of taking the boat around the Isle of Wight for a couple of days if nothing turns up to interfere with that idea."

We shared one of those all-knowing, all-recognising smiles that convey a degree of deviousness known to occur in higher management circles but never passed down to the ranks below. It was he who next spoke.

"I have a placement in mind for the IAEA thing, which I'll get on to straight away. As for the 1979 thing, with a previous Director General, are you intending to open an inquiry into the matter, or will you allow me to use the information regarding Trubnikov, in GB's best interests?"

"Too ancient to have any relevance in today's world to be worth an inquiry, John. However, there may well be some mileage you can back me up with, apropos of the trade figures. Other than that, it's all in your good hands to deal with as you please."

* * *

I had briefly spoken with Fraser over the selfsame Indian Office sub-file and the one Dickie had covered his back with, which was safely locked away in the vaults at the Foreign and Commonwealth Office no doubt. Dickie was several things and one of his most important characteristics was being ultra careful. I said nothing of my visit to St Michael's Church to Fraser. Again it was not through lack of trust, it was because I needed to glue everything together in my own mind in order to get where I wanted to be. In any case, I told myself, if Dickie wanted his old fishing partner, Fraser Ughert, to know what he sent to the church, then he would have told him.

* * *

It was my contention that Sir Russell Macintosh did not die accidentally from an allergy to penicillin. Health records of staff employed at GB's embassies are stored on files lodged where the Foreign Office send their diplomats. This has always been the case, since the inauguration of the Foreign and Commonwealth's Office. Two copies are kept; one at the F&C here in London, and one wherever the diplomat was assigned. I found the original paper copy at the Foreign Office. Someone had redacted all the information about allergies. There was an autopsy report redacted where it should show the cause of death. Neither Fraser nor I were great believers in coincidences. Fraser had his own theories.

"Maybe that was what Dickie was trying to avoid—a quarrel between the diplomatic and the intelligence services that was building. There would be few walking away from that unscathed. Certainly Sir Russell would have rocked many boats if the affair between his wife and the head of MI6 was ever made public. And, of course, if Grant had done his job properly and found the sordid love affair Macintosh was having with a Russian spy in India, then we would have had another scandal on the Philby scale.

"Nobody would want another disgrace of that magnitude so Dickie quietly removes one of the problems, leaving Vyacheslav Trubnikov in place, undisturbed. I'm guessing of course, but maybe Dickie was ordered to hide it and he didn't fully agree. That's why he sent Miles Faversham to collect those Solidus papers from Kudashov using the Macintosh name. He left it out there for someone to find if they ever looked hard enough."

"I think you're correct, Fraser, all apart from the bit where you said someone to find if they ever looked hard enough. I think Dickie left it out there for when someone *did* look hard enough, and I'm coming round to the opinion that he meant that person to be me.

"In May 1979, the general election returned Margaret Thatcher for the first time and a Conservative majority in the House of Commons of not many. If this sordid affair would have broken in the early days of her government, then who knows how history might have changed.

Anyhow, there's no point us looking for the reasons behind Dickie's decision; they were multitudinous in everything he touched. But there is something else I want to do with Vyacheslav Trubnikov before we push him aside and deal with what I found at St Michael's Church." He could hardly contain himself as I heard the frantic intakes of tobacco from his pipe. "I shall keep you guessing until later tonight. What time are you and Molly arriving?"

"Is your memory going, Patrick? You arranged the transport to pick us up from here at four, so allowing for the traffic, I guess we should arrive around five, or thereabouts. The show starts at eight, but Molly's meeting her friends in the American bar at The Savoy at seven-thirty. She'll have plenty of time to rearrange your kitchen in the apartment and your life in general, before she leaves. I'm surprised she's allowing the housekeepers to cook for us and didn't insist on doing that herself. When we were there she insisted on cooking."

* * *

From Vauxhall and Sir John's lavish surrounds, Jimmy drove to Group's more modest and functional headquarters in Lavington Street, at the Borough, where we arrived by the time I had finished speaking on the phone to Fraser. Michael Simmons had temporarily returned to Group to access the AIS decoding machinery at Greenwich more effectively. I didn't ask for the technical reasons, I just nodded when he told me and left him to it.

As instructed, he had transferred all intercepted coded messages from the signalling facilities at RAF Menwith, originating from Delhi, India between 1975 and 1979 and intended for Moscow Centre. There were seventy-three in total. They had been worked on at the time of sending, but remained unreadable for Menwith Hill; however, with the facilities at Michael's fingertips, the encryptions could be deciphered and read.

I felt a tear in the corner of my eye as I walked past the office Hannah once occupied before we had married. However, by the time I was settled in the screening room I had composed myself and was ready for work. I had restricted those who attended to three: Michael Simmons, myself, and the station officer at Group. The screen showed a sequence of low-grade intelligence passed on to Moscow, then it stopped before automatically reloading with more images and began again each time a message had anything of a higher classification than a C rating. This filtering method went on for around thirty minutes, until the screen cleared and A+B rated messages were listed in date order. All was running without incident until a signal dated fourteenth of April 1979 appeared with an A rating beside a decoded CIA company insignia. It read: *Soviet planning, preparation, operation, etc., gone.*

Under normal circumstances I wouldn't have given it much more than a cursory inspection before passing it on to Sir John's desk. It was from a CIA officer operating in an Eastern Bloc country, signalling a Russian foreign intelligence agent stationed in India, who relayed the coded signal on to Moscow Centre. But it was the originating country that hit me hard in the stomach. It was sent from Prague in Czechoslovakia. From inception to finish I was led to believe there was never a CIA ground presence anywhere in

Czechoslovakia. If that presence existed in 1979, why would it have disappeared by 1982 when I went there and why would there be no record of them being there held in the United Kingdom? If my initial thoughts about Dalek Kava's weakness being used by the CIA were wrong, then he was in no position to get movement intelligence of Soviet planning in 1979. No, Dalek Kava might well have had a connection through his father to the Czech secret intelligence, but he was not connected to America's overseas intelligence. There was a Soviet double agent inside Czechoslovakia in '79 that Dickie was showing us. The trouble was we needed to rid ourselves of the blinkers that were narrowing our vision.

* * *

I wanted a few more answers from Kudashov, whom I was sure would be more inclined to open up on the things he was holding back after a successful raid on the Zaragoza laboratories and a triumphant extraction of his granddaughter for Moscow. However, if he continued to withhold information, I would be in a stronger position to force his hand by threatening to turn Cilicia loose and anonymously notifying the Russians of a botched abduction by some Chechen rebels with whom they were at war.

Despite feeling more optimistic than ever in finding the reasons behind 'the mystical ball' that Dickie started to roll in 1982, my apprehensive feeling persisted for no discernible reason. I put it down to just butterflies failing to settle with all that was going on around me. I wanted to run some things past Fraser before confronting Kudashov, and if my suspicions were right, then I needed to do that before Sunday's operation took precedence over other matters.

Chapter Twenty-Eight: Two Russians

Molly had left to rendezvous with her old friends from Fraser's service days at the American Bar first, before enjoying the Gilbert and Sullivan dramatic operetta of *Iolanthe* at the Savoy Theatre. The three of us had dined together and afterwards she commended my housekeepers on their culinary skills and thoroughness in their other duties.

"I'm impressed," she declared emphatically when her PPO escorted her to the waiting car for the short journey. As soon as the car pulled away from the courtyard below the panoramic windows of the apartment, Fraser lit his first pipe since his early evening arrival and I fetched the Jura.

We smoked, imbibed, and exchanged a variety of thoughts over the Macintosh, Grant, Trubnikov trilateral affair and reached an agreement that my theory of Grant's omission of Macintosh's indiscretions was done purely to save reputations, especially that of Elizabeth Macintosh. We went through Major Swan's operational plans for Sunday and even examined the funeral plans that Hannah's brother had supervised, before the real fun started.

I showed Fraser the confidential signal of April 1979 that I'd seen earlier that day, explaining how, in my opinion, none of what Michael discovered in the signals from Menwith Hill was easy to understand unless we both thought along the lines that Dickie Blythe-Smith would adopt in the early eighties if he wanted a name to be hidden.

* * *

In June 1981, an intelligence information report was addressed to the Russian counter-intelligence desk from an untraceable relay point in Warsaw, Poland. It provided an in-depth study of long-term and short-term planning, preparation, operation and evaluation of Eastern Bloc exercises. Included in the paper was an explanation of the purpose and nature of each series. In essence, it was a follow-on from the signal of

April ’79, but this report had far more significant detail. Among the many attachments was a calendar plan of the ‘Most Important Training Enterprises of the Soviet Armed Forces’ for one year, and an orientation plan for the following five.

Seeing the ’79 draft, I can say it was good. High quality stuff, but insignificant compared to its big sister of ’81. That one was red-hot material with intelligence information ranging from the training of technical communications troops to the training directive of the Soviet Ministry of Defence, and the list of joint multi-national Air Defence exercises. It would have blistered fingers of the top-floor analysts when they handled it in 1981.

The CIA staffers in the decoding rooms at RAF Menwith Hill said the signals of ’79 and ’81 were virginal. Unblemished by any outsiders’ dirty prints placed on them. Although I have to reluctantly believe that to be strictly true, I’m of the mind that somehow Dickie Blythe-Smith had the information of both signals as they went out from Czechoslovakia and then the one from Poland. If I was right, it would explain how the

Polish colonel that Jana Kava contacted could have known the GCHQ insider.

Carrying along the line of my hypothesis, the sensitivity of those '79 and '81 signals could have been why Kudashov messaged the name the Polish colonel had given Jana in the Odessa coding straight to Dickie on the top-floor. That was logical, if I could ignore why Dickie would take all this trouble to hide a name that at least one other person would know.

I could understand how Kudashov did not know the name of GCHQ's insider, because the name was written in the new code, the key to which I had only just relayed on to London. If the signal containing the CIA insider's name had been sent in the Soviet Union new military code, then eventually all at the Russian desk would know it. That would not be Dickie Blythe-Smith's plan, nor was it his plan to show it to Kudashov and let him use Odessa rules and relay it on to the top floor—eyes only, Dickie. No, Kudashov would easily be able to decrypt the first Soviet coding working backwards from his Odessa coding.

That didn't sound like Dickie's way of operating. If you're on your own at the top of the tree, then you're on your own if you come down to play with other people's toys. Dickie had another code, and I was betting someone outside of my narrow vision had given it to the Polish colonel.

There was only one person who could do that—the rogue CIA foreign intelligence agent who sent London the '79 and '81 Warsaw Pact information report. Both were important turning points for British intelligence but, as I said, the '81 was dynamite, whereas for my theory to work, the '79 intel was a Russian-inspired ticket to buy into our complete organisation and I thought I knew where that ticket took the Russian agent. Something happened between 1979 and 1981 that changed the philosophical political leanings of a CIA operative working for the KGB into working for us. Easy, eh? All that was left was to find out what that was.

* * *

I went looking for a file Hannah had been working on and had taken to Sussex on her last journey; the one on Geoffrey Prime, whilst I left

Fraser to begin to read the parts of the 1981 document, entitled *Diagram of Conversion Needed For Soviet Command Structure To Move From Peace To War.* Heavy reading for most of us, but to Fraser with his Cold War background and thirst for conspiracies, an Enid Blyton *Famous Five* novel.

The Warsaw Pact Joint Enterprise Plan consisted of a schedule of all joint exercises—combined Armed Forces, special forces level, army level, air defence, long range bombers, naval squadrons and rear services. The plan also included scheduled meetings of Warsaw Pact Military Council: chiefs of the General Staff; chiefs of Intelligence; heads of branches of arms and services; directorates of reconnaissance; air defence, and; anti-aircraft troops. Also included were radar installations along with their communication systems. Air force divisions and numbers. Naval squadrons and rear echelons. Numbers of rocket and artillery troops, engineering troops and chemical troops and to crown it all—communication log-ins for daily encryptions and online relay signal stations. The Holy Grail!

Exercises and deployments with the cryptonym 'ZAPAD' were organised and conducted by the General Staff of the Soviet Defence Ministry. These were seen as the eve of victory over the West using conventional forces and, if necessary, limited first-strike nuclear weapon. When in the ultimate final throes of this coded exercise, or as was foreseen, the real thing, command would be handled by the Central Politburo only.

The report went on to say that as of the end of 1981 there had been only two ZAPAD exercises, and they differed from each other so much that really they were two different types of exercises under the same cryptonym. The first exercise was conducted in May 1977 on the territories of the USSR, Poland, Czechoslovakia and the German Democratic Republic. It utilised the command structure, staffs and designated units of the Soviet armed forces from the Group of Soviet Forces in Germany and the western military districts of the USSR, as well as armed forces of Poland, GDR, and Czechoslovakia.

The second ZAPAD exercise was conducted in September 1981, exclusively on Soviet territory. The only participants allowed were Soviet armed forces from the Baltic and Belorussian military districts, the Soviet Baltic Fleet, and Soviet Strategic Rocket Forces. Delegations of leaders of the respective defence ministries were invited as observers. Very importantly—no Warsaw Pact forces were involved.

The purpose of the first ZAPAD exercise in 1977 was to test the new concept of management by the Soviet Supreme High Command and the commanders of the divisions of the military, the strategic deployment of Warsaw Pact forces for war and the conduct of those forces for offensive engagements in the long-term theatre of military operations. Conclusions drawn from this exercise subsequently helped the Soviets to force through a new wartime command formation.

The aims of the second ZAPAD exercise in 1981 were not clear. From fragmentary information, it appeared that the more important aims could have been: testing of the newest weapons systems and equipment of the Soviet armed forces, and the then development of recommendations for further technical improvement by the internal armaments industry. It could also have been for the testing of new concepts of conducting offensive operations by the use of a new concept called Operational Manoeuvre Groups (OMGs). Fast moving troop deployments aimed at securing identified Western key command centres. The report contained those centres.

Conclusions with command configuration, along with points of incursions and seizures, were listed on seventeen sheets of decoded script. In essence, where the '79 intelligence opened a window onto various Soviet military based organisations, the 1981 report gave the USSR's exclusive plans for war. The status required to access this magnitude of classified material must have been at the highest level of command. Possibly this was a Russian American who could speak and behave as a Russian of influence and had a background in espionage. The information was so good, he could even have been a member of the Politburo.

* * *

Christopher Irons telephoned at the prearranged time for a three-way conversation with his old boss, Fraser, and his new one, me. One new piece of information was added to the puzzle as we went through the details of Cilicia Kudashov's staged abduction. Fraser had unearthed some information that was missing about the Director of the Communication Centre where she was departmental head of a separate 'K' section, monitoring the decryption machines that dealt exclusively with NSA/CIA transmissions. The head of the department's name was Anatoly Vladimirovich Malikova. More important than his name was his status; he was a nephew of Nikita Sergeyovitch Kudashov's wife, Anna.

At first I queried Fraser's information, believing that Kudashov would have told me that it was his wife's nephew who was holding Cilicia, but then I remembered his warning about how the plan would be jeopardised if he was not told before it went ahead. Could that have a bearing on the family relationship Anatoly Vladimirovich Malikova held?

Fraser had come across it during his continued interest in Victor Rothschild and the spreading influence he had on the society that Guy Burgess, Donald Maclean, Anthony Blunt and

Kim Philby moved in, but more so in the case of Kudashov's newly exposed relative and his connection to John Caincross, the fifth member of the unholy Cambridge five. It was here that I realised Dickie had a big ball rolling and all I had on it was a fingertip.

* * *

Caincross was a translator and integral part of Bletchley Park, the WWII codebreakers, who was considered to be the British intelligence officer who leaked details of German army lines of attack at the Battle of Kursk to the Soviet Army, and thereby delivered a massive defeat to the German High Command. According to archives discovered in 1945, Caincross supplied the Soviets over five thousand documents, mostly about the Nazis, but a considerable amount concerning the future capabilities of Great Britain and the Commonwealth in peacetime. Included in his treachery were future plans regarding sovereignty issues over India and other such commitments in the Far East. His contact inside the KGB for all the information he sent was a Major General Vladimir Anatolyevich

Malikova, the father of Anatoly Vladimirovich Malikova. Neither of us believed that to be a co-incidence.

Chapter Twenty-Nine: Prime Time

RYAN was the four-letter name Dickie sent under the cryptonym of NOMITE and I found his full name, Randall Ryan Cavershall II, first recorded at GCHQ in May 1973, listed under the following account: vetted January at Oxford. Leading language graduate, honours and distinction, Russian dialect translator, attached to J Division. In 1977, following Geoffrey Prime's resignation from GCHQ over his dislike at delivering lectures about message analysing, Ryan was moved up to fill the gap Prime left in the J30 section of Special Sigint that dealt exclusively with Soviet intelligence.

Ryan became one of only three officers allowed into the vault at J Division, but unlike Prime he was not allowed to take documents home. There was yet another vacancy left open by Prime's 'untimely' resignation—that of leading a team of twelve transcribers in another part of J Division, the Higher Intelligence Specialist part. Ryan volunteered and was promoted to it. As I looked closely at the areas of his responsibility, it became clear that he was accountable only to himself. Who better to expose a spy than another spy, and then take his place?

I showed Fraser what I'd found in the records from Cheltenham after Molly had returned from her night out and was safely in the adjoining apartment sound asleep. If she smelled her husband's pipe tobacco or heard the clinking of glass as the lip of the Jura bottle kissed the whisky glasses, then I think she might have demanded their return home to Chearsley in Buckinghamshire immediately, but as she didn't I thought the two of us could play at solving mysteries until the puzzle was tired of us.

It was almost three in the morning when we decided that enough was enough. We had ideas of what could have happened, but we were short of people who could confirm those ideas, However, there was one perhaps who could tell us if 'Ryan' was the traitor Dickie suspected, and if we could jog his mind a little further, perhaps confirm my idea that Ryan was the CIA operative in Czechoslovakia before I arrived there.

* * *

Being married as long as Molly and Fraser, almost forty years I think, was something I could never have imagined for myself until I had the great fortune to meet Hannah. I had known her for such a short while in measurable time, but an eternity in unquantifiable painful memories. I suppose there must be several advantages of a long marriage and one certainly must be the telepathy between the couple who have survived the years. I experienced Molly's clairvoyance in knowing that Fraser was not going home to Buckinghamshire straight away as she finished breakfast and then bade her husband farewell with a kiss to his cheek and one to mine.

"Look after him," she said to me, adding, "he's a complete idiot when it comes to looking after himself. Don't let him smoke too much and don't let him drink as if he's trying to save all the distilleries in Scotland." Then to Fraser she said, "Just be careful please, and come home in one piece."

With that, she disappeared through the door, down the steps to the apartment's gated entrance and the waiting car. The comfort inside would be scant recompense for her husband's company, but a journey I guessed she would have made a hundred times before—on her own. There is a difference in how one can be alone whilst in the company of others, or alone in one's own company. I thought no more of it, leaving the harmony of self-sufficiency to another day to explore when loneliness for companionship overtook this lazy body of mine. For now, we had Geoffrey Prime to see and then, if time permitted, off to Beaulieu and a reluctant Russian who'd said nothing of a relative named Anatoly Vladimirovich Malikova, whose father had a prolonged period of contact with a traitorous man to this country.

* * *

Prime's record was not easy for me to read. He was sentenced to a total of thirty-eight years imprisonment in November 1982 when he pleaded guilty to seven counts of espionage, and three counts of sex offences against children. Thirty-five of those years were passed down for his spying activities and only three for the sex offences.

I calculated his release date to be some time in 2020, not 2001, as in reality it had been.

He served only half his sentence. Eighteen months for indecently assaulting three girls aged eleven to fourteen, and seventeen-and-half years for giving away some of our secrets to the Soviet Union. I know I'm a cynic. I've recognised that illness in me for a good many years, but the disproportionate level of justice for the children and their parents carried the stench of a social, privileged order that made me want to weep for justice. Social stratum considered the affairs of state far more important than the wellbeing of the working-class.

I had read that when Geoffrey Prime was posted to Kenya, in the late fifties, early sixties, he was so disgusted by the poverty he saw in the countryside, along with what he perceived was the exploitation of Kenya by the British colonial authorities, that he turned towards Communism as an answer to man's inhumanity to man. Had there been many as sensitive onlookers to Prime's lenient punishment for the sexual abasement of children he confessed to, then maybe the ranks of Communists would have been swollen by people who thought likewise when justice was dispensed so unevenly that day in November. Despite my cynicism and obvious abhorrence, I had to move on and interview this man.

On leaving prison, Prime moved into his deceased mother's house situated within nine miles of The Doughnut, the appellation of the Government's Communications Headquarters in Cheltenham, Gloucestershire. He registered with the police and was put on the sex offenders register; other than that, he was free to move around the same as anyone else. I didn't plan to stay long in his dead mother's house.

* * *

He was a tall, unshaven, gaunt man, with a grey receding hairline, ashen-faced with blue-framed spectacles through which two brown eyes stared at me, wishing I would disappear from his present into his past, but I wasn't going anywhere other than through the front door his left hand held only ajar.

I thrust an open wallet with a plastic card denoting I was Chief Superintendent Pritchard from the War Office Constabulary, at his face.

It was a plainclothes police officer from the War Office who arrested Prime, and I doubted any amount of time would erase the memory of that warrant card.

"We're coming in and you're not going to stop us, Geoffrey. Stand aside or you will be hurt." The file said he was sixty-eight, but on first impression he was nearer eighty-six or older.

"Have you a warrant?" he asked in a soft voice.

"No, I haven't. Nor am I known as being patient. But I do possess a very loud voice. Open the door or I'll use it to tell the neighbours exactly what you are, Prime, in case they don't know."

As the door opened, I was hit by the smell. Cats have never been my choice of companion. Not only for the way they tend to take everything for granted, but because I've encountered the same smell of litter trays that are hardly ever changed. I know that it's not the cats' fault, but that doesn't alter my view. Next to strike me was the shabbiness of the place matched by his own lack of self-respect. The shirt he wore was threadbare in places as were his trousers, making his whole musty stale smell irritate my nose. I sneezed loudly and noticed his bare feet. Dirty feet and smelly litter trays; where else would I rather be? He disgusted me.

His mother had passed away in this house whilst her son was detained in prison. She had few friends at the time and, as a consequence, her body was not found for six days after her fall, which according to the autopsy led to a painful, agonisingly long death. Geoffrey had no other close family. Of the not-so-close, not one attended her funeral to stand at the graveside with her convicted son. When I read that detail, it crossed my mind what had kept her nieces and nephews, her brother and sister away. Was it his treason or his perversion? I was already in a bad mood when those thoughts crossed my mind again and they did nothing to help.

Inside the three up, three down, grey pebble-dashed, terraced house, there was ancient faded wallpaper hanging from corners in the hallway, and in one place hanging more than halfway down. The room Prime showed us into was dark and dank with a worn, indistinct patterned carpet on which stood two armchairs and a faded sofa where lay four cats in various modes of repose. There was a low coffee table between the two soft chairs either side of an imitation log fire with a small, square piece of wooden furniture on top of which was a television. It was from beside that item of furniture that the smell originated: two fouled cat litter trays. In the other part of the long, undivided sparse room were four hard-backed, timber chairs and a dining table. I sat on one of the chairs at the table and indicated to Prime to sit opposite me. Frank opened the two windows onto the rear neglected garden and took a deep breath.

Prime offered tea. At the time of offering he smiled, adding a comment of how important he must be to justify a Chief Superintendent paying him an unannounced visit. When I failed to answer either his question or pass a comment on how important he was or not, he asked if he had done anything wrong. He was a squalid man in equally squalid surroundings and I had no intentions of hiding my hostility towards him.

The force of language I used and the volume of my voice in replying to his pointless question caused Frank to rapidly close the windows, adding, "Careful of the neighbours, boss. Remember what we said."

"Yeah, you're right, sergeant. We had better keep it down for Mr Prime's benefit. At least for now, Geoffrey, hadn't we? It's up to you if I remember that when we leave. I've only a few things to ask of you, Prime, and if you deliver straight, honest answers, I can move you out of here, give you a new identity, and offer you a new start in Canada or Australia."

His facial muscles went rigid as his hand rose to remove his glasses. My eyes followed the hand that was holding them; they were twitching involuntarily between his forefinger and thumb. He carefully placed the glasses on the table. He rubbed both eyes and replaced the blue-rimmed spectacles on his face, leaving his gaze to look through me as though there was something new for him to see. His eyes then narrowed into a question. "How do you mean?" he asked, in a hesitant voice.

"What do you mean by what do I mean? I mean what I said. The office told me you were intelligent. You had better be, Prime, for your sake. Listen carefully to what I'm saying and open your effing ears. New start, new place. First question, and do something with that effing window, sergeant. I'm suffocating in here. Ever thought of cleaning the cats' shit up, have yer?"

"I do most of the time, but I haven't been well lately. Oh, was that your first question?" His face had relaxed into a stupefying look. The vacancy of his expression made me think that he could have taken sedatives for the illness he spoke of.

"No, it effing ain't, you piece of shit. My questions are a lot more serious than about effing cats and if I don't get the right answer to the right ones, I'll see to it that the only thing you can afford to eat will be cat shit. No, of course you won't be eating cat shit. How silly am I? You won't be able to *pay* for cat shit. There is another consideration of course, before you stop thinking about the aforementioned shit and that is, will you have any teeth left after I have your name and the word paedophile painted on every blank wall anywhere near here. I'll even add your address for good measure, Prime. I might be able, sergeant, to get it in the local rag. Can you see the headline, Geoffrey? A convicted nonce living at blah, blah, blah. How does that appeal?

"Perhaps your neighbours don't know what a paedophile is, but they soon will once I get started. But, no, don't look so worried. What I want is not that difficult to deliver. If all you say ticks the boxes, then I'll go back to the Ministry of Defence and recommend to the Minister you get that new life I said you would. What I recommend gets done, no problems with that. Okay, here we go? Are you ready for this life-changing opportunity?"

His head was nodding like one of those toys on the back shelf of cars.

"What incentives were you offered to name Randall Cavershall II as an American CIA spy, Geoffrey?"

There then followed the confirmation I was after. Without any further inducement he pointed the finger at Cavershall and gave some further insights behind Dickie's reasoning why he was shown so much leniency inside the prisons where he was kept segregated from those who might cause him harm on behalf of those helpless children and their parents. I was following Frank along the narrow hall towards the front door when I stopped suddenly, causing the following Prime to close on me. I turned and 'inadvertently' trod hard on one of his bare feet. Of course, I apologised.

* * *

As Frank and I praised each other for our thespian skills playing the hard cops in a Cheltenham movie, Jimmy put the car in gear, and away to a waiting Fraser in Whitehall we drove. Neither of my PPOs bothered to ask if the relocation I'd promised Prime to his favoured Canada was going to happen. They both knew me too well for that.

* * *

"Are you saying that once Dickie was certain there was another mole at GCHQ, he offered Prime a protected prison sentence if he got the mole's name? And you are further assuming it was this CIA/Soviet double agent who supplied the teaser from Czechoslovakia in 1979. Is that about right, Patrick?"

"Yes, that's where I'm going with it. The CIA planted Cavershall in GCHQ without knowing he was already under Russian influence. The

CIA's idea behind having a spy inside Cheltenham was to gain additional information their Frosting programme was short on. They wanted a way into our most secret communications. One would have been the internal scrambled link between the Prime Minister's office and the War Department. Another was the link between the office of chairman JIC to the Strategic Command Centre in the Admiralty. Both those two, and four other vital UK defence issues, were handled separately through a division of GCHQ manned solely by the Director General's handpicked staff. Cavershall would be automatically co-opted into the staffing role once he was made head of J Division.

"As the Russians never had an ear inside the government's communications headquarters, they wanted everything Cavershall could get. In respect of the '79 information document, I'm working with the theory it was simply a taster in order to get the Russian 'spy' accepted by top floor at Century House. It's intriguing as there's no record of Cavershall leaving the UK. What there is, if you look closely, is an abnormal signal routed through a CIA relay outstation in Lucknow, India, on to their central command West Berlin Station and finally, so the AIS machinery in Greenwich tells us, to a hand receiving set with the coordinates registering to an address where Cavershall lived not far from Prime, in Cheltenham. That first originating signal that reached Lucknow was apparently a shortwave micro signal with a distance of no more two hundred kilometres.

"I'm presuming this signal originated from Vyacheslav Trubnikov's desk in Delhi following a command from the KGB at Moscow Centre. Who knows? That order could have come from a department where Putin worked. Obviously, Dickie did not have our facilities at Greenwich to work with. We must bless old Hardballs for that, Fraser, which I'm doubly sure you do. I reckon Cavershall told Dickie all about Trubnikov and the Delhi link when confronted with Prime's accusation."

"Excuse me if I'm missing something, Patrick, but where did the '81 report come from if there was no logistical officer working the ground and focusing on that amount of detail that is in that report? Are you saying the Russians gave up their crown jewels in a message sent to a hand receiver near GCHQ, and all the millions of pounds worth of monitoring equipment missed it? Do you honestly believe there was that amount of incompetency at GCHQ at the time?"

"No, Fraser, I would never accuse GCHQ of being incompetent. To my way of thinking, Dickie turned Cavershall when he found out he was a CIA plant but with Soviet loyalty. How he did that is open to all kinds of conjecture, but remember this: in the late seventies, early eighties, the world was hanging on to sanity by a strand of hair. We were fast approaching a nuclear war between the great powers of Russia and America. Dickie was almost three times young Cavershall's age, so I think he played the patriotic card. 'You're playing the protagonists against each other and it will only end up one way—world desolation, son. Work for us and we will be able to keep the USA and the USSR apart. Give us the power to do that, because we are the only sane ones left in the world.'

"Cavershall was given all the tuition that fifty years in the intelligence trade had taught Dickie. He guided Cavershall's every step it took in convincing Vyacheslav Trubnikov that London bought everything Trubnikov wanted to sell … with one enormous condition."

Fraser's impatience interrupted me. "You're getting almost as good as me at telling stories. Come on, laddie, let's get that condition on the table."

I smiled at the old form of address he had for me. Although I had been the instigator in asking that it was dropped since my elevation to the top chair, I missed his familiarity in that regard. Who knows for sure, but perhaps it was to do with marrying Hannah and not wishing her to think Fraser was disrespecting my position. Another possibility, and in all probability the truth, was my ego's need of massaging, having arrived at the throne of power that Fraser held before retiring. I ignored the use of 'laddie', and hoped for more, but I would not admit that to any examining psychiatrist in case they thought I put my ego before my wife's death.

"The condition was that Cavershall forced Vyacheslav Trubnikov to defect to our side, Fraser. Otherwise, none of this has any meaning."

Fraser stood from the sofa that Hannah normally occupied when we were together talking generally about this or that, and at once I was reminded of the normality of a life we had both spoken often of, away from secrets and lies, deceit and consequences, living as an ordinary couple in Sussex, enjoying a country way of life. I realised that form of normality could never be now I was on my own, but not at that moment. Now I had Fraser staring down at me, daring me to expose my explanation on how anything like that was possible. Someone of Trubnikov's importance to be turned and nobody else in the know other than a young CIA double-spy and the practised hand of Dickie Blythe-Smith on the verge of retirement, pension, untold fishing stories and the knighthood the old bugger deserved. I was ready to turn my back on the spoken normality and return to the nefarious life I chose.

"He did it because of the love affair Dickie told Randall Cavershall Trubnikov was having with a Polish colonel that was known by Dalek and Jana Kava. Ask me how I know that, Fraser." I hadn't meant to change the tone of my voice, but it had changed. I was demanding he ask that question like some dog barking to be let out. However, it was never my intention to give him a chance to reply.

"I think I told you that I was unsure, but thought I heard another voice in the background when Faversham contacted me on the embassy scrambled phone link after my elimination of Dalek's message hit Faversham's fax machine. When Miles started the first-phase debrief over the phone, it was a question he put to me that prompted me to think I was right and there was someone pulling Faversham's strings. He asked if either Dalek or his sister had said anything about a Russian? I told him a story Dalek had told me of a First Directorate KGB officer that had been on intimate terms with a Polish army colonel Jana and he regularly met."

Fraser was still standing but by now looking out of the huge windows overlooking the splendour of St James's Park. The window was open and he was consciously puffing his pipe so the smoke left the office. Lazily, I wondered why.

"If that's true, and I'm coming round to believing your tale, Patrick; why did Dickie need the information from Jana Kava's Polish colonel about who the traitor was?"

"Precisely, Fraser! That's where I've got to. Dickie didn't need the name of Cavershall. He had that from Prime. But when Trubnikov knew we knew about his love affair, his price for coming over to us was the Polish army colonel's life. Dickie's enticement was straightforward, *'Show me what you've got and we'll point the finger at your lover for you. If not, well, sorry about that, but we'll have to tell Moscow Centre what you and a colonel of the Polish army got up to. We have you hook, line, and sinker, old chap, but fear not; either way we will leave a series of clues leading back to a Czechoslovakian who was on the receiving end of military secrets given to her by your ex-Polish lover. The KGB will either love you as a patriot or shoot you as a spy. Your choice?'*

"And he did choose, Fraser. Trubnikov joined us with Cavershall holding his hand. Cavershall is told by Dickie to alert the American Embassy in Prague about their asset, Jana Kava, seeing a Polish army spy who's on the verge of jumping ship into their laps, but he's scared rotten of being caught. The Embassy is to give Jana Kava a lethal pill with instructions to pass it on to the colonel—*'in case things turn nasty and we cannot get you out.'* The only way Cavershall can get that message out and cover his back is by first using the Berlin station and then the Lucknow relay one until it hits Delhi. Dickie starts turning the screw on Trubnikov. He asks a simple favour. *'Tell your lover in Prague to give his Czech contact a message'*."

Fraser's impatience was showing in his voice and on his face, but I firmly believed my theory would not be something Fraser would enjoy hearing, so I never stopped him asking his questions before I elaborated on it further.

"I'm still confused, Patrick. If Cavershall's name was in Dickie's pocket, why did he keep that to himself? He never mentioned it to me, nor did I see it in any classified documents. Was Dickie still having a dig around after finding Prime and then Cavershall, do you think?"

"I can't be sure, but I don't think so." I didn't have time to finish my sip of whisky before Fraser fired another question at me.

"Why so much chicanery over this name Cavershall? It was current to the day, not now!

Why did it need being hidden in the cryptic message sent to the church where Jack Price and Job are buried? In any case, why leave it to chance that you would come along and work out his convoluted puzzle?"

"I haven't completely solved Dickie's puzzle, Fraser; there is still a considerable way to go, but I believe we're closing in fast. There are several things confusing me at the present. One is I'm not one hundred percent sure the name Dickie sent to St Michael's is the only name he wants us to have. I don't mean us, as in you and I. I mean whoever found it.

"Using the computers at Group and the AIS facilities at Greenwich, Michael Simmons has found that when Cavershall was at university he had a nickname derived from his father—Ryan Cavershall. Apparently, Ryan was preferred to Randall. In the preface to The Warsaw Pact Joint Enterprise Plan of 1981, there is a code for Ryan on the final sheet of that report. It's not obvious. It doesn't say 'Coded Ryan' or anything as plain as that, but read that final paragraph again, Fraser; it says, '*The purpose of operation Raketno Yadernoe Andropov Napadenie was to collect intel-*

ligence for potential contingency plans if the Reagan administration launched a nuclear first strike against the Soviet Union.'

"That piece of text comes from a programme initiated in May 1981 by Yuri Andropov, then chairman of the KGB. The 1981 report you read was sent to London one month later. Raketno Yadernoe Andropov Napadenie is an acronym for RYAN."

"How on earth did a foreign operative get the Russian military to headline an operation with the initials of his code name?"

"Easy when you have friends in high places, and Vyacheslav Trubnikov had some of the highest friends at the time, and that hasn't changed in twenty-five years. So, yes, Randall could have had it worded in such a way. Are you with me, Fraser?"

"Oh, yes, laddie, every beautiful step of the way."

"In that case, here's the first one to mull over. From the photographs that went to Image Recognition, I circulated a cut-out of Jana Kava's killer's face and had it sent to all friendly intelligence services. I didn't say why I was looking. We had one positive recognition. It was from the CIA at Langley. They pinpointed him as assigned to an outstation from 1979 until 1985. It's the same place where Black-Op G3 forces were registered as operating from when Mossad informed us of an insertion by a G3 agent at the Iraqi's nuclear power project at Kirkuk back in 2003. Different time but the same players, Fraser. Jana's killer was definitely CIA special forces. Michael contacted the outstation in Delaware. The signal we had back claimed he died on Operation Eagle Claw in 1980 when President Carter authorised that failed attempt of the rescue of fifty-three hostages held inside the US Embassy in Tehran, Iran.

Chapter Thirty: Friday's Drive

The vaults at the Foreign and Commonwealth Office contained a myriad of compelling documents, memorabilia and written accounts of deeds best left unmentioned in public. Fraser had access to these vaults when chairman of the JIC, and there's no doubt he visited them and made use of what he needed in there, but during his tenure the code name Ryan was not known by him, nor relevant to any operations mounted in GB's name, nor was the name Vyacheslav Trubnikov important for his enquiries. However, Trubnikov was now important to me.

Fraser had returned home to Molly, leaving me alone with my thoughts in the back of the ministerial car on the way to Beaulieu from Whitehall. I was closing my eyes, at times playing recognition games of whereabouts we might be on the oh so familiar journey, when I opened them. I was right a few times and wrong just as many, but in my dealings with Kudashov, I could not afford to be wrong by having my eyes closed in guessing games. That awareness would equally be applicable in my conversation with the Russian Ambassador to India, whom I planned to see very soon.

* * *

There were not many more 'missions' carrying the insignia RYAN filed in the vaults under Dickie's surname, but one of those that did, happened the year after the '81 report. It was allowed to be discovered by the CIA, who attributed it to a known Soviet defector and not to any agent named Ryan. This trick was successfully instigated one other time whilst Dickie was gainfully employed by the government of the day. Another of Ryan's operations was to leak a report in February 1983 of a top-secret KGB telegram to the London KGB residency, which was encoded and forwarded on to a personnel fax machine at an address accessed only by Dickie Blythe-Smith.

The telegram stated: *'The objective of the assignment is to see that the Residency works systematically to uncover any plans in preparation by the main adversary USA and to organise a continual watch that will be kept for indications of a decision being taken to use nuclear weapons against the USSR or immediate preparations being made for a nuclear missile attack.'*

An attachment to that message listed tasks for London-based Soviet agents to complete and report on. These included: the collection of data on potential places of evacuation and shelter. An appraisal of the level of blood held in blood banks. Observation of places where nuclear decisions were made and where nuclear weapons were stored. Observation of key nuclear decision makers. Observation of lines of communication, post office activity, reconnaissance on the heads of churches and banks, and surveillance of security services and military installations. Added on was the activation of all the Soviet-funded infiltration of Trade Unions in the UK. Taken as a whole, this leaked message was devastating.

When Dickie released the report, it was the view of the intelligence service that London was under immediate attack by the Soviet Union. I was unable to find two other faxed messages Dickie made reference to, but without the address or name of the sender—*Two messages filed in vaults*—was all I could find. Within the files I'd found there was nothing injudicious. All of Dickie's work was transparent, but in certain circumstances some files had been made difficult to find, given the normal set of conditions applicable to searches through top-secret archives. I vowed to search again for those missing two when time was less demanding.

When President Reagan deployed Pershing II nuclear-armed missiles in West Germany and then, almost immediately, began the Strategic Defence Initiative, it added up to more concerns for the Russian military and Politburo. Ryan reported on a crucial meeting between KGB high-ranking officers and the Main Directorate for Reconnaissance of the foreign intelligence service of the Ministry of State Security of the German Democratic Republic. That meeting concluded that a further 300 positions within the KGB were needed to combat what the Russians saw as American dominance of Europe. Each one of those posts was named and highlighted by Ryan in a signal of June 1982 that was lodged in file and signed off by Dickie, who retired that year.

As well as the above, Ryan listed parts of confidential plans being drawn up in the USSR to launch a satellite containing various smaller ones, all capable of firing laser beams and designed as a countermeasure to anything the Americans might deploy in this SDI—Strategic Defence Initiative. It had huge costs involved and according to Ryan's source, a cost the Soviets might not be able to sustain. A serious position had arisen.

Ryan's report suggested that a first strike policy might be the only option left to the Soviet Union if Reagan went ahead with the SDI programme. Fortunately for the world, nothing came of the Strategic Defence Initiative programme to antagonise the Soviet purse. We came close to the eradication of this earth that Ryan had little influence over, but Dickie Blythe-Smith did, with Bernard Nicholls and his Delineated Signal Intelligence Gathering having a lasting effect on the Soviet Union when the American President initiated a military exercise under NATO authority, coded Able Archer '83. That politically expedient exercise brought this planet as close to destruction that it had ever been.

The last mention of agent Ryan was in a message dated 17th July 2000. It had been consigned to the vaults four days later and signed in by Sir Richard Blythe-Smith. Taken at face value the wording of the coded message held little of sensible content, being in some kind of cryptic form more suited to a crossword puzzle than an intelligence signal, but bearing in mind Dickie's reputation of never wasting words, it needed my unmitigated attention. However, the prospect of solving it was not close to hand: *A Stone guards the money as it drains to the sea. The Russian is a danger, but it's the Finnish man you need to fear.*

Why the capital letter to Stone? The second part of the message referred to something I was already aware of. However, being aware of it made it impossible to forget.

It seemed as though the falsified agent coded Ryan that Dickie and Randall Cavershall developed along with the Director General of GCHQ, was responsible in so many ways for stopping the world's self-destruction. As far as I knew, Bernard Nicholls was still alive, enjoying his fishing in Alta, and the name of Ryan, along with Randall Cavershall, was allowed to retire from its connection to the British SIS to any part of the world Randall chose.

For the time being, I kept those final thoughts on Cavershall and his SIS-coded alias as Ryan to myself. I thought there was more to the open message that had been sent to St Michael's Church than a simple coding based on the middle name of a double-agent Dickie had discovered at GCHQ, but for now I wanted that left to me and me alone.

* * *

Despite my efforts to distance myself from my once marital state, all the thoughts spilling over in my mind were of Hannah. I could not shake the memory of those last shared moments with each other in the apartment, with me answering a call from the Prime Minister and her on the way out for the journey to Sussex. One of the fondest memories I had was of our first meeting in the offices of Group. Our awkwardness in me being her boss and she not wishing to jeopardise her job by having an unwise love affair. For most of my life I'd indulged in many sports and I confess, one of those sports was the pursuit, and hopeful capture, of attractive women. The chase was the adrenaline booster needed before one could enjoy the fruits of one's labour. Sadly, not always, was that the case. Sometimes I was the prey, but not every time was the thrill of being hunted rewarding when cornered.

The same applied when I was the hunter. Such things were on my mind when I saw Hannah. I was the boy playing at life and she was my beautiful quarry. However, it didn't work that way. For no logical reason that I could acknowledge, we fell into that place that poets bewilderingly call the state of love, the same place I had spent my life successfully avoiding. Four years is not long for lasting memories, but long enough for the painful loss of no more to come.

* * *

A few days after Hannah's passing, the Cabinet Secretary, Sir Nigel Hicks, the same man who had telephoned after her assassination and said nothing about taking things easy, came to see me in my office. The purpose of his visit was to offer the professional expertise of the in-house Ministry's medical 'therapy' services. During the first five-year period in the intelligence business, I had the misfortune to be 'invited' to visit the psychology practice five times over deaths that were either of persons close to me or someone I had killed in the line of duty. The purpose was to see if my psyche was damaged in any way because of the perceived 'trauma' involved in such occurrences.

I was not traumatised by any of them, neither was I traumatised in a psychological way by Hannah's murder. I did not take up Sir Nigel's offer. However, by one of those contrived accidents that are too obvious for everyone's benefit, the psychologist Sir Nigel had in mind was a very presentable young woman of fewer than thirty years' experience of everyday life and a mere ten years' experience of vocational training. She bumped into me the Thursday evening following Hannah's assassination when I was on my way to meet my wise and all-knowing colleague in the Foreign Office before I met with Sir John Scarlett.

I had never met this particular psychologist before; she was far too young for that. By anyone's standards, she was courteous and polite in a professional manner. It crossed my mind that she could be of help in silencing those voices in my mind.

* * *

Kudashov was not yet a memory, nor was there a place reserved in any corner of my mind for his name, but as I played this childish game of 'guess where we are in the car', I did wonder if he would become a bad or a good memory.

Word from his handlers at Beaulieu was that he was unhappy and impatient with whatever they did for him, asking time after time when next he was going to see me. Although this visit had to happen, I had arranged it on the spur of the moment due to the constant pressure the Foreign Office was apply regarding the Indian situation, and the one the Prime Minister asked me personally to deal with, that of the International Atomic Energy Agency in regard to America's plans to invade Iran. Sir John Scarlett had made contact with the Director General of the

IAEA through an emissary at the United Nations and put the suggestion that Iran be declared unstable in the eyes of his organisation.

Unfortunately for the powers that be, those that make up *the invisible government that control the machinery of elected governments* that both the British Prime Minister of 1878, one Benjamin Disraeli, and a little later in time, the American President, one Theodore Roosevelt, spoke of, the Egyptian lawyer who headed the International Atomic Energy Agency could not be influenced. He spoke as he found, and declined to tell a lie to appease those with hidden agendas, some of which were contained in that Gladio B file.

On the surface, none of that was of any concern to Kudashov, but he knew of the corrupted file and as yet I did not know how much he knew. He did know of Henry Mayler and the plans he and another Rosicrucian, a Lebanese Assyrian billionaire, drew up to build a home for Armenians, Assyrians and Kurds in the once Kingdom of Cilicia in the south of Turkey, bordering the Mediterranean. Did Kudashov know of the plans to invade Iran and lessen the western world's dependence on Saudi Arabian oil, thereby creating a vacuum for unrest in that crucial Islamic country?

If the invasion of Iran went ahead, and the Gladio plans were realised, parts of the world would then be controlled as if they were pieces on a chess board, being moved by unaccountable and invisible hands for nothing more than their greedy gratification. For a time, I took tremendous pleasure in knowing that Fraser and I had stopped these people four years ago, but it was our intervention that directly led to Hannah's death. Those chilling words on the scrap of paper about death being the most grateful recipient of life were stencilled in my mind that, despite my childish game of peek-a-boo at the countryside, just would not stop rattling around.

Michael Simmons had run every feasible check available to certify Kudashov's assertion of being responsible for the case files on the Kavas at the beginning of Operation Donor. There was nothing to disprove his claim; in fact, there were more positives showing his hand to them than not. For the May '81 report, and then the one on the first of March 1982, Kudashov was in Vienna, Austria on 'Police Business.'

Technology beyond my comprehension unearthed two microwave signal messages emanating from a one-way, single-use dispatch radio corresponding to dates in both March and May from an address in Vienna of a company used by the SIS in the early eighties. That MI6 company, registered as a specialist art-framing business, then filtered it and sent it via an art gallery in Old Bond Street, London to the Russian counter-intelligence desk, seventh floor, Century House. Again, this amounted to no more than circumstantial evidence of Kudashov's story being true, but very seldom in my line of work is there any indisputable evidence of certainty.

* * *

When I arrived at Beaulieu, Kudashov was under the shade of a silver birch in the rose garden looking every inch the English country squire I imagined he would like to become. That's where I started our interview.

"Where do you see yourself after Cilicia has been liberated from Moscow and she's here with you in England, Nikita? Is there a special place where you'd like to settle down?"

He mentioned a place I knew vaguely, just over the border with Scotland in what's called the Lowlands, a place my father had taken me to when he and my mother were alive. It was a good many years ago, but I remember it being summer and very hot. We stopped for lunch in a restaurant, the outside of which was festooned with hanging baskets and window boxes of flowering plants of every colour. My father ate fish. I remember the day well, as after finishing his meal he had a severe attack of what he said was just indigestion and nothing to be concerned with.

A few years after that trip to Scotland, he went to see his local doctor and complained of another attack of indigestion. Just hours after seeing his GP, and he agreeing with my father's diagnosis, my mother found him dead on their bed at home. The same GP was summoned and he diagnosed my father had died from a heart attack. Apparently, the symptoms of indigestion and an oncoming heart attack are quite similar.

I have always wondered if it was a slight heart attack he suffered in that pretty restaurant. In my case, I prefer to think of myself as ignorant at that lunch rather than to know and accept I was utterly useless. I smiled as I wondered what that pretty young psychologist would make of my thinking I should have saved my father.

* * *

Whilst on the subject of saving people, I'd had a peek at one report a psychologist had written on me. It was after an incident in Ireland where I'd witnessed a prolonged death and been the cause of a quick one. The incident I'd spoken of was the one that gave me the most pain until, that is, Hannah died. Again, it had been my fault. I had allowed a woman to get too close and I hadn't arrived in time to save her. When I got to the warehouse when she'd been taken, there was only time to watch as her tortured body slowly drifted into death's outstretched arms that no paramedic could push aside. The effect that her death had on me was vented in a way that protocol strongly ordered never to do, nevertheless, having broken those rules I found that killing her killer had not removed the pain and nor had the therapy.

The psychologist I'd told this story to suggested in her report that I attend the Harley

Street practice of the retained civil-service medical therapist. Although it was only a 'suggestion', it was not one it would be wise to refuse. When I stole that glance, I didn't recognise who she was speaking of until I reached the end.

His highly developed intelligence coupled with his direct motivated characteristics of determination, mixed with a single-minded selfishness and complete inconsideration for others, make West's case most interesting and his condition almost impossible to treat. His one redeeming quality is his complete devotion to and love of his job, and the pride he has in his personal performance both within and outside of its constraints. Although these emotions fall short of tempering his inconsiderateness in achieving his role and objectives, his recent display of ruthlessness is in my opinion an integral part of his self-absorption. It is my professional view that Patrick West is unreservedly suited to the role he is currently employed at.

* * *

My searching into Kudashov's future with his granddaughter resolved nothing. I hoped for better results as I moved the conversation on to both parts of Operation Donor.

"I need to get everything down on tape," I stated as the debrief began and I produced the small service issue tape recorder.

"Most of what we'll be covering today we will have touched on or spoken more fully about already, but you know what institutions like the SIS are—red tape and paperclips. Everything in triplicate and then some more. Sorry, if this is all at bit tedious, Nikita, but you know how it is?"

He made a few grimaces reminiscent of a man in pain when doing something he doesn't want to, but they'd disappeared by the time I began.

"I'm going to start with Jana Kava. You were her handler on both parts of the Operation Donor that you were instrumental in setting up. Are we up and running with that, Nikita?"

He moaned that we were covering old ground, but kept up with the story that had been told, until we came to Warsaw, the Polish colonel, and Gdańsk. I told him part of what I knew about Ryan without mentioning any detail. I said I knew Jana had fingered the colonel to keep our source, Vyacheslav Trubnikov's name, out of circulation from the KGB. He looked surprised and made no attempt to disguise it.

"I'm impressed, Patrick. Yes, Dickie had a runner inside the CIA with access to the KGB. It was an enormous coup on his behalf. I'm a bit of what you English call a snob. I'm afraid I hate the word agent being used to describe me. The snob in me started in childhood, then it developed into something far deeper than mere pretentiousness. I was hubristic from birth of course with my bloodline, but my self-confidence grew stronger on marrying into the Romanov royal connection with Anna.

"When Dickie Blythe-Smith had your chair, I was his special artist at the performance of espionage. Our relationship transcended any tradecraft instruction book platform. Together he and I wrote the sequence to that book, and you and I will write the novel that closes the series, Patrick.

"Yes, Trubnikov needed protection but, more importantly, Dickie's inside runner needed Trubnikov on the stage and playing, not locked up in the Lubyanka or some version of it in India. Over the years, Dickie had his source reading signals, dossiers and picking the pockets of the rich, famous, and wicked. GB's SIS credentials were looked upon as the vertex of the shrouded world that no other nation could come close to toppling. I hope somewhere he wrote out in full all of what he did for successive governments of your country, and perhaps one day you may find where he hid his memoirs and go on and publish them."

"I hope I do. That would very nice, Nikita. Would I find your name in those documents?" I asked.

Chapter Thirty-One: Hammer and Sickle

"You said Dickie only mentioned Kudashov's name once to you, Fraser; are you sure? Only Kudashov's story is that he was much more than just Dickie's ears and eyes on selective intel. He's implying he was Dickie's number one overseas intelligence agent in all spheres of interest until Dickie retired."

I called Fraser as soon as we were pulling away from Beaulieu on the homeward bound journey to Whitehall. Kudashov had answered all my queries with varying degrees of satisfaction. On more than three occasions he repeated his insistence of having another vital piece of information to reveal only when he had my confirmation that Cilicia was free from Moscow and en route to London. But I left Beaulieu still uncertain about his true reasons for wanting his granddaughter 'rescued'. I had no doubts as to her communications value, that had been proven, but I sensed another agenda brewing in his motives. He was an extremely persuasive and experienced intelligence operative, and I was reminded of my own explanation to Fraser of how I thought the equally experienced Dickie Blythe-Smith had led Randall Ryan Cavershall by the hand in turning Vyacheslav Trubnikov. Was Kudashov using the intelligence services of this country, hoping to conceal something of his own making?

* * *

Fate played a card as it often does, and as always happens, nobody could stop it or tell where it would lead. Fraser had been studying for the tenth time everything he had and everything else he could find on his pet subject of the Cambridge Spy Ring that existed from the thirties until the late fifties. He was looking at the fifth member who was identified as a part of that infamous passage of history: John Caincross.

Caincross studied languages at the Sorbonne in Paris as well as at Trinity College, Cambridge. French, German, and Russian were his specialities. When he was in his final term in Paris, he had a brief but intense affair with an American girl who was studying the same languages as he. When they both came to England their relationship continued, but at a steadier pace until the outbreak of WWII when the love of his life, Patricia Jacobson, returned home to America, where she followed Caincross's eventual footsteps by becoming a translator for her country's intelligence service.

Before the war started, Caincross worked for both the Cabinet Office and the Foreign Office and sometime in 1937, he joined the Communist Party of Great Britain. Around that time, Communism had become an attractive economic ideology in America and, again, nobody can be absolutely sure of the precise date, but Patricia joined the Communist Party of the United States of America. As Cold War tensions fuelled fears of widespread Communist subversion in the labour unions of America and then spread to government institutions, a list of possible subversives was put together, which became the starting point of McCarthyism in America. Patricia Jacobson's name was on such a list and, in time, she was due to appear before one of Joseph McCarthy's investigation committees into Communist affiliations within the FBI, for whom she worked.

Joseph McCarthy's investigations led to a political opponent committing suicide because of pressure McCarthy was exerting on his homosexual son. The Democratic politician's suicide led to McCarthy's witch hunt being immediately discontinued. Fraser found records lodged in Washington DC, through his contacts in the FBI, of Patricia's active role in the Communist Party of the USA. She had escaped investigation by months.

Fraser's searching did not end there. By 1941, Patricia was married to an army physicist working for the US Army Corps of Engineers at Oak Ridge, Tennessee, on what became known as The Manhattan Project, or put more simply, working on the production of the world's first nuclear bomb. Whilst her husband worked in the army laboratories, she worked at the nearby Signal Intelligence Service as a translator of signals emanating from Oak Ridge to unrecognised transmission points. The Signal Intelligence Service suffered from an unescapable weakness in its lack of coordination with other communications services, notably that of the Department of State and the FBI. Meaning that nobody controlled the signals to and from Oak Ridge other than those who worked in the Signal Intelligence Service.

Between 1941 and the end of WWII, Caincross worked at Bletchley Park, Great Britain's Code and Cypher School, where he passed on German military decoded secrets to the Russians and added to them when he joined the counter intelligence services at MI6, where his translation skills were put to use. When another of the Cambridge Five, Guy Burgess, fled Britain for Moscow, written notes from Caincross were found in his apartment.

Those letters, Fraser told me, were never allowed to leave the vaults I've spoken of, and when I was back in my office at the Foreign and Commonwealth building, I accessed those vaults and read those letters. When finished with them I could just about hold myself back from calling Fraser. I decided to wait to tell him to his face.

In them, John Caincross mentions his American married girlfriend, and how she had let slip a couple of messages to him using his Soviet code name of *Liszt*, containing specific details of core elements of the fusion component to the nuclear bomb her husband was working on. In one message she added: *I believe what Joe is working on should be shared to those less fortunate than us. Maybe you could help in that way, John. Try to make sure the Russians have what the Americans have otherwise I fear for the safety of this world.* That message was in plain text with no effort made to disguise its meaning.

The man she called Joe was her husband. His full name was Joe Joseph Cavershall. When the Cavershalls had their only child, Randall, in 1942, Joe Joseph added the numeral of I after his own surname, giving his son Randall Ryan the honour of having the II after his.

* * *

By the time I reached Chearsley that evening I was fit to burst with what I'd discovered, along with something connected that Michael had found. My investigations came first.

"Can you see the reason behind Dickie's cryptic NOMITE message, now, Fraser?" I breathlessly asked of an equally excited pipe-puffing guru.

When he answered, "No, Patrick, I can't," I swooped like an eagle when ready to attack its prey.

"It's the 'each', at the end of Jack Price's acronym of No One is More Important Than Each, Fraser. Joe Cavershall was the first and Randall the second part of each. Together they are two parts of a three-part puzzle, with Patricia making up the third part. Dickie was able to turn Randall into working for us because of what his mother had done. He told Randall that if he disclosed anything about the operations, Dickie would have the Hammer and Sickle flag with the Russian emblem permanently added to the family name."

Michael Simmons had found that Randall Ryan Cavershall II was posted to Germany in October 1991 to witness the last of the Wall coming down. He was there as leading GCHQ representative, waiting to co-read the signal traffic from Berlin Central travelling east. It was rightly expected to hit new heights in transmissions. To allow for what was technically named open-space-impetus, Randall had his office full of signal intercepting machinery away from Berlin, in Cologne, Germany. From retirement, Dickie Blythe-Smith had selected its location, on an empty floor of a block of offices next to the one occupied by the German Federal Intelligence Service, to one of which Kudashov was a regular visitor.

"There's no record of the two ever having met, but wouldn't it be strange if they did?" Fraser asked, expecting me to agree, but I failed to reply.

Between a few glasses of Jura and possibly the same number of pipe refills, but not as many as the Dunhills I smoked that evening, the taped transcript of my earlier meeting with Kudashov was combed through, then re-examined under Fraser's finely tuned ears whilst I drew the first of my square grid panels to take on the flight to India.

On the first sheet of paper, I had the names of all those who benefitted from the demise of the Polish colonel Jana Kava pointed out to the CIA's Black-Op G3 assassin. During my nine-hour flight to India I planned to draw as many grids as I needed to maximise the answers to the remaining questions of what each had in common, and to find the missing strand that pulled them together. Fraser's view on Victor Rothschild's career as a concealed Soviet spy was changing, partially due to the evidence I'd uncovered in the Foreign and Commonwealth vaults misfiled under Ryan, and not with the plethora of papers categorised under Cambridge Five.

Fraser showed me papers he'd had for years in the quest for truth of the Cambridge Spy Ring, which had been hidden by Philby when he fled to Russia. They showed Victor Rothschild, Guy Burgess, and Anthony Blunt being members of the Apostles, a campus society characterised by Marxist intellectual speculation and homosexual activity, but there was nothing to suggest Rothschild was under Soviet control. Rather, the evidence Fraser had amassed implied Rothschild was pursuing another aim entirely—the creation of a Jewish State in Palestine, a family dream fulfilled in the aftermath of the Second World War. Stalin was among the first to support the fledgling State of Israel; after all, a large portion of its immigrants had come from the Eastern Bloc and he wanted a Communist state in the region. Perhaps it could be proven that Rothschild advised the Soviet leadership on affairs to do with Israel and, in so doing, help to hasten Britain's weakening grip on the Palestine Mandate, but it was an inevitable outcome, no matter how it was dealt with.

Fraser was coming round to believe that it was through Rothschild's actions that Kim Philby was finally exposed to be the ringleader of the Cambridge spy ring because of Philby's published antisemitism. Flora Solomon, an ardent Zionist whom Philby unsuccessfully had attempted to recruit in the 1930s, became incensed at his pro-Arab, anti-Israel journalistic slant and decided to reveal what she had known for decades. Solomon reported Philby to a figure perched high in the British security establishment: Lord Victor Rothschild.

All that made interesting reading before my flight to India, where I had no intentions of staying long in Delhi. My idea was to meet with Vyacheslav Trubnikov tomorrow lunchtime, Saturday, and fly home on the 10:20 flight to Heathrow leaving Delhi on Sunday morning. I was to be out of England until Sunday afternoon. If the flight was on time, then I could meet Major

Swan and his team at the SBS barracks in Dorset by four in the afternoon and catch up with Kudashov at Beaulieu, early evening, when I could inform him of the mission at Zaragoza. I would be tired, but that tiredness might keep thoughts of Hannah aside.

I suggested to Fraser that sometime over the weekend he contact Samuel Rothschild, praising his relative's judicious handling of foreign affairs when advisor to the governments of Edward Heath and Margaret Thatcher, and praise him for his continuing contribution to the UK's relationship to Israel. I implied that could be the gesture that would open the door to his Circle of Eight families.

* * *

My sleep that night was again plagued by nightmarish visions of the bullet hitting Hannah's head last Thursday. This time I cradled her head, turning her face towards mine as she smiled, then drifted from my grasp. The nightmare continued with me on the floor of an unfamiliar large, ministerial limousine searching the open space for signs of her, but all I could see was a headless body sitting bolt upright, supported by a seat belt. When I couldn't find her, I opened the car door and left. I never saw which direction I went in and that's what woke me. I was sweating even though the air conditioning was working, and alcohol never had that effect on me.

I showered, dressed, and packed my overnight travel bag, making sure I had all my diplomatic travel papers, then opened a grid, this one with the name of Vyacheslav Trubnikov in the centre of it, and then I added the names of those who benefited from an association with him. I spent the four hours I had before I was due to leave with the computer off and my mind focused on what was to happen in Delhi.

Chapter Thirty-Two: Petr Tomsa

I escaped the torment of nightmares during the flight. Even so, the thoughts that filled my mind certainly bordered on them as I could not see any motive for Dickie Blythe-Smith altering the place where Kudashov's wife died. Why change the place from where it actually happened, in Moscow? The reason he gave me seemed reasonable at the time; misinformation to lead Jana Kava's killer off Kudashov's back, but the more I thought about that the more absurd it became. Dickie was never empty-headed in his line of thinking, so there must be another reason. Either way, someone was lying. Among the questions that still required an answer was why now did Cilicia need rescuing? I wanted more background information on her before I listened to any answer her grandfather would give me, but it was proving very difficult for Michael Simmons to come by, no matter what data he used in whatever computer system.

As a form of last resort I'd asked Liam Catlin to get a fingerprint sample from something she touched when at one of their sightings in Moscow. One of his lamp-burners had successfully lifted one from a cup she'd used in a coffee house last Wednesday. This was processed and sent to Group on Wednesday evening. Everything we had was thrown at it, but by the time I boarded the flight, nothing had turned up.

* * *

I had two names that kept staring at me from the paper of the three grids I'd drawn: Kudashov and his relative, Anatoly Vladimirovich Malikova. Neither fitted into the threads between any of the others. Kudashov in particular stood out by a country mile. Almost all the others had a connection to at least one other name than just Dickie Blythe-Smith, but Kudashov only had Dickie as a common denominator. Malikova only had a tenuous connection to Caincross through his father, and a family connection to Kudashov and Cilicia. Maybe it was the turbulence we encountered whilst halfway to India that made me think of Ryan once again. I had a sneaky feeling that Kudashov was pushing me for a mention of the codename Ryan when we met. If Kudashov and Dickie were as close as Kudashov told me they were, then I could think of no rational thinking behind why Dickie would not have told him the name as Kudashov might have benefitted from Ryan's disclosures. But there were things Dickie never told Fraser, so being the person he was, private and extremely careful, then I could understand why the Russian might not be told.

Could the reason Kudashov seemed to be trying to prise Ryan's name from me be attributed to plain curiosity, or was there something more sinister going on? Despite there being so much to consider in this labyrinthine puzzle, one question overrode everything else: why did Dickie go to so much trouble to hide something that, if it had threatened the security of Great Britain, should have been disclosed far sooner than now?

The flight was on time and the ambassador's car was a welcome refuge from the heat and the never-ending throng of hustling people, and the suffocating air that had nowhere to escape through the static haze that hovered over the city.

* * *

I met with the Russian Ambassador to India, one Vyacheslav Trubnikov, in the shaded cool gardens of the British Embassy on Saturday morning at 11 o'clock. He was punctual for the prearranged contact. As a normal rule of thumb, it is almost impossible to confirm any foreign national's birthdate, and from what used to be known as the Eastern Bloc countries, doubly difficult for obvious reasons, but with Trubnikov that rule did not apply. From an undisclosed source, his complete background was included in a paper file I found in the Foreign and Commonwealth vaults filed under the name of Macintosh. Had I needed any more confirmation that Faversham's use of the Macintosh disguise was a Dickie Blythe-Smith inspiration, then there it was and, alongside it, was an autopsy report on Miles Faversham. He had indeed died from an inherent heart condition made worse by his obesity. One of my worries had been put to bed.

Trubnikov was born on the fourth of May 1944, but he looked a lot older than the sixty-three years he was. He was a short, stooping man, appearing comfortable with what seemed to be a deformity, although his filed description contained no reference to it. It did, however, mention his lack of height and the penetrating stare of his icy, blue eyes. He had a thick crop of lacquered grey hair, cut close to the forehead and neatly around the ears and shirt collar. There was a distinct parting on his left side with not a single strand of hair out of place. He was not overweight. Neither did he have an appetite for the traditional English elevenses of tea with a selection of biscuits. We were alone in the secluded garden, where no directional microphone could reach. I had insisted on total privacy.

He knew who I was, as that would have been impossible to hide, and there was no reason to try. Even so, time was not an issue so I played the game of being a UK emissary, open to suggestions of how to address the imbalance of trade Russia had with India at the cost of the United Kingdom. We jostled with the problem for a while until eventually I injected some realism to the issue, introducing the subject of agent Ryan, and at once he gave me the name of a pliable government figure who was, in Trubnikov's opinion, open to bribes. I judged the time right to reminisce about days when Ryan's influence on world affairs was beneficial to Trubnikov and the United Kingdom. I asked him directly if he had regrets about his Polish colonel's death.

"I guess you would describe your feelings as confused when we offered to eradicate your Polish indiscretion in return for your compliance with certain Soviet originated classified material, Vyacheslav, is that right?"

He appeared sad when he agreed with my laconic summary, but offered no detailed explanation why that might be. I pressed him more on the Polish colonel and how he thought the man may have got hold of the lethal pill he used to commit suicide rather than face interrogation by the KGB for the traitorous acts he had committed against the USSR. He was very open about that.

"It was my suggestion he got his hands on one. I never wanted him to suffer. He told me the Czechoslovakian girl he was giving secrets to gave it to him. I asked him if he would ever use it and he was emphatic that he would. He said he had seen what the secret state police had done to a young naval rating at the Kaliningrad base who had been caught passing a copy of a list of Soviet submarines he had worked on in the dockyards; that's why he wanted the pill. Innocently he told me the rating had only passed on a list of supplies the boats took on board. He never knew who the information was passed on to, but he said he'd heard two separate rifle volleys fired. One the day following the rating's arrest and the other two days later."

I asked Trubnikov if the colonel had said where his Czechoslovakian girl had got the pill from, and he said she had told him, "It came from her handler—a Petr Tomsa."

How on earth, I asked, had he remembered that name for so many years and he turned the question around, asking me if I would ever forget the name of the person who killed the one I loved. I never answered him. I just looked into those steely blue eyes and I knew what he was saying was true. It must have been Kudashov who had handed over the lethal tablet to Jana and she had passed it on to the colonel. No harm in that, but why not tell me, and why did he not give another pill to Jana?

We chatted about how his life had changed since his days in the First Directorate working with Vladimir Putin and whether those former days the two had shared had assisted his appointment as ambassador. He thought there might be some truth in what I said. I kept on about Putin and asked if they were still close friends, to which he politely replied that he was now too far removed from the corridors of power to be of any use to British Intelligence. That patently was untrue and, to me, sounded too rehearsed to be left alone.

The conversation turned back towards bygone days and the two odd pieces to my matrix of names: Nikita Sergeyovitch Kudashov and Anatoly Vladimirovich Malikova. He knew of both. One, he said, was the departmental head and the other was the grandfather of the female deputy at the Eighth Chief Directorate where they monitored and managed national, foreign, and overseas communications, cryptologic equipment, research and development into making Russia even stronger than she was now. He knew of them and their positions because it was his department before becoming the Russian ambassador to India. It went one better than that. It was he who had selected them. He told me how Anatoly Malikova's father was a famous Russian General during WWII and it was he who won the battle at Kursk, perhaps the turning point of that war, for which he was awarded the Gold Star medal of the Hero of the Soviet Union.

Trubnikov had met the general when he was eleven at a grand parade his father had taken him to. At the end of the parade, there was an unveiling of a commemorative memorial to the Glorious Dead of Mother Russia. The memorial was not what he remembered; it was the tall general in his bright shining ribbons and medals with the Gold Star one making him the most prominent officer he saw that day. He was given an opportunity to speak to the general, and he asked what the medals were for. The general looked at young Trubnikov and recited what battles they represented but none, he said, were important. What was important was that he and his comrades had defeated Hitler, who wanted to kill every Russian there was. He added something that had stuck in Trubnikov's memory. He said that it was intelligence rather than muscle that would defeat any enemy.

The deputy head of the Eighth Directorate, Cilicia Kudashov, was, he said, the foremost university student of her year, majoring in the languages that earmarked her for a career with the foreign communications directorate in which she had shown herself to be invaluable. Then, from nowhere, his haunting blue eyes narrowed and he took on the appearance of a gloating parent at a passing out ceremony before he announced, "I know a secret about her grandfather, Nikita Sergeyovitch Kudashov, and I will sell it to you for the right price."

I didn't jump at his offer at first; in fact, I didn't mention it for quite some time. Of course I was interested, but I wanted to know more about the man who was walking beside me and how reliable his information might be. The source to his file had recorded his loyalty and honesty as changeable, by which I assumed he could be bracketed with the corrupt Indian trade official. I wanted confirmation for what I believed happened in Warsaw with the colonel that led to Jana's death in Gdańsk the following day. I feared the worse but, nevertheless, I needed to know if Trubnikov asked his fated lover one other thing London required passed on to Jana Kava. Unfortunately, I was right. Ryan had made it happen as I believed.

"The first signal came to me in mid-August '82. It originated from a desk in Cologne, went via a terminal at a place called Correos, and I forwarded it on to what was coded as Gladio. It contained one word: Ready. The second one came by exactly the same route and again had one word: Gdańsk. I forwarded both on to the same recipient at this Gladio point."

However disillusioned I was, I had no choice but to move on to other things done under the name of Ryan that I'd discovered in the Foreign Office vaults, one of which was that last filed message under Dickie's Knighted first name as Richard. I asked Vyacheslav Trubnikov if he had ever seen a signal from Ryan with the name of Richard anywhere in it. He said no, adding with a disconsolate voice that Ryan existed in a yesterday's world no longer relevant today. I told him in no uncertain terms that, although the days of the intelligence exchange handled by Ryan had dried up, the reasons that he had so willingly agreed to meet me had not vanished with the death of any Polish army officer. He remained inextricably connected to a Soviet traitor. Information I suggested that his friend President Putin would not be aware of. The motivation for him to readily agree to meet me was on the table. Yes, he thought, London was still fully aware of the past.

* * *

Part of what I learned from Trubnikov was how Ryan's intelligence value to all sides was in his unwavering ability in hiding names. In not one report, stolen or given to any side, did he divulge the names from whom the reports came, or referred to. Except once.

I, like Dickie twenty-five years before me, had made an alliance with Trubnikov, and mine was a simple trade whereas Dickie's was far more intricate. I would keep Trubnikov's secret liaison when much younger and his subsequent dealings with the GB's intelligence service confidential for eternity by wrapping it up in obscure files and hiding them under a perpetual directive, if he told me the secret he had on Kudashov for a discounted price rather than the figure he first asked for. When he saw the sense of my offer, he accepted the terms. The agreed price for the secret Trubnikov held about Nikita Kudashov was a sum of money that could be channelled from part of Sir John's designated budget into an account our Indian ambassador could manage for that purpose.

The two of us worked out a deal of mutual benefit. One of the things I would do for him was to keep all mention of Trubnikov's help in past projects safely hidden away from discovery, and one of the things he would do in return would be to make sure the government official he recommended would be a long-term 'asset' for British trade because if not Trubnikov, or whoever came after him, would have him killed. Trade negotiations seemed remarkably easy to me.

* * *

The British Embassy's duty officer in the communications room was busy. He sent one message to his opposite number in Moscow, then one to Sir John Scarlett at Vauxhall with a copy of that signal, plus some separate material I needed to look at addressed to Michael Simmons, and another to the private IP memory address on a computer at Chearsley, in Buckinghamshire. The one to Fraser did not contain what Trubnikov told me was in Ryan's last communiqué, nor what he said about Nikita Sergeyovitch Kudashov.

Before I left to catch the morning flight home, the duty officer brought me a decoded signal address that pinged on his fax machine just after six that morning. It read: *Lights Out.* On a more troubled flight home than the one that took me to Trubnikov, I wondered how what had happened in India was to affect all those concerned. The one I worried about the most was Fraser Ughert.

Chapter Thirty-Three: Kallebrann

Sir John was the first call I took as Jimmy put the car in gear and we joined the convoy waiting to escort us away from the terminal at Heathrow. He was full of thanks and congratulations at the job well done, not only in respect of future trade figures with the sub-continent, but also it was his name I'd accredited to the top of the agreement I'd left with the ambassador to sign with Trubnikov's Indian government official. Although the documentation was only in the Sunday pipeline, Sir John had already notified the Cabinet Secretary who, being more prudent by nature, advised Scarlett not to release any notice of the deal with Rolls Royce and British Aerospace worth billions of pounds until confirmation of the contracts being signed was received at the Ministry of Trade.

Michael Simmons was the next to call from his desk in the office next to mine. He asked if I'd received the Delhi signal okay and told me Major Swan and his team had arrived safely at the naval airfield at Poole in Dorset sometime after eight o'clock that morning. Being slightly ahead of my estimated time I was hoping to join them three quarters of an hour earlier than I'd imagined.

* * *

The six-man SBS team the major had put together left Kallebrann, Norway, at one o'clock Sunday morning, crossing the Russian border where Norwegian engineers had repositioned the electronic beacons that covered the whole borderline without interrupting the constant signal. It was a manoeuvre practised several times on their own equipment, but this was a first on the Russians. Clothed in specialised non-reflective thermal imaging body armour, they quickly travelled through the perpetual daylight, overland to Ozero Kuets'yarvi Lake. Once there, they unloaded the three two-man submersible vessels from the SUV vehicles, riding them beneath the surface of the lake and through the river system of the Reka Kolosyoki until they reached the Zaragoza laboratory site. The SUVs returned to the Norwegian side of the border to await orders for the return.

The journey to the periphery of the laboratories took one hour and twenty-one minutes. Another hour was spent in surveying the area. As there was no indication of an attack being planned on the complex, only four armed guards were posted as security. These were silently killed from close range before access was gained to the main building and the two tunnels. Fifty-three pounds of Semtex explosive were placed in strategic points around the building and tunnels, and the timers carefully set. As Major Swan's team returned and reached the pick-up point for the SUVs, the bombs they'd planted detonated with such force, it was said the blast was heard over thirty miles away at the port of Murmansk.

The destruction of the site was photographed by a small drone developed for the use of designated special forces UK, which I authorised. The pictures came straight to me from an untraceable field relay point without passing Sir John Scarlett's desk or anyone else at The Box, or the Home Office. I had the heat image analysed and it was confirmed that the temperature generated would have destroyed any virus being developed in the laboratories.

* * *

Everything had gone as the major had planned. He showed me more of the before and after demolition photographs of the tunnels and laboratories. To my professional eye, it added up to an intensive research and development site which was stacked with some highly dangerous and restricted chemicals, the purpose of which the Home Office analysis had corresponded to Nikita Kudashov's claims. Although my usage of the government's secret installation at Porton Down to evaluate the two small, cylindrical glass bottles meticulously packed inside the parcel shipped by the Royal Airforce from Norway, which arrived at RAF Northolt just outside London on Saturday morning, was done through Group's mandate, the notice it triggered had not been sent straight to me to validate and then add any response. Its first posting was to the Home Office, and then it landed on the desk of Prime Minister's private secretary, who passed it on to the Cabinet Secretary, who wanted to know what purpose there was behind my need for some weird chemicals being examined.

"Are we likely to be under some kind of terrorist inspired chemical attack, Patrick?" he asked, flustered, on the car telephone as we were pulling through the gates at the Royal Marines, Hamworthy Base at Poole.

I managed to moderate his concerns by bending the truth somewhat, saying they were mere names of samples Porton Down wanted on a watch list issued to Special Branch to be aware of in the forthcoming months as a consignment of each had apparently been stolen from premises in Amsterdam, used by GlaxoSmithKline. Interpol was working the case and, so far, had a highly likely destination marked in as Kashmir with the recipients being a rebel group that were on the Indian government's Defence Intelligence radar. He accepted my false explanation, but knowing him to be an assiduous pursuer of unfavourable political news relating to the government, I wondered how deep Sir Nigel Hicks would look. Just as I thought I had gotten rid of him, he asked if I'd seen the psychologist he'd recommended. Just at that moment, Frank held aloft a faxed message from Fraser and my mind jumped from the back of the car where I sat moderately comfortably, to inside Fraser's office. I might be in need of Sir Nigel's suggestion before too long.

* * *

The professionalism shown by Major Swan and his men thoroughly deserved the accolade they received in the Mess Room on their return and the one I laid on for them later that night. I had other places to go but wished I could have stayed with them, away from the consequences of my visit to India and Kudashov's granddaughter's coming evacuation from Moscow tomorrow.

I also had a briefing of the Defence chief of staff to attend in the morning, at which I was sure I would be questioned on the operation I authorised, undertaken by a contingent of an elitist naval marine company that could have flagged up on any of their desks. To have kept the arrangements for the Zaragoza raid secreted away for so long was a fantastic logistical achievement, but once the major's team entered Norway and from there into Russia, protocol would have been breached, with several branches of the Defence Ministries possibly warned. I wondered if I would be walking into an ambush on Monday's intelligence meeting, but from what I learned so far, I hoped I was in the clear.

The major was adamant that his squad had left no evidence of British involvement at the site. Weaponry used was the same as the Russian military, AK-74 rifles firing 5.45mm bullets and if, as planned, small parts of the mission's conversation was overheard and taped from the concealed microphones; it was in a Chechen dialect they had spoken. Everything was good about Zaragoza, but I couldn't say the same about Kudashov, Fraser, or me with Tuesday's funeral fast approaching. I had worries over Kudashov as well as Fraser, and I was far from certain how to deal with either of them.

Chapter Thirty-Four: What's not Remembered Cannot be Forgotten

The East Berlin Stasi desk heard of the proposed demolition of the Wall through an intercepted NSA signal four days before it started to be pulled down. Trubnikov had been given a heads-up about the demolition two days before them. A spokesman I contacted at the BBC from India said it was his telephone call to *Die Welt* newspaper that alerted the western press to its forthcoming demise. Trubnikov told me he was ordered by the high command at the KGB to leak that information, but no reason was given.

Dickie Blythe-Smith was retired when the Wall came down. Or rather a more precise way of describing Dickie's condition of unemployment would be to say: his remuneration, derived from his pension when his salary ceased to be the main source of income on the eighteenth of August 1984. However, Dickie being Dickie, he kept a hand on the wheel of matters that concerned his main adversaries throughout his service life—the KGB, in all its many manifestations. One of those selections he made related to the conduct of Vyacheslav Trubnikov, to whom he had given something special for those days that Jack Price called *those days when it rains and nobody is giving away umbrellas.*

Dickie had seen the same NSA signal that Trubnikov had seen because Trubnikov sent it on to him, using the once private Odessa coding that now four people knew. The fourth person was Hugo Glenister through whom the signal was sent. But Hugo never knew how to decode it. He just knew the signal had to end up as a telegram addressed to Dickie's private post box at The Travellers Club in Pall Mall, a place the then widowed Sir Richard Blythe-Smith used every day.

By using the Trubnikov route, Hugo Glenister sent the Odessa coded signal to Kudashov, telling him of the open NSA terminal point at Mannheim and to go and find what he could. Unfortunately for everyone, Kudashov was too far away to get there before the leaking terminal was shut down; however, he was also too far away from his own terminals to read the cancelation signal.

The following day, Kudashov received another message from Trubnikov, this time initiated by agent Ryan. Into the body of this message Trubnikov was instructed by Ryan to include the encrypted NSA telecommunications Kudashov was later able to pass on to his granddaughter. The files containing the signals that Cilicia Kudashov decoded were authenticated when presented to the cryptanalysts at GCHQ.

The luckless visit Kudashov undertook to Mannheim was further complicated by the innumerable cameras the CIA had around the site. They snapped away merrily at Nikita Sergeyovitch Kudashov, adding his previously unlogged face to their classified files.

* * *

Glenister's longevity as Director General on the Soviet Satellite desk was not entirely due to Dickie's patronage and influence, but it did Hugo no harm to have such a heavy-hitter on his side. He had left Hugo to carefully tidy away any loose ends that had been left exposed to any CIA or

KGB interference. But there was one that had been missed, though not by Hugo, because not only is it true that a secret one is unaware of cannot be disclosed, equally true is that which one does not know, will always be forgotten.

Dickie, now knighted, hid himself away from direct contact with Glenister through normal channels, preferring to meet in far-flung rendezvous places away from Westminster eyes. For a further six years following Hugo's retirement, Dickie ferreted away at old friends for insights into Russian politics, carefully making sure his name was not coupled to any Ryan inspired message.

* * *

As a direct result of Nikita Kudashov's ill luck in having his face photographed at the NSA's Mannheim relay station, another signal was sent. This was the one Hugo knew nothing of. It originated at a console address in Kent County, Delaware. It first went to the same Correos address as used in 1982 by Ryan's Cologne address, where after it was encrypted into a different code, it was sent on to Trubnikov who, having accepted a great deal of money from an American he refused to reveal, changed the coding once more before forwarding it on to the Central Intelligence Agency, Directorate of Science and Technology in Washington D.C. That signal was sent in 2001, and the person who it was sent to was a CIA agent named Marcus Stoneman.

* * *

As this investigation of mine encapsulated more and more of what I held dear, the more I had to rely on random assumptions rather than rational ones. For some reason that I could not fathom, the Stoneman family and Nikita Kudashov had bad blood running between them. I knew that to be true because Trubnikov had kept copies of open text signals that went one way and then the next between Kent County and Marcus Stoneman's CIA desk.

Paulette Simona had confirmed the name of Nikita Kudashov to Marcus Stoneman when she recognised him from the photograph she'd been given when he approached her at Torp Sandefjord airport. But the face in the exact copy of the photograph was not known by that name at the Kent County end of these transmissions. In the home in Delaware, he was known as Klaus Mecklenburg. It did not take the Stonemans an eternity to discover the family name had been changed from Mecklenburg to Kudashov. Apparently, for reasons known only to himself, Nikita was Kudashov to some people and Klaus Mecklenburg to others.

That was, I thought, the logical way of interpreting what Trubnikov told me of the Kent County signals. But where was the logic in sending an agent from a CIA department, who was working at a clandestine laboratory, to meet with a man known to be a British intelligence officer? Ignoring logic, as it seemed obvious I had to, where would random thoughts take me if it meant Kudashov was being drawn into the open for a purpose only the corrupted part of the CIA knew? If that was so, then my random thinking opened another labyrinth of conflicting solutions to the Cilicia problem. One of which was exacerbated by the arrangement Dickie had made with Trubnikov. And that was the one giving me the most trouble!

* * *

I had asked that Kudashov be transferred from the residential area of Beaulieu to the far more secure detention area whilst I was in the British Embassy at Delhi, waiting for my flight back to the UK. There he would remain until I had the time to visit. I was conscious of his demand for prior knowledge of his granddaughter's extraction, but I could not securely do that by telephone or fax. That needed to be told one-to-one. Although I thought I knew the true reason for him bringing his case to the SIS and not presenting it to the Americans, it mattered not to me, as in my opinion Cilicia Kudashov still remained in need of rescuing. However, there were many considerations of the Moscow operation to be reviewed by those on the ground before it could take place, leaving me helpless other than to hope my belief in Liam Catlin and Christopher Irons was not misplaced. Other than that, my foremost concern lay to the north of Poole, in Buckinghamshire with Fraser Ughert. It was in that direction Jimmy pointed the car and our flying motorcyclists escorted our three-vehicle convoy. I wished beyond the boundaries of hallucinations for the comforting words and supporting smile of Hannah to be sitting once again at my side, stroking my hand with her soft slender fingers and my eyes closing in sleep, but sleep was impossible ... as were the words and smiles of my dead wife, Hannah.

* * *

The knowledge of having suspected some of what I learned from Trubnikov gave me no feeling of pride or vanity; if anything, the opposite was nearer the truth than that. There was no sense of superiority when realising the earth that supported my feet had opened up and swallowed all the reason there was for the world I existed in.

When I finally retire from the intelligence service I would like to leave a less intricate legacy than the one left by Dickie Blythe-Smith that I was trying to unravel. Whatever it was that Dickie was hiding, not only was it well hidden, but I was beginning to ask myself whether I really wanted to discover it.

Chapter Thirty-Five: Correos

Fraser was reticent in his greetings and I had expected no different from him given the circumstances.

"Were you aware I had a visit from St. James's Palace yesterday at more or less the same time as you took off for India? Rather convenient you'd left, don't you think? But let's forget that for a while and look at all this rubbish you sent me from India. Are you serious in any of it, Patrick? Because if you are, I think you're having a breakdown with all that occurred with Hannah's murder and the complications you experienced on being shot once again. How is the leg by the way?"

I just about managed an okay, before he was off again.

"There was a woman involved in two of your shootings, wasn't there? I bet any psychologist would love to pick at what's going on inside that head of yours because of that. Never mind! Some people can live with being mad. But I doubt it's a qualification needed for the joint intelligence committee."

I thought that last remark about being mad to be a bit on the low side, but he had a right to defend all that he held in the highest esteem. I said nothing, leaving him directing the discussion. He hadn't finished with the prospect of me being insane.

"I spoke to the Cabinet Secretary this morning. His wife tried to fend me off, being Sunday and all that, but, as I suspected, he took my call when I mentioned the name of the visitor I had from the Palace. He agreed with me that a breakdown could well be what's making you act oddly. He said he'd recommended a psychologist already, but you'd refused to see her. In the light of your message from Delhi, I think you should change your mind on that subject and make an appointment with her as early as you can."

Fraser finished as abruptly as he had started, leaving me uncertain of where to begin my defence. I didn't start with my knowledge of his caller from the Court of St James's visit, nor did I tell him of the similar message he'd heard from his visitor, being delivered to me immediately when I arrived at the British Embassy by an embarrassed ambassador. What I did do was try to extract something I very much doubted Fraser wanted to confess, by beginning the account of the Trubnikov story nearer what in a straight portrayal of time would be called the end of the puzzle surrounding Cilicia Kudashov, but equally it could be said to be the place where it all began. I kept my depiction of what happened in India as concise and correct as I could, without cutting too many corners or including facile facts that were superfluous to the puzzle.

When Trubnikov mentioned the surname of Stoneman in connection to the Zaragoza site at Nikel, along with the site's owner, the Russian oligarch Bohdan Dimitriyevich Valescov, the adrenaline in my veins started to pump my heart rate higher and, at the same time, lower my rate of breathing as it always does when I'm faced with excitement and danger. Four years ago, without this disclosure Fraser and I failed to equate Valescov's importance to the Rosicrucian fraternity that we knew he and Tucker Stoneman belonged to. I thought perhaps my trip to India had presented us with another chance.

* * *

After the embarrassment of the faxed message from St James's Palace that he'd been required to read to me, the British Ambassador in Delhi assisted in my enquiries of the United States Foreign Service, and it was through him I found the name of the US Ambassador to Poland in 1982. My message to Michael Simmons was a request for an in-depth research into the Stoneman family. There were three sons. The youngest was called Marcus, the middle one Spencer, and the oldest brother was called Tucker. This was the exact same Tucker Stoneman of Gladio B, 2002 vintage. The head of the family's name was George Thomas Stoneman, of Kent County, Delaware. George was the American ambassador who met Jana Kava in the park in Prague when she inadvertently left her reel of microfilm.

George died aged seventy-seven years on the same Sunday Paulette Simona's plane came down in northern Norway. And his, not her death, was directly linked to Nikita Kudashov showing up at Fraser's reunion dinner at the

Savoy two weeks ago this coming Tuesday, the day of Hannah's funeral.

* * *

To begin with, Marcus Stoneman's interest lay solely with the laboratories his father and his fellow Rosicrucian, the Russian, Bohdan Dimitriyevich Valescov had funded and how they had evolved at the old nickel mines in order to process the Ebola virus they had conspired to release in Sierra Leone. That was to be their testing ground from where they wished to witness and log the escalation of its effects both in the continent of Africa and alongside its intercontinental growth. And then someone, presumably within this depraved section of corrupted CIA officers, sent Nikita Kudashov's photograph to the Kent County home of George Thomas Stoneman and the bells rang inside George Stoneman's memory.

The introduction of Stoneman's name to Fraser had lightened his expression from one of belligerence to one of slight exhilaration. The fact that Tucker Stoneman had lost the presidential nomination because of his involvement with the objectives contained in the Gladio B documentation was satisfying to a degree for us, but all we had really was just circumstantial, without any hard evidence. The official reason for his withdrawal from the presidential race was due to a medical condition he suffered from flaring up again, or so his wife wanted the public to believe, but it was our belief that it was simply because of not wanting to face awkward questions over his alliance to that corrupted file. If his relationship to the laboratories at Nikel could be proved, it again did not help, as the destruction had obliterated all traces of Ebola virus being manufactured there, or any other virus, along with the verification of eugenic engineering.

We needed concrete corroboration of the Stonemans' involvement in cataclysmic activities and maybe Kudashov could supply it. However, Kudashov's involvement was hardly without complications and it was some of those complications that now required explaining.

"There was no message sent to London from Warsaw by Jana Kava or Nikita Kudashov, Fraser. The Polish army colonel did not know the name of an insider at GCHQ. That's the obvious reason why nothing showed on anyone's screen at Century House. There was no Odessa coding.

"You said yourself that Dickie had the name of the insider before the operation went live in Warsaw. Part of the truth behind Jana Kava seeing the Polish officer on the thirty-first of August 1982 was to save Trubnikov's life. He and London needed the colonel dead to obliterate the knowledge of the love affair the two had been engaged in. By fingering the colonel, it allowed Kudashov to gain a certain degree of aegis with Polish authorities and we got future favours from Trubnikov. The other reason why Jana had to die was that she knew a secret that just could not be allowed to become known beyond the few that knew it. I will tell more of that secret later."

"If you wanted to shock me, Patrick, then, yes, I'm shocked but, after all, death is part and parcel of the world we live in. Dickie obviously took a long-term view of the relationship we had with the Soviets and other Eastern-Bloc countries at the time, as someone in his position must. Incidentally, did we give that colonel the cyanide pill?"

"No, it came from Kudashov, but Kudashov was given it by the Americans."

The expression on Fraser's face showed how surprised he was. "Why them?" he asked in a raised voice.

"Because Dickie got them to supply it, Fraser. In that way, he distanced the secret intelligence service of this country and removed us from a show of involvement. I firmly believe the reputation of this country was Dickie's primary concern in everything he dealt with. Some people may say that went too far."

"That seems an odd thing to say, Patrick. Any substance to that caustic remark?"

"No, no! There's nothing he's done that either of us wouldn't. I'm just saying that not all are as patriotic as Dickie."

Before I was allowed to continue, there was a loud, disapproving *hmm* from Fraser.

"Two messages went to Trubnikov from a remote exchange an agent working exclusively for Dickie had fictitiously set up in Cologne, in West Germany. From a secured, specially designed encrypting machine inside J section, GCHQ, the signal was bounced to an isolated relay point in Correos, Spain. It then went without showing its sender or its recipient to Trubnikov's *Pravda* newspaper desk in India. Following Dickie's directive, he sent his doomed Polish lover both instructions. The first was for him to ask his contact to obtain the lethal pill he wanted to take to avoid a painful death when he was discovered, as he knew he would be.

"The ability to use that Spanish relay point came from Kudashov. You will have to live without proof for the time being on that, but it should be clear as we plough on, Fraser. Dickie wanted Kudashov to get that pill from the CIA because he knew the Polish secret police were watching the Americans and when they followed Kudashov back to Jana Kava, they watched where she went and handed the colonel on a plate to the Polish police and then the KGB. Why they waited three days before they arrested the colonel is for them to know and us to guess at. I would hazard a guess and say they wanted to see if he contacted any other army officer in the Kaliningrad barrack before they went for him."

When I told Fraser the second message Trubnikov received from Dickie and passed on to the

Polish colonel, he was overtaken by sadness. I didn't think for one moment it was for himself. I knew it was for his friend. He removed the pipe from his mouth and slowly placed it in the ceramic ashtray he kept on his desk, then stared at his whisky glass in his left hand as though that was where he would find the answer if he looked hard enough. He did find an answer of sorts.

"You can never forget loyalty, Patrick. You may in time forget how a person looked, or even their idiosyncrasies, but you can never forget how loyal they were to you and how much loyalty you gave them. If Dickie did order that, then he had a very good reason."

"Yes, he had a reason, but I'm not sure how good it was, Fraser."

* * *

Whatever else Trubnikov was, a couple of things were abundantly clear; he was clever and practised in living as much by his instincts as his intellect. He was also a practical man. The only commodity he had to sell was secrets and in order to sell them he needed to accumulate as many as he could. He smelled an opportunity when so many messages were coming his way. Although he was far removed in distance from Poland, that would not stop his search for stock to sell. That was exactly what he was doing when he sent that last message to Warsaw. He was thinking about why anyone would send an agent to their death. What made it more bizarre was the fact they were sending a woman agent to her death. What did she know that needs to be silenced, he thought.

'*First they send this woman to point my lover out to the KGB. Then they send her to another place in Poland, this time the city of Gdańsk. The motive for sending the message in open text must mean the man who sends it wants it to be read. She is being sent to her death, but why?*'

Trubnikov became embroiled in the mystery he found himself involved with and, using the extensive connections he had within the First Chief Directorate of the KGB, it took him no time at all to discover the connection there was between Correos in Spain and Nikita Kudashov. It had taken George Stoneman a lot less time, as it was Nikita who initiated George into the Rosicrucian fraternity whose spiritual home, if folklore were to be believed, was where a Knight Crusader saved the life of Richard I, King of England, when he was returning from the Crusades to reconquer Normandy. That place was Correos in Barcelona, Spain. The difference between Stoneman's discovery and Trubnikov's was that Stoneman knew Kudashov as Klaus Mecklenburg.

There were other things that Stoneman knew about Kudashov, that originally Trubnikov did not know. One of those was that his ancient family were the founders of Fraser's Circle of Eight. By the end of WWII, the Mecklenburgs had business interests that stretched from one side of the globe to the other. There was no country in the whole world where one could not purchase a product manufactured by some part of the Mecklenburg empire. George Stoneman was not the only person who was aware of the far-reaching Mecklenburg's power within this intriguing story of Machiavellian deceit and manipulation.

The 'umbrellas' Dickie gave Trubnikov were the complications that glued the whole thing together. One of the parts to the umbrella was the indisputable facts Dickie passed on about how

Kudashov had murdered his wife in the Prague apartment they shared when he was chief of police in that city. Jana Kava knew of the murder and that was the motive behind the reason she was sent to Gdańsk to die.

Dickie protected Kudashov from apprehension by changing the files after Jana was shot. He had the photographs of her murder, taken to further lay the blame on the CIA, but he took precautions to evade repercussions coming Kudashov's way. Those precautions fell apart when George Stoneman recognised Nikita Kudashov as Klaus Mecklenburg.

Chapter Thirty-Six: The Fascist Butcher

I was playing back the tape recordings from the British Embassy gardens to Fraser, whose mood had not changed since hearing of Dickie's compliance in sacrificing Jana Kava for the real reason of keeping Anna Kudashov's murder by her husband a secret. He was listening, but I suspected his mind was working on the possible reasons for Dickie to protect Kudashov. Fraser was renowned for being impatient and I had no wish to keep him waiting too long, so I fast-forwarded to parts I thought might interest him more. When I found what I wanted, I pressed the play button again.

"The head of your secret intelligence service, a Mr Blythe-Smith, and I met in Berlin when only a few bricks of the wall remained to be taken down. We had cross-messaged each other twice in the past, but this was our first face-to-face meeting. We had a few drinks at a restaurant on the west side of Berlin called Bar Schuschnigg.

He was most insistent I spelled that name correctly, asking specifically to meet at that restaurant and stressing more than once that it was on the west side of Berlin. He said he'd been there once and wanted to meet somewhere authentic, not some plastic bazaar where the whisky tasted of the River Spree. But it was his assertion of the word *west* that now seems to have had a hidden purpose.

"I found the place after some difficulty. I asked about five taxi drivers, none of whom had heard of it until the sixth one remembered where it used to be. He was surprised to find it where he remembered it to be, as it was in an area where all the properties had all been demolished. Your man was waiting inside. He was very uneasy. During the half an hour I was there, he kept looking over my shoulder to see if anyone had followed. No one entered the place and no one was waiting outside when I left."

I was watching Fraser, expecting to see some sign of recognition when Trubnikov pronounced the difficult name of the café, and then spelled it out loud in case his Russian accent confused the German name, but there was none. Then

I remembered I was alone with Dickie in the Travellers Club when I first mentioned the name Schuschnigg. It was in relation to what had occurred in New York with Jack Price. I believed the family named Schuschnigg were related by birth to the parent family of our present monarch—the Saxe-Coburg and Gotha side.

When I was recuperating near Brighton after returning from America, I had plenty of time on my hands for research and I found my earlier suspicions to be true. There was a family connection dating back to a marriage between an Ernest I, sovereign Duke of Saxe-Coburg and Gotha, the great-great-great-grandfather of Queen Elizabeth, and his bride Charlotte Schuschnigg, a direct descendent of Leopold V, Duke of Austria. The same Leopold who held King Richard I, the Lionheart, for ransom.

* * *

The coincidence of the restaurant's name and place of meeting did not pass my attention, nor did Trubnikov's reference to the two crossed messages between him and Dickie. Perhaps they were the two fax addresses he'd used that I had failed to find in the vaults. They were possibly filed under the name of Schuschnigg. I vowed to look if time permitted.

'West' side of Berlin and Schuschnigg: the clues were there, but what lay behind the purpose? The net might be widening, but I felt it was closing in as well. The Embassy garden tape was still running.

"Your Blythe-Smith looked tired, not through normal day-to-day tiredness, but more through a weariness of life, holding secrets that are not your own. You must know what I mean by that. It's the lies you have to remember and remembering to forget what the truth was, in case the two get mixed up. Anyway, he wanted all I had on Vladimir Putin. I had many names in my pocket that made larger bulges, but no. He wanted none of them.

"Vladimir and I had spoken often and the last time we did, he told me that he saw his future elsewhere than the foreign intelligence service, and had resigned. He was to enter politics in St Petersburg as soon as he was sure he had all the right backing of past colleagues of the KGB that he needed. He asked for mine and I willingly gave it. We were close friends then and still are.

"In public, he said he'd resigned from the KGB because of the coup against Gorbachev. He said he did not agree with what had happened and did not want to be part of the intelligence community in the new administration. But shit to that. If that were true, then why did Boris Yeltsin, who overthrew Gorbachev, allow Vladimir to carry on? Anyone with common sense would have thought Yeltsin's first move would have been to instruct the KGB to shoot those with a high profile who did not support him. Blythe-Smith told me he was watching the situation in St Petersburg and Moscow very carefully. The only thing I could think of was your man believed as I did; Putin had something on Yeltsin that kept him alive and would accelerate his journey further up the ladder.

"I asked your man for money for what I knew. It wasn't a lot that I had on Vladimir and it all happened a long time ago in 1977, two years after we both joined the KGB, but your head man listened to my outline and then offered me something far more valuable than money."

I stopped the tape and asked Fraser if he wanted to go on and hear things about his family he wouldn't want to hear. He told me I was stupid and just to carry on, regardless of personal feelings. "At my age, laddie, there's nothing that needs special treatment. I've used enough honeyed words as well as harsh ones during my time, and my admiration for my old friend will not be destroyed by anything a Russian will say. Let the tape play, Patrick, there's a good chap."

Yes, there was a degree of scepticism in his voice without some of the conviction he had previously, but Fraser was Fraser with all the bravado in the world still inside his angina-ridden body. I knew what was on the tapes and I suspected he did too, and although I would have preferred him to disclose it, his pride would not allow him to give in and tell tales of the past. He wanted to see the fight through, so I rewound the tape to the *something far more valuable* bit.

"He said it was to be my ticket for life. I could play the kingmaker at any time just by knowing it. He said it was no use to British intelligence as they would never be able to use it effectively, but I could if I ever needed to. It was about a German who adopted a Russian legend to hide his family's secrets. His real name is Klaus Mecklenburg and he is still alive. During the war, it was his family's money that bought him and the rest of his tribe their liberty from the Red Army.

"Once I had the name of this German, I did not leave it there. Your man would have known that. He knew the type of man I was. There is no money for me in secrets that I know nothing of, is there? I traced as much of the Mecklenburgs' family history after the War ended as I could. Dietmar Mecklenburg was the first of the family who interested me.

"He was a Nazi staff general. Came from some aristocratic military academy that I've forgotten the name of. He never saw action; he never stood trial. His money saw to that. I have the names of those who accepted his bribes, if you want them. Somehow, though, I doubt anyone inside your SIS would be very interested, as the British intelligentsia fared well with his money."

There was a pause to the tape here when he stopped walking and picked a peach from one of the trees, eating it as he scrutinised my face, looking for signs of any gallant riposte showing in my eyes. Finding only a mirror of his own absence of chivalry, he carried on in both his consumption of the peach and his recollections of his studies.

"In 1945, Dietmar held his grateful hand out to the Americans for their largesse and, with their money freshly invested in his businesses, his profits soared to unbelievable heights. His three remaining soldier brothers returned to their palatial, unscathed homes and likewise continued making money, as did the sons of those mentioned. But there was one Mecklenburg who did not fare well when the hostilities ended and sense prevailed. His name was Adelar, an SS colonel and elder brother to Dietmar and Klaus, but younger than the two others. Nearing the end of the war, the German High Command named him the Slav Eater.

"The Tito-inspired partisans fighting for their freedom in Yugoslavia, knew him by another name—the Fascist Butcher of Communists. He was captured at the end of that theatre of war, and interviewed by a British army intelligence officer who—after hearing his testimony and then the evidence from some twenty odd survivors of his men's torture of the Slav men, women, and children— summarily executed him by firing a single round into his head from under his chin. The execution was concluded away from witnesses, deep inside a forest a few kilometres from Zagreb. A private matter between a man with an idealistic conscience and the other, a pernicious exponent of evil. You see I had a long time to do my homework on what happened to the Mecklenburgs, and my research was done confidentially, without any witness to what I'd seen. I'm a keen advocate of keeping research personal."

He stopped walking to look at me. "Do you know who that British army intelligence officer was, Mr West?"

* * *

"Did you know then that he was talking about my father, Patrick? Is that why you thought I might prefer you not to run the tape?" Fraser asked whilst he refilled my glass and his.

With the tape recorder stopped, Fraser told me more or less exactly the same as what Trubnikov had said, who had every detail of what happened to Major General Adelar Mecklenburg, of the Waffen SS from the account given by Major General Stuart Ughert at his court-martial at Aldershot Officers' Academy in December 1946, where the youngest major general in the British Army was found innocent of all charges on a directive received from the Ministry of War, co-signed by the Prime Minister, Clement Attlee. The only witnesses to the crime of murder was the dead Adelar and Major General Ughert himself.

* * *

Fraser leant across the occasional table, switching on the tape-recorder.

"The transcript of the military hearing, along with the document sent by Prime Minister Attlee is readily available, you know. I was told it was safely kept in the Ministry for Defence vaults. Can't be much of a secret if it's as open as that, can it? This information comes free of charge, as long as you leave me alone to hold the real secret that Mr Blythe-Smith gave me and do with it as I please. If you interfere, then I think those human rights activists you hear more and more of nowadays might kick up a storm and embarrass a very close friend of yours. In today's cordial world between the East and the West, I would not like that to happen."

* * *

"I appreciate the earlier thought, Patrick, but I did know of that episode of my family history. Something you would not know is that when Tito became President of Yugoslavia, he invited my father to visit the country where they had added his name to a roll call of honour to the dead in Belgrade. I think I was sixteen when he, my mother and I went to the ceremony. What struck me the most was the devastation of the place.

"During the war, my mother and I moved from our home on the outskirts of Edinburgh to a place called Fortrose, on the coast not far from Inverness, to escape the bombing. Apparently, we had been offered evacuation to Canada, but she turned down the offer. She was a very forceful and proud Scottish lady, was my mother. She undertook some of my education, leaving the essentials to the Fortrose village school. The two together must have done something right as it was because of them I managed to graduate to university. It was that background of small-town life on the coast in the Highlands of Scotland that made Belgrade so stark and unusual to me. The time I had in Yugoslavia opened my eyes, not only to the devastating destruction of war, but also to the fact that different cultures must exist together in order to survive.

"I had read some material I'd found on this man Tito before we left, and although his politics were alien to what I'd been brought up to believe, when I was given the opportunity to listen to a couple of public addresses he made, I could understand how difficult the blending of so many aspirations must be for a politician. We were guests in the country for about a month. I don't remember much, other than it being stiflingly hot with only dust to breathe in the towns, but fresh delicious fruit available throughout the tree-lined countryside, and my mother bitterly complaining how there was no tea anywhere and the coffee was like treacle. My mother died within a year of our visit and father went downhill quite rapidly following on from her death.

"During his service life he was a very smart man, but at home he was the exact opposite, dressing in an infuriatingly casual way that brought many a rebuke from my chapel-going mother, but he took no notice. He told me in a loud voice to not let anyone tell you how to dress. I think I got the 'scruffy' reputation from him, but I'm proud my stubbornness came from both of them. My mother was always clipping me around the ear for not polishing my shoes or tying my tie incorrectly for school. If she had lived to see how I dressed when at university, then I think she might have killed me."

"Did you know about Kudashov being related to the Mecklenburg of Yugoslavia, Fraser?"

"Not until we had this conversation, but if your next question is going to be will it make a difference to how I react when I see him next, then no. My professional approach will not change; however, psychologically, I cannot help but think of the past, but we are both different from his relative and my father. Time has moved on, as they say, laddie."

The pride the young Fraser must have felt on seeing his father's name being honoured in a foreign land had overshadowed the despondency he'd shown when listening to Trubnikov's account of how and why he was so highly thought of in war-torn Yugoslavia. On lighting another pipe and pouring another glass of our whisky, his smile had returned. I had no wish to see it disappear; nevertheless, the issue over the visit of an aide to the Court of St James's at his and Molly's home in the rural splendour of Chearsley, and the delivered court dictum read to me in India, was hanging over both our heads and had to be addressed. It wasn't I who opened the discussion. Nor was it approached in the delicate way I thought was warranted. Fraser dived in with all guns firing in all directions.

"I'm not sure that the load of rubbish I got was the same as the load you did, but does anyone really expect us to believe that about Kudashov and Dickie, because I don't and I never will. How on earth did the Palace get involved?" he asked and I wished he hadn't.

Chapter Thirty-Seven: 1987

When George Stoneman saw the microfilm fall from Jana Kava's cigarette packet as he strolled into the Letna Park in Prague that sunny spring lunchtime, a catalogue of events were put in motion, leading me to where I was in the understanding of the importance Dickie Blythe-Smith placed on Nikita Sergeyovitch Kudashov. It was Kudashov as Klaus Mecklenburg who invited Stoneman to join the Rosicrucian fraternity and enjoy the benefits that association would bring. Enjoying himself making money was what George did best. He needed no second invitation.

George was fifty-two years of age when he and Jana met on that day. He was flattered by her attention and, in return, she was more than gratified by his. His marriage was not an insurmountable problem for his wandering eye and use of casual acquaintances to satiate the increasing sexual appetite he enjoyed into his later stage of life, but for the obvious StB reasons, their meetings were sensibly conducted with appropriate guile so as not to bring attention to themselves. Although Jana could not be described as ugly, she could not be described as beautiful either. Her greying hair and chubby face were not unattractive; indeed, she had an air of breeding about her that turned many a male head in her direction. However, as many as there were that looked, there were more who did not.

The file that Kudashov had crafted for MI6 summed her up entirely accurately: comely. Jana was someone's mother and aunt in the waiting. She was not a long-term American ambassador's mistress, but she was a spy. George quickly parted from Jana, leaving her troubled by the withdrawal of his affections, but never attributing that to anything other than the sexual impulses men suffer from. After all, she told herself, she had the bed of an ex-Prime Minister of Czechoslovakia to keep warm when he could escape from his evil wife. No consequences from the normal separation of paths that happen with men and women contributed to Jana's death. Even so, there was a separation—one made permanent by Anna Kudashov's murder.

* * *

The attributes George offered the Rosicrucians were of a material kind and far more than they actually required. He moved inside the circles of power that controlled a military machine that one half of the civilised world worshipped as the possible saviour and the other half despised, as one would despise the school bully in the playground. Nikita, as Klaus Mecklenburg, offered George an alternate playground to the Rosicrucians which, although they would be beneficial, were not really offering the things at the top of George's list. Klaus Mecklenburg offered the patronage of a group of eight families who moved in a constructed circle for the elite only. One where the Stonemans could be rewarded with privileged positions that would be advantageous to those who made up the core of the Circle.

Before George Stoneman left Czechoslovakia for America in March 1983, Klaus Mecklenburg introduced him to Bohdan Dimitriyevich Valescov, a native Russian of immense wealth and influence. Bohdan had plans way beyond those of the old men on the Politburo of the Soviet

Union. He wanted to rule the whole world without blowing it up to achieve that objective. He had made friends with a young man full of visionary ideas of being able to dominate the world without fracturing the infrastructure, a young Vladimir Putin. Bohdan was the Russian government minister for oil and gas production, who had already become a dollar millionaire without anyone noticing. He needed somewhere safe to relocate his growing pile of money from the seven Russian banks he presently used.

George Stoneman was Bohdan's answer. George had been called home to take up a position inside the US Treasury as advisor on investment inside the Eastern Bloc countries. He was specifically tasked with formatting a committee to undergo a thorough analysis of the future when the lantern of Communism would be extinguished and the pragmatism of democracy would be adopted. Domination of the world would be a harder proposition than dominating a committee, but George was soon able to open the accounts in the Panama banks into which not only a special Russian's money was funnelled, but also legitimate American funds—a large part of the trillions of dollars from the US defence budget that went missing.

The Stonemans were diverse in their business portfolio. Compared to many American families they were wealthy, but in comparison to the Mecklenburgs they were as poor as a slave on a cotton farm when slavery was accepted as the norm. George Stoneman was a greedy human being, not one to settle for the wealth he had. He sniffed the Mecklenburg opulence and was resentful through jealousy. He heard the tales of corrupt opportunities that Bohdan waved under his nose and he signed on the dotted line. Tucker Stoneman, the eldest of his three sons, was earmarked for the top job available on the world stage, from the chair of which the world could be driven in the direction the invisible government wanted to go. Stoneman's eldest would be the crucial element to supremacy sought by the inner sanctum of eight.

George pinned his colours to the imperious military leaders disillusioned with the appeasement they saw in their country's foreign policy that armed the future enemies of America, forcing them to order troops to die as American ordnance rained down on them. They wanted to control where the weaponry went and who lived and who died, not the ever changing politicians on Capitol Hill. It was not long after Marcus Stoneman, George's second son, joined the Central Intelligence Agency that he found like-minded agents with high-ranking military relatives who had constructed a tentative blueprint based upon an existing confidential NATO file that they said needed polishing with clean dollar bills before it could deliver the strategy that all true isolationists needed to rule.

Spencer Stoneman, George's youngest son, left Harvard University, making a name for himself in corporate law before being headhunted for a branch of the United States legislative where, for a time, he served on Tucker's presidential campaign. The Stonemans were well placed to have the singular edge one needs to succeed.

* * *

As a family, the Mecklenburgs looked at Gladio B and saw some advantages to do with future trade, but not much else. They had affiliations to most powerful institutions owing to their established Rosicrucian association within the larger Freemasonry fraternity. They were content with the ever expanding markets the Rosicrucian fellowship presented, which were far less confrontational to conquer. There was one other member of the Circle who was satisfied with the fraternity they belonged to, without having the need for the desolate aims advanced by the escalated Gladio B file.

But sadly, the two member families were outnumbered and the balance became even more uneven when the formidable remaining six persuaded Klaus and the other Mecklenburgs that Gladio B was the only way forward. That left one family unwilling to concede to the aspirations of the bastardised NATO file. Despite the separation of ideals, the exiting family were unable to completely sever links to the Circle, owing to past arrangements in areas of combined interest.

The family of Bohdan Dimitriyevich Valescov looked, and the five other families who were bored looking inside their bank vaults looked, and with one accord they all agreed on the future formula—divide the world's populace into those they could continually squeeze more from and those they could only bleed dry once. The ultimate formula was based around the concept of breeding more of those that would become of use and obliterate the strain of human genome of those that would become a drain. With the two objectives achieved, all else would fall into place. When ready to proceed, they would start with Iraq, move on to Iran, then when in control of the oil from both, they would weaken the Saudi grip on the Western world. The life of the planet would be extended they argued by the population management as decreed by the Circle, who would conserve the world's energy by managing the numbers of those who used it.

However, with Tucker's demise, the families that made up Fraser's Circle were forced to reassess their position. The seven who were left participating within it concluded their business in 2003 by agreeing their time to control the foreign policies of America would come again when a suitable candidate, acting as their puppet, could be identified. Meanwhile, Bohdan Dimitriyevich Valescov was to be left alone to effect what ambitions he could, using the chemicals he had developed. It was all Bohdan's money that had financed the Zaragoza complex with the knowledge of the President of Russia, Vladimir Putin. When the plant was at full operation, the Circle could preside over a reviewed Food for Oil programme—this time for the displaced Kurdish population of the corridor from southern Turkey across northern Syria, Iraq and Iran, contaminating the supplied food with the eugenic mutilating drugs devised at Zaragoza.

Tucker had been stopped by British intelligence intervening prior to the Iraqi invasion. The photograph of Klaus Mecklenburg was one thing to handle, but the tracking down of Nikita Kudashov was an entirely different proposition, which by August 2007, George was incapable of pursuing as it was on the sixteenth of that month he met his end, quietly as he slept. The job of tracing Kudashov's whereabouts was left to his two sons, with Marcus in the vanguard through his CIA connections.

* * *

I now knew part of the meaning to Dickie's final message that I found in the Foreign and Commonwealth vaults. The date was insignificant as he filed it a long time before George Thomas Stoneman's death. But although the capitalised letter 's' to Stone obviously stood for Stoneman, at this stage I did not know about the Panama banks, nor did I know what the word Finnish signified; some of that knowledge was shortly to come.

* * *

Time had moved more quickly than I hoped, being much later than I'd planned for; nevertheless, there was a heavy Monday to navigate without any failure or complications occurring in Moscow to deal with. Then there was the meeting of the Defence Chiefs alongside their boss, the Minister for Defence. Military men are trained to fight battles in wars, not to sit in an air-conditioned room discussing areas of conflict they cannot have an impact upon. Yes, they needed my intelligence reports, but none of those in the room on Monday wanted to hear me telling them of a botched extraction from Moscow or, come to that, the UK's involvement in the successful destruction of Russian property on Russian soil. Notwithstanding any of that, my main meeting with Kudashov could not wait until tomorrow when his granddaughter's life was at stake.

My plans were to tell him of the operation being set for 6 o'clock in the morning Russian time and report on progress from my office in Whitehall via a video link that was being set up in his rooms at Beaulieu, which was one of the reasons for moving him. The other reason I moved him was for his safety. I could only be happy to a certain extent that nobody outside of my extraction team knew of what we planned to do. Unfortunately, I could not be one hundred percent certain as I could only take the words of others regarding the security of the Moscow family helping on this operation. Kudashov had no knowledge of them when I'd asked, but that meant nothing overall. I had to accept Liam Catlin's approval of their use, and that made me feel a little nervous. Nervousness was not an emotion I could show in front of Nikita Kudashov and, partially because of that, I invited Fraser along with me for the ride and the company. I gave my word to Molly I'd look after him overnight and send him back to her safe and sound by Monday lunchtime.

Chapter Thirty-Eight: Beaulieu

Kudashov could not have known I'd been to India to meet Trubnikov, but from the moment we arrived at Beaulieu he was unusually defensive. He had eaten by the time of our arrival, which was fortunate as dinner would have delayed our deliberations. I thought he would be perturbed now there was less time than he'd said he would need to prepare before his granddaughter was rescued, but any disappointment he had was quickly tempered by the pleasure the video link installed in his sitting room gave him, accepting that as the reason for the temporary change of accommodation. It was one of them of course, but the other was more important.

I'd planned to leave a mobile phone with him when we left, which he would suspect I'd bugged in some way. If he was half the man I imagined him to be, he would strip the phone down to see if there was a device fitted inside. There was none. However, the whole residential area including the grounds of this part of the

Beaulieu estate was tuned to this phone. There was nowhere he could use it without my people able to monitor the call. I hoped he would be open about why he needed prior knowledge without making that call, but I couldn't risk not knowing who he would contact. For now, I started at why Dickie had altered the files about the death of his wife. When I had first asked, Kudashov had described it as protection. I asked him: *from whom*?

"I had enemies who would have loved to know all the details of my life, Mr West. It was merely a ruse we thought up that might confuse some of the less vigorous followers," he replied in a more heavy and introspective voice than I could remember of him.

"I will have to disagree with you. I think it was to do with one of the three reasons why Jana Kava had to die. One of which was because she knew you'd murdered your wife in Prague, Nikita. Is that right? And was that behind Dickie's reasoning?"

Fraser tried to look nonchalant and aware of my accusation, but it did not fool me or Kudashov. "I would assume that we will be here forever if that's the substance of your accusations this evening, Mr West. Either forever or until one of us dies of surprise."

He was looking directly at Fraser when he said that. Fraser smiled, which made every grainy tissue of skin on his face demand attention, as it was he who put the next question. "No, we have good reasons behind that assumption. We would simply like to know why it was Mr Blythe-Smith who would want to protect you from anyone or anything?"

"Now, here we have what you English use a strange word to describe a puzzle, a conundrum, and I hope I have pronounced that word right?" He quickly looked at our two faces to check what already he knew was correct before continuing. "Dickie spoke highly of you, Mr Ughert, but he kept things away from you as he regarded you as what we say in Russian as—*vysypaniye*, and you mean—rash. In Russia, rash people are regarded as seditious. Not people to rely on. In actual fact, I was closer to him during his passage through the British secret intelligence services than you were. I was a valuable asset working in hostile areas of the world. I would not expect my name to have been voiced much as if it had been, it would threaten my cover, but my contributions were of immense value. There you have the basic reasons for him wanting me protected. I was important."

Fraser's smile degenerated into a grin he held firm throughout Kudashov's explanation. When Kudashov finished speaking, Fraser filled his pipe and prepared to light it. I kept an eye on him, as I believed the ritual he'd adopted was one filled with nervous energy, not knowing where to explode if the pipe was no longer an available choice. His and my drinking habits I attributed purely to being sociable. I lit a cigarette more from frustration than desire, as I had cut down on smoking for the time away in India and the absence of nicotine was harder to accept now home.

"It doesn't seem to me that Dickie had your importance in mind when he notified the CIA of you showing your face at the NSA establishment in Mannheim, Germany, and then sent a copy of the photograph they took of you off to your old friend George Stoneman in Delaware USA. What do you think of that?"

Fraser had found the whisky and an ashtray, and I'd found the chink in Kudashov.

"Not sure I know a George Stoneman, Patrick, but if Dickie did do such a thing I'm sure it would have been for a valid reason."

"There's no point in playing game, Klaus," I let that name sink in for a second before continuing. "All that will do is delay the end slightly. I know most of the story and I know for certain that it was Dickie who sent the photograph, as he was the only one who knew you both. One of George's sons has found you and that's why you're scared stiff for Cilicia, isn't it?"

He looked at the wall clock before he spoke, but I got in before him. "I don't anticipate being here for long. Tomorrow is a worrying day for you and me, and sleep would be very welcome tonight. I will leave you a phone when we leave. It's not bugged, but I don't expect you to believe that without checking. You'll have at least six hours to arrange whatever it was you needed to do. I went to India over the weekend to meet another friend of Dickie's. One I don't believe you've met, but you will have heard of his name if for no other reason than it was he who appointed Cilicia to her position, a Vyacheslav Trubnikov.

"At one time I could have been persuaded about the importance you represented to the British intelligence community, but that was shattered when I learned Dickie gave away your most classified secret to Trubnikov. That was the one you only told Blythe-Smith about, when he threatened to expose you to the Polish StB after your refusal to kill Dalek Kava. That's why there was a necessity for Operation Donor and for my involvement.

"The man he gave away your crown jewels to was not the most dependable man to keep a secret. He makes a living by selling them. But for an objective only known by him and Dickie, he kept yours until I asked him for it. Then he gave me everything, Klaus. Now why would someone who thought of you as important give up your name to a man he knew would go looking for you, as well as telling him that same man your holiest of holies?"

I was not going to give him a chance to speak. "When I asked him why it was he gave Cilicia her job as deputy head of the Eighth Directorate, where you must be proud of how she has worked her way up to become the head of a separate section, he just smiled and never answered me. Quite honestly, I had all I wanted from him. There was really no need for me to know. Besides, I'd have no way of knowing if it was truth or lies he told me. But perhaps you might know and be able to tell us, Nikita? Perhaps you might also like to tell us more of your murdered wife's relative, Anatoly Vladimirovich Malikova, while you're about it?" I was not giving way. "But before we get too far into that one, hopefully not jeopardising tomorrow's abduction, let's tackle your references to Henry Mayler and his and your connection to the Rosicrucian fellowship?"

I gave way and smoked my cigarette and drank my Scotch.

"Yes, I can start there, but I doubt either of you will enjoy what I have to say. Your prized Dickie Blythe-Smith was a Mason like me, Mr Ughert."

"Yet again, you fail to impress me, Nikita. I'm a Mason as well. Most of the British civil service, along with most members of Parliament, are Masons. About the only person I know who's not is

West here," Fraser declared with both pride and amusement.

"Maybe all what you say is true, Mr Ughert. Or maybe the Ugherts' truth is different to other people's truth. Yes, I am Klaus Mecklenburg. A relative of the Adelar Mecklenburg your father murdered. And you dare to insinuate I murdered my wife when you befriend a murderer yourself, Mr West." His accusing look darted from my face to Fraser's and then back again. When neither of us answered, he carried on with his submission.

"You might well know the story of Adelar Mecklenburg, but what you have never known is that I introduced Blythe-Smith to a very important person who was central to the Circle of Eight you are, as I'm given to believe, obsessed with. Dickie knew the potential those families, who include my own in their number, represent."

"Yes, I got all that from Trubnikov, Nikita. Despite the past with its ramifications on the present, I also discovered how Dickie shared all the intelligence Trubnikov gave us on the young Vladimir Putin with the CIA. You didn't know that, did you?"

Fraser's missing smile reappeared at just about the same time as Nikita Kudashov's face took on the ashen glaze of shock.

"Hmm, I can understand your worry, Nikita. Especially as Cilicia is still in Moscow, but back to your wife's connection to the Romanovs, and Anatoly Vladimirovich Malikova, for a moment. Could he not have helped his niece to escape from Russia? He must have many connections? Could it be that he knows the truth about Anna, and doesn't want to help? Does he have the same inside knowledge as Jana Kava had, knowing you murdered your wife? And was the consequences of that brutal act covered up by Dickie Blythe-Smith's story of papers stashed away by General Ivan Aleksandrovich Solidus, proving Victor Rothschild's treason? Is that the cover story that did the rounds of those that had to know?

"These are some of the mysteries that led Fraser and me to other mysteries we cannot solve without your truthful replies. Perhaps there are numberless mysteries that will cloud our vision between now and 4 a.m., forcing us to call it off in Moscow and see who gets to Cilicia first? Would it be the corrupted American branch of the CIA who write files on proposed genocides and kills for fun, or perhaps the President of Russia gets there first, either because we call him up and tell him? Or possibly Trubnikov will call his old friend, being unsure what I will do now I know your secret? Either way, we can watch as Putin kills your granddaughter in retribution for your acts of espionage against the old USSR, not forgetting any you may have committed against his new federal state of Russia. Would it be fair to leave Cilicia to pay for your acts? We live in interesting times, Nikita, don't we?" I watched Kudashov as he looked into space and I knew we'd won.

"We do, Mr West, but I fear they will be more interesting for you than me."

"Tell me about George Stoneman's contribution to your Circle of families and how he and you fit into this blessed Gladio B file that just won't go away. Then I want to know who the Finnish man that's so important to it is? How does he fit into this story? Remember Moscow when you consider my questions, my friend."

* * *

At first we covered what he did and did not know of the 'leak' at GCHQ. He knew of Geoffrey Prime, but not how Dickie coerced Randall 'Ryan' Cavershall to act as our double and turn Trubnikov into a conduit British intelligence could use with impunity. He suspected his own name could have been circulated, but had no idea by whom; least of all did he suspect Dickie of being his Judas. He had read of George Stoneman's death on the same day as Paulette Simona's plane was shot down, and he strongly believed it was someone from the Stoneman family who was responsible.

What then followed was a detailed analysis of the cooperation the Circle of families enjoyed until they were presented with the Gladio B file that friends of George Stoneman wanted financing. Nikita Kudashov, as Mecklenburg, introduced Bohdan Dimitriyevich Valescov into Stoneman's thinking and, hey presto, Panama was up and running. Now I had the answer to Dickie's obscure reference to the: money as it drains to the sea. We next addressed who the Finnish man was. Fraser had heard the name from somewhere, but was unable to remember from where. He left the room to contact Michael Simmons, who set about running the data through the computers at AIS. Whilst Michael was available Fraser checked on the situation in Moscow with him and was reassured that all was calm and set for the time arranged.

Chapter Thirty-Nine: A Circle

Anatoly Vladimirovich Malikova, the person whom Nikita Kudashov implied that if ever his granddaughter disappeared from Moscow would probably launch nuclear missiles if able was, in reality, as timid as a church mouse. Or so it said in the report Christopher Irons sent directly to Group before it found its way to me last Thursday. Kudashov did not look sufficiently surprised to satisfy either Fraser's or my curiosity. However, in another part of Christopher's report, it stated that he was as KGB as blood was red and very much part of the Federal Security Service, the KGB's replacement.

Anatoly's patriot father, Major General Vladimir Anatolyevich Malikova, was the department head of the Soviet counter-intelligence from 1955 until his honourable retirement in 1981, aged just sixty-six years of age. He had travelled to Prague a year after his retirement not only to attend his sister's funeral, but also to investigate her death. A gunshot to the head was the cause and the handwritten note, found beside her body, attested to her state of mind preceding her apparent suicide. But by the time General Malikova arrived, the note had mysteriously vanished and there had been nobody other than his brother-in-law to vouch for his sister's handwriting.

He had a letter from Anna in his pocket, where it said her husband was having an affair with a woman who worked at the central policy committee of the chairman of the Communist Party of Czechoslovakia. She had seen them together several times so her letter went on to say, and she did not believe him when he told her, in fits of anger, that the woman was a police informer who only worked for him. Her brother questioned Nikita about the 'affair' and those fits of anger, accepting the explanation of stress for the anger and the importance of secrecy for informers, strenuously denying any infidelity, which the general, a man of the world, understood implicitly. Nevertheless, more doubts started to creep in, especially after he'd returned to Moscow and saw Kudashov in the company of a seductive younger woman a few months after his sister was buried.

He was not in a position to approach Kudashov that day, when he saw his brother-in-law arm in arm with the woman from his hospital bed, where he lay with the cancer that was eating his body away. Sadly, he died three days later. His son, Anatoly, took it upon himself to continue to look into his aunt's suspicious death and when asked by Nikita Kudashov to care for his parentless granddaughter by arranging a position for her somewhere within government ministries, he knew exactly where her qualifications would be suited. He asked his colleagues in the upper echelons of the Federal Security Service and Vyacheslav Trubnikov, owing a favour to his father, and in the process of taking up his role in India, agreed to appoint them both to the communication hub in Moscow Centre. It was as simple and as fortuitous as that. There was no ulterior motive, or hidden agendas. Simply luck that Cilicia was able to read the NSA signals.

But luck had nothing to do with Nikita Kudashov's wish for the time he desired before we went ahead with Cilicia's extraction. That was to exact retribution on Anatoly for what his father had done to Nikita when he was frustrated over his sister's death.

The major general had let it be known that the reason for Nikita Kudashov's change of name from his rightful German one was not as Nikita said—in order that he could ingratiate himself into the Western intelligence services in order to spy for Mother Russia. The major general alleged the opposite to be true—he was an American spy. The allegation brought trouble to Nikita's door. He was recalled to Moscow to answer the allegation, but Dickie Blythe-Smith had seen this coming immediately after Kudashov had admitted killing his wife. That was the reason behind Nikita being seen encouraging Jana Kava to point out the traitorous Polish army officer.

'There,' Kudashov said at his hearing, 'is your answer to my hate-filled, vindictive brother-in-law's slur on my character. Did I not point out the traitorous army officer? I am yours, as my money has shown, and I will continue to contribute as long as I have your trust.'

The scar left by that accusation was deep and angry, needing lancing by the death of the accuser's son in recompense. Kudashov had someone in mind to kill Anatoly Vladimirovich Malikova, but now, Kudashov said, it was too late for him to be reached and once Cilicia had gone, so had her grandfather's hold over his would-be assassin. Although I suspected something along those lines, I was far from sure; however, I proposed another way of dealing with Malikova to Kudashov, which I had discussed with Christopher Irons on the drive down to Beaulieu. After our discussion, Kudashov agreed that there was no longer a need for the mobile phone. Having cleared that away, I moved on to why Cilicia was now in so much danger from the George Stoneman's family and the third reason for Jana Kava's death, which Fraser was unaware of.

It was Jana who introduced George Stoneman to Karina Kudashov and her husband, Ludvík.

Karina was a beautiful young woman who had the same roaming eye as George. It did not take long for the two to form a secret partnership that was to last until Karina fell pregnant with Cilicia. Jana knew George was the father because Karina told her so. Similarly, she told him he was the father. But she told Nikita's son, Ludvík Kudashov, a different story. She told him he was their daughter's father. Nikita suspected what his son did not, asking Karina outright. She did nothing to conceal her infidelity. All was as well as things could be in the Kudashov family until George Stoneman told Kudashov about his position regarding the Gladio B file and his ultimate aim of the destruction of the world order in which the Mecklenburgs had prospered. That's when things went sour between the Stoneman family and Nikita.

In desperation, Nikita tried to hide his granddaughter away from the clutches of those who shared George Stoneman's ideals. He told Dickie his secret, but Dickie had a higher game to play than hiding Nikita's family's shame. When the time was right for the British interests to exceed those of Kudashov, Dickie told Trubnikov the truth of Cilicia's father in exchange for the information on Vladimir Putin. Trubnikov kept this 'umbrella' dry, but not unopened.

In her final year at university, Trubnikov met with Cilicia Kudashov under the pretence of interviewing her for the eventual role she filled within the Russian counter-intelligence communications department. He told Cilicia the truth about who her father was. George Stoneman, he said, was a senior CIA administrator. He showed her evidence of her stepbrother's presidential nomination campaign, and not being aware of corrupted files of demonic proportions, he played up the all-American Stoneman family to rival anything she may have known of American culture.

"You have two other stepbrothers," he told her. "One is a highly placed CIA agent who would adore to have a sister working on the inside of Moscow Centre. If you were to agree to the American overtures, I could ensure your grandfather's safety in the West. If you accept, you have my word, but if not, then who knows?" he said.

Being a man who used lies exclusively for the betterment of himself, Trubnikov sold the allegiance Cilicia declared for the CIA to former colleagues he knew from his KGB days. Anatoly Vladimirovich Malikova was one of them, and it was he who suggested to his superior that at the age Cilicia now was, twenty-five, she was ready to 'defect' to America and work there for the interests of Russia.

Nikita Kudashov did not know of Anatoly Malikova's intentions, nor did Anatoly know of Nikita's. But I knew of them both, as Trubnikov was a fountain of knowledge.

* * *

Fraser and I left Kudashov to his agonising worries of tomorrow morning and set off for Whitehall, filled with the same concerns, or so I thought. However, Fraser was occupied with others.

"We now know of two of the families who make up that Circle of mine. Is it our job to police what goes on in the world of legitimate trade and finance, or not? If all they're doing is manipulating prices and availability, then okay, it's a moral issue when it comes to the less fortunate, yes, but is it our role as intelligence gatherers to intervene? I know you had the same question when we were dealing with Henry Mayler and what he represented. I'm quite convinced Kudashov and his part of the Mecklenburgs have nothing to do with Gladio B, Patrick. As for the Court of St James and the House of Windsor, etc., they too have a right to form advantageous allegiances to further their state ambitions. I'm equally convinced of their non-participation in Gladio B.

"From what you have told me, I can only conclude that Samuel Rothschild's hands are also clean, along with the Lebanese Assyrian billionaire, Aaron Simonin, the man he was working with to create the home for displaced Kurds, Syrians, etc., in Southern Turkey. Which leaves us with three names that we know of: the Russian, Bohdan Dimitriyevich Valescov, the Indian in charge of SanMonto, the Israeli with the pharmaceutical company, and we have the Finnish name to come, which completes the Circle of Eight. Now, however, I'm not absolutely certain of what we should do.

"Dickie was always promoting GB interests, as all good servants of this country should. I hope I did the same when on the JIC, and I'm sure you do, and will do, now you have the chair. I've said it before, but it's worth repeating: the world of espionage is never a straight path to tread. But returning to what we have here, there are several things I'm still unclear on, Patrick. The main things are—why did Dickie go to all the extent he did just to name a double-agent dating back to the eighties? Where exactly is the benefit in that? The question about how did he know you would still be around has not been answered and probably never will be, and possibly the most important question of all is why give the Americans all what Trubnikov gave him about Putin? Dickie saw the potential Putin had; otherwise he would not have worked so hard on Trubnikov."

I spent a few moments thinking in what order I should answer Fraser's questions when the car phone rang and it was Michael with an identity to the name Kudashov gave us of the Finnish man in Dickie's last signal, locked away in the vaults at the Foreign and Commonwealth. Fraser was right in the line of thinking he was taking. What could British intelligence do with four foreign nationals taking advantage of financial situations to dominate the markets they were in? Our role was to protect British interests around the globe. There were no rules attached that obligation, nor should there be. I decided not to tell Fraser the latest and last name to his Circle. I could see no good reason why.

Chapter Forty: Key Fitzgerald

Exhaustion and the consumption of whisky overtook me on the car journey home, forcing me to apologise to Fraser for falling asleep and only waking on our arrival at Whitehall. Apparently, I'd slept for a solid forty minutes from the time of taking Michael Simmons's call. It felt as though I'd had a full night of sleep as I was wide awake and raring to go. That couldn't be said of Fraser who, despite or maybe because of staying awake to speak to both Frank and Jimmy on the drive from Beaulieu, looked debilitated on the short walk from the lifts to the spare apartment. I enquired about his health and was told to mind my own business in a deep Scottish voice he normally reserved for Molly when she likewise enquired. In many ways I needed that show of affection, even allowing for its alcoholic doctoring, as it took me nearer to the lost affection I had with Hannah. Be that as it may, I had a job to do that in five hours' time that could cost a life, or more, if not done correctly. Fraser asked to be woken early and then waved goodbye, leaving me to reflect on what I knew.

There were a few files attributed to 'Ryan' that I've mentioned and would have mentioned to Hannah had she been alive, but there was one that I have not disclosed to you or Fraser. It went a long way in answering Fraser's main question of why did Dickie give the Americans all the information Trubnikov gave him on Vladimir Putin. It also explained why Dickie did what he did in constructing such a hugely elaborate web to conceal one name—the only name agent Ryan ever sent in plain text. It also had a lot to do with why it was hidden, but not completely concealed from anyone who looked hard enough.

I had wanted to tell Fraser of it from the moment I made the discovery, but other considerations arose before any indulgence in self-congratulations seemed appropriate. The old saying of pride goes before a fall, has haunted me since schooldays, be they primary days or university ones. Too many times have I tripped over my self-pride to allow it now to be of significance.

Despite any feeling of importance, there was nobody left alive who could categorically say that Dickie's magical, sleight-of-hand illusion was meant to be found by anyone, least of all me. Nevertheless, the coincidence of the names of Jack and Jacqueline Price, alongside the handwritten note found at St Michael's Church, were names and places known by both Fraser Ughert and me, but the message contained in the anagram of NOMITE was something only I knew and would have taken note of. Putting aside my friendship with Fraser, built over more years than I care to remember, the two people who were most influential in my formative time in the intelligence service were Jack Price and Dickie Blythe-Smith. Both were precise and thorough men. Men who believed that clarity, although most often disguised as a necessity in our way of life, was essential for the full comprehension of any procedure. They preached and sought the ability to look beyond the obvious.

It was the privilege to be able to look behind the personal clues that compelled me to dig further than someone outside would have and, in following those directional hints, I found the misinformation that Dickie was renowned for in the signal that was sent in his retirement years about an unknown Soviet 'defector.' Not the one they knew of in 1981.

This was the one-worded Ryan communication in the vaults hidden under the file name of Cilicia. A name unknown to any other chairman of the Joint Intelligence Committee until Fraser and I found an obtuse reference to it five years ago at Hannah's and my wedding. Had Cilicia's grandfather not come here, then in all probability I would never have looked and Dickie's masterstroke would never have been discovered.

It was a secret that perhaps had to die, to enable a false sense of stability to fall upon the person Dickie had in his pocket to be resurrected whenever circumstances dictated. I had to wait until Moscow had been concluded before I could pull back the curtains and reveal the Blythe-Smith trickery to the world.

* * *

By 07:28 UK time, Cilicia Kudashov was in the air on board a Norwegian flight bound to Oslo from Moscow, sitting beside Christopher Irons.

From there she was due to board a British Airways flight to London, arriving mid-afternoon our time. The rest of our 'rescue' group had their own unhindered ways home. Everything had gone to plan.

The need for the appearance of it being an abduction had disappeared when I'd spoken to Trubnikov in India, where he'd told me of the conversation he had with his former KGB personnel. When Trubnikov told me that Anatoly Vladimirovich Malikova had put forward the idea that he could construct a false defection to America for Cilicia, and then 'handle' her from either inside Moscow Centre, or better still, he said, 'If I were to travel after her.' That was an offer that no doubt caused some deliberations within the equivalent of the KGB First Directorate. I appropriated that idea of his to attribute Cilicia's disappearance to his well-constructed plan. In that way, I figured he would be the centre of any investigations and nobody would look for her until it was far too late.

On my instructions, Christopher had given Cilicia a sedative to put in any drink Anatoly might have the night preceding her 'defection.'

With Liam Catlin working miracles on a copy of a computer-generated scenario, we provided error-free details of Cilicia's adopted American identity with such things as a driving licence number, details of a fictional bank account, medical insurance, and an address of residence in New York State. This we left in Cilicia's apartment on open view, to be found when her absence was noticed. Catlin and his helpers were able to install a copy of the scheme onto the hard drive of Anatoly's computer at the Eighth Chief Directorate. As an additional form of satisfaction for Nikita Kudashov, he agreed to reimburse the small sum of money that purchased the single air ticket to New York in Anatoly Vladimirovich Malikova's name that Cilicia had managed to conceal in Anatoly's desk. When Anatoly found her gone, he had two choices, from neither of which could he escape the charge of incompetence. At best, his career was ruined and at worse he was locked up as a traitor.

Nikita Kudashov loved the proposal I put to him, greedily accepting it, pledging his undying support of GB for eternity. He was even more pleased when I told him that it would be impossible for Cilicia to be traced once she was clear of her apartment. We had supplied a wig with hair extensions that exactly fitted the photograph on her new passport she carried, along with stacked-heeled shoes that made her two inches taller than her real height. Films from the cameras at Moscow airport would not show a Cilicia Kudashov, nor would boarding control. All that was seen was a tall, black-haired woman named Georgia Wallis, an American from Syracuse, New York, returning home from a short holiday in Russia. Nikita's granddaughter was safe from harm. At least as far as the Russians were concerned.

* * *

Part of the jubilation we all felt was shared by the Prime Minister when we met as part of my duties on Monday morning. I confirmed Klaus Mecklenburg's decision to move the headquarters of his family's specialist military signalling engineering company from France to Swansea in South Wales and his computer terminal block manufacture from Germany to Coventry in the

Midlands of England. He was, I told the PM, contemplating signing a contract worth billions of pounds sterling and providing thousands of jobs in Belfast, Northern Ireland, to build oceangoing yachts for sale. If he had the right incentives, he told me, he would resettle the family's small but highly profitable ship-building industry to Belfast. The Prime Minister was speaking on the telephone to the Minister for Trade as I left his office with a huge smile across my face.

The weekly intelligence sharing meeting of the Defence Chiefs was completed without any mention of Zaragoza or Moscow, finishing in sufficient time for me to explain to Molly Ughert why I hadn't fulfilled my promise of sending her husband home on time. She accepted my explanation and my offer of the ministerial car with an overnight stay at the Foreign and Commonwealth guest suite before the solemnity of Hannah's interment at the Hesse family home in the New Forest at Brockenhurst. Not a day I looked forward to, I told her, adding that I needed her close to me to get through it all without blubbering too much. In the meantime, I had Fraser to myself and closure to Dickie's Byzantine mystery ready to explain. I chose my club for the exposition.

* * *

"Do you remember telling me, Fraser, of Bernard Nicholls and his great invention that identified Soviet subs entering international waters, and how you and Dickie travelled out to Langley to sell the idea to the Americans? Well, it wasn't only there that Dickie went, was it?"

"No, it wasn't. Dickie left me one day to enjoy that hospitality I seem to remember mentioning. They certainly do know how to entertain all right. To tell you the truth, I can't remember how they got me back to the hotel."

I laughed with him as I could imagine that happening to either of us.

"I bet you can't! Maybe we can have one or two out there at the expense of the CIA when this is all over. But, for now, I want to take you back to when Dickie left you and went to see the ex-husband of Patricia Jacobson. Do you recall who that was?"

"I'm not quite senile, laddie. I wasn't aware they divorced, but her husband was the physicist

Joseph Cavershall, who worked on the Manhattan Project. The one they pinched from us and then wouldn't share."

"I won't get into politics, Fraser, but, yes, that's him. Joe Joseph Cavershall, to give him his full name. They divorced after only three years of marriage because of his adultery, and that wasn't declared through a sense of chivalry on his part to spare his wife's blushes.

"The woman Joe committed adultery with bore him a son, born the year after the war was finished by the bombs he and others worked on. Whether it was because of the horrors the first detonating nuclear bomb unleashed upon the world, or whether it was the guilt he felt because of his ex-wife's treachery with John Caincross, I cannot be sure, but Joe changed his name from Cavershall to Elliot, never insisting or suggesting his first son Randall should do the same. But Randall did. He became Randall Ryan Elliot the same day his father became Joe Joseph Elliot. It was with Joe that Dickie met, near where he and his wife lived in Baltimore, not far from your hotel in Washington.

"Dickie held nothing back. He forced Joe to acquiesce to all his demands by threatening him with public exposure because of his ex-wife's treachery that we know of. Dickie was after Joe Joseph Elliot's second son, Bradley Scott Elliot. He was roughly thirty-five when he became crucial to all of this.

"Bradley had followed in his father's footsteps somewhat by working for the American government. Only his choice was not to become a physicist. He trained in the technology of computers and the understanding of their nuances. He was one of three departmental heads of the complex known as the Asian desk, inside the National Security Agency Headquarters in Maryland. Bradley was virginal. No outside agency hands had touched him. He had no background away from the NSA headquarters. He could supply what Ryan could not. Bradley had his feet in American intelligence and Dickie wanted him to grow.

"Randall knew nothing of this of course and nor did Dickie want him to know. He swore Joe to secrecy, threatening him again, this time using his eldest son as leverage. Dickie held every card in the pack and Joe had no option but to submit. To sweeten the pill, he gave Joe some reasonably toxic intelligence to do with the Soviet fleet anchored in the Baltic Sea off Tallinn, in Estonia. It concerned the conduct of the captain of the Russian small missile ship, the *Passat*. This was a type of boat popular in the Soviet navy around that time because of its low radar profile carrying a hostile threat way above its size. It was a boat the West knew little about, but envied. Joe passed this intelligence on to his son when the two met at Joe's home on the weekend following yours and Dickie's departure. Joe's conversion of his son is one we can only speculate on of course, but whatever approach he made, it worked.

"The name on Ryan's only ever signal carrying one was Key Fitzgerald. If Randall made any connection to Scott, the middle name of his stepbrother, it was meaningless without knowing that Dickie had him on a leash.

"When Bradley told his superiors of the captain of the Russian ship *Passat*'s indiscretion, it caused a slight panic inside the NSA until they spoke to the CIA, who metaphorically rubbed their hands together whilst adding Bradley's signature to their books and begging him to carry on. Dickie passed relatively small snippets of intelligence to Bradley throughout his retirement years, stuff that was just enough to keep his American mole burrowing away in Langley, supplying Dickie directly with intelligence the CIA were gathering throughout the world and using the NSA transmitters to carry it on.

"We came to know about the improvements that were made to the Frosting programme this way. Bradley was also able to supply the technical breakdown on the guidance system used by the Space Shuttle, which was later adapted to several satellite launches. Bradley was invaluable to the secret intelligence service of this country and it didn't stop with guidance systems."

Fraser interrupted me. "What happened to Bradley's intelligence when Dickie passed away, Patrick? Did it just dry up?"

"It did. And that, I believe, was one of the reasons it was left to be found. By my calculations, Bradley is sixty going on sixty-one. We tracked him down to a part of the secret service called the Presidential Central Security. Amongst other things he's director of the White House signal intelligence, Fraser."

"Are you going to leave him alone?"

"I don't think so, no. I've given Sir John Scarlett what details I can, without exposing any of Dickie's original operative. Just enough so he can twist Bradley's memory a bit if needed. Michael is doing some family background checks as we speak."

Fraser fell silent. Perhaps he was wondering why his old boss hadn't shared Bradley with him when they met in Dickie's retirement years, or maybe he was contemplating what to add, if anything, to his eulogy for Hannah's burial tomorrow. I chased the demons in my head away and turned back to whisky, cigarettes, and work.

"The real sting to Dickie Blythe-Smith's operation came in 1991 after he and Trubnikov met in Berlin. Dickie passed a portion of the intel that Trubnikov gave him about Putin on to Bradley, with precise instructions of how he and Trubnikov were to use it. The part of the information on Putin that Dickie kept exclusively for GB use only was not given over to anyone inside the SIS or inside the Foreign Office, or any other part of HM government.

"There were, as I said, two parts to the last message Dickie sent to himself using Ryan as its preface. The part about Stoneman's connection we have already covered. It's the second part that holds the answers you wanted, Fraser. Dickie's signal was coded using the letters of NOMITE to represent numbers on a periodic table of elements, as issued by the Royal Society of Chemistry. I managed to decode it.

"I have always suspected Dickie offered me a position in the service because I'd got a degree as a qualified chemical analyst. It would certainly prove my theory of why I got Operation Donor and why NOMITE was used twice to conceal Dickie's workings. Sorry, Fraser, I've wandered slightly from disclosing who Dickie gave Vladimir Putin's secrets to. It's the reason why we were both reprimanded by Palace officials. He gave it to the man who in the year 1991 headed up the Court of St James's security, Viscount Richard Temple, Sir Richard Blythe-Smith's sponsor and relation dating as far back as King Richard I days—one God, one King, one Country.

"Viscounts don't have a retirement date set in stone. They tend to go on until they fall. However, Richard Temple did retire in the same year as Dickie passed away. At that date, Vladimir Putin's history became the property to the new Master of The Royal Household and so, presumably, it will be transferred in perpetuity.

"The Royal House of Windsor have had a controlling influence over many international events since changing their name from its Germanic heritage. However, the connection to other Royal houses through the Saxe-Coburg and Gotha line continues to this day, encompassing my wife's Landgft surname, within the European House of Hesse, and onwards to the last Tsars of Russia.

"Although Putin could never be called a Royalist, his commitments to Communism had not always been the paramount thoughts behind his actions. In the first ZAPAD exercises of May 1977, mentioned by Ryan in a leaked signal from Trubnikov, the twenty-five-year-old Vladimir Putin was assigned to the General Staff of the Soviet Defence Ministry, stationed in the German Democratic Republic in Schwerin, the capital of the state of Mecklenburg-Vorpommern. By chance, he met Anna, wife of Klaus Mecklenburg. The Mecklenburgs had a palatial home there. Anna and Vladimir had a passionate, all consuming affair inside and outside that home, without Klaus's knowledge.

"But according to Trubnikov, Putin told his friend, who was serving in the USSR during this ZAPAD operation, that he knew Anna Mecklenburg was related to the Romanovs, not only because she'd told him, but she secretly showed him some Romanov jewellery she'd kept with some family photographs of the Tsar and Tsarina that included her. Trubnikov gave Dickie the original transcript of those messages from Putin, declaring his involvement with a Romanov. Putin never reported her to his superiors. He also complicated his life by visiting her whenever he could when the military manoeuvres finished in the GDR.

"I can only surmise some parts of this story, but Jana Kava told me that Anna Kudashov had a secret and Jana believed she had a child somewhere that was never spoken of. Jana saw

Nikita Kudashov on the day she believed he killed his wife. He was acutely angry, mouthing the name Schwerin over and over again whilst punching his hands together as he made his way past Jana on his way home. Dickie did not know of that and I only remembered it as I was listening to Trubnikov's story, and remember Dickie had a head start by at least sixteen years, but I got a signal off to Michael Simmons about Schwerin, asking him to look into records of illegitimate births registered around February1978. And guess what, Fraser? He found the one Dickie gave to our Royal Family's equerry. An illegitimate Romanov son born to Vladimir Vladimirovich Putin on the twenty-six of February 1978! He actually signed the hospital's register and it hasn't been destroyed. How's that for arrogance?

"I checked with the present Master of The Royal Household, Lord Tennyson Gravel, before attending the Defence meeting this morning. He was reticent as first, as you can imagine, but I was right. As far as he is aware, the young man in question is the only Romanov connection alive today. Lord Gravel asked me to meet with him and the Prince of Wales on Wednesday. When I'm there, I will ask if our knowledge of this birth has been used in any way to impact on Vladimir Putin's world decisions. I said it would be nice to know.

"As far as I'm concerned, if Dickie Blythe-Smith was happy handing this revelation over to the Queen's equerry, then so am I, Fraser."

There was an additional part to Lord Gravel's conversation that I never mentioned, but by the canny look in his eyes, I would not have been surprised if he had already guessed. As we finished our arrangements to meet, not only he, but as he put it *his boss*, he apologised for the terse letter the British Ambassador to India was forced to read to me, and also the heavy-handed visit to Fraser and Molly's home.

He then added, "The man in question has always had someone looking out for him, and that will always be the case." Without a sense of intimidation, but with an unnerving edge to his voice, he added, "The Firm always looks after their own, Mr West, and they now include you amongst their number. The Prince of Wales sends his sincerest regrets for the loss of your wife, Mrs Hannah Landgft-West, but hopes you will keep the house at Hassocks in Sussex, enjoying all it offers. There was just one thing his Royal Highness requested and that was for you to have an open mind when the two of you meet on Wednesday."

* * *

A covenant can be a concise contract where the understanding of a pledge is paramount. However, any agreement or pledge entered into by a spy is never underwritten by rules or regulations. This case is different. The pledge between the SIS and the Royal Family is one of a greater substance than any political allegiance or signature to an official document.

Indebtedness incurred purely through status or rank could be ignored or pushed upon someone else, but as far as I, or Sir Richard Blythe-Smith before me, are concerned, the House of Windsor has always honoured the obligation it owes to the state of Great Britain over any other consideration. The responsibility to provide guidance and protection to a present day bloodline relative to our Royal Family was better suited away from the public eye and politics. It is not my duty to inform the present or any future government of this arrangement. My covenant will always be to serve the best interests of this country.

The End

Dear reader,

We hope you enjoyed reading *A Covenant of Spies*. Please take a moment to leave a review in Amazon, even if it's a short one. Your opinion is important to us.

Discover more books by Daniel Kemp at https://www.nextchapter.pub/authors/daniel-kemp-mystery-thriller-author.

Want to know when one of our books is free or discounted? Join the newsletter at http://eepurl.com/bqqB3H

Best regards,
Daniel Kemp and the Next Chapter Team

A Covenant of Spies
ISBN: 978-4-86750-494-9 (Large Print)

Published by
Next Chapter
1-60-20 Minami-Otsuka
170-0005 Toshima-Ku, Tokyo
+818035793528
16th June 2021

CPSIA information can be obtained
at www.ICGtesting.com
Printed in the USA
LVHW111912290621
691470LV00001B/56